KESTREL

ADRIENNE LOTHY

BOOK ONE OF THE STARHAWK TRILOGY

AN MM ENEMIES TO LOVERS SCI-FI ROMANCE

ISBN 979-8-9904977-0-2 (e-book)

ISBN 979-8-9904977-1-9 (print)

Book cover by Seaj Art.

First edition 2024.

For Noodles, who has always been there

The Starhawk Series Reading Order

Kestrel

Killjoy

Starhawk

CONTENT ADVISORY

Dear reader,

This story contains themes which may be upsetting to some, including: on page violence and murder, deaths of characters' family members, references to trafficking, slavery, sexual assault, and descriptions of domestic abuse. Sexual assault is occasionally directly referred to by a four lettered word, beginning with R. Some of these scenes are depicted with very mild and limited description.

Stories are meant to entertain, inspire, and provoke thought. Not every story is meant for every reader, and that's okay. There's no shame in deciding one just isn't for you. Whether you choose to read on or end your journey with this series here, thank you for taking the time and consideration. Take care of yourself, and never stop believing in the magic of stories.

This book is intended for adult readers only. The author does not condone acts of violence or murder outside of fiction.

With respect and gratitude,
Adrienne

CHAPTER ONE
I'VE GOT YOU

NIKO NEVER THOUGHT HE'D be back here again.

He pursed his lips and glanced around the conference room of Station Twelve. It had been over three years since he'd last stepped into the crowded little city-moon of Kaapra-19's Galactic Police headquarters. Its arched ceilings towered above him, warm light cast back upon itself in the mirror-polish of marbled floors. Old faces had greeted him enthusiastically at every step back into this building, people who he'd once known as friends and colleagues.

Several of them had actually stopped him along the way to ask how he was or recount some of his past triumphs at hunting—cornering one fugitive on an abandoned colony moon by bringing down the derelict buildings around him with explosions, catching another after a four-hour nonstop pursuit through an acidic alien bog. He'd been stalled under all the attention for a good twenty minutes before Zann, Station Twelve's lead investigator and Niko's half-brother, came and waved everyone away and dragged him back into the conference room for a private briefing.

"So," Zann started. With a lazy wave of his hand, he summoned a holographic menagerie of grisly case file images that spanned the length of the entire wall. Their pale light washed over the room, painting everything a ghostly blue in stark contrast to the warm lights of the station. "You're going to help me take him down, right?"

"I don't know, Zann," Niko said. "I never really planned to go back to bounty hunting."

It was a lie and it wasn't. Niko missed hunting. He craved it like he craved air—brimming with adrenaline as he slowly wore down the galaxy's worst fugitives until they had nowhere left to run made Niko feel alive in a way nothing else ever had.

But he also knew what hunting did to him. Years later, he still bore the scars, some deeper than others. It took a toll on him, each job a little more than the last, each reckless injury a little harder to get back up from.

The last one had left him unable to get up at all.

"Then why keep the ship all this time?" Zann asked.

"Sunk cost fallacy. I've put thousands into modding it."

"That's bullshit and you know it. You practically worship that thing. I know you've been training with the suit, too. You even showed up in it. Besides, if money is an issue, I've already spoken with the chief and they gave authorization for Galapol to fund any supplies you'll need for this."

Zann leaned back against the long, shiny oak conference table and crossed his arms. Niko glanced at him. They made quite the odd pair. He didn't resemble his brother much—next to Niko's muscled frame and bulky suit of tech-armor, Zann stood skinny and sleek. His short-cropped hair grew in glossy, tight coils, his rich, ebony skin and high cheekbones favoring his father over their shared mother.

Niko, on the other hand, had a deep bronze complexion, just like their mother. His straight, shaggy, dark brown hair favored a man Niko had no memory of.

But both shared the same dark, perceptive eyes which peered out at the scattering of case file holograms that hovered before them now.

Zann raked his hand over his face. "Look," he started. "All I'm saying is that I know you want this. I'm going to be blunt with you here, and I know you don't want to hear it. But ever since you stopped hunting, you've been a shell of a person. You don't even leave your fucking apartment, except maybe to go see Dad. You haven't gone out in years. You're just letting yourself waste away. Why do you think I got you the suit?"

Niko grunted. Everything Zann said was true—since he'd given up bounty hunting, Niko had sunk into a dreamless haze that could only clinically be called living.

He had never resurfaced since.

None of it changed the fact that bounty hunting was a deadly game and Niko knew all too intimately the sort of consequences it often led to. He didn't need a fresh reminder of that.

"That doesn't matter, Zann. I retired. I'm out of it now."

"Yet you showed up when I called on you." Zann smirked, his eyes forming smug, dark crescents. "Niko, you see this guy's files." His expression sobered up as he gestured to the holographic photos before them. "And I know you've been watching the news about him. I know you. I know it's got to be eating you up inside. This might just be the biggest asshole this galaxy has ever vomited up so far. He's our number one. If anyone needs to be brought down, it's him. And if anyone's actually capable of doing it, it's you."

"Zann—"

"Niko. There's nobody better than you. You know I wouldn't be asking otherwise." Zann pushed off the edge of the table and looked Niko in the eyes, imploring. "The Kestrel has killed five planetary leaders, a renowned philanthropist, and a well-loved actor to date. Clearly the guy isn't about to stop any time soon. Unless somebody makes him."

The Kestrel.

Niko sighed. Zann was right—again. He'd been glued the past four months to the reporters, witnesses, and talking heads of non-stop news feeds as they'd chattered, wide-eyed and with hurried words about the elusive assassin who had quickly earned his spot as Galapol's number one most wanted.

Ever since, Niko hadn't been able to stop watching, listening, and reading about the gruesome assassinations of influential figures across the galaxy, all flawlessly executed by a mysterious figure known only as the Kestrel. The title was all they currently had on the guy, gotten only from a message left spray painted in near illegible writing on the brick side of a rooftop utility shed near his first kill: *TELL THEM THE KESTREL IS COMING.*

The handwriting was so egregiously awful that Niko was baffled how someone with a hand steady enough to snipe a perfect headshot on several different occasions could also scrawl out whatever abomination that was. How anyone had managed to work out what it even said was a whole other miracle.

Zann looked over at the holographic scattering of autopsy images and crime scene still frames captured from security feeds and drones, the name KESTREL hovering above them all in a wash of headache-blue text. Niko's gaze drifted to a photograph of the third district senator of Delan-6, Nurun Jia, the lavender-skinned Heenva politician crumpled onto himself, prone on the ground, the aides flanking him forever frozen with panicked hands and fearful eyes. Around him was a dark puddle of violet-colored blood. Next to that image were several close-up photos of the bullet from his following autopsy. It matched with the same sniper rifle model utilized in the other assassinations.

Niko hated guys like the Kestrel—haughty, cruel, egomaniacal. People like him felt they were above the law and had a right to take the lives of others into their own hands. The murders a single man had committed had sent shockwaves of fear, trepidation, and unease throughout interstellar societies. Each new death sent entire governments scrambling, forcing hasty replacements of dead leaders. It was unprecedented, each death on a galactic scale that had never been witnessed previously.

Looking at the aftermath of his kills—the panic, the grief, the violence, all plainly on holographic display—made Niko's insides twist with tight rage. He would love nothing more than to ruin the Kestrel's day.

Once upon a time, Niko had lived for bringing garbage like him down. But ghosts of the past clung heavy to his legs now, dragging him back down to sober reality. He glanced away.

"Zann," he said. "It's— After everything that happened before— I'm done. I'm not a hunter anymore."

His brother's voice softened. "Niko. I know. I wouldn't ask you to step back into that world if it was anything short of this. This guy is making public spectacles of killing the most influential and powerful figures out there. People who lead nations and planets. People who everyone is looking up to for guidance and stability. He needs to be stopped. I'm asking you to help me stop him. We've thrown everything we have at him so far and he just evades it every single time.

"I'm out of options, Niko. You're my trump card."

Niko winced. He could feel himself caving. "The chief really authorized funding? I've never seen anything like that before."

"They did. I got it in writing. This is big, Niko. Probably the biggest case you'll ever be put on. Even if you never hunt again after this, imagine finishing your career on this kind of bang. He's out there unchecked and nobody can take him down so far. And he's got that tech shit too. Impossible to get near him and he can straight up go fucking invisible."

"Yeah, that'll make it difficult."

"If we could get our hands on some of that, though..." Zann whistled. "Imagine Galapol with stealth cloaking powers. Or society as a whole. Maybe nabbing this guy could be a silver lining in more ways than one."

Niko swore under his breath. "This feels like... before, all over again."

"It does," Zann agreed, his expression growing tight and unreadable. A memory, haunted and ripe with roiling grief, threatened to surface between them, drawing the air out of the room. Both men stood in silence until Zann spoke again. "Which is why we both know how important this is." After a pause, he added, "And why you need to be the one to stop him. You're the best we've ever had, Niko. I'm not saying that as your brother, either, so don't try to give me any of that 'bias' shit. You know the reputation you built. Everyone here knows it. It's all they've been talking about since you walked in these doors.

"Ivrieet Talanari? Vasra Kolaryl? Roland Mausca? Dozens of other infamous criminal assholes we'd been trying to take down for years? You were the one who finally got them, Niko. *You*. I need you to do the crazy, incredible shit you did then again. This one last time."

Niko nodded, looking over at the scattering of holographic files, security camera stills, and portraits of the deceased. None of the people in them had done anything to deserve losing their lives in such a violent end. An old itch was starting to resurface in him—the need and want to protect. To make a difference.

To wake from his three years of sleepwalking and live again.

Niko knew he was far beyond saying no now. He closed his eyes for a moment, relenting, before asking, "Okay. Who do we think he's going for next? What's the intel?"

He tried to ignore the way Zann brightened, how he stood a little taller. "So, we've got a few leads, but it's a matter of narrowing it down. We've been curating a list of upcoming big events for leaders, celebrities, everyone we can think might make it as this guy's next target. But the truth is, it's still just guesswork so far. Guy appeared out of nowhere one day and killed the Prime of Ghalaecua.

"After that, it was just one after another. But it's not just leaders, right? It's actors, philanthropists. There's no certain basis or motive for why he's doing it other than what we can guess is sheer ego. He never goes after these guys in secret. He takes them out where everyone can see it. The spectacle is the point."

Niko nodded. "Right. Taking out the biggest and the best just to show he can."

"You've dealt with the type."

"So why not just advise canceling upcoming high risk public events?"

"Can't cancel events forever, Niko." Zann shrugged. "And it's a big galaxy, with a lot going on. We did put out a warning but we can't force anything. Some of them did cancel. But others are going on about how they won't live in fear, that sort of bullshit. If I had to guess where he'll end up next, though, it'll be at the Grand Sovereign of Yhanwe-ha's annual address." He swiped a small portrait to the center of the room, then expanded it. Niko found himself staring back at the enigmatic, pious leader of the Quwa-quay people—skin of pale, pearlescent gold, an ornate and colorful veil hanging down over their sun-sensitive eyes. "Pattern recognition guys are predicting that one. Big event, big crowd. Huge public figure."

"How do we—"

Niko was cut off by the groan of the old, heavy conference room door as it opened, followed by a surprised laugh. He tensed automatically, shoulders rising as he turned to see another detective—human, with near translucently pale skin, dark hair and thick black eyebrows—all but gaping at him. He was one of the new faces Niko hadn't recognized at the station. "So, you're the one who everybody's going starry-eyed over."

"Uh, yeah, I guess so," Niko said.

The man's gaze ran up and down along Niko's armored body, openly mocking now. "Wow. What the hell's with the power armor, though? This isn't the battlefield, mate."

Charged silence fell over the room before Zann snapped, "Fourier. Haven't you ever seen a bounty hunter before? Is this your first goddamn day?"

"Right, sorry," Fourier laughed again, clearly not sorry.

"What do you want? We're busy," Zann said.

"Came to tell you there's been an update on the Kestrel case. He just killed Horu Duu'mari at the Diamond Comet Awards."

"Fuck," said Zann. He and Niko looked at each other. "This wasn't supposed to happen."

"Wait. The director of *Twenty-One Toliai?*" Niko asked. He had been an enthusiastic fan of the action classic growing up, reenacting several of the most famous fight scenes as an excited boy on his hapless stepfather.

"Yep," Fourier said.

"Alright," Zann said, his face a landscape of tension and stress. "I'll be out in a minute."

Fourier disappeared through the door again, giving Niko a little salute and grin. Niko shifted his weight uncomfortably. Maybe he shouldn't have come in the suit.

"Fuck," Zann said again, voice hoarse with a fatigue Niko hated hearing.

"Yeah. Wow."

"Hey. Don't worry about the suit. Fourier's newer here, so I'll talk to him. Besides, you look cool in it. It's fitting that you show up looking like a big armored badass. You're the one who's going to end this, after all."

Niko was fully self-conscious now, though he appreciated Zann's enthusiasm. "It's fine, Zann. It's not a big deal at all."

"Look, I have to deal with this new kill," Zann said, already moving towards the door. He waved the holographic files away, and the room dimmed in the absence of their blue light haze. "I sent you everything we have so far. I'll update it with what we learn about Duu'mari."

Niko moved to exit after him, and as he reached the doorway, he could see the station was now alight in frenzied commotion: officers, investigators and researchers all undoubtedly scrambling under the freshly devastating news.

Zann glanced back over his shoulder before heading towards the swarm of activity. "You know what to do. Bring him down, Niko. End this quick. Do what you do best. Just like old times."

Being back on the *Soñadora Despierta* again was strange. The sleek, heavily-modded ship, which could bypass thousands of star systems in a matter of hours, had sat unmoving in Niko's rented hangar for three years—though was frequently maintained and visited. Zann had recommended over the years that he take it out, have fun with it, that it might put a crack in his depression. But Niko hadn't been able to bring himself to. It would have only reminded him of something he'd loved but had closed the door to.

He hadn't been able to bring himself to sell it, either. Nor any of his weapons or gear.

Doing so would have locked that door permanently and thrown away the key.

Niko sat now in the pilot's seat of the *Soñadora*, parked among thousands of other ships, all pilgrims who had come to hear the spiritual address of the Grand Sovereign, whom the Quwa-quay people looked to as the mortal incarnation of their deity. The Grand Sovereign's annual address was a source of inspiration, guidance, and hope for many Quwa-quay and even some members of other alien species. And the Kestrel was, likely, aiming to silence that hope forever.

Not on Niko's watch.

Every foreign craft had been checked for registration as a precaution, since the Kestrel had begun picking off leaders around the galaxy. Once Niko had given the local authorities his registered hunting license number and explained he was working in contract with Galapol, he was cleared for entry.

He peered through the windshield up at the huge, looming twin moons of Yhanwe-ha, one scarred and deep red, the other pale, gray, and smooth as a polished stone. They looked down on the holy grounds, parking lot, and city beyond like mismatched, watchful eyes. Before him spread miles upon miles of intricately carved, ornate alien architecture, twisting pearlescent spires decorated with pale gold. He tried to steady his breathing. It had been a very long time and a lot was resting on his shoulders now.

Niko stood, clad once more in the thick, protective veneer of his armor, and walked to the back of the ship where the weapons lockers were, each step heavy and clanging against the floor. He leaned forward towards the leftmost locker, pulling his glove off, then pressed his hand against a biometric scanner. The lock clicked open with a satisfying, crisp sound, and before Niko lay a variety of firearms and grenades of various sizes and impact, each one appreciated and oft-used in a previous life. Taped on the inside of the locker door were the old, familiar photos of his favorite nude male models.

He opted for the rifle—his favorite, and a classic. High impact, explosive shots, messy, got the job done quickly. Though Niko usually tried to bring his bounties in alive (it was better to send them through the judiciary system and make them face the consequences of their crimes and maybe, *maybe* reflect on what a horrible person they'd been) it wasn't out of the question to resort to more permanent means of stopping his mark, either. Galapol's contract had given him clearance for using any means necessary.

Whatever it took to make sure the Kestrel didn't hurt anyone ever again.

Niko fastened the rifle to the back of his armor, where it snapped into place with a magnetic lock, then grabbed two more pistols as backup. He closed the locker, casting his gaze towards the exit door of the *Soñadora*.

In addition to the anxiety gnawing away at him, Niko felt something else beginning to culminate—something even greater, more overpowering. He felt a *thrill* now, intense, private, and hungry. Something that had long laid dormant, sleeping in the depths of him.

That same thrill and eagerness had always driven him on his jobs, had made him unable to capitulate until he was the last one standing. It was the need to bring down the worst the galaxy had churned out, the scraps and slime from the bottom of society's general offering of people. Those who would hurt, wreck, and ruin.

It was personal for Niko. And Zann.

He had a feeling about tonight, something ephemeral but electric. He knew he would see the Kestrel here. Every cell throughout him buzzed, quiet and subtle, yet charged as the air before a lightning strike: the instinct that they would meet tonight.

He knew the assassin was here.

Niko pulled his helmet on and locked it in place, with another metallic snap, then stepped out of the ship and down its ramp, where his feet stood now on the gold-inlaid pavement of an alien world for the first time in what felt like eons. The door slid closed and locked behind him.

A crowd of people moved around and ahead of him, weaving in between their parked ships, funneling their way through check-points and into the holy monument where the Grand Sovereign was due to speak. Their waists terminated in a long, serpentine appendage instead of legs, on which they gracefully propelled them-selves—the Quwa-quay species, who originated from here on Yhan-we-ha.

Their long, spindly arms and necks of iridescent white were adorned in a variety of gold bangles and ornately cut gems. Niko was unused to seeing their large eyes left bare, pale like luminous pearls. Yhanwe-ha was a planet tidally locked to its star, and the Quwa-quay people evolved steeped in the eternally dark side of their planet. Niko was used to the ornate and diaphanous veils over their eyes that protected them from foreign suns and harsh, artificial lights.

Some of the Quwa-quay noticed him as they slithered by in the distance, curious pearl eyes falling on his armor before turning away and moving on.

Niko imagined he wouldn't be the only other bounty hunter here tonight.

His helmet chimed, and a portrait of Zann appeared in the right corner of his visor as a call came through.

"Answer," he mumbled.

"You're there?" Zann said, breathless. Niko imagined him run-ning to and fro in the station, probably not having sat down once in several hours.

"Yeah, just got clearance and landed about ten minutes ago. Anything I should keep in mind?"

"Be fucking careful," Zann said. "That's what you should keep in mind. The guy's good. Maybe the best we've ever been up against. We have agents stationed around the grounds as well as local sec. No one has spotted him yet, but that's nothing new. We don't know how he's getting in and out unnoticed, but he is."

"Got it," Niko said.

"You have good instincts, though. Figure out where he is and tag his ass," Zann said. "And, Niko. Welcome back."

"Roger that," Niko said, terminating the call and glancing around the holy grounds. Niko shook his head—the setup of the event was a tragedy begging to happen. The monument was built atop the burial grounds of the First Sovereign's bones, all open, flat terrain with a gilded platform for the Grand Sovereign to stand upon for their address. And it was, in this particular case, fatally flanked on all sides by towering spires and skyscrapers that glittered darkly under the dim light of the large twin moons.

If they weren't willing to cancel the speech, they could have at least moved it elsewhere. Religion and tradition didn't work so simply, though. The address had always been held here, and would always continue to be, regardless of how many nearly-unhindered opportunities it would provide the Kestrel tonight.

The assassin obviously favored sniping from a distance, particularly seeking out high vantage points. Keeping the address here was basically a nightmare waiting to happen, but in the end, the Grand

Sovereign had been one of the leaders to respond that they would not live in fear before others.

Have it your way, he thought.

Niko was determined to end this before it progressed any further, regardless. Horu Duu'mari would be the Kestrel's last victim.

He peered up at the twisting, alien skyscrapers, trying to slip inside the Kestrel's head. His gaze turned towards a particular skyscraper at the far end of the burial ground borders. If a sniper wanted a good shot, that was the best place to do it from. It was technically outside of the active grounds, but to a sniper with a phenomenally steady hand and a reliable rifle—both of which the Kestrel were proven time and again to have—it would be solid gold.

Niko knew where to go.

He made his way through crowds of Quwa-quay. A scattering of other species was mingled in—primarily either religious converts or foreign press and media, little camera drones hovering by, at the ready. Security stopped him a few times and he impatiently presented the same information he'd given before landing. Each time he was stopped, Niko became antsier and more frustrated. He felt every second that crept by in a keenly physical way—they crawled around through his suit, along his skin, pulsing with the beat of his heart. Driving him towards the high tower in the distance.

Foreign, scripted letters spelled out a puzzle along its side in a gentle glow of neon orange. Niko couldn't read Quwa-quay, but given the antennas along the top which pierced the sky like great needles, he guessed it was some kind of broadcasting building. A quick search on his visor's map as he closed in on it, finally past the thickest crowds, confirmed it as the Aman-aii Broadcasting Center.

Once he reached it, Niko pushed through the glass entry doors and into the dim but glittering reception lobby, full of its curving gold-edged counters and crystal-lined benches. The security staff immediately rose at the sight of him, fully armored and armed, but not drawing their weapons. They eyed him warily.

"You're not supposed—"

Niko sighed, reciting his well-worn line. "Bounty hunter. License 44-8783-332, working in contract with Galapol of Kaapra-19. I need access to the roof."

"There's nothing on the roof," the security guard to the left responded in heavily-accented Galactic Standard, their pale eyes looking him up and down. He saw another guard run a check on his license number, a pale blue hologram hovering before them. "We've run checks every ten minutes. And we've had personnel guarding the elevator. You're wasting your time here."

It pained Niko to be delayed like this, and it was all he could do to keep from groaning audibly. Their argument would be acceptable in any other circumstance, but the Kestrel had an uncanny way of simply *showing up* in places he didn't belong. Places, even, that had been under strict observation preceding his kill.

"I understand that. But I still want to check it out. It's a potentially critical vantage point I want to keep an eye on."

The security guards all stared dully at him now, clearly not thrilled to be told they weren't doing their jobs. They mumbled to one another in Quwa-quay, one giving a soft, almost musical laugh. Niko could tell they weren't a fan of him, but at the moment, he couldn't spare any fucks to give. A guard to the right of him shrugged and responded in even more heavily-accented Standard, *"This* is what Galapol sends. Enjoy the view."

"Thanks, I will," Niko managed to grunt out before heading to the nearest elevator. The building was kept so dark that without the aid of his visor, he likely wouldn't be able to see much at all. The visor also allowed him to catch the smirk that flashed across the elevator guard's face.

I need to thank Zann for this suit, he thought.

The elevator was unsurprisingly empty, except for him. A single, dimly-glowing crystal dangled from the ceiling as a light source. The floor selection interface was written in Quwa-quay, so he jammed his finger into the topmost button, figuring that indicated the roof, or as close as he was going to get to it. It was a crapshoot with alien architecture, especially with a species who didn't utilize stairs.

The doors slid shut and Niko was left to an agonizingly long ride up sixty stories, accompanied by alien elevator music that he figured must somehow sound pleasant to Quwa-quay ears. To Niko, it resembled a cat in heat yowling, set to a minimalistic twang of string instruments.

It wasn't to his taste.

And then the doors opened again, freeing him of his aural hell and revealing an upward-ramping passage that terminated in a single door. He pushed through it and out into the open air of the roof. Above him, the moons filled most of the sky, lingering huge and ominous, almost as though pressing down on him. They felt closer than before.

A breathtaking view spread before and below him—a tapestry as wide as he could see of twinkling lights, dim neon signs, and glinting gold designs which comprised the cityscape of the Yhanwe-han capitol.

Far, far below were the hallowed grounds where the Grand Sovereign was about to speak. The height was dizzying—cars, ships, and people all resembled little more than ants crowding around a single, sacred spot. Niko's heart began pounding heavy and fast inside his chest, as an old, familiar adrenaline spiked through his veins like a drug.

I remember this.

He reached behind himself, unlatching his rifle from its magnetic lock and switching off the safety. Each breath flowed in and out of him consciously now, steady and setting a rhythm to every crucial second that passed.

He glanced around, gaze sweeping over the length of the building. Just as the security guards had said, there was nothing here. No one. The roof was empty, quiet, and still, save for the rhythmically blinking lights of the great antennas it bore.

But something didn't feel right, and it pricked at Niko's skin.

That intense lightning-strike breathlessness still hung heavy in his chest. Every instinct from his earlier days hunting told Niko the Kestrel was *here*. The feeling screamed, sang inside him like a beacon.

This was the spot. It had to be. But where was he?

Niko stepped forward quietly, head tilted as he scanned the building again with standard visual, then thermal readings, then even ultraviolet. He looked up at the grand broadcasting antennas as he moved swiftly and cautiously around utility structures, gun first. And was met with nothing but stillness, silence.

Celebratory fireworks began erupting in the sky around him then, shattering the heavy silence, heralding the commencement of the Grand Sovereign's address. They painted the mirror-windows of nearby spires in myriad colors, and filled the air with roaring booms that sounded a bit too close to gunfire for Niko's comfort. He knew that below, the Grand Sovereign must be making their way to the sacred platform.

Something was wrong.

This was the perfect spot for an egotistical sniper to take out his victim with little interference to contend with. The best spot, in fact, in the entire surrounding area.

But no one was here. Had Zann and the Station Twelve research team misjudged where he'd end up next? It was certainly possible—after all, Zann had seemed outright thrown for a loop when Fourier announced Horu Duu'mari's death. Galapol was running off of guesswork here.

Maybe the Kestrel had no interest in the Grand Sovereign. That didn't feel right either, though—the holy leader of Yhan-we-ha was an immensely influential entity in the galaxy. If the Kestrel were truly driven by ego and some sick notion of fame, this would be too much to pass up.

Niko had one more thought. Something else he could try as a last-ditch effort before returning to the ground and trying a different building.

He began rotating through different frequencies of his helmet's wireless radio. If the Kestrel was in communication with anyone, and was nearby, he'd be able to pick up his private frequency. He was far enough away from the ground that other nearby devices wouldn't transmit this far, and the huge antennas around him stuck to certain powerful, public frequencies.

Niko rotated through several, with nothing but static, until suddenly his helmet was awash in a startling sea of sound. It wasn't talking, however. It was music—the middle of a pop song, a shimmering ocean of buoyant melody and rhythm, wrapped around a woman's voice.

"Baby, I've been looking for someone like you,
Now that I've found you, baby, I'm never letting go.
You're in my orbit, caught by my gravity. I'm your star.
Your star, your starlight burning.
When you're lost, my love will guide you home.
I've got you, baby."

He was here. He was on the roof somewhere.

Niko raised his gun, frozen, ready for a fight. His pulse hammered in his ears, louder even than the song itself. He stared straight ahead, something catching his eye now—a distortion of the air itself, as though it curved and bent subtly. In the silhouette of a man. His heart leapt into his throat the moment he realized he'd been up here the whole time, so close to the very killer he'd been hunting, and hadn't even seen.

He could barely make out details; looking from the corner of his gaze gave a clearer picture than trying to see him straight on. The figure before him was distinctly male: lithe and agile, elegant.

I've got you.

Niko aimed at him, but as he did, the man twisted in a single, fluid movement, looking directly back at him now, his own sniper rifle raised. Niko hadn't even made a sound.

Niko had been walking around the roof all this time. But it wasn't until he'd aimed his gun that the Kestrel had turned to face him. He had a feeling this guy possessed the same level of instinct Niko himself did, the sort of skin-prickling tension that came with knowing you were being watched or, in this case, aimed at with a gun and malicious intent. Until now, Niko hadn't even registered as a threat to him.

He could just barely make out the odd contours of the man's head—he was wearing a mask of some sort. It protruded out from his face, terminating in a sharp point like a bird's beak, obscuring whatever lay beneath.

"Not again," the Kestrel growled.

The contempt and condescension in the man's voice drove Niko into an instant, white-hot rage. It was the way someone would talk about a stain on their shirt, or dropping a glass.

Mild irritation, annoyance. Maybe even exasperation. Nothing more.

Niko was better than *mere inconvenience*. And he was determined to show the Kestrel as much. He fired first, an explosive shot straight to the chest, the sound swallowed up by the fireworks show around them.

Nothing happened.

Or, rather, it did. But it wasn't anything Niko had expected.

The very air around the Kestrel distorted and rippled in a shockwave from the impact, eidolic. He had a shield or energy barrier of some kind, tech that seemed to only exist in movies. Niko had never seen anything like it in all his years of hunting, and it had stopped a bullet easily in its tracks.

The Kestrel fired on him too, and the bullet ricocheted off his armor.

This wasn't going to work. Niko changed up tactics, relying now on an old, brute force move. He liked it best up close and personal anyway, liked fighting people one on one, body against body. There was something primal and thrilling about it, something he craved and missed more than he'd wanted to admit. He wanted to tackle the Kestrel, throw him to the ground, and break through all his tech and defenses. Maybe break him too.

He rushed forward, charging the other man. He fired once, then twice more as he rapidly closed the ground between them, all three bullets ineffective and uselessly stopped in the air, eliciting similar shockwave effects as before.

The Kestrel turned away before Niko could reach him and leapt with the elegance of a competing diver off the edge of the skyscraper. It was all Niko could do to stop his charging advance before going over the edge himself. For a brief moment, he was bewildered—had the Kestrel decided to take the easy way out on his own terms, once cornered?

But that didn't seem right either. The man had come off as far too prepared, far too arrogant, and simply unafraid of Niko. *Unfazed*, even.

But how could anyone survive a jump like that? Niko looked down over the side of the building. The Kestrel was gone. His frequency and music were lost as the distance between them rapidly grew, and Niko was left with only static in his ears. His gaze fell to the sea of people far below, gathered around the Grand Sovereign as they delved into their address.

The assassin was somewhere among them now. Any of those people could be in danger, the Grand Sovereign in particular.

Shit.

Niko ached, every cell in him on fire with desperation and panic. He had to go after him. Had to catch up. He wouldn't—couldn't—let a killer like that win. The Grand Sovereign's life was in his hands now.

For a dizzying moment, something wild and dangerous called for him to follow, to leap right off the edge and figure out what to do from there. He'd always had that kind of self-abandonment during hunting.

There was a time before when he would have done that very thing.

But a vivid flash of memory—of falling, of broken glass and the devastating shatter of human vertebrae—ripped through him, raw and visceral as a bullet to the gut. Niko found himself dizzy as he stumbled away from the building's edge, the world swimming around him. It was hard to breathe.

He would have to find another way down.

Niko ran back to the elevator, jamming the button for what appeared to be the first-floor symbol repeatedly. The doors closed, agonizingly slow, and the yowling music started again. The sound grated against him, clawing his patience into ribbons. He needed to be back out there, needed to be pursuing the assassin who'd come to make another devastating kill. Instead, he was trapped in an elevator, nowhere to go, left simply to stand and wait.

He had been so close.

Niko should have jumped. He knew he should have jumped. That's what had made him so good before—he threw himself away, a cruel exchange that always caught his bounty at any cost.

But the cost had been himself, once, irreparably. And so now he had backed down, gotten scared. And lost the Kestrel.

It was all Niko could do to keep from punching the elevator interface, but he knew tantrums wouldn't make it go any faster.

I should have jumped.

Jumping was suicidal. It was destructive. He knew this. Yet the line repeated itself like a deadly mantra through his brain now anyway.

His thoughts were churning together, coalescing into an intense, spiking headache. Niko felt hot sweat running down the back of his neck, under his helmet. He didn't know where the desperation and adrenaline of his encounter with the Kestrel ended and the nauseous horror of past trauma began. It all warred within him in a sickly skirmish.

He knew he would be too slow now, knew he had lost this battle. The Kestrel was surely long gone and every part of Niko screamed inside, demanding justice. Demanding blood. Another life was about to be lost, and it was all due to his hesitation. Inside the suit, it was getting hard to breathe.

The doors slowly slid open, and Niko pried them apart, forcing himself through. He booked it through the lobby, the security guards looking alarmed as he flew past. Then he burst through the front doors, the air in his lungs liquid and burning, when a single firework rang out in a roaring boom.

No.

It wasn't a firework.

The fireworks had stopped since he'd made his way back down. This was something else. A shot, singular and precise, and followed now by screams which only grew in intensity as more and more voices joined in.

The crowd gathered across the holy grounds erupted into chaos: people trying to flee the scene, Galapol agents rushing towards the stage, and at the center of it all, the Grand Sovereign of Yhanwe-ha, slowly sinking to the ground in a limpid, gentle motion as their private security gathered tightly around them. Their blood trickled off the platform, feeding the sacred grounds below.

Desecrating them with the violence of their death.

Niko slowed to a walk now, and then stopped entirely, dazed and shocked. There was no reason to run anymore, no reason to hurry. The world swam and spun around him. All the adrenaline in his body melted away into a slurry of icy shame and horror, the taste of unpalatable, rare defeat on his tongue.

He had failed.

The Grand Sovereign was dead.

Chapter Two

A PREDATORY BIRD

"So, what happened?" Zann's voice was strained over the phone, the signal fraying his words with faint static. When at his apartment, Niko's phone was set to project through his Autonomous Assistant Bot, T1-N4. The round, orange bot hovered in the air with a tiny, softly purring engine as Zann's demoralizing question sunk heavy into him.

I didn't jump after him. That's what happened, Niko thought. *I hesitated. I should have jumped.* He knew it was a poisonous thought, something borne of old habits he should have long learned from by now. But he also knew it was the truth—if he'd let himself be a little reckless, he would have caught the Kestrel. Niko knew it, plain as day.

"It's been a while, Zann. Guess I'm rustier than I thought," he said instead, rubbing a calloused hand across his face. Niko peered around his apartment from where he lay across the couch. The newsfeed played on his TV hologram, where a green and betentacled

Gheroun reporter anxiously rambled about the Grand Sovereign's death and the devastation it meant for the people of Yhanwe-ha. "I shouldn't have hesitated."

The same walls—pale dusty sage with no discernable decor except for old, framed family photos—bore down on him as they did every day, year after year. Niko had sunk into these walls, had become another piece of furniture decorating the small apartment. He'd barely left in three years. Going to the station and then on an actual bounty job had been the highlight of his year so far. Even if it had ended in tragedy. And failure.

Niko didn't want to be having this conversation.

On the other end of the line, Zann sighed, the sound emerging from T1-N4 as a static hiss. "It's not your fault, Niko." He sounded disappointed and tired. "We've thrown everything at this guy we can, and he just keeps surviving it like a fucking cockroach."

Niko's chest ached as frustration spiked within him. He struggled to sit up on the couch more, as though somehow doing so would grant him more presence, more weight in this conversation. Earlier, Zann had said he was the best. Now he was lumping Niko in with every other failed attempt. "It won't happen again, Zann. I'm learning the guy. He's slippery. And he has some kind of energy shield I've never seen. But if I can get through that, he'll be vulnerable. Next time, he's mine."

Niko's gaze wandered from the newsfeed's looping footage of the Grand Sovereign slumping to the ground amidst a shockwave of panicked crowds, instead resting on the nearest hanging portrait. It was his favorite, from back when his family had been whole. Niko was younger in the picture, about seventeen. Ryen, his younger half-brother, was there too, eleven maybe, with a soft and springy afro and a wide smile beaming on his face. Their mother's countenance bore its familiar, generous smile, and the warmth in her crinkled eyes and radiant bronze skin made something eternally inconsolable ache inside Niko.

His stepfather stood beside Ryen, wearing a look of contentment on his dark features that Niko hadn't seen on the man's face in years. He could be an older copy of Zann, who despite the better times captured in the old photo, still wore an edgy, suspicious look. Zann never smiled in photos. He was too cool for that.

I should visit Dad, Niko thought. *See how he's doing.* He knew the answer to that—it was the same as it had been for a long time. Not well.

"Niko," Zann murmured, pulling him out of his reverie. Niko could imagine his face perfectly. They'd been inseparable for years, closest in age of all the family members, and left to pick up the pieces of tragedy. Where their father had shut down and turned inward, Niko and Zann had instead taken action. "I know. I'm only saying that this guy is a real son of a Toliai. I still believe you can get him. Just... He's become a pain in my ass, if you know what I mean."

"Yeah. I can imagine," Niko said.

"Now you see why I'm at my wits' end with this bastard."

The newsfeed caught his attention again as a Quwa-quay began talking, their pearlescent, wide eyes wet with heavy tears. "It was terrible," they said, words thickly accented. "I can't get it out of my head. One moment, the Grand Sovereign was praying, then the next, they were just gone. What did we do to deserve this?"

"Listen, Zann, I have to go," Niko mumbled. They said their goodbyes and he hung up. The same moment of devastating failure played from different angles, before cutting to a live video of the newly anointed, auxiliary Grand Sovereign vowing to avenge the previous body's death. Niko didn't fully understand the Quwa-quay religion, but knew it had something to do with the Grand Sovereign being one ancient soul that inhabited each new vessel. They pledged personnel and resources to the investigation, and to monetarily contribute to spiking the bounty on the Kestrel's head. Then they prayed for the wisdom of the previous vessel.

"TV off," Niko mumbled. T1-N4 disabled the hologram and the living room fell quiet.

T1-N4 chimed in her perennially pleasant, digital tone, "Niko, you seem to be lethargic and depressed today. Would you like to view the top-rated video of 'kittens misjudging how far they can jump?' It is considered by viewers across the galaxy as 'heartwarming' and 'funny'—"

"No." He groaned, struggling to push his legs off the edge of the couch. He gave them both a hearty shove and both feet settled onto the floor.

"Perhaps you would prefer 'puppies greeting their owners after a long absence?'"

"Knock it off, Tina," he grunted.

"Okay, Niko. I won't show you any animal videos."

Niko rubbed at his face, a sour sensation verging on nausea creeping through his gut. His mood was slipping lower, and a string of resilient anger still sat heavy, stubborn, and searing in his chest. He didn't know if he was angrier at the Kestrel or himself. Failing a job never sat well with him. Niko had always taken his bounty work very, very seriously. When he'd been regularly hunting, Niko had been one of the galaxy's best. He'd been relentless in bringing down his marks—at any cost. He didn't know how to rest, how to let something go. Especially something like this.

His thoughts wandered again to the Kestrel. The man had made it all seem so effortless. He was hardly even concerned by Niko's presence. He had seemed more irritated, frustrated than anything. Like Niko was just one of many who'd tried inadequately and failed stunningly. The Kestrel was dancing circles around everyone—Galapol, planetary authorities, bounty hunters. They were mere nuisances to him.

Not again.

The words rang like a bell through Niko, reverberating. They made him sound like common trash who had merely gotten in the Kestrel's way. And it was true; that was all Niko had really been the night before. Something merely in his way. Thinking about it only fed the tight and bitter resentment in his chest. He'd never used to be so sloppy, so timid in his work. He wasn't used to failing.

Niko's pulse hammered against his neck and in his stomach. He hated everything about this guy, from his haughty, cool arrogance to his taking lives into his hands and snuffing them out dispassionately.

He even hated the man's next-gen tech. Not to mention that vapid, catchy music. And that fucking bird mask.

Kestrel. A predatory bird.

The conceit of it, of having a *theme* as though the whole thing were a game made Niko hate him even more.

This was getting him nowhere, he could see now, other than sending his pulse into a frenzy and his mood sinking further into the mired depths of spiraling shame and contempt. With a sigh, he scooted towards the edge of the couch and took hold of the wheelchair sitting beside it. He swung himself into it, a move that seemed effortless now, but relied on strong arms and three years' worth of practice. Once he was settled in, Niko reached down and adjusted his legs into place.

Two years ago, Zann had gifted Niko the glossy, black tech armor as an astoundingly invaluable gesture. It was uniquely customized, equipped with cutting edge neurotech sensors built into the legs and spine of the suit that allowed him to ambulate and move the legs that had gone three years without feeling or control.

It was the only way Niko could walk again for the rest of his life. He still had no sensation while in the suit, but several months of stubborn training and grit had allowed him to relearn how to balance, walk, and even run again.

Even so, retired from hunting, Niko hadn't had any real use for the suit. He'd trained in it regardless, unable to give up the hope that one day he might be able to return to the hunt. It had all remained little more than a fantasy. Something had always kept him back from actually trying again.

Until now.

He wheeled out into the kitchen, blearily looking around at its contents. White cabinets and a faux-marble countertop stared back at him. His mother's holiday cactus sat drooping in the corner window by the sink. He needed to water it again.

The familiar purr of T1-N4's engine whizzed by. "Do you require help with items on the top shelf?" she sang at him.

"No."

"Would you like me to order from your number one ranked restaurant? I can replicate your last order of one party tray of chicken nachos, large soft drink, and family-sized pan of brownies from Ch'ua's Chicken."

Niko winced through T1-N4 regurgitating his last depression binge order. *Party* in his case often consisted of one attendee and an action flick rerun.

The owner of Ch'ua's Chicken was a Dvaab, a little leathery and time-worn, olive-toned alien whose species honored its members by bestowing them horrifically long names. The more esteemed a person was, the longer their name. Ch'ua was—to Niko's chagrin—merely a nickname for Ch'uachial'nenauani'nii'eenanvi'coenan'ssche'dewerr. He could never remember it past the first few syllables though, and probably couldn't if the fate of the galaxy depended on it.

Ch'ua's Chicken was cheap, though, and it was tasty in the way food drowned in salt, sugar, and partially-legal alien spices often was. Zann was convinced the "chicken" was actually Yeuronean desert-frog meat, but Niko didn't care to think too hard on it, and didn't ask. He and his brother were both shamelessly constant patrons of the little food joint.

Still, it was tempting and he knew the easy serotonin hit would marginally improve his shit mood. Loaded chicken nachos were the fuel to his days more and more often lately. Any sort of rich, saucy meat piled on chips reminded Niko that life was still worth living.

Sometimes it was the small things. And he didn't have the wherewithal to prepare an actual meal right now.

"Sure. No drink or brownies this time, though." Niko tried to maintain some semblance of self-respect.

"Okay, I'll—" T1-N4 started.

"No, I want the brownies. Family-sized." *Fuck self-respect.* Niko was angry and miserable and wanted carbs.

"Okay. I'll add brownies to your order."

He grabbed a beer from the fridge and waited for the food to arrive.

Niko had to stop moping. The more he told himself that, the more he could believe it. He needed to take action. He had to make sure this didn't happen again. Next time, he would be more prepared. He would knock the Kestrel down from his high tower and make him pay for everything he'd done. Every death, every senseless tragedy.

Once the food came, he wheeled back out into the living room, this time to the small desk in the corner, and cracked open the beer. After a few swallows, he glanced at T1-N4, who had drifted into the room after him, tentatively hanging back.

"Play Royce RG."

The silence of his apartment was instantly replaced with melodic, heavy rap from Niko's favorite artist, the bass so intense it made T1-N4 vibrate with each beat. It was all he could do to push out the catchy, sparkling pop song the Kestrel had been listening to; its chorus had wormed into his brain and begun looping like a parasite. Maybe now he had a chance at getting some actual work done.

"Pull up the files from Zann. Display them."

T1-N4 did. Myriad text, video and photo files from Galapol's tireless research on the Kestrel began appearing one by one in the air before him, suspended in the telltale blue light of T1-N4's holographic projection. Niko knew these files were something he *probably* shouldn't have in his possession, and by probably, he knew that he definitely *shouldn't*. But he and Zann had done plentiful favors for and relied on one another to get things done and bring in criminals throughout Niko's bounty hunting career, and in the end, who the hell was Niko going to share this sort of intel with, anyway? It only served to make his job easier, and Niko would take every advantage he could get to save the life the Kestrel deigned to be next in his crosshairs.

The files appeared to be updated, with footage and documents on last night's death of the Grand Sovereign.

Niko sifted through them, opening and making his way through greasy nachos and chocolate crumble brownies as he did. Alongside the crime scene photos, autopsies, and images of the hasty and near illegibly scrawled *Tell them the Kestrel is coming,* grainy and unclear shots of the Kestrel—with his stupid, *stupid* bird mask and sniper rifle—were littered throughout the files. It seemed he'd managed to occasionally be glimpsed on security cam feeds before disappearing under stealth. Many had various observations hand-written directly on them by Galapol investigators.

Young, male presenting. Human or Heenvan biology. Likely aged 18-35 was scrawled under an enhanced close up of the Kestrel, which amounted to little more than a humanoid-shaped set of pixels.

Another said, *Observed to have advanced tech.*

"No shit," Niko murmured, taking another swig of beer before moving on.

Tech = wealthy corporate sponsor? Big company behind murders, backing Kestrel???

Niko sighed. Somehow, that didn't seem right. He had no proof, nothing to go off of other than instinct. This guy was working on his own. He knew he could always be wrong, but his gut said the Kestrel was a loner. Besides, when it came to big, wealthy and corrupted companies, there were far subtler ways to wreck and ruin lives than indulgent assassinations carried out in the bare public eye.

The newer files from Zann revealed that there had been two false leads taken in and questioned recently, both human men—an Ezrah Carragher, aged twenty-four, and a Loren Faulks, aged twenty-eight, who stared blankly at Niko from dead-eyed portraits. Both men had past criminal histories that implied a specific hatred towards author-ity and celebrity figures, as well as a penchant for violence. In the end, both had solid alibis to prove they'd been engaged elsewhere when the murders had happened. They'd been subsequently released.

The data continued, stating the Kestrel had been assassinating galactic leaders and public figures for roughly over four months now, every kill carried out with the same type of bullet, fired from a sniper rifle. Niko knew that already. The Kestrel had taken eight lives publicly, before the eyes of billions. Niko knew that too. Before Zann had called him in on the hunt, Niko had found himself just as glued to the newsfeed as—if the internet was any indication—most people had become. Something in him had itched at seeing each development, each new death. Something that had been put long to sleep but had resurfaced again now, restless and insatiable. The need to make this right. The need to be the one to take him down. Despite all his reservations, despite swearing off hunting, some part of Niko had silently begged for Zann to call him in.

And then he had.

Niko sighed. "Close the files."

The dim glow of the dozens of holographic images and documents blinked instantly from view. Niko rubbed at his eyes; sometimes staring at holograms for too long gave him a headache. He could already feel one beginning to form, a hazy pain pulsing in his temples. Or maybe it was just from the pile of salt, sugar, and carbs he'd just ingested.

"Tina, compile and display a list of upcoming public events of politicians and celebrities for the next quarter."

"Here you go!" T1-N4 chimed, and the single most despairing list of data Niko had ever seen appeared, hovering before him in illuminated text.

"Shit, this has to be a hundred pages long. At least."

"Excellent guess! The list is ninety-two pages long with 2,344 unique events. I've covered the next three months for you in detail."

Three months. Over two thousand high-impact public events across the galaxy in just three months. Niko's head swam. He glanced over at an old portrait of his mother, sitting atop the desk, and silently begged her for strength. Niko was beginning to see why Zann always looked and sounded so tired working with the Kestrel case.

"Alright. Tina, reduce the list to only the members with extremely wide appeal and recognition across the entire galaxy. Anyone who would have a sixty-percent recognition rate or higher."

"Okay, I've updated your list."

The hologram blinked and refreshed itself, revealing a much more manageable and precise list of potential targets for the Kestrel's next kill—no. Next *attempted* kill, Niko corrected himself. There wasn't going to be another death.

He sifted through the data from most recent to furthest out, marking and highlighting certain ones. The truth was, the Kestrel could be at any of these events. But Niko was going for the biggest, most high-profile ones. The Kestrel wanted to be seen. Niko couldn't shake the feeling. The assassin wanted people to know and witness when he took lives. He wanted to either frighten people or gloat, Niko wasn't yet sure which. Maybe a bit of both. Either way, if it were merely about getting rid of someone, the man would kill them anywhere and any way.

The spectacle of it all was more than part of it, he knew. It was the point. The Kestrel's work was steeped in vanity.

Niko began researching a particular event—it was one of the soonest approaching, and easily had the highest potential attendance. *Starlight Burning*, it was called. A concert set to become the single biggest entertainment event in the galaxy to date, held at the Vhesa Station Arena that orbited the giant, rocky world of Yeuronea. Niko was shocked at the projected number of attendees: well over two million people from all across the galaxy. The event was sold out, and had been for several months since the moment it was announced.

Two vogue, alien music starlets who'd had years of legendary public feuding were now holding a concert together. They were set to perform not only new and previously unheard material, but were debuting an album they'd collaborated on. *Starlight Burning* was all the rage, enough that as much as he'd wanted to ignore the world of celebrity pop idols, Niko remembered seeing the ads several times over the past few months, had seen it mentioned again and again in internet forums, and had even heard some of the staff at the Galapol station discussing it in excited, breathless tones.

Even now, as Niko researched, Kuliedi Taan and her former rival, Hayura, peered out at him from dozens of glamorous promotional photos together. In each, the antennaed Heenva vocalist and green, betentacled Gheroun pop star looked like they loved nothing more than each other's company, despite apparently having disdained one another for years before this. Such was the power of carefully-curated public imagery.

Niko opened the website for the official event and goosebumps pricked along his skin, the air growing chillier. Holograms of both performers singing their hearts out filled the air before him and an eerily catchy, familiar chorus replaced the rhythm of Royce RG through T1-N4's speaker.

"I'm your star.

Your star, your starlight burning.

When you're lost, my love will guide you home.

I've got you, baby,

I'll be your star, your star, your starlight burning,

When you're lost, my love will guide you home."

He was going to be there. Niko knew. The song, bright and melodious, continued playing, though it only made his skin crawl, cold and clammy. This was all a game to the Kestrel. He'd been having fun, listening to their music, planning to silence them permanently after he'd taken down the Grand Sovereign.

Niko had his next destination.

"I have a feeling about this concert," Niko said. He was back on the ship again, in his wheelchair as his armor charged. He wanted it to be in prime condition for the concert. His favorite rifle—the one he'd taken with him on Yhanwe-ha and the one that had seen the most use throughout his hunting years—lay disassembled, each piece spread out carefully on the table as he cleaned them.

Zann's voice cut through the ship's comm speakers. "Look, I don't disagree with you that it's a high possibility. It's on our list.

But I have to go with Deura-11. There's a political parade there that several big Toliai politicians are going to be in."

"But this has a bigger impact, Zann," Niko said, examining the barrel. Satisfied he'd de-gunked it, he reached for his oiling cloth. "He's going for who has the biggest turnout. If we're talking ego, he wants to show off. Not to mention the music. It was the same song."

"Could just be the guy has shit taste in music."

Since he'd called his brother to announce he'd found his next target, Niko had been met with surprising opposition. Zann's research team had firmly argued the Kestrel was most likely headed to the Deura-11 parade and hadn't budged since. Both events were happening on the same day, and roughly at the same time, but in vastly different corners of the galaxy, and therein lay the crux of the entire argument.

"So, there's been talk at the station lately," Zann continued, "and they think there's a distinctly political motivation to his killings. We're putting a lot of brains together to try and predict him. The common conclusion is the parade."

"But he's killed celebrities. An actor and a movie director. The human philanthropist lady. What was her name? Nadeen Narradi? It's not all political."

"Nadeen Navarri. And sure, but when you really delve into the actor's and director's pasts, they both had strong political affiliations. Even the philanthropist did. Every one of them were tied to politics somehow. They all donated to campaigns, too. There's some kind of connection going on here, a web we're not quite yet seeing."

Niko paused, shaking his head, though Zann couldn't see it. Frustration crested in him at knowing his brother had begged him to join in this hunt, only to now brush aside his judgment. "No. I don't buy it. I don't think this is political. If it was, he'd just be getting rid of them by any means. But he wants everyone to see. There's ego in this."

"I'd say a political parade is pretty fucking public, Niko. Look, I trust your instinct. You've always been good. My guys are going to be focusing on the parade and I know you'll have the concert. It's better to split up anyway, so we can take both. I'll get a few undercovers posted with you too. They'll keep an eye on anything weird. In the end, we'll see who's right. Maybe it's neither of us and we end up with another death."

"That's not going to happen."

Once he was off the phone, Niko's thoughts strayed again to the Kestrel. It was hard *not* to think about him at this point. What had previously been a curiosity that Niko had kept up with in the news was now taking up all his headspace. Hunting did that to him. He became solely focused, driven, until nothing else mattered but bringing in—or taking down—his mark.

It had been a long time since Niko had started the tumultuous slip into this particular kind of all-consuming obsession, and it was happening fast and hard to him now. When he wasn't researching the Kestrel, he was watching newsfeeds discussing him. When he wasn't doing any of that, and was trying to separate himself from it all and get some quiet time napping, his mind went back again and again to the assassin. The easy grace of him, the tone of his voice when he'd dismissed Niko. *Not again.*

Whatever the man's reasons, he was a peerless assassin. The best Niko had ever encountered in his life. He was obviously young, and agile, and to say he was good at what he did would be a gross understatement. It had been years since Niko had encountered this kind of challenge—and this kind of thrill. It had been even longer since he'd had someone who could keep up with, even outmaneuver him.

There was something darkly intriguing, even *fascinating* about the Kestrel. Something about the audacity of him. The shroud of mystery surrounding him. Niko wanted to know more, wanted to understand. Wanted to know how a single individual in this vast collection of gravity-bound stars could devastate entire worlds and shake off the best officers and hunters in the galaxy like a dog casually shaking water from its fur. He played a clever and skilled game, whatever it was.

Niko wanted to be the one to match him, to meet him, to take him down and end his dark brilliance. Some selfish part of him hoped he was right, that the Kestrel would go for the concert instead of Zann's parade. That he would be the one to eradicate the arrogance the man espoused. Skill for skill. Niko had once been among the best hunters out there, and the Kestrel was quickly proving to be the galaxy's most formidable, evasive enemy. He hadn't felt so alive—so *awake*—in a long time.

There was something heady about that. Something, maybe, sensual.

Niko pushed the thought away quickly, burying it, refusing to give it a single second more of consideration. The Kestrel was a bastard, and nothing but. He was a murderer who thought he was better than everyone else in the galaxy. The man clearly had no reservations whatsoever about terrorizing and killing innocent people.

Two million sets of eyes from every alien species would soon be watching the stage at *Starlight Burning*, and probably a hundred times more from their homes or places of work. Hayura and Kuliedi Taan were just living their lives, creating music, making others happy. Both artists were so young. They didn't deserve to die.

Niko wasn't going to make the same mistakes he had on Yhan-we-ha. The next time he met the Kestrel, there would be no hesitation.

At any cost.

CHAPTER THREE
STARLIGHT BURNING

NIKO KNEW THE VHESA Station Arena was huge, but somehow, he hadn't accounted for just how massive the entertainment venue really was. The station was a tangle of high-ceilinged corridors, wings, and smaller arenas all surrounding the main attraction concert hall, and every free space his gaze fell on was either full of little opportunistic pop-up merchandise shops or brightly neon holograms showing the singers and hyping up the show to come. The entire station was surrounded by a parking dock ring, which was full to the brim with ships of all sizes and shapes. The traffic to get in had been almost more challenging to navigate than the job itself would likely be. Even the exterior of the station had been covered in various animated holograms of the bedazzling Gheroun and Heenva star celebrities.

Just as he'd done on Yhanwe-ha, once Niko had presented his bounty hunting license and collaboration with Galapol, he'd been let in to walk the endless wings of the labyrinthine entertainment station. He was grateful for the map Zann had managed to snag and send his way; Niko had it loaded into the visor interface of his helmet now. Without it, it would have been all too easy to get lost, swallowed up in the chaos of a galactic crowd.

There were other bounty hunters out there stalking through the crowds too, Niko could see. They stood out from the fans and staff alike, usually carrying multiple weapons on them. Their aesthetics tended towards the more eccentric and extreme, too—myriad tattoos, brightly colored hair, clothing that made a statement. They made a generally rougher, more rugged looking crowd. Niko could hardly judge, though. He knew he must look intimidating walking about in his full armor, rifle attached at his back. He shared the other hunters' fondness for tattoos, his body covered in them from neck to toe, though none of that could be seen beneath the suit.

Niko wouldn't judge them on their appearance, but he definitely *would* judge them on another criteria, the very thought making him grimace. Likely many out and about for the concert, weaving their way through crowds and trying to figure out how to find the Kestrel in their own way, were fully mercenary, working for themselves without a sanctioned contract with Galapol nor any local authorities. Niko had always been wary of them. They operated in a rapacious sort of way that he found often straddled the line between cold disregard and outright brutality.

He craned his neck to follow a mean looking lavender Heenva, armed to the teeth in every which way. The man appeared to be hassling a group of music fans who had crowded in and blocked his path. Voices began rising as the group refused to capitulate now that the Heenva was demanding them to. Niko began walking towards them, wondering if it was going to progress to the point of needing to break it up—

—and was nearly knocked off balance. A short human woman shoved past him, her hair a shade of pink that Niko could only think of as bubblegum. Off her back hung a frayed, magenta backpack covered in obscene patches and pins. She eyed his armor up and down as she walked by, not stopping, and sniped over her shoulder, "Out of the way, dipshit."

She was several steps past him before Niko could retort. Bubblegum—Niko's brain imprinted the name on her—was coming right up on the altercation before them, but didn't seem fazed. Instead, she spared no effort in shoving the snarling Heenva out of her way, just as she had with Niko. The man looked so shocked at her audacity that he just stared, too. Then she was gone as the same crowd who'd blocked the Heenva parted quietly to let her through. Nobody, it seemed, wanted to get knocked on their asses.

Another hunter? Niko shook his head. He'd never seen so many in one place before. The idea made his pulse quicken. Every one of them was after the same bounty he was. Every one of them wanted to be the one to get there first. Niko wasn't about to let that happen.

He turned and began making his way to what the map overlay indicated was the central arena. A congregation of young Gheroun women dressed in glamorous, sequined outfits looked at him and giggled. They wore sparkling bracelets on their tentacles.

"What's with the armor?" one asked. They couldn't be older than adolescents. If the Kestrel really was here tonight, they'd all be witness to his violence.

"Security," Niko grunted back, before moving on. It wasn't entirely a lie.

When he reached the main arena where the concert was due to be held, a wave of trepidation flooded over him. He paused, scanning the vast area and crowd ahead of him. There had to be a few hundred thousand people on this station already, if not more. And almost all of them were gradually crowding their way into this arena. Finding a single person—especially one who was exceptionally good at not being found—among this many was daunting, to put it lightly. The arena was vast, with an arching glass ceiling several stories high that granted a straight view of the hazy blue Yeuronea against a backdrop of stars. The walls of the arena curved, forming a colossal circle. Just like the halls outside, nearly every surface was covered with bright, fast-moving holograms that advertised the singers, refreshments, and upcoming shows. Niko couldn't stare at them for long or the telltale ache behind his eyes began to threaten him.

Instead, he glanced upward. He had to be smart about this. The countless crowds filing into the arena, the constant onslaught of color-pop of the holograms meant nothing. He did his best to tune it out like the visual static it was. If the Kestrel was here tonight—and Niko couldn't shake the feeling that he was—the sniper would again go for high ground. There were no rafters to maneuver across—Zann had revealed that out of an abundance of caution with the Kestrel murders, though the show hadn't been canceled nor postponed, the lightwork infrastructure had been dismantled and light-tech bots and drones deployed instead.

That left one other option.

Hanging along the room in a great circle were dozens upon dozens of private balconies, undoubtedly for those with an extra bit of clout and a lot of money to pay for them. Niko pulled up the map again and maneuvered towards one of the private elevators that led up to them.

A hefty Dvaab wearing her own thick armor pads and plates—all stamped with the Vhesa security logo—stepped in his way. "You got a pass?" she asked warily.

"No," Niko said, projecting his license and other relevant info from his visor, "but I'm working in contract with Galapol and I have cause to believe the Kestrel may be here tonight. I'd like to scope out the private balconies."

The Dvaab processed his license number, running it through a quick check for authenticity, then murmured into her radio too quietly for Niko to hear. Finally, she turned a bland gaze on him again. "No one's up there yet but they're due any moment. Station sec says you can take a look at this one but not for long."

Niko nodded to her in thanks and stepped into the elevator. Several seconds later, the doors opened and he stepped out onto the balcony, looking down now at the arena below. It was easier to think up here, but he had limited time.

Niko turned his attention to the other adjourning balconies. The Kestrel could be on any of them already, watching him like the predator he was. He could be on *this* balcony, mere feet from him, just like he had been on the roof before. The thought of being so close, of being observed by something so deadly made goosebumps creep along Niko's skin.

But something didn't seem right. He ventured forward further onto the balcony. It was, for the size of the arena, shockingly small, with only ten seats per, all crowded in beside one another. This was a sold-out show. Every one of these seats would be full. And even if the Kestrel had managed to buy himself a seat ahead of time, there simply still wasn't enough room to set up and make a shot with a sniper rifle. Not without it being left completely empty, and an empty balcony would be sure to draw the attention of every security guard and bounty hunter present.

The balconies weren't feasible.

Then where? Niko glanced up. He was on the highest spot in the arena, above two other rows of balconies. There were no other doors, no hidden panels, no platforms on which to stand.

For the first time since he'd seen the concert website, a pang of doubt speared through Niko. Had he misjudged?

No. He just had to think harder. Be cleverer. Crawl into the Kestrel's head and think like he did.

Somewhere else, then.

He entered the elevator and descended, skirting along the edges of the arena at ground level once more.

If Niko were the Kestrel, he would take extra precautions not to make the same mistakes twice. Though the assassin had still completed what he'd come to do and had killed the Quwa-quay leader, Niko had at the very least thrown a wrench into his plans. He'd been found out. Uncovered. It was a thought that pleased Niko a little—he hadn't managed to stop the man, but he at least had forced him to flee and think on his feet. That was more than almost anyone had accomplished so far.

He had to think this time of what the Kestrel wouldn't do as much as what he would. It was one thing to predict a skilled assassin; it was another to predict how a clever mind might learn from and react to almost being caught. Even if the balcony seats were viable, the Kestrel might not go for them anyway. It would be too easy to be found twice.

In the precious few minutes Niko had spent on the balcony, a flood of people had made their way in. He was barely aware of voices calling out announcements over an echoing speaker. The show's start was imminent. Maybe he had gotten it wrong after all. Maybe Zann and his team of researchers were spot on, and the assassin was a trillion miles away, lining up his shot at one of the Toliai politicians this very second.

All around him, a sea of music fans, security guards, and hungry bounty hunters who'd had the same idea he did maneuvered through the station.

Niko couldn't shake the feeling his first instinct was right, even though there was no sign of anything amiss whatsoever, and absolutely nowhere for a sniper to work. The Kestrel could find some level of anonymity among the crowds, but hiding something as big and obvious as a sniper rifle among them wasn't feasible either.

A voice rang out again across the arena, so loud and intense now that Niko felt it in his chest. The warm-up act was starting, welcoming everyone for coming and asking if they were ready for the show of a century. The arena was beginning to pack in now, more seats filled than not at this point, and as the music began, so did a neon array of nearly psychedelic, rapidly dancing colors and imagery through the air and along the walls, projected by various hovering tech. The colors changed with each beat of the rhythm, and Niko's headache pressed in again, dangerous and stabbing and threatening to grow into a rare migraine. Niko felt like he was rapidly spiraling into a dreamlike, hyper-sensory experience that blended sight and sound. Around him, the music hammered relentlessly, loud and jamming the thoughts out of his head.

Everything was drowned in music; the combined voices and deep bass and drums of alien music were enough to vibrate the floor and walls. There was still absolutely no sign of anything off, no presence lurking in the rafters. Around him, the crowd thrilled and cheered at the warm-up band and growing hype. Niko was at a loss. There was simply nowhere the Kestrel *could* be. Nowhere felt right. Taking out the singers in their changing rooms before the show made little sense either. His kills had always been as public as possible. Maybe Niko really was wrong. Maybe the instinct he had always so easily relied on had dried up and vanished completely in his years of quiescence.

Did I lose my spark?

It wasn't impossible. He may have once been one of the best in his field, but three years was a long time to sink into stagnation and stop honing his skills or doing much of anything. Three years was a long time to not think fast and in the moment. To have let himself go in several different—and damaging—ways.

The warm-up band finished their act to screams and applause, and the real event of the night took center stage as the two alien singers Niko had seen on every commercial, in every hologram, stepped onto the stage.

"Are. You. Ready?" The lead warm-up singer screamed, and the crowd erupted into shrieks and cheers so passionate that every voice bled together into one great, hungry roar. Hayura—the pale green of her tentacles dotted with glinting diamonds, likely collected from the rain of some gas giant—clung to a keytar as she grinned at the crowd. Beside her, Kuliedi Taan sported an asymmetric, pink bob and barely concealing shimmery dress. Her branching antennae were swathed in strings of jewels, a detail Niko could see when he magnified his visor's view.

She gave an elegant bow and the crowd screamed again. Both women began addressing the audience, thanking them for all their love and loyalty, before going on to compliment each other. Niko's heart was in his throat. He could barely pay attention to any of the showmanship, and hardly cared. It wasn't why he was here anyway. If the Kestrel was here, now would be the time. Niko felt ill, the beginnings of a nauseous migraine churning through his gut, tightening its grip on his head. One part of him felt acutely alive, buzzing with the anticipation of tragedy about to strike. And another part was just tired that he had fallen so far out of instinct, out of skill. Out of *everything* that had once been the greatest passion of his life.

The introductions gave way quickly and the real treat of the night began. A pulsing heartbeat rhythm shuddered through the air, louder than over a million excited screams, the holographic and surreal twisting colors, shapes, and phantom dancers even more intense than they had been with the cover band. The music was pure camp—the same plasticine pop Niko had heard from the Kestrel's frequency.

Its pulse pounded so heavy through his chest that he couldn't tell where it ended and the anxious hammering of his heart began. Maybe they were one and the same.

Zann's argument began to sound more and more convincing, but there was something in the air—that electric rainstorm tension—that Niko just couldn't shake.

As though Niko had summoned him, Zann's contact photo appeared on his visor screen, the beeping notification of an incoming call nearly inaudible against the music. Niko answered, straining to hear his brother.

"Niko. We've got a lead here. Rooftop figure has been spotted at the parade—"

Shit. No.

An uncomfortable tangle of emotions wormed through Niko. Humiliation, surprise. Disappointment. Deep, deep disappointment. He hadn't wanted to be wrong. He'd wanted to be the one to stop him, to—

"He's got a sniper rifle. My guys are closing in now," Zann continued. Niko winced. He knew he should be happy about this. He should be thrilled. Relieved. They were about to bring down the man who had wrought unspeakable horror across multiple civilizations. Having this guy off the streets and unable to hurt anyone ever again should have been nothing but a relief.

Should have been.

But his string of misjudgments and failures since coming back only told Niko that hunting wasn't meant for him anymore after all. He should have left it behind for good. Niko just wasn't what he'd used to be.

He wanted the glory, the satisfaction, the recognition that he was still at the top of his game. That he still had it, even after his accident.

Accident? Is that what we're calling it now? He shook his head, trying to clear it of the cruel, biting thought.

It had been a risk to return to hunting. It had always stirred up dark habits in him. Self-destructive ones. But he'd taken that risk, because the truth was, life had felt empty without the hunt. It had felt meaningless. Niko needed to know he was still capable. Instead, all he would ever get now was a failed job and a wrong prediction with the data he was given.

Niko didn't like to lose.

"Be careful, Zann," he warned, swallowing down the oily cocktail of wounded pride. He knew first-hand how slippery this guy could be. How dangerous.

"They've got him. He's down. You owe me a beer, Niko. I was beginning to doubt we had the right idea over here. You actually almost had me convinced." Zann laughed. "Threat has been apprehended and neutralized."

"That's great. Good." Niko hated hearing the strain in his own voice.

"Got a little bit rusty, Niko," Zann said. Niko didn't respond. "Listen, I need to go. But I wanted to let you know we finally got the fucker. I'll call you."

He hung up with Zann, peering out at Hayura and Kuliedi Taan as they sang on stage. Both women seemed to be genuinely enjoying performing together. Either that, or they were incredible actresses. The music was especially grating on Niko's nerves now that he knew all the time, effort, and certainty he'd had in this being the target was wasted.

"*It can't keep me down, can't hold me,*" they sang.

He felt hollowed out, scraped clean inside. But there was another feeling too. One that remained, persistent and nonsensical: that instinctual alarm, the feeling that something was off. That something was wrong. That Niko had picked the right place.

Yet Zann's guys had found the Kestrel. They had him under arrest now, were bringing him into custody. He'd been exactly where Zann had predicted he'd be. There was nothing left to guess at or feel anxious about.

But then—why wouldn't his skin stop crawling?

He thought about what Zann had told him. The Kestrel had been spotted and subsequently taken down on a rooftop near the parade, sniper rifle in hand. It was exactly the thing a skilled and clever strategist would want to *avoid* after being discovered once already in the same situation. These were middling mistakes expected of an amateur.

And Zann had said they'd spotted him. The Kestrel had been plainly visible to Galapol's spec ops team.

The Kestrel had stealth tech.

Oh. Shit. The hair on the back of Niko's neck rose and he looked up, purely by instinct. Another phone call began ringing through his helmet, Zann's image filling the corner of the screen. He answered.

Zann sounded breathless, his voice coming in torn and desperate. "False alarm— *Niko—*"

Something caught Niko's eye: a misty spray of crimson, scattered through the air, spurted out from atop one of the balconies. It caught peculiar and uncanny in the shifting neon lights, like alien rain from the stars above. Then a body followed, a man with his throat sliced open in a red, macabre smile who fell—no, was pushed, Niko could see now, with particular force—from one of the private balconies above.

It happened fast. So fast that Niko barely had time to unlatch his own gun and fumble in shock with its safety.

"—some sort of copycat—" Zann panted. "He might still be there, Niko. You have to hurry before—"

A scream filled the air, louder even than the music around him. Niko realized it was his own voice, hoarse as he shouted unthinking at the people below.

"Move! Get back! *Move!*"

None of them could hear him. The man dropped, dead weight, and struck the ground well behind the nearest floor level seats. If he'd somehow survived the initial injury, by the sight of his contorted and broken figure, Niko could see there was no chance life still inhabited the man's body. Several seconds passed, painting the scene sur-real as holographic colors danced around the mangled body. The people nearest glanced behind them at him, briefly confused at what they were looking at. Beyond the nearest attendees and closest security, no one even knew a life had just been taken.

The music continued on. *"Gravity can't touch me when I'm with you."*

"Niko?" Zann said.

"Oh, he's definitely here."

"*Shit!* Niko, you can't let him get away."

"I'm on it."

Niko was already moving. He knew he could never find the Kestrel in a crowd this dense—especially now that the realization of what had just transpired was beginning to spread like a shockwave. Concert attendees were screaming, trying to back away from the body. Some were frozen in place, openly staring, while a disturbing number were trying to make for the exits. He hoped this didn't turn into a stampede.

"Free me, love me, take me, remake me—"

The singing stopped abruptly as security flooded the stage to whisk Hayura and Kuliedi to safety. The background music track ground to a halt, the dreamlike, dancing holograms and neon lights still sweeping across the arena, ghostly and wrong against the lack of music.

It could have been anyone. It could even be another copycat, just like Zann's team had encountered. In over four months, the Kestrel had never once killed with anything but a sniper rifle. But Niko *knew*. He felt him. He'd known the Kestrel would be here tonight.

He'd had to use another method. It was that simple. Where there had been no room to take a shot, the man had simply used a different means instead.

Niko summoned the map again, pinpointing which balcony the body lay under. B64, whose private elevator opened near an exit to a series of corridors and branching offshoots and—

There.

—eventually Gate E64 to the parking deck ring. This was a station and the Kestrel was just as trapped as anyone else there until he could get to whatever transport out of there awaited him. But he wouldn't be for long. Niko burst into a run, pushing himself hard, electric jolts of pinpricked nerves singing up through his legs as he moved. He had no time to think about the pain.

It felt strange to run like this, to push himself again on two legs until his body ached and lungs burned from the effort. It was disorienting, too, though—he had no feeling in his legs, having to trust and rely on *imagining* himself running in a visceral, physical sense, trying to send the sensations of moving those muscles and nerves into the suit for it to respond properly. It was a technique that had taken months to master, but right now, it was worth it.

Even if he would have to pay for it tomorrow.

Nothing was going to stand in his way now. Not limitations, not pain. Niko wasn't letting him get away this time.

"Zann, I need to go. Get a hold of your undercovers and tell them he's here. Gate E64."

"Niko, be careful—"

Niko cut the call, no seconds to waste. He sorted through frequencies as fast as he could while running until he reached the one used by Vhesa security, if the cacophony of panicked orders and questions filling the line was any indication. It seemed the Kestrel had thrown them for a loop as well.

"You need to close Gate E64 to the ring. I am in pursuit of the fugitive and believe that's where he's heading."

A pause on the other end. "Who is this?"

"Hunter 44-8783-332, in contract with Galapol. You need to close the gate."

Another flurry of voices and the security officer he'd spoken to addressed him again. "Gate E64 is locking down. We're sending backup. Good luck out there, hunter."

Niko pushed himself harder, willing himself forward. The Kestrel was fast—infuriatingly so—and if Niko had any chance of catching up to him, he'd have to be faster. Each stride was exhausting to a body unable to run, let alone walk on its own for years. Niko was too close to let himself stop now, though. He wove through confused and panicked bystanders who turned to stare at him as he bolted past.

"Find a security officer. Get yourselves somewhere safe," he called out several times as he ran, but the crowds paid his warnings little mind, some even filming him.

The further he ran, the more the crowds began to thin out. Niko's lungs burned, desperately thirsty for air. His body ached, covered now in a thick sheen of sweat beneath the suit that he wished he could wipe off. His map told him he was nearing Gate E64. It wouldn't be long now. It was going to be a crapshoot if security had managed to get the large gate sealed in time. If Niko had been too slow to get the message through, he may have just shot himself in the foot, putting six-inch-thick steel between himself and the fleeing assassin.

He rounded the last corner, the gate falling into sight in the distance. It was still closing, the thick metal plates grating loudly as they came down, a red light flashing above it in warning to keep clear. Even this far out from the arena, several people stood around, gazing at the gate nervously. They had likely arrived late to the show.

Then Niko's gaze caught on something else. A distorted image, transparent and difficult to follow, moving swiftly down the hallway towards the gate. A slender, athletic figure gliding ahead of him, ethereal as a ghost.

It was him.

This ends here.

If he stopped and took aim, Niko could hit the man before he reached the gate. It was descending rapidly, the gap leading into the vast parking deck beyond growing smaller by the second. But it could go either way still. The spectral runner could still just make it at this rate.

Niko couldn't stop, though. And he couldn't shoot. The scattering of civilians around the gate was too much of a risk. He no longer possessed the lung capacity to command them out of the way, pushing himself to his limit to keep up now.

A bullet whizzed past him from behind, exploding on impact as it collided with the gate. The explosion was strong enough to make the floor and walls of the hallway shudder, and those who were scattered around ducked and cried out. Some had the smarts to run.

Niko stumbled but caught himself, turning quickly to find the source: Bubblegum.

The small woman had caught up to him, her whole body heaving with heavy breaths from her exertion. In her hands was a thick, short-barreled gun of some sort that Niko didn't recognize. Something homemade or black market custom. She pumped it and aimed again.

"Hey—no! There are *civilians* here," Niko shouted at her.

"Then they can get out of the way. So can you," Bubblegum said. She fired again, the shot eliciting another round of cries from the now terrified bystanders. Niko bristled immediately. This was why he hated unlicensed hunters.

Instead of hitting the gate, this time the shot exploded mid-air, a distorted shockwave rippling outward from the bullet's impact before it fell to the ground. Like Niko had before, she'd hit the Kestrel's barrier with no result.

"You're mine now, you little bitch," she snarled, and pulled a neon green grenade from her open backpack.

Niko's heart leapt into his throat at the sight. He recognized that vibrant, toxic green for what it was: bog-theun corrosive, a rare toxin harvested from its namesake endangered alien swamp animals, dealt in black market trades for exuberant credits.

It digested almost anything it touched.

"Oh, fuck no. There are innocent people—" Niko started. He surged forward without thinking, running straight towards Bubblegum and body-slamming her.

He was too late. Behind them, near the closed gate, the telltale stench of bog-theun toxin spread through the air, followed by screams of pain and panic, then the sizzle of the floor and walls as the corrosive substance began to eat right through them. Niko craned his neck, glancing up over his shoulder to see the damage, and Bubblegum took the opportunity to slip out from under him. She delivered a solid kick to Niko's side, and he took a small satisfaction in knowing it probably hurt her foot more than it had his armored body.

He struggled to pull himself to his feet. *Come on. Just like you practiced.* It took longer than he'd have liked, but soon Niko had his feet planted beneath him and stood. He turned to assess the damage ahead of him with dismay.

The floor before them was slowly dissolving, its melted, foaming pieces dripping down into the growing hole. Gate E64, which had managed to close and corner the Kestrel, now had a similarly growing series of holes. Most of the terrified concert goers had managed to flee in time, but Niko could see a few had clothing that was already beginning to singe away.

Niko disdained hunters like Bubblegum. This was exactly the kind of carelessness espoused by the unregistered and those who were only in it for easy money. They didn't care who else got pulled into their destruction. Niko at least had the pride to say the only person who ever got wrecked in his pursuits was his mark. And, sometimes, himself.

Niko opened the comm channel to security again. "You're going to need medics. We've got injured civilians at E64."

At the center of the chaotic scene stood the Kestrel. His barrier faltered, the air rippling and shuddering around him as a layer of neon green corrosive clung to it, until finally it fell away completely, whatever powered the stealth tech going with it. The man behind so many assassinations stood vulnerable and revealed now, clear as day.

A few drops of caustic green from the broken forcefield landed on his masquerade-styled bird mask, the plasticine material of it sizzling and smoking as it began to melt. With a panicked grunt, the man grabbed wildly for it and pried it off, tossing it to the ground.

There was a brief second when everything around Niko paused. He looked at the Kestrel, and the Kestrel looked back at him.

He was the most beautiful thing Niko had ever seen. The face that peered back at him now was so perfect it made him ache. It stole his breath away. He hated it, hated the leaping twist it gave in his chest and the burning heat it bid in his cheeks.

Niko especially hated that such breathless beauty was wasted on someone like *him*. It only made him despise the assassin all the more.

The Kestrel was clearly in his early or mid-twenties, with a pale complexion and equally pale blond hair that hung around his face in messy cowlicks and loose curls where each strand ended. He had a strong nose, his mouth twisted downward in frustration, his eyes a stunning gray-green Niko had only ever seen before on the oceans of Eanan. Right now, those eyes were boring right back into Niko, both wickedly intelligent and very, very pissed off.

Then the Kestrel tore his gaze away and glanced towards the wounded. He then stared at Bubblegum, his expression darkening into a deep disgust—disdain, even.

"You fucking asshole," he said.

Rich, coming from you, thought Niko. He remembered how to function again, aiming his gun towards the Kestrel.

"Oooh, you're a pretty boy," Bubblegum retorted, her own homebrew gun trained on him as well. "Look at that face."

Niko wasn't the only appreciator of fine art, it seemed.

He fired, but the assassin was already moving. Bubblegum had erred in more ways than one and the Kestrel took the advantage as it presented itself. He slipped through the expanding hole eating its way through the gate, bursting into a full sprint through the parking deck. Niko's bullet pinged uselessly off the gate.

"Little shit," Bubblegum growled, slipping through right after him.

Niko paused, frozen, glancing again at the wounded. Should he stay and help them, make sure they were alright? Or pursue the Kestrel and make sure he never killed again? In the end, Niko had no medical training beyond basic first aid to adequately know he was helping rather than harming, and medical professionals would be on their way soon. With a silent apology, he pushed through the gate in pursuit.

He didn't want to give Bubblegum the satisfaction of claiming the bounty either, after the damage she'd caused others. To be awarded money and fame after sacrificing civilians was contemptible to Niko.

Yeah, she's definitely not registered.

The parking deck was vast, forming an infinite, curving hangar that ringed Vhesa Station. Side by side, ships of all different make and size were parked. Some were like Niko's—small and meant for one to two people. Others were hefty carriers equipped for transporting groups of several dozen. The one closest to him was a mid-sized Dvaab craft, its hull twisted into the sacred spiral designs typically favored by their people.

Every ship here only served to make Niko's life harder, forming a compact maze miles upon miles long. He pushed forward, weaving between packed-in vessels, following the heavy sound of Bubblegum's boots as they echoed through the parking deck. Niko grimaced at his own heavy footfall giving away exactly where he was. With the armored suit, it couldn't be helped.

A voice rang out from somewhere ahead, breaking the tense and heavy quiet. Masculine and clear as a bell. "The two of you are really the best they could send?"

There it was again: that same arrogance from before. It irritated Niko to be lumped in with somebody like Bubblegum—a messy, unregistered hunter who clearly only gave a damn about money. He moved towards the voice, rounding another wide-winged silvery ship, but stopped up short when he saw Bubblegum. She wasn't running anymore, her body still as she tilted her head around to try and decipher the direction of the Kestrel's voice. Something shifted inside Niko, an old and paranoid instinct that had kept him alive on his jobs. Something wasn't right. The voice had had something to it, something uncanny—

"I'd say it was a good effort, but it really wasn't." The Kestrel's voice came again, and Niko could hear—and see now—that it emerged from off to the left of Bubblegum. A small, rectangular two-way radio lay on the ground. "In fact, you were pretty pathetic resorting to banging up civilians just to get your way."

"The fuck?" she asked, kicking the radio and turning on heel, her gun raised.

She was too slow.

The Kestrel was already on her from behind, a flurry of pale gold hair and black clothing. He drove the blunt handle of the same bloodied knife he'd used to kill with against the side of her head, and Bubblegum crumpled instantly, unconscious.

Niko wasted no time, charging towards the Kestrel with everything he had. He closed in quickly on the assassin as the man staggered back from Bubblegum's collapsed form, taking him by surprise and slamming him to the ground before he could escape. He heard the air escape the Kestrel's lungs in a sharp exhale as both men struck the floor. The Kestrel was quick, though, and rolled to the side before Niko could get him pinned down. The blond man sprung up and sprinted further into the parking ring, disappearing behind a bulky, pearlescent Quwa-quay ship.

Niko hauled himself up—more quickly than he'd been able to after tackling Bubblegum—and followed, every part of him threatening to collapse in exhaustion from burning, pleading muscles. An insatiable need to finish this carried him through the pain and fatigue now.

"Why?" he panted out, weaving around a tiny but sharply designed two-seater ship that belonged, possibly, to another hunter somewhere on the station.

To his surprise, the Kestrel answered as he ran, forever several steps ahead. Niko caught him in glimpses—a swift peek of darkly clothed limbs here, a flash of wild, pale gold there, before disappearing again around another ship. He sounded tired too, the words pushed out in a huff of air. "Why what?"

"Why kill these people? What do you get out of this?"

The Kestrel ducked under a colossal, blocky ship that nearly took off Niko's head as he stooped to keep up and breathlessly follow.

"What do *you* care?" the Kestrel spat. He sounded just as breathless, despite how easy he made it look to keep ahead.

Niko knew the implications of the question—he was, after all, a bounty hunter. To anyone who didn't know him personally, he came off as little different from Bubblegum, he was sure. Bounty hunting was typically about the pretty bounties it paid out, and many were called to the siren song of getting those credits, no matter what shortcuts they had to take to be the one to get there first. To Niko, it had never been about the money. Something greater called him to bring in the dangerous and cruel.

"I—I want to understand," Niko said, his voice dripping with sincerity. He did. It was easy to pin ego and fame as the reasons for the Kestrel doing any of this, just as easily as it would have been to pin Niko as a money hungry trash hunter with only self-interest at heart. But the Kestrel hadn't come here tonight for the two biggest, easiest, most high-impact targets. He hadn't gone after the obvious star attractions. Instead, he'd come for someone in the audience. Kuliedi Taan and Hayura were left unscathed.

The Kestrel did something Niko never expected, then. He stopped running.

He slowed to a pause between two towering fleet ships and turned to regard Niko, chest and shoulders heaving as he panted for air. It was so bold—and open and shocking—that Niko stopped in his pursuit as well, wary and waiting for what came next. He kept a several yard distance between the Kestrel and himself, gun half-raised.

The assassin looked tired, those painfully beautiful seafoam eyes watching Niko back just as warily. His unruly hair hung around his face, damp with sweat, his cheeks flushed from exertion. Niko couldn't comprehend it. Stopping here was madness for the Kestrel. Security was likely to catch up at any moment, as well as the undercover Galapol agents Zann had stationed and the myriad bounty hunters Niko had seen prowling about before the show. And Niko himself had been clearly intent on bringing the man down. Something settled uneasily in the air around them, a brief trust between Niko and what was almost like a wild animal: cagey, dangerous, and feral, but pausing to consider you instead of fleeing or attacking. This moment was fleeting and liminal, and Niko could feel it.

The Kestrel's eyes narrowed, serpentine distrust creeping back in, and he spoke again, pushing a long curl of disheveled blond from his face. "I don't believe you."

Niko swallowed, holding his ground. It took everything in him not to shatter the fragile moment and take the opportunity to tackle or shoot the Kestrel again. Every second he spent here, waiting, listening, doing nothing, was giving the other man the chance to get away and kill again in the future. But every instinct told Niko to *wait*. Told him he was on the precipice of learning something vital, some piece of a puzzle he couldn't even see the whole of yet.

"Why do this?" Niko chanced. "Is it fame? Do you get some kind of thrill from killing?"

The Kestrel's expression closed off again immediately, hard and cold as it had been in front of Bubblegum. Niko had said the wrong thing.

"Oh, I get a thrill, alright." His tone was laced with malice.

Niko scrambled to keep him talking. He couldn't lose this when he was so close to grasping... *something*. "But why? Why hurt innocent people?"

"Innocent? That's where you're wrong."

"What?"

"They know what they've done," the Kestrel continued. He looked as disdainful as he had when gazing at the wounded people Bubblegum had deemed collateral. "Every one of them—"

Gunshots tore through the air, bullets ricocheting dangerously close off the side of the ship nearest them.

Their conversation had come, painfully, to an abrupt end. Niko was out of time.

"If you don't want to end up dead too, then stay away," the Kestrel said, already turning to flee again.

"I can't do that," Niko said, raising his gun.

A searing flash of light exploded across Niko's vision and he scrambled to switch on his visor's darkening feature, but it was too late. Imprints of swimming light and color danced across his blinded eyes, temporary damage from what Niko recognized as a flash grenade.

Without being able to see where he was going, he was all but useless, unable to follow. The Kestrel must have grabbed it off of Bubblegum when he'd assaulted her from behind. The deftness of his hands was—grudgingly—impressive to Niko.

By the time backup arrived, the Kestrel was long gone, leaving Niko only with the feeling that he'd stepped off an invisible ledge and was caught in freefall, no ground below to catch him.

CHAPTER FOUR
EVERYTHING YOU HEAR

NIKO HAD GOOD DAYS and bad. The bad ones were never something he could control entirely, and they would always be here for the rest of his life. A good day left his legs numb or with occasional rippling twinges of nerve pain. A bad one found Niko in agony as the nerve pain erupted into what felt like fire. On those days, sensation in his legs ebbed and flowed from a tingling numb to feeling like he was standing in searing flames, the pain sharp, vibrant, and unlike almost anything else he'd experienced in life since the fall that had rendered him paralyzed.

Sometimes the worst days came along, unexpected and cruel. Other times, he triggered them by overexerting himself—like he had the night before at the concert. Running down the Kestrel had brought about the worst day he'd had so far.

His legs spasmed and ached, sending electric jolts up his shins and thighs, and phantom burning in his feet. He had definitely overdone it by running so much, making demands of body parts that had nothing left to give. He had never been merciful to himself, extending all his care to others. Niko threw himself away in the process, and he knew that he did. But he could never stop himself from doing it. Once he was caught up in the moment, the only thing that mattered was reaching his goal.

It was why he'd been so afraid to come back to hunting.

Niko preferred to spend the worst days inactive and lying on the couch, watching a comfort movie and drinking enough beer that he didn't have to think anymore, but today, he was scheduled for rehabilitative physical therapy, and with being back in hunting again, he figured he couldn't afford to miss it. So he was, instead, pushing through the worst of the pain.

The morning and early afternoon were spent in Loolae's little state of the art, mirror-lined studio—so called Destination: Reclamation—where she guided him through exercises and stretches. Morning hours had been for walking, running, learning coordination in the neurotech armor. When afternoon came, he was back out of the suit and working on therapeutic exercises to keep his legs healthy and his body in prime condition.

Loolae was a Xermotl, an alien people who hailed from the torrential, oceanic world of Valaevanas. Amphibious, their skin was rubbery and smooth, with four long tendril-like legs built more for water than land, but capable of maneuvering on both. Loolae was teal green with bright yellow stripes and patterns. Xermotl weren't capable of speaking Galactic Standard, but she wore a small translator chip at her spindly neck and Niko could see her natural excitement each time he succeeded at a set of exercises by how her yellow patterns lit up brightly, the bioluminescence rippling across her.

Niko had gotten to meet Loolae when Zann introduced them shortly after he'd gotten out of the hospital, and considered her one of the only friends he still held closely left in his life.

Normally he wouldn't have gone to an alien with vastly different biology for delicate and intensive physical therapy, but Loolae was the best at what she did, and she took pride in helping grievously wounded veterans, officers, and others injured in service of protecting others. In fact, it was Destination: Reclamation's specialty—the empowerment and discipline Loolae espoused present in the studio's name itself.

Niko didn't regret it for a moment.

"Hellooooo? Niko? Are you still in there?"

Niko twitched, his attention returning to their exercises as he found two wide, golden pairs of alien eyes staring at him curiously. He cleared his throat.

"Yeah, sorry. There's been a lot on my mind."

"I can see that," Loolae commented, leaning back slowly, her patterns dimming to a gentle blue. "Try it again," she counseled, carefully moving his leg into position so Niko could grab his ankle and stretch forward. He did, wincing into the pain that sizzled up along his leg at the movement. "So, I heard you're back into hunting now."

"Yep."

"Does this distraction have anything to do with that assassin by any chance? The Kestrel."

Niko grunted, reaching forward to stretch more intensely into the pain, a flare of frustration sparking in him. "Yeah. The guy is impossible. He thinks he's better than everyone in the damn galaxy and evades every chance I have to get at him. It's been driving me nuts."

"Hmm," Loolae hummed neutrally. "Other leg now."

Since she'd asked, Niko couldn't stop talking. It was all falling out now. "I'm doing my best. I'm giving the best I can. And it's not good enough. He just keeps getting away. The guy is pretty much untouchable. I thought I was better than that, you know? Different from anybody else who wants a shot at him. But every time I get close, he shit-talks me like I'm nothing before disappearing again and it kills me."

"I can't tell if you sound more like a jilted ex-lover or someone who's angry they can't get their turn dating him yet."

"Oh, hell no." Niko balked at the idea, insulted at being linked to this asshole in any kind of sexual or romantic way. He had no interest in fucking the galaxy's number one most wanted criminal. He wanted to punch him and drag him into the station for the judgment and punishment he deserved.

That's *all* he wanted. Even if the Kestrel was infuriatingly, disgustingly good-looking. It only made Niko hate him more.

"Niko, please be careful. I've been following the news on him. He's incredibly dangerous and you have to remember that while you're very capable of hunting, you're still learning how to do it all over again in a different way after your injury. It won't be the same as it was before."

"Yeah," Niko sighed. He had no way of telling her what, exactly, the Kestrel *did* to him, though. The need he had to see this through, to best him. How he'd been called upon to put an end to this and kept slipping up again and again. "You're right."

"I heard about the human man he killed yesterday. Some big CEO."

Niko grimaced, focusing on the quiet burn of his stretches to blot out the sting of what he was unable to forget. "The owner of StarSeam. Guess he was a big fan of Hayura."

"Right, the shipping company. Do they know why it was him? Everybody's surprised it wasn't the singers."

Yeah. Me too, Niko thought. He couldn't *stop* thinking about it. The brief and bewildering exchange with the Kestrel filled his thoughts all morning. They had robbed him of virtually any sleep, tossing and turning, feverish half-dreams, half-memories of the blond man pausing to assess him, to tell him every victim was somehow guilty of—of something. Niko had been frustratingly robbed of whatever the Kestrel had been about to say.

They know what they've done.

As if the universe were wreaking some cosmic irony on him, *Gravity* began playing softly over the speakers, filling the studio with its effervescent beat, the same debut song at Vhesa that had been ground to a halt by the Kestrel's little game. *"Gravity can't touch me when I'm with you."*

Niko barked out a bitter laugh.

"Niko?"

He grunted, murmuring another apology. "No. They don't know. I'm sure Zann's guys are working on it though."

"You were there last night, right? I saw footage on the news somebody recorded of you running and telling people to get to safety."

"Yeah. I was so close, and then I—I messed it up again."

"You're doing the best you can, I'm sure," Loolae graciously offered, her glow shifting to a soft lavender Niko had come to recognize as trying to soothe. "Let's go back to the left leg."

Niko wasn't so keen to agree. Guilt and shame flooded him, melting with the sting of another failure. If he'd really been doing his best, he wouldn't have hesitated. He wouldn't have given the Kestrel a moment to talk. The man had been standing right in front of him. Niko could have taken the opportunity, could have broken through the bizarre trust the Kestrel had given him. If he had, the man would be dead or in custody right now, and whoever was next on his list would be safe. The galaxy wouldn't have to worry about him ever again.

Instead, Niko had listened, and not taken action. And now the assassin had vanished again.

"Good job today," Loolae said once they finished up, patting him on the shin with a rubbery tendril. "Even if your head was in the clouds most of the time."

Niko wiped his face and neck down with a towel when his phone rang. A caller ID hologram of Zann's photo appeared before him. For a brief moment, Niko hesitated, his gut icy and crawling at the idea of talking to his brother. His shame deepened at the thought of avoiding him, and he answered. "Zann."

"Niko, hey. Good call on the concert, after all. I guess I'm the one who owes you a beer. Even if Kestrel got away last night, we gained some invaluable info on him. A treasure trove, really."

"You mean *the* Kestrel?" Niko blurted out automatically, then winced at himself. It was the most pointless and unnecessary correction he could have said. He rubbed at his face.

"Uh, actually, no," Zann said. "Listen, you'll want to be here for this. Can you come out to the station?"

"Yeah, I'm just finishing up with therapy." Niko glanced at Loolae, who waved in the background, her patterns flashing a bright and rosy, mottled pink. "Loolae says hi."

"Well, I say hi back. Get down here, Niko. This is big."

"Should he be here? Should we be sharing any of this with him? He's not Galapol," Fourier asked, his thick eyebrows rising as Niko entered the conference room. Niko saw a cluster of exhausted-looking investigators sitting around and murmuring, their features brightly illuminated from a wall-to-wall scattering of holograms. He paused briefly, stricken, at seeing several images of the Kestrel staring back at him—personal photos and professional ones. Clearly, they'd found who he was.

Niko had come in the armor again. He'd worn it to physical therapy and came straight to the station, but this time Fourier didn't say a word about it, nor laugh. Zann must have explained the situation to him, or at the very least, had chewed him a new one for mocking Niko over it. Fourier, instead, had chosen to single out and question Niko's legitimacy.

"He's on the case," Zann said with a clipped air of finality. "Besides, this is about to be public knowledge by the end of the day."

Fourier shrugged but quieted down.

Niko sank into an empty chair, glancing again at the dozens upon dozens of holographic files that lined the presentation wall, including the photographs of a face so beautiful it still made Niko's chest ache. It was jarring to see. He forced his gaze away.

"Alright. To catch Niko up, this is Elliott James Kestrel," Zann started, bringing one of the man's professional portraits front and center. Someone whistled a catcall from the back of the room and Zann stared at them before continuing. "It wasn't a nickname or title. That was his actual fucking name. He'd written *'tell them that Kestrel is coming.'"*

A couple detectives chuckled around and behind Niko. He winced at the holographic image of the atrocious spray-painted message as it was brought to the forefront now. It *could* say 'that' instead of 'the'—if one were squinting, drunk, and had a generous imagination. Another image of the man's professional signature was moved next to it, matching the illegible chicken-scratch.

Zann continued. "Signature matches. Age twenty-six, from Delevia, out in the Ourros System. We were able to match facial recognition from security cams and DNA tracing from the damaged mask. Now handwriting too. This is our guy."

He held up a vacuum-sealed transparent bag which contained the half-melted remnants of the avian masquerade piece Niko had come to disdain so much. Up close like this, bare and unconcealed by the—no, by Elliott Kestrel's—usual cloaking tech, Niko could see it was simple, flimsy, plastic. Something that likely came from a cheap costume store. It was oddly surprising to him; he'd expected something more elaborate, somehow.

"He was actually born Elliott Johann Kestrel, after Daddy, but filed for a legal name change on his eighteenth birthday," Zann continued, setting the evidence back down. "Earned fantastic grades at Graceleaf League Uni. Graduated top of his class *and* early. Then worked as a robotics engineer at LaraTech. We already have guys out to interview his old boss and coworkers. His old professors. We'll try to see if he has any close confidants too—best friend, girlfriend, the like—and talk to them."

Niko peered at several photos lined up, most professional in nature. Carefully curated images taken from business cards and security badges looked back at him, a clearly tepid but admirably cordial smile on Kestrel's lips. Some of the photos were personal in nature, likely grabbed from old social media accounts. He looked much happier and more relaxed in those, eyes painfully beautiful, his smile easy. The same blond cowlicks fell around his face, albeit marginally more maintained and shorter trimmed. He looked like a perfectly normal person who didn't regularly engage in killing sprees of planetary leaders, celebrities, and mega-corporate CEOs.

Aside from how exceptionally handsome he was. It almost hurt Niko to look at. He couldn't express how much he hated that, how much it made something deep inside him squirm uncomfortably.

"Now we get to the juicy stuff. We've acquired reports on his medical history, and there's a lot. Childhood history of psychological treatment and therapy. As an adult, he suffers from delusions and mental illness. He had to be hospitalized for a month and a half over it. Delved pretty swiftly into conspiracy theories and went off the deep end about three years back, after his sister, Cleo, supposedly cut contact with him. He lost his job over it and became estranged from most of society.

"Behold, Cleo Marie Kestrel."

Images of an equally beautiful, radiant woman appeared on the wall now next to Kestrel. Cleo had the same coloration as him, right down to the seafoam eyes. Long blonde hair fell around her face and shoulders in fluffy waves. In almost every picture, Cleo was smiling—sincere, lovely, and bright. Many of them had a distinctly professional, beauty industry sort of look to them.

"Fashion model with mid-level renown. We've been able to contact and question their parents, and they claim they thought she dropped out of the public eye just over three years ago and went no contact due to her being afraid of her brother, but we're not ruling out the possibility that he killed her too. We've been trying to contact her at all her last known numbers but they're not turning up anything. Her industry colleagues claim she stopped showing up for work, too. Evidence is pointing to him disappearing her, unfortunately."

Zann brought up another picture, this time of Cleo and Kestrel embracing each other. They grinned jubilantly on what appeared to be his graduation day, both faces so resplendent with obvious joy it shook Niko to his core. It felt almost perverse to see this personal moment. And it felt absolutely nothing like the deranged, cold killer he'd been hunting.

It told a different story of two siblings who had loved—and trusted—each other intimately, of a sister who had come to celebrate her brother's milestone achievement in life with him. They looked unburdened, faces pressed together as they hugged, Kestrel clad in a dark cap and gown and Cleo in a vibrant sundress. Cleo had clearly taken the picture herself, one arm extended forward, disappearing out of the edge of the image.

The idea that Kestrel had likely turned on his own sister, had hurt her, had maybe even taken her life made the photograph feel haunted rather than the celebratory moment it portrayed. Just like the pop music Kestrel had been listening to, it shone and glimmered on its exterior, but held a dark and eerie truth deep beneath the surface.

"Interrogators brought in and spoke with Mary and Johann Kestrel this morning, just preceding this conference. Mary says both children have been estranged from them for years, and that Elliott had problems when he was a child, including lashing out with a history of violence towards them and Cleo. She says Elliott frightened her, though, even as a child, and that she believes Cleo went into hiding because she was afraid of him too. They don't seem ready yet to accept that Cleo might be deceased."

Kestrel's history looked bad. If he was delusional and unwell, it certainly wasn't out of the question that one day he could be functioning just fine, and the next, having a violent breakdown. The very person who loved and celebrated with his sister in one moment could be tearing into her with a hurricane of violence the next. Niko knew very well the cruelty some people were capable of.

And Kestrel had dove into conspiracies, parroting them enough to estrange him from his coworkers and cost him his job at a renowned tech development company.

They know what they've done. Every one of them—

"Folks, it looks like we have a case of delusional conspiracy, mixed with a persecution complex. Throw in mental illness and a lifelong history of violent outbursts and there's a glimpse into our motivation," Zann said.

"The guy was a ticking timebomb. Typical nutjob," Fourier said, "but with an unusual skill for building neat toys that make him invisible and bulletproof."

"Something like that," Zann said.

"Makes you wish being able to execute minors you know are just inevitably going to be a shitstain on society was possible sometimes."

The room went silent, the other investigators craning their heads to stare at him.

"Fourier," Zann said. "You might want to shut up."

"You want to execute *minors?*" Niko said, appalled.

"What?" Fourier asked, holding his hands up defensively. "If we were able to, creeps like this wouldn't be walking around as adults, ruining everybody's lives. I'm not talking about every juvie who commits a crime. I mean the obviously fundamentally broken ones you can see turning into destructive, messed up adults from ten miles away."

"I'm gonna pretend I didn't hear that," Zann said dryly. "Because that's beyond fucked up. Let's move on."

"So," Niko started, shifting uncomfortably. If he'd disliked Fourier before, it had sunk into disdain now. "Where's the guy live? Is he still on Delevia? Can we do a raid?"

Zann shook his head. "Says he sold his property just over two years ago in a private sale and disappeared off the map, couple of months after Cleo disappeared. They used to share the house together. We don't know where he's staying. We sent guys out there to surveil anyway but it belongs to an Anong Saetang now. We're questioning her too."

"Did we send out some cadaver dogs to sweep the place?" a Dvaab investigator asked, scratching a clawed finger around her face in a gesture Niko interpreted as frustration. He didn't recognize her; she must have been one of the new transfers to the station since he'd retired from hunting.

"Not yet, but that's happening as soon as possible."

"This can never be easy, can it?" the investigator lamented.

Zann smiled. "Never is, is it? But we're on the right path now." He brought up a video this time, of another Dvaab interrogator speaking with an exceptionally thin, brown haired human woman and pale blond man in the station's interrogation room. It was quite clear whose parents they were—both siblings had favored their mother's mildly aquiline nose and father's hair.

These guys work fast, Niko thought, shocked at how quickly Galapol was able to get all the little working parts in motion to piece this months-long puzzle together overnight. The DNA sample must have been confirmed sometime throughout the night; Kestrel's parents must have been contacted immediately after and escorted to the station within hours. It was dizzying how rapidly it had all transpired. While the station had been in a chaotic frenzy after the concert, Niko had been sleeplessly tossing and turning through all of it. He glanced at Zann. His brother looked exhausted, wearing deep creases under his eyes, a mug of coffee sitting half-drank next to the evidence bags on the table.

The recording ran through the usual formalities, where both individuals being interviewed swore their honesty and granted permission to be recorded.

"Interrogation Officer Kulna'vuan'deii'vulman'de'caaa. I'll be speaking with you today regarding Elliott James Kestrel. What can you tell me about your son?"

"He was always problematic," Mary Kestrel began, one elegant hand on the table, her fingers absentmindedly touching at its surface. "Johann and I were honestly afraid of him, even when he was very little. He'd have tantrums. Violent ones. Would throw things, try to hurt us, attack us. He choked Cleo once and almost killed her. We tried to keep them separate and even considered surrendering him to some sort of foster care or detention center. We tried to educate ourselves and get him help but nothing stuck. I was honestly terrified of what he'd turn into when he became a man."

"See?" Fourier spoke over the recording.

"Shut up," Zann said.

"He was delusional too." Johann spoke now, clearing his throat often as he talked, his words halting. "After he'd go through these violent episodes, he'd get confused, and start accusing us of doing to him what he'd actually done to us. I'd try to show him the marks and bruises he'd leave on me, and say, 'Elliott, you were the one who did these things, not me,' but he would get mad all over again and say we were lying to him. That we hurt him and hurt Cleo. He was always getting mad, and getting confused. He had a hard time keeping track of what was real and what his broken brain had fabricated."

"He was always blaming and accusing other people of being violent, or bad somehow," Mary interjected. Unlike Johann, who stared down at the table as he spoke, her eyes were wide and intense, darting around and often landing on the camera, as though addressing it straight on, instead of the interrogator. "As he got older, it turned into complex conspiracies and theories and just delved into all kinds of craziness. I think he found them on the internet."

Officer Kulna leaned forward, tilting his head. "Our research shows Elliott not only got into a prestigious university, but he graduated top of his class. How is something like that possible with the problems he was espousing?"

"Oh, he was always very smart," Mary said.

"That was probably the crux of the problem," Johann added. "Sometimes I wonder if his brain was too sharp and it just started turning on itself, making and inventing things where there was nothing. But yes, Elliott has always been exceptionally smart, despite his problematic grasp on reality. To be honest though, we haven't spoken to Elliott since he was thirteen. He left home far too young and cut contact. I—I only just learned he changed his name, even."

"Were you aware he and Cleo had been sharing a residence prior to her disappearance?" Kulna asked.

"Yes," Mary said. "She was trying to reconnect with him, though we cautioned it was a bad idea. She thought she could even help him. Whatever he did or said to her, though…" Her voice trailed off before she spoke again. "She stopped reaching out or answering her phone too."

Something about the interview didn't sit right with Niko. Something barely perceptible, hiding away between the words. Everything Kestrel's parents said was logical, matched with the man's sordid actions and medical records. But Mary kept staring at the camera, eyes afraid, as though trying desperately to convince someone of the validity of her words. As though begging someone to believe her. It could just have been the guilt and horror of realizing the very person you'd created and released into society had gone on to do terrible things. He knew it could be Mary merely pleading to whoever was watching that she hadn't been a bad mother, hadn't directly contributed to what her son had gone on to do.

But there was something more. Niko had seen it plenty of times, that same bewildered, tense pleading from criminals he'd cornered on his jobs when they'd realized they had no way out except a last-ditch effort to try and bargain.

He glanced around the room at the other investigators, but whatever they were thinking was a mystery to him. No one else looked particularly suspicious, some shaking their heads at the abuses Mary and Johann described. Many were taking notes. Zann, for his part, just continued to look tired.

"When you told us he was *the* Kestrel— I thought it was a nickname, you know, and nothing to do with our actual surname," Johann explained. "The killer. I thought— Well, I hate to say this. I really do. There was some small part of me that wasn't even surprised. I mean, I was very shocked, of course. But I—"

He paused, exchanging glances with his wife. "Mary and I always knew Elliott wasn't, well, right."

They both looked at the camera.

"You— Officer, earlier you mentioned protection in exchange for cooperating," Mary said. "Is that still on the table?"

"Of course it is," Kulna said.

The rest of the interrogation went as Niko expected—they didn't know why Kestrel was killing galactic leaders, but had plenty of theories with past violent outbursts and a tenuous grasp on reality. Officer Kulna brought up—gently as he could—that they couldn't currently rule out the possibility that Kestrel had killed his sister and Mary began crying again, this time requesting a break.

When it was over, Niko said his goodbyes—goodbye, really, to Zann, with an obligatory grunt towards another couple of faces he recognized and a pointed snub of Fourier. Zann promised to send him everything from the updated files. Then Niko headed back home, only then allowing himself to give in to soul-deep exhaustion from the devouring pain he'd been enduring all day long in his feet and legs. Even now, they punished him with a barrage of constant phantom flames clawing up through his nerve pathways.

He sprawled on the couch and started to open the compressed file that Zann had dutifully transferred over before Niko had even gotten home, but the day's pain and exhaustion had raked him hollow. Niko was simply far too spent to go there right now, closing it all out instead before it overwhelmed him. For several moments, he simply lay with his eyes closed, brain empty and numb, nerves drenched in acid. He wondered if this was what it would feel like to get splashed by bog-theun toxin.

"Don't forget to eat today, Niko!" T1-N4 cheerily reminded him from beside the couch.

"Mmh, not hungry," he mumbled, already slipping into the hazy twilight that lay between consciousness and sleep.

Dream imagery danced a fever with memory, intertwining until they were one and the same, indecipherable. Niko was back on Vhesa Station, running after Kestrel. Always running, always pursuing, always too slow. The lithe, blond figure was clad in black, ever maddeningly out of reach, but always in sight.

Niko surged forward with the last of his strength, knocking Kestrel to the ground beneath them. This time, the other man didn't slip away, didn't outmaneuver him. This time, Niko pinned him down with his own weight, body against body. He held Kestrel against the cool floor beneath them, the other man panting, cheeks flushed with the exertion of his run, his fight, his effort to survive.

Niko kissed him.

He pressed his lips to Kestrel's own—warm, wanting, parting for him—and slipped his eager tongue inside. Exploring him. Claiming him. Kestrel moaned into Niko's mouth as his body went limp in surrender.

Had it really happened this way? Or maybe Niko had once dreamed that it had. Maybe he was dreaming now. It was too hard to tell anymore as he slipped out from the tight grip of nauseating pain and sank into the honeyed warmth of Kestrel's arms instead.

It had been so long since anyone had held him.

Kestrel combed his fingers through Niko's hair, the touch divine and sending pleasurable chills racing through him. They weren't on Vhesa anymore, but somewhere safe and hidden away, with dim lighting and a soft bed. He didn't need armor here. Kestrel brushed his mouth against Niko's ear, breath hot against his neck.

"You don't believe everything you hear," he whispered. "Do you?"

CHAPTER FIVE

UNDER THE SKIN

TRYING TO DECIPHER THE pattern behind Kestrel's chosen targets mystified Niko. What he'd at first presumed to be either political or ego-based murders were now instead appearing to follow invented conspiracies. Niko combed through endless files on Matteo Ricci, the CEO of StarSeam. The man had a fairly clean history other than some shady dealings with tax fraud seven years ago. He was well known for regularly donating generous portions of his income to charity. Whatever reason Kestrel had cooked up in that labyrinthine, dangerous mind of his to judge another philanthropist deserving of death left Niko puzzled. But madness rarely worked in ways that could be clearly labeled or understood.

Kestrel's words ran through his mind again and again.

They know what they've done.

He shook his head. Elliott Kestrel had a broken view of reality—if Mary and Johann were to be believed. Despite everything, Niko felt a pang of sympathy. The man needed real help, not the gratuitous public execution that would be inevitably waiting for him when he was finally brought in—if he wasn't killed on the scene by hunters or authorities first.

If Kestrel hadn't gone so far, they could have tried to get him the help he'd needed. But he had crossed a line that he could never return from, and had kept running. An entire galaxy had its eyes on him now, and it was frightened, angry, and vengeful.

And in the end, though Niko was sympathetic—he and his father, after all, suffered from severe depression themselves—mental illness wasn't a pass for hurting and killing others. It would never justify his actions.

Niko researched endlessly as the days passed, each hour seeping into the next, illuminated in a haze of hologram headache blue. T1-N4 hovered around him all the while, pressing urgent reminders to eat, drink, take breaks, take showers, or even take care of himself at all. It wasn't until a good three days in that Niko realized his face had grown rough with a five o' clock shadow. In the end, he was no closer to having any answers than when he'd started.

Zann sent along new content as well, interviews with others who'd known Kestrel in his life before he'd embarked on a galactic killing spree. One was a recorded interview with a slender and bony, middle-aged Heenva with widely branching antennae who had been Kestrel's superior at LaraTech. He blandly gave a similar story of the man seeming like a fantastic worker at first but quickly unraveling to the point of his eventual hospitalization. They'd had no choice but to let him go, even fearing the safety of some of their other employees.

The man's expression and tone were so dry and lifeless it pained Niko to even listen to him. He clearly didn't want to be there and had little interest in being interviewed, giving Kulna only the most basic details unless pressed for more, until bluntly asking if he could leave now.

The second interview featured a human man who identified himself to Kulna as Kestrel's ex, Liam Soren.

Oh. So, he's gay, thought Niko. *Or queer, at least.*

Kulna asked Liam the basic questions about himself. He was currently twenty-six and had met Kestrel just before he'd graduated university. They'd both attended Graceleaf League Uni, with Liam a year behind. He had majored in Statistics. They had dated a year and a half before he'd had to give up on Kestrel.

Niko paused the video, leaning forward in his wheelchair to eye the finer details of the man. He wanted to study him, to see if by looking at the people who had once been part of Kestrel's life, he could somehow understand something about the assassin that he'd missed, as though the still frame would whisper its secret to him.

Kestrel had managed to hold employment at a prestigious company, one of the biggest tech developers in the known galaxy. He'd attended and completed a master's degree from the top STEM university out there—and in fewer years than was the standard. He'd had relationships too—Niko didn't know the full extent of Kestrel's tastes, but Liam was a human. He was handsome, with hollowed cheekbones, dark curls, and sun-kissed skin. He wasn't as athletic or strong as Niko, though. And Niko knew he had a better jawline than

Liam. The man's style left a lot to be desired, too, basically scream-ing *I'm a smarmy douchebag.*

Niko was confident he would have stood a chance—

He cut the thought off, suddenly uncomfortable, self-con-scious, and painfully aware of what he'd been doing, and resumed playing the video. Liam continued talking with Kulna, wasting no time in condemning his ex-boyfriend.

"Elliott was a piece of shit, yeah."

The rest of the interview followed the same pattern as the oth-ers, with Liam offering up a testimony to Kestrel's generally chaotic nature, inability to track reality, and penchant for violent outbursts.

In the following weeks, two more events on his list—a ben-efit full of actors and famous authors to raise awareness of a rare genetic disorder that the Heenva sometimes developed, and a speech given by Uru Taal, crown prince of the Toliai homeworld of Thoro—came due. Niko went to both, ready, armored and armed, only for each to go peacefully and without interruption. Kestrel was laying low—that, or whatever basis drove his hitlist hadn't found those actors, authors, nor the prince worthy of death. An ever-growing flock of other bounty hunters circled the event grounds like ravenous sharks who'd caught a scent of blood in the water.

Eventually, he found himself sitting yet again in his living room, at the corner desk, staring at the same list. The sun of Kaapra-19 had recently set, giving way to bruise-blush dusk. Niko kept the window cracked, the scent of evening settling into his small apartment, the quieted sounds of nighttime cars and small ships humming past his window.

The next approaching event was another charity gala, on Uula, a planet that shared the same star as Yhanwe-ha. It was the only known solar system to have natively, independently developed two sets of sentient life, with the tentacled Gheroun hailing from a large, resource-rich moon called Haneen that orbited Uula. Uula was a gas giant that the Gheroun claimed as part of their empire, and the several dozen floating settlements there that kept to the atmosphere, suspended among pastel, buoyant clouds miles high had since made Uula a luxury spot among the galaxy.

The Gheroun leader, Imperator Khaathra, was expected to attend the gala to accept an award for her donations to various charities around the galaxy. In many ways, finding out Kestrel's history had only *complicated* trying to parse his next target and motivations more than not. Niko had no way of being sure anymore at this point—every event was guesswork now at best—but decided it wouldn't hurt to be there, just in case. He hated wasting his time milling around events where nothing happened, often supplied with several Galapol undercover agents by Zann. But it was better than the alternative: not attending and later learning another death had happened in his complacency.

Niko leaned back in his wheelchair, looking over at the portrait of his mother, with her ample smile forever frozen in time. Her dark eyes glittered affectionately, crow's feet forming in the deep bronze skin around them. Her hair, glossy, black, and full with curls, was just beginning to show fine streaks of silver.

Mom, he thought. *I don't know what to do. How do I help people? How do I keep them safe?*

He looked back to the files, his chest panging with grief, and tried to focus on the Starlight Burning concert. Kestrel had gone for a CEO in the crowd, ignoring the main attractions of the night. There was still a flare for drama there, in that he'd killed the man at a highly publicized event. He always killed at big events. He could have gone to Ricci's home, could have taken him out quietly. But he didn't; Kestrel cut his throat and shoved him over the balcony in front of over a million people. It felt, in fact, more and more to Niko like he was doing it to send a message.

Oh, I get a thrill, alright, he'd said.

Zann was probably right. This was some misguided persecution complex. One question remained, though: why? What connection between each person were they missing?

He ran countless searches online for connections any of these members could be supposedly involved in. What he found only grew more and more insufferable and ridiculous to read, and not a single one linked every individual who had been killed. What could the renowned screenwriter and director of *Twenty-One Toliai,* a cult classic action film, have to do with the deeply spiritual, elegant, and always composed Grand Sovereign of Yhanwe-ha? And what could either of them have to do with the CEO of an interstellar shipping company?

T1-N4 chimed, making Niko jump as he startled from his thoughts.

"You have one unread message from Zann. Would you like me to read it?" she said.

"Yeah."

"*The day's coming up, you know.*"

T1-N4 reading out Zann's dry text in her digital, merry tone left Niko disconcerted. He craned his neck to peer out into the kitchen, where a ship-themed calendar hung on the fridge. This month's image featured an ultra-fast XR-193 model racer that usually made Niko salivate a little whenever he looked at it. This time he ignored the image entirely, his gaze falling onto a single red X sloppily scratched onto the 14th. It marked the anniversary he never wanted to think about.

Niko's heart dropped the moment he saw it. He sank further into his chair, every bit of Kaapra-19's gravity felt profoundly.

"Message him back: yeah, I know. I'm going to visit. Send it."

Zann replied almost instantly, which T1-N4 dutifully read, her bright tone relentlessly uncanny. "*Good. He'll need it. I can't make it out that day. Lots going on here.*"

It hurt, but Niko wasn't surprised. He ignored the dull ache and instructed T1-N4 to respond. "I'll keep him company. Don't worry."

He looked back at all the research hovering before him: the event list, documents from Zann and the ongoing investigation. An old professional photograph of Kestrel, looking like a blond, pedigree dog. All of it blended together like visual noise, pressing in on him. With a quick, angry wave, he gestured the holograms away, sitting now only in the dim light of his desk lamp.

He glanced again at the photo of his mother. He needed to see her like that, see her smiling. See her alive, and not left bleeding on the side of the street. He swallowed, gripping the edge of the desk, the sound of his pulse filling his ears as the suffocating memory of loss consumed him.

Two days later, Niko sat in his parked car outside his stepfather's apartment complex. The complex was nice enough, with several stories and big windows, and was located in the same district of Kaapra-19 as Niko and Zann.

Oliver Delamar was the only father he'd ever known, and had loved and raised him as his own since Niko had been two years old. Niko's biological father had abandoned him and his mother, and in thirty years of life, Niko had not once so much as found a text message or birthday card from him. Nor did he care. Oliver was the man he called *Dad*. He was the man who Niko cherished as family.

Oliver's blinds were drawn tightly closed, and tended to stay that way. Niko could imagine him in that dim apartment, wallowing, wasting away with each day that ticked by. It hurt him to think about it. For the last three years, Niko hadn't been too different from his father.

He exited the car and wheeled to Oliver's unit, grateful for the elevator that took him to the third floor. In his lap sat a six pack of cold beer and a big bag of Ch'ua's Chicken that smelled like salt and grease, its brown paper already freckled with translucent oil stains. He rang the doorbell and Oliver appeared a moment later, the man's expression hollowed out, eyes empty and glossy.

He's been crying.

"Hey, Dad," Niko said. "I brought some food."

The older man let him in. He really was an aged portrait of Zann, if Zann had had the life and soul ripped right out of him and left only the body behind. Over the past decade, Oliver had sunk into a state of simply existing, sleepwalking through life. He had better days occasionally, but this particular day was always the worst.

For all three survivors of the family.

Niko swept his gaze through the apartment as he entered, forever worried about the state of it and if his father was taking care of it, and of himself. It seemed clean enough, though, and only then did he realize that he'd been holding his breath, shoulders tense. Oliver lived in a little one bedroom, with a cushy but worn-out couch and even more family portraits and memories hanging than Niko had at his own place. Where Zann resembled their father with the same black skin and short cropped, coily hair, Niko had grown to be a lot like the man in personality: steeped in sentiment and grief he could never get past that pulled him down into the depths, forever clinging and heavy. The last three years had left Niko sinking into similar habits of aimlessness. Of soul-deep numbness.

Niko extracted the boxes of saucy chicken-heaped nachos onto Oliver's coffee table by the couch, his father sinking down into a recliner. He handed Oliver a beer, then opened one for himself.

Both men ate in relative silence, only with small conversation. The ghost of what had transpired a decade ago today had stolen any enthusiasm for eating, leaving both containers eventually abandoned, half-full of cold chicken, congealing sauce, and soggy nachos.

In the background, an old action movie played its ending scene on the TV, which neither Niko nor Oliver could quite remember the name of but had seen countless times before.

"Is Zann coming out today?" Oliver asked, the quiet hope in his expression betraying his nonchalant tone.

"No, Dad. Sorry. With all the Kestrel shit, he hasn't had any time off." It was, of course, an excuse. But Niko couldn't bear to stomp on the heart that was already broken.

"Oh, of course," Oliver said politely, nodding.

The old action flick ended, the credits scrolling to a powerful soundtrack.

Then *Twenty-One Toliai* began playing, the famously beloved cold opening cutting right to a beaten and bloodied Xermotl pushing himself up to stand on jagged, wet stone, torrential rain and roiling, great waves filling the shot. Niko choked on his beer, coughing as he watched the title appear. Almost two dozen gargantuan, mean looking Toliai gangsters surrounded the Xermotl, looming in silence before they broke into dramatic fighting. It hit him then that the previous movie was Horu Duu'mari's work too. This was an entire tribute marathon.

What had once been thrilling entertainment now felt all wrong, especially here in this place, on this day. The movie was just another memento mori of someone gone from this life.

"It's been a decade now. I should go on and get over it," Oliver said.

Niko winced. "Grief doesn't really work like that, Dad. You shouldn't expect yourself to 'get over' the people who were your world."

"I know. I know that." His father turned the can of beer over in his hand.

Niko struggled to find the words. "But you also deserve to live your life too. You deserve to go out and experience things and enjoy your time, still."

If only he knew how to take his own advice.

Niko's father looked back at the movie now. The cold opening was past, and now the film journeyed on to its most widely-quoted scene, in which the Xermotl began recounting to Gheroun interrogators his revenge mission against the twenty-one Toliai mobsters responsible for killing his two wives.

Niko wished they could turn it off.

"What about you?" Oliver looked at him now. "I hear you're back to hunting again, even after what happened."

Niko's heart dropped. "This is a special case. It's just a one-time thing." He didn't know if he was trying to convince his father or himself at this point.

The older man looked pained, hunching forward in his chair. "Since this day, ten years ago, it's been nothing but pain begetting pain begetting pain."

"Dad—"

"First I lost Yessie and Ryen. Then you went on and got ruined hunting their killers—"

"I'm not *ruined*," Niko interjected, a tumultuous mixture of hurt and frustration coursing through him. He forced his voice quieter, realizing he'd raised it. "Things are just... different now. But I'm still here."

Oliver's face crumpled up in grief and shame. "I'm sorry, Niko, I— This day always does bad things to me. I shouldn't have said that."

"Come here, Dad." He pulled his father into a hearty embrace, holding tight to one of the very last tethers he still had to home and family. Niko didn't know who parented who more these days. Oliver had become so worn down that Niko often felt he was scrambling to pick up the man's pieces when he could barely keep himself together. Zann had become less and less helpful every year on that front, his own grief manifesting as a locked door behind which he retreated deeper and deeper. Last year was the first time he'd skipped visiting their father on this painful anniversary.

They hugged for a solid minute, the dramatic soundtrack and explosions of the movie keeping the silence at bay.

"It's okay," Niko said, wishing he had someone to tell him the same. "It's going to be alright, Dad."

It was a tradition to visit the graveyard on this day, though in previous years, it had always been with Zann and their father. This was Niko's first time alone—even Oliver couldn't bear the grief of going, too worn down—and the sorrow and sting of how deeply the fissure throughout all their lives ran clawed through him. Niko sat in front of two small gravestones, staring at the names etched in. They felt so impersonal, so cold, two lives summed up in blunt roles.

YESENIA MARÍA ESTRELLA-DELAMAR
CHERISHED MOTHER AND WIFE

RYEN LORENZO DELAMAR
BELOVED SON AND BROTHER

Niko lifted a spray of red roses from his lap and dropped them gently between the two graves. All around him, the soft green grasses of the graveyard swayed in the warm wind. The planted trees made dappled light dance across the ground as their leaves shook. This was one of the few green spaces on the entire moon. It was peaceful here.

A memory came to him of a time when he was younger, unburdened by the stunning pain and loss that lay ahead. He remembered picnicking with his family at Saanas Park, one of the other rare, curated green spaces that cut a rebellious hole into miles of endless city. It had been a warm day like this: windy, with the sun warming them. Niko had shown Zann how to fly a kite that looked like a ship, while on the blue blanket, his mother and stepfather sat together, talking quietly.

His mother held Ryen, who was just a baby then. His dark eyes were wide with astonishment as he stared at their kite. The world had been new to him then, and full of wonder.

Another memory came of his mother. Everything about her had been larger than life, ample and giving. The meals she'd made, her smile. The full, wild curls of her dark hair. Even the shape of her body, which had seemed made for hugging.

He remembered being ten, coming out to her as he'd tearfully confessed a crush he had on a classmate. There was no shame about such things in their household—it was never like that there. But Niko had been so afraid, terrified to the point of being unable to sleep, simply because he'd worried at somehow disappointing his mother that he wasn't what she'd assumed he was, the need for honesty and transparency always vital to him. He'd been scared that by being different, that he would let her down.

He smiled sadly at the memory of how terrified he'd been, how worked up he'd gotten himself at the idea of revealing his secret to her that had sat so full in his heart. She accepted him perfectly, as she always had, with open arms and a smile. Nothing had changed. It seemed so trivial now, looking back on it all. So simple. But at the time in his young and limited life, it had been the most important thing to him. It had been larger than life itself.

Niko didn't even remember the other boy's name anymore. But he remembered how the love and acceptance of his mother had made him feel.

Even in the silence of the years that followed, he would never forget that.

He wanted to see them this way, to remember the times he'd been privileged to share with them. Not the single, painful memory that concluded their lives. It was hard, because so much was built upon that memory and the agonizing pain it had inflicted in its aftermath. He'd had love in his life. He'd had joy. So had his father, so had Zann. And someone had decided to take it away, simply because they could.

He opened his mouth to speak, struggling to know what to say, and knowing anything he did say would change nothing anyway.

"I miss you guys. We all do. Zann's doing great things. He's been promoted again to Lead Investigator and they have him on a big case. He's looking out for the galaxy. Dad's... Dad's getting by, and I'm keeping an eye on him. He's getting a little better every year. He's been contemplating working again. I'm—"

His words drifted off. He had nothing kind to say about himself. "I'm—"

A small chime startled him out of the moment, and Zann's ID appeared. Niko read the text waiting for him.

You still at Dad's?

No, Niko replied. *But it would've been nice if you'd shown too,* he wanted to write.

Take a look at the news.

Niko's heart leapt into his throat. He started to open a hologram of the newsfeed but stopped himself, looking over at the two small, marble graves before him, and the dramatic spray of red he'd left on the ground between them. This wasn't the place.

"I love you," he said quietly to them.

He wheeled his way back to the car, taking his time to get strapped in and adjusted. Niko's heart pounded in his ears, the only sound now filling the silence of the car and the stillness of the graveyard beyond. He sat for a while, letting the moments pass, anxious and afraid to open the news. Whatever waited there wouldn't be good. It couldn't be.

He opened the hologram and a single headline filled it, crowning several photographs, including the blandly smiling professional portrait Niko had in his case files, and a delicate, rose-pink Xermotl wearing an ornate headdress.

KESTREL KILLS AGAIN

BELOVED YEURONEAN PRINCESS FALLS AT TEA SOIRÉE

Witnesses describe 'harrowing scene' as assassin chased, cornered, and killed Princess Vhee-vaala

Niko swallowed, leaning forward and resting his forehead against the steering wheel in silence. This wasn't supposed to happen. A tea soirée hadn't even made his list of events. Tightly constricting rage and anxiety clawed through his body, making it hard to breathe. He felt nauseous.

Kestrel's reasons meant nothing. His judgment meant nothing. All that mattered was that Niko made him face the justice he was due—even if it meant taking the man's life. He knew firsthand what it was like to witness lives ended by apathetic, cruel hands. He knew the indescribable pain of those who were left behind.

It was always personal.

But now it was under his skin.

Chapter Six

LET'S DANCE

For most of his life, Niko had wanted to visit Uula. He'd dreamed about it as a boy, dreamed of running across its floating platform cities, and of gazing out into endless miles of churning, layered clouds around him, wild winds caught in his hair.

He'd just never imagined when he finally set foot there, it would be like this—fully armored, rifle strapped to his back, grenades at the ready, on the hunt for a cold-blooded murderer.

He was tired of being outsmarted and outmaneuvered by Kestrel. This time, he came with a few extra *gifts* from his weapons dealer—including electromagnetic pulse grenades that would disable the man's tricky layers of tech defense.

Uula was, at least, as beautiful as he'd always imagined it to be. It surpassed any picture or video; the exotic and abstract clouds of the gas giant's atmosphere made every angle, every view painterly, graced in hues of lavender, pinks, blues and tinges of soft green. Several tiny moons—including Haneen, homeworld of the Gheroun—could be seen hovering above, little pale crescents that passed in and out of view.

The charity gala was being held in front of a dazzling conical conference center atop a large, airborne platform. Tables were set up everywhere, with party favors and hors d'oeuvres. Golden string lights hung crisscrossed between lamp posts and from layers of decorative floating platforms, casting a warm glow over the gala. Waterfalls trickled from the edges of the platforms, spilling from each to the one below it.

The press, a swarm of Galapol agents, and an additional number of Yhanwe-han security personnel—donated by the newly anointed Grand Sovereign to help in the efforts against Kestrel—prowled the grounds, making an odd mixture with the formally dressed gala attendees. With each new event, security both tightened and learned from the past mistakes. Drones now trawled the skies above, keeping a close eye on the gala grounds.

As always, Niko didn't have to look far to find another bounty hunter, either. With each kill that Kestrel carried out, his bounty spiked higher, often contributed to by the offended government, business, or association linked to the deceased, and matched by Galapol. Niko had never seen a number like it, not in any of his years hunting. The press reported it as the highest ever reached. He'd stopped paying attention a few kills back, but it had hit a solid four hundred million credits as a reward for killing or apprehending Elliott Kestrel.

Niko had never been after Kestrel for the money. But with a number like that, he couldn't help but think of how he could repay Zann for all his help after his injury. Repay him for the suit, the contribution to his surgeries and physical therapy. Then he could buy their father a luxury apartment, or even his own house. He could donate to Destination: Reclamation and contribute whatever remained after that to the charities Kestrel's victims had favored.

Niko looked up at the decorative platforms, with their string lights, gentle waterfalls, and sprays of colorful, decorative alien plants. They would be easy vantage points and vulnerabilities, and Galapol had caught on to the idea too. Every one of them was stationed with an agent who possessed their own sniper rifle. They crouched in uniform at the edges, peering out at the gala grounds below. Whatever they weren't able to spot, the constantly circling drones would.

If Kestrel was going to be here, he had vastly less to work with than he did before. But Niko knew enough about the bastard to predict that would hardly stop him from stunning them all, in the worst way.

The gala was starting to get underway now, the first guest speakers thanking everyone for coming and delving into current topics as attendees made their way to their seats, quieting down. Imperator Khaathra was due to speak soon, and Niko was antsy and tense, his eyes scanning again and again for potential ways Kestrel could wreck someone's day. The skies were all but covered, thanks to the drones present. The platforms were all handled by Galapol agents and counter-snipers, and the sharp, conical shape of the conference center—typical to most Gheroun architecture—gave no purchase to stand on. If Kestrel was going to pull something now, it would have to be particularly clever.

But Niko didn't expect him to disappoint on that front.

The audience politely applauded around him as the first introductory guest speaker stepped down to allow a tall, veiled Quwa-quay to take her place.

Niko scanned the platforms again as they began speaking about galactic orphan outreach programs—but paused midway through. Something was off. He glanced through again, looking towards the southeast platform. Something was different there, something about the agent. He magnified his visor's view until he got a clearer but still blurry visual of the agent. A shock jolted through his chest at the sight.

The man had had tan skin and red hair. Niko knew he did, had noticed it during an earlier visual sweep of the area. The uniformed agent who perched at the edge now, plain as day, had ivory skin and hair of gold. He wasn't using his usual stealth tech—this time, he was hidden in plain sight, disguised.

So that's your game, he thought. *Let's dance.*

All around him, the gala continued peacefully, no one aware yet of the presence of Kestrel other than its possibility. Niko moved quickly, his body responding by reflex before he could even think about what he was doing. He needed to get up there. He pushed his way along the edge of the gathered crowd until he was below Kestrel's platform. It hovered hazily above him, dozens of stories up, suspended in the air by small and elegant engines of alien technology, water raining down from its edges. It was the highest platform, well above several layers of others.

He'd have to make his way up a little at a time.

Niko moved to the next closest platform, hovering lower but still far out of reach. He unlatched a compact but hearty grappling hook from his belt and aimed it towards the edge of the lowest platform—another *just in case* item he'd requested from his weapons supplier, frustrated at how Kestrel favored high and hard to reach places. It was just long enough, nearly stretched to its limit, but the anchor clamped itself on the platform's edge and he pressed the trigger, reeling in the cord and propelling himself quickly up to the platform.

A Galapol agent was stationed there, turning wildly in place, gun trained on Niko. He'd clearly spooked her. "What the fuck? What do you think you're doing up here?"

"He's here. Top platform." It was all he could provide her; pausing to give his credentials would only cost him time he couldn't afford to lose. He aimed the grappling hook for the next platform and pulled himself up again once it secured. Another agent was there as well, who gave one of the most colorful strings of curse words Niko had heard in a good while, but he didn't have time to commend the man on his creativity—Niko was gone just as quickly.

As the rope pulled him ever higher, the ground and gala shrinking further and further below him, he felt his pulse hammer in his throat, the furious rhythm of life written one beat at a time. Every part of him was on fire now, searing with adrenaline, with anticipation. He was close now.

He pulled himself up quickly to the platform once he reached it, knowing every second he took was a second Kestrel had to react. The Imperator's life was in Niko's hands now.

Across the platform, half obscured by several strangely curling trees and succulents, was Kestrel, crouched low, his sniper rifle lying beside him. He wore the semi-armored uniform common to Galapol's tactical field agents, and clutched two devices, one in each hand. Niko quickly realized one was a two-way radio, the other held against Kestrel's lips as he spoke, his voice emerging double—his own, and another over the radio, foreign and unfamiliar and nothing like what he'd sounded like when he had paused to speak to Niko at Vhesa Station.

"All clear. No sign of Kestrel, over."

The agent who had been there moments ago was nowhere to be seen.

You fucking killed him. Of course you did, you prick.

Niko's pulse spiked. He wasted no time taking aim, unloading a sloppy, quick shot. An explosive round detonated against Kestrel's energy shield uselessly, the air around him rippling and distorting under the impact. Niko definitely had his full attention now, the man's head whipping in his direction. Kestrel grabbed his rifle and aimed back at Niko, quickly standing.

"We really have to stop meeting this way," he said.

"Shut up," Niko spat. He reached down and grabbed one of the new EMP grenades he'd brought and pulled the pin, hurling it straight towards Kestrel. Kestrel tried to dodge, but had reacted too late, and the detonation quickly fried his shields, leaving him bare and vulnerable. The barrier around him glitched, visual static dancing around him before fading entirely. The grenades had cost a good chunk of Galapol's allotted sponsorship budget, but in this moment, it was worth every credit.

Kestrel stumbled from the impact. An expression of shock, followed by genuine fear flashed across his face before he clamped down hard on it, a cool scowl settling in instead. The satisfaction of getting the upper hand over him drove Niko forward and he took another shot. It missed as his foot caught on something solid and hard, sending him crashing hard to the ground. Kestrel was on the move again, slipping behind one of the curling landscaped trees for cover.

Niko recovered quickly, rolling over to stand back up, when he paused. He'd tripped over something that wasn't *there*. Nothing but carefully curated, flat ground lay beside him.

He leaned forward and saw it then: the faint silhouette of a body, merely a distortion of the air itself in the vague shape of a man. He was almost impossible to see.

It was the original Galapol agent, laid out with Kestrel's stealthing device. There was something else, though—the man emitted a soft groan, mumbling incoherently as Niko stood. He wasn't dead, only unconscious. His voice matched the exact one that had emerged double, like a ghostly echo from Kestrel when he'd spoken into the radio.

A voice replicator. He'd been talking to Galapol, mimicking the agent's voice, giving the all clear.

Niko was up now, gun in hand. He aimed it at the thick tree, slowly moving in a wide semi-circle around it.

"Change of heart, I see," Kestrel said.

"What?" Niko snapped.

A soft breath of tired laughter escaped from the assassin. "Last time, you wanted so badly to talk. You were begging me." His voice took on a mocking, cruel tone. "'*I want to understand,*' you said."

"I'm done talking to you. You're a murderer."

"Then what are you?"

Before Niko could answer, Kestrel seized his chance and sprang up before leaping off the edge of the platform with the same grace he'd done the night Niko had first encountered him. He had some sort of tech that gentled the impact of his fall, Niko could see now.

This time, Niko wasn't going to hesitate. He wanted to finish this.

He took a few steps back and ran towards the edge, launching himself and hoping the momentum was enough to take him to the lower platform after Kestrel.

Niko landed hard. Harder than he'd anticipated. An all too familiar shudder of pain shot up his numb legs and along his spine, knocking the breath from him for a precious few seconds. He watched as Kestrel moved quickly onto the Galapol agent stationed there, dispatching him. Like the agent above, though, he didn't kill him. He had yet another device at his disposal—some kind of taser, likely. The agent dropped, lying limply on the ground, eyes lulling closed.

Kestrel kept going and Niko shouted at him as they both ran, all white-hot rage.

"Don't compare me to you. This isn't the same at all. I stop garbage like you from ruining lives."

"We're more alike than you think." Kestrel launched himself again, and Niko was forced to follow. He winced as he jumped, dreading the impact as the platform below rushed up to meet him. The pain of it shook him to his core and rattled his teeth. Niko's ruined nerve endings fired in bursts of electric, scathing fire. This was beyond him, beyond the boundaries of his new existence as a permanently injured man. But he wasn't about to stop now.

Niko gritted his teeth through the pain and took another shot at Kestrel, missing. He was forced to reload and Kestrel dispatched the second Galapol agent as she tried to call for backup on her radio, once again stunning and disabling her, dropping her to the ground too. He was vexatiously fast, making quick work of Galapol's special ops agents and outmaneuvering Niko at the same time. Niko struggled to keep up with him now, each breath ripping painfully through him as his legs and back howled their protest and plea for him to give them mercy. The pain was making him sluggish, his body soaked now with sweat that swam unsettlingly within his armor.

There it was again, though, haunting Niko's brain: that appeal to justice from Kestrel, that what he was doing was somehow *good*—that they were somehow alike in their work. He dangled the enigma of his motives before Niko like a carrot. It was bewildering. Niko felt he was falling somehow, being drawn into some sort of trap, but he couldn't help it. He wanted to follow his thread of logic.

He would play this game. For now.

"What the hell is that supposed to mean?"

Kestrel had slipped behind another thick tree for a moment to recover. Niko took a shot at it but the thing still stood, even with an explosive round, likely transplanted foliage that had evolved hardy to withstand the deadly climate of a harsher world than Uula. Two more bullets pinged off the trunk in succession, likely from Galapol's counter-snipers on distant platforms.

"Every one of these people were traffickers. Slavers. Rapists. Murderers. They were never going to stop. I'm doing you all a *fucking favor!*"

It was incomprehensible. Kestrel really was insane. He thought his actions were helping, that he really was doing what Niko was—hunting down and removing actual monsters from society. But these weren't criminals—they were leaders, artists, and philanthropists who a broken mind had deemed as evil. In another life, if Kestrel weren't unwell, maybe he would have eventually gravitated to a line of work like Niko's.

"You're trying to tell me Princess Vhee-vaala was trafficking slaves?" The mental image of the delicate alien princess holding a carved shell teacup while doling out the worst crimes one could do to another sentient being was absurd beyond humoring.

"Yes. They all were."

Niko felt a sympathy crawling in that he didn't want to feel again. Everything Kestrel was doing was wrong. But there was a difference between killing for ego and fame, and killing because you delusionally thought you were legitimately stopping someone evil from harming others.

He had seen Kestrel's history. He'd heard Zann's presentation of his descent into broken fantasy. The man was certifiably nuts. Delving into conspiracy theories, going on violent tangents and delusional rants that had cost him his career, his professional and social standing, and had landed him in a hospital. Clearly, he hadn't gotten much better since then. What the man needed was help, not unfettered access to a gun, next-gen tech, and a roster of galactic luminaries.

"Even if that were true," Niko said, "why not just go to the authorities? Why not report it to the media?"

"You think I haven't tried? Every time I have, they've silenced me. The police and the media are bought."

No, thought Niko. *They just knew you were spouting nonsense.* "You're off your fucking rocket."

"They're above the law, and they all protect each other. They're untouchable." Kestrel huffed out a breathless chuckle, his tone turning dark. "Or they *were*. I'm fixing that."

Niko had had enough. He rounded the foliage and took another quick shot. Kestrel ducked out of the way just as he did, the bullet close enough to stir his hair in its wake.

"Why don't you tell me where Cleo is?" Niko ground in every word, like a blunt knife, hoping it hurt.

"She's not anywhere anymore. She's dead."

Fuck. At least he'd admitted to it—and with shocking ease. Zann's guys would be having a field day when they found out.

"You kill her?" Niko pressed the dull blade further. "I think you did." Kestrel emerged from his makeshift cover, face ashen pale, eyes vibrant with wild fury. He took a sloppy shot at Niko, the action messy and exposing him. Kestrel missed.

Niko fired back, taking the opportunity, but his bullet only grazed the hearty trunk again, sending a spray of fibrous, woody debris into the air. Another of Galapol's sniper shots lanced through the air too, this time missing the tree—and Kestrel—entirely. If Niko could keep wearing him down, keep driving him into making mistakes, he would have him.

Kestrel ducked back behind the tree. "Believe it or not, I don't really want to be doing this with you."

Niko ignored him and pushed further. "Why'd you kill Cleo, Elliott?"

"Why would I kill my own sister?" His words came slow and oddly calm, the sort of slow talking Niko recognized as barely contained rage from someone who didn't want to lose control. "You know so much about me, it seems. So why don't you tell me?"

"Maybe you thought she was one of those traffickers."

"You're wrong."

Niko needed to get him out again, needed to get him into view so he could take him this time. "Or maybe she just said something you didn't like. Maybe you had a fight, and she wanted to leave, so you killed her."

"Wrong again. You're not even close."

"Then what happened to her?" Niko readied himself for another passionate slip up, but Kestrel was a fast learner, and whatever rage was fueling him now, he'd managed to force down a tight rein on.

"You won't believe me anyway. Or maybe you won't care. No one ever does."

He felt himself falling deeper into it again—that little gnaw of empathy, of self-destructive curiosity. Niko knew he was letting himself be baited along, deeper into this game of conspiracies. He knew the *why* didn't matter. But he chased it anyway.

"Try me."

Kestrel was silent a moment, before murmuring so quietly Niko thought he'd misheard him. "Honeybliss." After another pause, he added, "You won't find anything on it. Anywhere. They pay people well to make sure of that now."

"Honey... Bliss?" It sounded like something from a diet sweet tea commercial.

"You should be careful who you say that word around, or they'll silence you too."

Before Niko could reply, Kestrel broke into a sprint again and leapt off the platform, down, this time, to the ground below. Niko braced himself, leaping after him again.

Don't think about how much it's going to hurt. Don't think.

He plummeted to the ground, landing so hard on his abused legs at the wrong angle that he tumbled, a cry of pain escaping him. Old habits of wild self-abandonment had gone past creeping back in now; they had gotten inside him everywhere. He was lucky something wasn't broken, and wouldn't be surprised if he found the next day it was and that he had kept going anyway. It didn't matter to him right then. He was tired of this cycle, of coming close but never succeeding. This time, he was going to win. Nothing else mattered. Niko didn't matter, then—not even to himself.

Kestrel broke into a quick run the moment he landed, darting away from the crowd and conference building, back out through the edge of the gala grounds and into the winding, curved alleyways that spread around jutting, cone-shaped buildings of the floating city proper. Niko struggled to stand, falling once, before he managed to get back to his feet. He pushed through the pain and exhaustion, a small, betraying yelp escaping him as he broke into a jog, then ran. He didn't have the time to let himself start falling behind now.

He was gaining on Kestrel. All he had to do was keep it up, but that was easier said than done. And it was only possible through sheer recklessness. Niko didn't want to think about tomorrow, or even an hour from now. The pain he was in now would be a whisper against the roar it would be later. Right now, none of it mattered. Only taking Kestrel down did.

He followed Kestrel out down the twist and turn of alleyways. The alleys were empty, giving Niko a clear shot straight to Kestrel. He wanted to take aim at the man, but couldn't without losing ground, and he was already far enough behind.

Niko spoke again, his words fragmented by heavy, breathless pants as his lungs burned, ragged. "Even if this were all somehow true, deciding you can carry out public executions isn't right. I still have to bring you in."

Why was he humoring Kestrel? Why did some small part of him wonder if what the man said had truth to it? The strained, nervous look in Mary Kestrel's eyes flickered through his memory. The way she'd stared at the camera as though she'd known someone specific would be watching it. As though she had been addressing them and not the police. It hadn't been the usual mannerisms of a distraught mother; rather, it had been the anxious plea of the cornered.

They'll silence you too.

All the evidence was so clear—Kestrel had fallen into a deluge of conspiracies. He'd decided to take action and persecute the ones he thought were doing harm. Yet something about it wasn't adding up now, and Niko didn't know what. There was something they were missing to all of this. It gnawed at him, ate away at the corners of his mind. Everything in the files had pointed to Kestrel being clearly unhinged and broken, someone with no control over their actions.

But there was a terrifying *clarity* to Kestrel that Niko couldn't deny. Someone fully in charge of all their faculties, someone who possessed a deadly sharp perception.

None of that lined up with the portrait painted of a troubled boy and man who confused reality with fiction.

Every interaction Niko had with him went the same. The man was sharp, quick-witted, and in control. He'd even managed not to rise to Niko's attempts at baiting him into rage, clamping a tight and controlled lid down. Something wasn't right. The man before him didn't match at all with the turbulent, chaotic abuse and lack of self-control described again and again in his files.

Believe it or not, I don't really want to be doing this with you, he'd said.

No.

No, Niko couldn't afford to hesitate or doubt again. He'd done it once before, and it had cost him.

Even if there was somehow a shred of truth behind Kestrel's claims, this path of vigilantism was still wrong. Horribly, horribly wrong. Niko pushed himself harder, closing the distance between them as Kestrel ran.

Kestrel began speaking, but whatever he'd been about to say was cut off as Niko sprang forward and crashed into the slighter man, sending them both to the ground. Niko grabbed hold of his shoulder, tightening his grip hard. Kestrel wasn't ready to surrender, struggling fiercely under his grip, writhing and twisting and driving his fist sharply into the joint between Niko's helmet and chestplate. The force of his hit ejected a spasming cough from Niko.

Niko grabbed him by the arm, wrestling it back and slamming Kestrel's hand against the ground. The other man cried out in pain, then made a grab for Niko's neck again, this time stabbing his fingers upward under the rim of the helmet instead of punching. He pried it off, tossing it away from them. It rolled and dropped right off the railed edge beside them, into the churning clouds below. Niko was briefly stunned—he hadn't even realized they'd been so close to the edge of the city platform. Had Kestrel planned to jump off there, down into the endless clouds of Uula, too?

Kestrel squirmed as Niko fought to keep him pinned down. He got in another good punch regardless, his fist driven straight into Niko's throat, making him choke this time. They both scrambled and struggled against one another, Kestrel kicking uselessly against Niko's suit, throwing his weight around and bucking beneath him. He worked the taser free, trying to drive it now against Niko's neck, but Niko caught it in time and gripped his wrist tightly, squeezing against the tendon and bone until with a grunt of pain, Kestrel dropped it. Niko grabbed it up and tossed it towards the city-platform edge too, where it fell into the infinite sky below.

Kestrel twisted then, coming loose from Niko's exhausted, slipping grip and leapt back up, already sprinting down another alleyway. Niko heaved himself from the ground, every movement feeling abhorrently sluggish and too slow, and took after him again.

He followed Kestrel to a dead end, the long curve of alleyway leading to a high, plaster wall lined with rusting utility pipes, and threw himself at him, but Kestrel dodged. Niko hit the wall hard, but turned quickly, keeping his balance. He took aim at Kestrel, but the assassin rammed into him this time, knocking the rifle out of his hands. Niko took a heavy swing at him, which was also infuriatingly dodged, catching only open air. He was drained and too slow, and Kestrel was still somehow impossibly fast. Kestrel punched him now in return, aiming right for the joint between armor plates at the side of his waist, the hit connecting. Niko grunted and kicked Kestrel, who stumbled backward from the impact.

Kestrel was good. Too good. And Niko was flagging. Kestrel was holding his own against Niko, but he too was panting, his hits coming less frequently, a sheen of sweat trickling down his face, dampening his hair. He wasn't trying to run anymore, either. Niko was wearing him down just as much.

Niko summoned the last scrap of strength in his body and surged forward, exploiting the opportunity. He caught Kestrel straight on, grabbing him by the neck, and throwing him into the back wall of the alleyway. Then he pinned him there with his own body to keep him from slipping away again. Niko's breaths tore from him, ragged and heavy and tired, his body heaving from the effort as he scrambled to find the pair of cuffs that hung at his utility belt.

It was over. It was finally all about to be over, whatever game all of this had been.

They were both tired. Kestrel fought him every inch still as Niko struggled to keep him pinned. It was nearly impossible trying to keep Kestrel from weaseling away and get the cuffs from his belt at the same time—the second he let go with one hand, Kestrel was already taking the opportunity to move. He broke one arm free of Niko's grip, weak and sluggish, and Niko's own hold on him was slipping. He looked at Kestrel, and Kestrel looked back at him, quiet desperation and fight rapidly ebbing but still alive.

"Give up, Elliott. It's over now."

"No."

"I'm bringing you in. You can tell Galapol all about Honeybliss."

"Eat my fucking ass."

"Present it, bitch," Niko growled.

They struggled more, Niko pushing against him with the strength he had left, Kestrel trying to throw him off. Niko's words seemed to give the man a stubborn second wind. Kestrel gripped at him with his free hand, tried to hit him unsuccessfully, then reached up and took a handful of Niko's shaggy hair. He didn't pull, didn't wound him. He just gripped it, looking at Niko, then tipped his chin forward, and kissed him.

It was viscerally shocking.

Niko froze. It wasn't like he'd dreamed it was, sultry and slow. There was a desperation, sloppy and ravenous, from Kestrel. Niko needed to stop him. He needed to pull away.

He didn't stop him.

He hated himself, hated the way a ripple of goosebumps prickled his skin beneath the suit, hated how his body and brain alike delighted in being touched—in having another man's hand in his hair, lips against his, wanting. Even here. Even now.

And not just any man. This man. This man, who matched him in skill and capability. The two of them were entangled, caught in a tether, always chasing and chased, always hunting and hunted. It made the brilliant lightning sweep of heady thrill—inappropriate, wrong in every way—only intensify. Niko parted his lips for him, and Kestrel slid his tongue inside. He was delicious.

He didn't know what he wanted more—to bring Kestrel in, or fuck him raw.

Niko's heart hammered in his chest, his throat. This was wrong. This was everything he shouldn't—*couldn't*—be doing. He forced himself to pull away and shoved Kestrel back against the wall again. The other man looked at him searchingly, lips still parted, wet from Niko. He ran his tongue along his bottom lip, as though trying to taste him still.

Niko couldn't help himself. Rapacious hunger overcame him like a flash flood—fast and intense, leaving him nowhere to run. He pushed against Kestrel and leaned forward to meet him in another kiss, insatiable. He couldn't stop. It was too much. He was lost in this strange, illicit moment. He lapped at Kestrel like a starving man, head tilted as he kissed him again and again.

He had to stop.

Every security guard, hunter, and agent wouldn't be far behind now. And what would happen if they caught him like this? Niko finally willed himself to pull away again. He'd come here to do a job, not...

Not...

"Why don't you send Galapol my regards instead, since you're so fond of them?" Kestrel murmured. A familiar, metallic *click* cut through the air and Niko's blood turned to ice.

No. *No—*

He tried to reach up, tried to grab Kestrel, but his arm wouldn't obey. The other man had—somehow—managed to work his deft hands and get the handcuffs from Niko's belt and around his wrist, the other loop closed tightly around a metal pipe that ran the length of the plaster wall. Niko tried to grab at him with his free hand, but Kestrel was too quick again, slipping out of his reach with a clever little smile, eyes narrowed in pleasure. It was clear he knew he'd won. He ran the back of his hand across his lips, wiping Niko free from himself.

"You're the only one who can keep up with me," he said. "But you're still in my way."

Shit. Shit. The humiliation—and horror—Niko felt was stunning. He fumbled through the small utility pack at his waist for the handcuff key, but it was difficult to feel it out with his hand covered by an armored glove. His whole body was numb with the shame of what he'd done.

By the time he had it in hand, Kestrel was gone. Like he always was.

Niko freed himself just in time to hear voices behind him—Galapol's agents and a scattering of hunters had caught up. He felt sick and strange, stunned by his own behavior, lost in a kiss that'd had no right being so electric as it was.

He'd never acted like this. He had always been a professional, through and through.

But instead, he had let himself... Had let himself *what?* Think with his dick? Let over three years of isolation and loneliness give way to Kestrel's clever hands, fascinating capability, and handsome face?

Niko wasn't worth the faith Zann had placed in him. Mistakes upon mistakes were all he'd made since he had started hunting again.

He wasn't even thinking anymore.

CHAPTER SEVEN

LIKE A GOOD BOY

"How the fuck did this happen, Niko?"

Zann's words came out in a pant. Both men were at the small, private gym attached to Destination: Reclamation for its clients to use. Though Loolae only served those in need of physical therapy, Zann was Niko's brother and Loolae's friend and got a pass when they went together. Niko lay across the weight bench, working on lifting while Zann stood near him, lifting his own smaller weights. Unlike Niko, Zann was wirier and lither. He preferred his work to be at the station, usually behind a desk.

Niko shook his head.

"I mean, you were so close to getting him. Three times now. How does this fucker manage to give the slip to a dozen Galapol agents and ten million goddamn bounty hunters? How does he manage to make it past *you*?"

Niko knew better than to respond, steadying himself before lifting the barbell again, the muscles in his arms trembling from the effort. When Zann was on a roll like this, it was best to let him rant it out. Interrupting or giving any kind of input usually just tended to make his mood worse.

"How does this keep happening?" Zann asked.

Niko lifted again, pushing up and fighting gravity. After how much he'd been struggling with Kestrel—a leaner man than himself—he figured getting back into a more rigorous weight training couldn't hurt.

"You're the best we have, Niko. What the fuck is going on?"

It took a moment for Niko to realize Zann wasn't continuing. He glanced over to see his brother staring expectantly at him and realized it was his cue to answer. He rested the barbell back down onto its rack.

"At least Imperator Khaathra got to go home that day."

Zann's full lips drew into a tight, thin line as he relented. "There's that. Good job there."

Niko shook his head, shrugging off the cheap consolation. He slipped to a different subject, one he couldn't stop thinking about. "Have you ever heard of Honeybliss?"

Zann paused in his lifting and scowled. A thin sheen of sweat glistened on his forehead. "Yeah. It's in his file under all the conspiracy bullshit. Why?"

"He mentioned it a few times as his motive. Do you think it's real?"

"Oh, for fuck's sake," Zann said. He set his weights down, wiping the sweat from his brow. "It, and a dozen other invented conspiracy groups. He changes it up constantly. None of them exist. We've had our best researchers on it."

Zann took a breath before continuing. "We've already established the guy is a lunatic. You were near him long enough to have a chat with him? Just shoot him in the head and shut him the fuck up. You have one job, Niko. What's the issue here?"

Niko didn't like where this was headed. His nerves pricked uneasily and he scooted on the bench to sit up. He scrambled for the first excuse he could think of. "His tech is the issue."

Zann opened his mouth to speak, but stopped himself. He eyed Niko oddly and Niko felt himself grow more uneasy.

Shit. He probably knows about the EMPs through Galapol's bill.

Silence fell between them briefly, before Zann sighed. When he spoke, his voice was softer. Tired. "I'm sorry, Niko. This piece of work has me in a bad place. It really is like Mom and Ryen all over again. I've never found another asshole who's so good at not being caught since."

"Yeah." Niko nodded. Before he could take it back, he found himself blurting the words out. "Is that why you wouldn't go see Dad?"

Zann froze, the uncomfortable looking one now. "I was busy that day."

"Yeah. Sorry. This Kestrel thing's getting to me too."

Another awkward beat fell over them before Zann spoke again. "Yeah. It was a little bit, actually. This whole thing is all just— It feels like it used to all over again. And not in a good way. I don't want to think about it anymore."

"I know what you mean."

"I shouldn't have asked you to come back, Niko."

That hurt. "What? No."

"You look like shit."

Niko reached up and touched at his neck, an echo of dull pain reminding him of the bruise that was still there. It had been four days since he'd encountered Kestrel on Uula, but his body still ached from everything the assassin had thrown at him. The day after had left him completely bedridden.

"Just part of the job, Zann."

"I know," Zann snapped. "Which is why I should have left you alone about it. I know how you get. You never stop when you should. You even knew it would happen. Just— This guy is the galaxy's number one pain in the ass. And mine. Nobody can bring him down. How does *one* guy wreck so much shit across the galaxy? I'd have felt better if this was an orchestrated group instead. And now everyone's terrified off their asses and he's all anyone talks about. I thought if nothing else, you'd be able to—"

"I will," Niko cut him off. "I *am*. I'm going to stop him, Zann. I prevented him from killing for the first time. I made him slip up. I won't let him kill anyone else. It's over."

I would have had him that time, Niko thought, *if he hadn't made me slip up too.* A fresh pang of shame gripped him at the memory.

Zann ran a hand over his face, looking exasperated and decades past his actual age of twenty-seven. "Yeah. Yeah, you're right. If I've ever had anyone to believe in in this life, it's you. You've always come through, Niko."

Niko punched Zann in his skinny arm, giving his brother the best smile he could muster. "Trust me, okay?"

The media had become intensely interested in Niko once drone footage from his initial confrontation on the platforms had spread and Imperator Khaathra had survived the event unscathed. (*If* that had even been Kestrel's intended mark—he could only assume it was her.) Niko was being billed as a hero, the sole man who'd been able to stop Kestrel and turn the tides for the first time since his deadly spree began. He wanted to laugh when he heard that; he hardly felt like a hero. He felt like a fucking moron.

It was sheer luck there hadn't also been drone footage of him with his tongue in the galaxy's most wanted killer's mouth.

Things were changing now. Something both inside him and out was shifting, like a tide being pulled back out to sea. Niko felt he was on a precipice, looking down. He'd had a poor history of throwing himself off ledges and ending up worse off for it. Uula had been his first victory over Kestrel, though. Even though the man had still gotten away, Niko had kept him from making his intended kill. He alone had Kestrel's attention now, maybe in the same way Kestrel had his. He was tripping him up, making his life difficult.

Niko was getting in his way.

Back at his apartment now, Niko groaned, stretched out across his couch, pillow propped behind his head. Sleep was evading him, his mind too full of a single blond bastard. He didn't want to think about Kestrel. He was tired of Kestrel.

All he could think of was Kestrel.

There were so many things not adding up. Kestrel had reacted with contempt when Bubblegum had hurt civilian bystanders. He could have killed any of them and made his life easier. But he hadn't. In fact, thinking on it now, Kestrel had no record of killing a single individual who wasn't an intended target. There were no messy, accidental kills. No moves of desperate cruelty. Everyone who had ever gotten in his way was dispatched, but left with their life. Even the Galapol agent Kestrel had stolen the uniform from and voice of.

Niko's stomach twisted. None of that behavior lined up with a man who had a violent history of losing his touch on reality and trying to murder his sister or beat his own parents in fits of rage. It was precise and deliberate, like everything else he had observed about Kestrel. It was intentionally, shockingly humane.

Niko didn't know what to make of that.

Humane was the last word he would ever pair with Kestrel. Yet here he was. It couldn't be denied—Kestrel had a sense of empathy. He chose his targets carefully.

Traffickers, he had said. *Slavers. Rapists. Murderers.*

Honeybliss.

The word was so strange. It sounded pleasant, like an indulgent candy or tea. He remembered seeing it somewhere before, though, in the case files like Zann had mentioned. Buried among several other conspiracy groups Kestrel had gone down the rabbit hole of was one called Honeybliss. The other conspiracies mentioned brought up countless theories and discussions online. A search for Honeybliss hadn't brought a single thing up, other than a few homemade recipes for honeyed snacks, though. But Kestrel had warned of that, hadn't he?

Niko turned over onto his side. If Honeybliss was just another conspiracy like the others, why wasn't there anything about it online? He was no stranger to the dark web, either. There'd been no mention even there.

So, what the hell was this supposed... group? Network? Cabal?

Kestrel had said he'd been silenced when he'd tried to speak about it. But he also hadn't shut up over the years about the other several obnoxious conspiracies, all with a visible presence among internet forums. It had cost him his engineering career. Had he been unlucky enough to stumble onto something rare and latch on? Something that had truth to it and had made him an unfortunate target?

None of it made sense and Niko was too tired to keep fucking with it right now. He let himself drift back into the haze of sleep when T1-N4 chimed from above the coffee table.

"You have one new text message from Unknown Number!"

Niko grunted. The press had been trying to contact him for an interview since he'd "heroically" saved the gala. He'd ignored every attempt. But none of the media outlets actually had his direct phone number. Rather, they'd tried to reach him through contacting Galapol, who held his contract. Zann had intercepted and politely told them, "He's not interested. Fuck off, thanks," during his initial post-gala briefing at the station with Niko.

"Read it."

"*You can't stop thinking about it, can you?*" T1-N4 recited mirthfully. Niko froze.

"What?"

"I will repeat the message—"

"No. No. Just—" Niko rubbed his eyes, his vision still blurry from half-sleep. He struggled to sit up as a chill spread through him. T1-N4 hung silently, awaiting his response, the gentle whirring of her engine the only sound in the room.

Who?

Had someone seen? Had there been footage after all, that Niko had missed? Was someone from the press about to try and blackmail him over this? His stomach twisted into a tight knot as a chill of unease trilled through him.

Another message chimed through. T1-N4 read it, her tone all wrong, too pleasant. "*I didn't think something like that would actually work. I thought you were supposed to be good at your job.*"

Whoever this was had Niko's full attention now.

Is it—

Could it be—

No.

"*44-8783-332,*" T1-N4 merrily recited. Niko's blood turned to ice upon hearing his bounty hunting license number. "*Niko Tomás Estrella.*"

"Tina," he said slowly. "Switch to private mode."

"Switching to private mode. Your messages will not be read aloud until you indicate otherwise."

Niko opened the text hologram, staring at the words. Whoever was on the other end of these messages was playing a dangerous game. And either it was someone who wanted to blackmail him, or it was—

Another message arrived and Niko knew at once who it was.

This time it was an image, a self-taken photograph of Elliott Kestrel.

All his breath left him. The picture was angled from above, looking down. The man was lying in bed, golden cowlicked hair fanning around him like a halo. Sea green eyes stared right back at Niko, gaze dull, bland even.

He was wearing nothing at all, his lithe body bare, patches of skin blushing with faded bruises from their last altercation. His hand was wrapped around his hard cock in mid-stroke.

Niko couldn't breathe. Heat flushed through his face and neck. It was an outrageous picture. It was insulting. It was—

He couldn't peel his eyes away. The idea of writing any sort of reply had vanished from the moment the image had filled his vision. Niko couldn't remember what words even were.

He swallowed as thought and sensation slowly came back online. A thousand questions hung half-formed in his mind, primarily *What the fuck?* And an inadmissible, possessed *Did you take this right now? Are you doing this right now?*

The thought made his face burn hotter.

Niko recognized this, now, for what it really was—provocation.

A taunt.

On Uula, Niko had tried to goad Kestrel into making mistakes. Now the assassin was returning the favor.

Another message pinged through. *I wonder, would you swallow it all for me like a good boy?*

And then another. *I think you would.*

It took a heroic effort of will to gesture the picture away, where it finally disappeared from view. Niko could think again, though only barely. His pulse was racing—he could feel it in his neck, in his chest, wild and anarchic. He hadn't been an adolescent sneaking his first illicit peeks at raunchy photos in a long, long time. But this had made him feel like one again.

Enough, Niko sent back. *Whatever game you're playing, I'm not having any part in it.*

The reply was almost instant. *You had a part in it when you kissed me back.*

Kestrel knew *exactly* how to get under his skin and inflict psychic damage. Niko was all out of sorts now, stumbling over himself, mind racing. Every word was a carefully aimed and executed sniper's shot.

Niko took a moment to center himself, to try and banish the tenacious mental image of the galaxy's most wanted killer lounging boredly in bed, pleasuring himself as he looked at the camera. As he looked at *Niko*. That picture had been taken with specific intent, meant for the eyes of no one else.

The more he tried to banish it, the stronger it burned through his mind. Niko opened his eyes, his gaze desperately wandering through the kitchen doorway, to the refrigerator calendar for a moment. It was bland enough with its ship and mechanical photos. His eyes drew towards the single crossed-out date, now weeks past.

No, I'm not doing this with you. Niko's fingers flew across the interface, trying to keep up with his rapid-fire thoughts. *This doesn't mean anything. You're a murderer and an asshole and it's a matter of time before you're brought to justice like you deserve.*

For good measure, he added, *Go fuck yourself up the ass, you pretentious dick.*

Kestrel was a fast typer. Or maybe he was dictating the messages if his hands were occupied. *Why should I, when it's what you wish you were doing? You're probably thinking about it right now.*

Niko groaned. He stared out again at the calendar, trying to memorize every detail, every streamlined angle of silver and white ship against a starry backdrop. Trying to replace the image that burned alive and feverish through his mind still. The small shadow that indicated Kestrel's elegant wrist bones. The dispassionate expression. The length of his ready cock.

Kestrel wasn't finished yet. The guy was obviously having a field day. *I think you like being tied up. You certainly made it all too easy for me.*

Niko was done with this conversation. It served no purpose but to get inside him, taunt him into making his work even harder. Kestrel wanted him pissed off, riled up. This was literal dick waving.

He was probably laughing at Niko now, at how badly he'd fucked up, at how a renowned bounty hunter had managed to let him get the slip over something so pathetic. Bound with his own handcuffs, stuck uselessly to a utility pipe after coming so close yet again.

Niko certainly felt pathetic.

And now he felt pissed, too.

He pushed away something else that was rearing its head—a fervid, hardening hunger. He didn't need that right now, didn't want to give it its acknowledgement. There was nothing to acknowledge.

What there was to acknowledge instead: the fatally dangerous fact that Kestrel had gotten Niko's phone and bounty license numbers, his name. The fact that he was studying Niko the way Niko had been studying Kestrel through his own files. The fact that Niko was engaged in a text exchange with the most elusive assassin in the galaxy.

And that very assassin had used the opportunity to send a fucking dick pic.

"Tina, try tracing the number."

"I'm sorry, Niko! This number is unable to be traced."

Of course. What had he even expected? Certainly not any part of this exchange.

Another message chimed and Niko managed to ignore it for at least thirty seconds before caving.

Let me know if you want to change sides. We would work well together. Consider this my invitation.

"What?" he blurted out. He paused, mind still reeling, before sending a reply. *I told you. We're not anything alike.*

You said you wanted to understand why I'm doing any of this. Do you still?

Niko stared at the message. The sudden shift from mockery, nudes, and cheeky messages to a more serious exchange was maddening. It felt dangerous. Had Kestrel finally had his fun and tired of the game?

Or was he only just beginning?

He hesitated, searching for the right response. He had a potential window to Kestrel now—a real window. And a transitory one. Niko decided to go for the heart of it all. *What is Honeybliss? There's nothing about them. Anywhere.*

This time, there was a long pause before Kestrel responded. *It was a mistake to tell you. If you've been trying to look them up, I suggest you cease immediately. Every search query you make leaves a virtual footprint leading right back to you.*

Another pause. *And I would hate for you to fall to assassins.*

"You've got to be fucking kidding me," Niko mumbled.

The audacity of this bitch, he thought.

He willed himself to stay patient and texted again. *Then why don't you tell me about them?*

Would you even believe me? Kestrel replied.

Try me.

The conversation ground to a sudden halt. The expeditious jeering from before was over. Niko sat as minutes ticked by, one after another. He massaged his hands, trying to free them of the ache that had set in since he'd returned to active hunting.

Minutes turned into a half hour, and then an hour. Niko had tried to reach, and it'd made Kestrel flee. He closed the phone hologram, too wound tight with anxious energy from the acute shock the whole interaction had brought. If he felt anything else, he pushed it away, deep into a part of him that he refused to turn his gaze upon.

Just as Niko began the awkward dance of pulling himself from the couch to his wheelchair, a single message chimed. He froze before opening it.

Meet me, it said. Niko's pulse spiked again, a chaotic rhythm conducted by the other man's whim and word. Several more messages followed in quick succession.

193 Tulnath Blvd, North Quarter, Sunorrna. Vialis system. It's a binary star.

Tomorrow night. I'll wait.

If you don't want to pull out.

Niko grunted, not missing the wordplay. This was a bad idea—maybe even the god emperor of horrible ideas. He could think of at least ten reasons why agreeing to meet with Kestrel in a private location with no witnesses probably wasn't good for his health. Then again, Niko rarely did what was good for himself.

He sent the message before he could think on it long enough for caution to override curiosity, every alarm within him already blaring. Something about Kestrel kept him from being *able* to back down, though—even when the hand extended was coated in poison. *I'm not backing down. I'll be there.*

We have a date, then, Kestrel sent back. *I'd appreciate if you didn't bring your Galapol friends.*

Yeah, I bet you would, Niko thought.

He sat in silence at the edge of the couch, stunned. The whole weird interaction had thrown him off balance and he couldn't regain his bearings. But every interaction with Kestrel did that, it seemed. And now he was being asked to meet with the very figure who an entire galaxy revolved around in outrage and fear alike. One who perched alone at its center, high above it all, like a malevolent king whose name was on everyone's tongue: Elliott Kestrel.

And he was going to do it alone.

It was an obvious trap. It was too easy. That Kestrel would ask him to meet alone made no sense. He could tell Niko whatever he'd needed to over the phone. No. This was likely a way to get Niko isolated and taken out. Or maybe it was all just part of another game where Kestrel would laugh at him for being so stupid as to actually show.

He glanced through the open bedroom door at T1-N4, the patient little bot drifting back and forth around his living room, one arm extended with a soft cloth as she dusted his furniture.

"Tina, call—" His voice dropped off. *Call Zann*, he'd been about to say. His first instinct was to tell his brother about Kestrel contacting him, about his request to meet, but something stopped him short. Was it really for the best to let Zann in on this? It would only lead to more questions. And undoubtedly, Zann would want to analyze the text exchange word for word. Some of what Kestrel had sent him sounded damning—even ignoring the ludicrous, baiting photograph.

Let me know if you want to change sides.

Consider this my invitation.

You said you wanted to understand.

Zann would *definitely* have questions about that. Niko was already about to prostrate himself before every known god and thank them for the lack of footage recorded of their alleyway fight and—

And kiss.

You kissed me back, Kestrel had written.

This conversation wasn't something Zann needed to know about. Yet.

Niko had been at his corner desk for three hours, a scattering of holograms detailing the planet Sunorrna and its North Quarter district hanging in the space usually occupied by Kestrel's case files. He couldn't concentrate. He couldn't think.

He had been staring uselessly at the text, photos, and videos of the planet while his mind wandered again and again to an image he only wanted to forget about. Niko knew he should delete the damned thing, but couldn't bring himself to, leaving Kestrel's text history closed. But in the hours since, his body had begun to wake up from a long internal slumber of its own, hungry and insistent. It wanted what had been given to him in small glimpses—touch, taste, connection. Niko hadn't had a lover in years—hadn't let himself, locked away in his own grief and self-consciousness. Kestrel was keeping him from being able to think, tapping into one of the deepest and most vulnerable wounds he held within himself—loneliness.

It wasn't going away, and he was tired of the distraction. Niko closed the research and opened a new browser. He sifted through videos until he found one of a handsome blond getting railed on all fours—then realized what he was doing and quickly swapped to a video of two men who very much contrasted Elliott Kestrel, all dark hair and tattoos.

He unzipped his pants and took himself in hand, hard and wanting, and began stroking as he watched one suck the other off.

He wouldn't think of Kestrel. He wouldn't think of the photograph, nor the way the man had tasted. The scent of him. The pitch of his voice and the way it might sound when he moaned.

Niko wasn't even paying attention to the video now, his focus surrendering instead to what was in his mind's eye and everything he wanted to avoid. It was pointless. He wanted a very specific thing, was driven by a single desire. He didn't want to let himself go there, but he did.

Niko swiped the video away and with a moment of hesitation and heady, aching thrill that throbbed with each beat of his heart, he opened their text history and scrolled up until he found the photograph.

Kestrel was fucking gorgeous. Niko hated how much he was.

A new thrill jolted through him, alive, electric, craving human touch. He wanted it so badly. Niko began working himself again, eyes only for the picture that gazed back at him so brazenly. He imagined Kestrel's hand instead of his own, then imagined himself giving this sort of attention to the other man. What would he feel like to take in hand? Glorious, probably. Niko wondered if he was as controlled as he was in their encounters, or if he would give way to soft sounds as he fell apart.

His mind was feverish, all over the place now, his fantasies switching again and again. He was back on Uula, with Kestrel against the alley wall. He didn't have the suit, didn't need it. He turned the other man around and pulled his clothes off until he was bare and perfect before Niko, then fucked him hard, legs pried apart, still standing.

It changed again as he got closer, to something uninvited—unwanted, even—but arriving on a thrill that gave him goosebumps. Niko lay on his back, Kestrel above him now, wearing the same haughty apathy from his photograph. He fucked Niko, beautiful cock buried full and wholly felt in him.

Good boy, Kestrel murmured against his ear as Niko took it all.

Niko hated it—hated the idea of being beneath him like that. And he loved it. He came with a low moan, an unusual sound for his self-pleasure. But he'd liked it that much.

Afterwards he sat, every cell glowing, body spent. He felt weird and disgusted with himself and quickly swiped the photograph away. His head hadn't been in the right place for a long time now. Since Niko had started this bounty, he wasn't himself.

He reopened the Sunorrna holograms and returned to the research that might help him actually survive this.

Chapter Eight

SAVING THE BEST FOR LAST

NIKO WAS GOOD AT making split second decisions. Niko was incredible in heat of the moment action. Niko wasn't so great at sitting around in silence, stewing in his own poor choices.

This had been a mistake. He knew it, down to his core. There was no explanation that could prove otherwise, aside from satisfying a morbid curiosity. In the end, it didn't matter why Kestrel did what he did. He was still killing galactic heavyweights by the week now. Zann had pleaded with him to put an end to it. His brother was relying on him.

So why, then, was he anxiously lying in bed, unable to sleep, insides crawling with dread and regret in knowing he would be leaving—*voluntarily leaving*—to the Vialis system to meet the very murderer he was hunting?

Niko would laugh at himself, if he weren't so annoyed instead.

He sighed, turning over again and opening a hologram. The pale light bathed the entire room and he squinted against its assault to his dark-adjusted eyes. He ran the search he'd run several times now, looking to find anything new: Sunorrna.

Sunorrna had once been a promising city-planet in the making, full of grand infrastructure and packed with grid-laced streets and compact living quarters. It had been abandoned when the planet's bizarre tectonic activity had gone haywire, resulting in mass casualties and structural loss in multiple districts. Readings revealed over time that further future investment would only lead to inevitable tragedy and lost income. The entire planet was a seismic ticking time bomb of phenomenal severity.

In the decades since, Sunorrna was gradually abandoned—by investors and citizens alike. It stood a silent skeleton of vast, nearly planet-wide city being reclaimed by the natural flora. Drone footage obtained by urban explorers revealed most of the structures still stood in the North and Southwestern districts—and probably would for another hundred years or more—but some had sunk and collapsed under the onslaught of violent earthquakes that occasionally ripped through the planet.

Was this where Kestrel was staying? Zann and his research team had gone mad trying to find where the guy's base of operations was.

Zann. Niko thumbed through images of Sunorrna, mindlessly scrolling through most of what he'd seen multiple times already. The smart thing to do would be to notify Zann. To get backup, hidden in the wings. To finish this as quickly and cleanly as possible. Niko considered messaging him but hesitated again—Zann would want to know how Niko had gotten to the point of meeting with Kestrel in the first place. And, despite every sign pointing to this being some kind of wicked trap with the same cruelty of his precisely delivered headshots, Niko couldn't help but want to see where this led.

He managed an hour of sleep before waking to the light of dawn yawning across his room through the shades. Niko's thoughts came slow and groggy and every part of his body ached and protested, fighting each movement. This was even more of a mistake—to meet Kestrel alone, running on no sleep. His reaction time would be slower, his wits dimmed. But he was dedicated now.

After a quick breakfast and half-assed shave, Niko left for his private rented hangar where he kept his ship. He opened Kestrel's contact in his list, which he'd since saved as 'Supermassive Asshole,' with a photo of the gargantuan, supermassive black hole that churned at the center of the galaxy set as his contact photo. There were no new messages—goading or otherwise. He grabbed the address from their last exchange and set the ship's course.

Niko suited up and brought his favorite rifle—which he'd recovered from their tussle on Uula—and a pistol holstered at his hip. He paused, then made sure to bring two of the EMP grenades for good measure. He had no idea what he would be walking into. He knew he was stupid for coming here at all, but at the very least, he wouldn't be going in entirely unprepared.

He landed the ship in an open space near the address Kestrel provided, in a wide and empty, mostly flat patch of dark red foliage that he surmised had once been a parking lot.

Sunorrna sprawled across the ship's windshield view, surreal and eerie and making the hair on the back of his neck rise. It was a planet of contrasts—towering, glimmering skyscrapers and crowded buildings all standing in perfect silence and stillness, untended garnet plants creeping up along them, curling into windows and doors, sprouting from lofty rooftops. There was no bright symphony of usual city scents—street food stalls, restaurants, sewer grates, factories—that Niko was used to on Kaapra-19. There were no sounds, save a gentle wind through the ruddy leaves and an occasional insect rubbing its wings together in summer song. The absence of the perpetual hum of traffic, car horns, distant alarms and occasional patches of music or conversation was profoundly jarring.

As Niko stepped out of the ship and into the deep red foliage—its color a likely result of the combination of two suns that traveled Sunorrna's green-tinted sky—he immediately regretted losing his helmet. It was a blatant and tragically unfortunate vulnerability, especially when meeting with an enemy whose preferred method of kills were headshots from afar. Kestrel could be camping him from any of these silent rooftops, hidden among the young trees sprouting there, wind whistling through them. He glanced around, feeling exposed and strange, half expecting to see him, occasionally mistaking clumping rooftop vines for a crouching figure.

Niko itched to hold the gun holstered at his back, but there was no point here, if Kestrel had him trained with his sniper rifle. And showing up with it out wouldn't be a particular gesture of goodwill, even were that not the case.

He checked the address again, moving along a back street that was as silent, still, and overgrown as the rest of the towering city around him. He paused before an apartment complex, a garishly orange building with several levels of balconies that spanned the length of the building, and an exterior staircase. According to his map, this was 193 Tulnath Boulevard. Niko raised a hand to his brow as a makeshift visor, squinting up into the twin suns at the building. His heart leapt in his chest as his gaze fell on a lone figure on the third-floor balcony—the single soul among thousands of miles of emptiness.

Niko's instinct was to reach for his gun and drop into defensive posture, to find cover, to—

There was nothing to hide from. Kestrel didn't have his sniper rifle aimed down at him. He didn't appear to have it at all. The other man stood, lazily leaning against the balcony railing, peering down at him from afar as though in bored contemplation.

Niko moved closer, each footfall heavy and echoing on the cracked, plant-laden concrete below.

When he reached the building, Kestrel let out a laugh, the sound seeming to split the oppressive silence of the empty world. A smirk spread across his face, the cloud of his unruly blond hair tossed about in the wind.

"Something funny?" Niko shouted up at him.

Kestrel's smile grew, and Niko could see now it wasn't something particularly pleasant. It reminded him of a dagger, surprisingly sharp. Bitter, even.

"You wore the suit," Kestrel said.

Of course I did, Niko wanted to say. *What the hell did you expect?* Yet, glancing down at himself, Niko realized the awkward imbalance between the two of them then—Kestrel in nothing but dark clothes, liquid against the balcony railing, his elegant, bare hand draped over it, and Niko, in full combat suit, armed to the teeth.

Kestrel's appearance hardly meant he wasn't armed himself, though. Niko knew better than to underestimate him ever again. And he couldn't imagine the other man showed up without any sort of protection or insurance of his own.

Not to mention, Niko couldn't walk without the suit on. He sure as *fuck* wasn't about to show up for this without it. And that was a fact Kestrel didn't know—nor needed to know, as far as Niko was concerned.

He didn't like this arrangement—Kestrel high above, looking down on him like he always did with his victims. Niko didn't like having to squint up, either. He moved to the stairs, climbing them quickly, each footfall a heavy, achingly loud *clang* that struck against the silence. On the third floor, he walked towards Kestrel before stopping, keeping several feet between them. Kestrel turned to the side, pushing up from the railing, his own body visibly stiffening as Niko closed in on him.

So, he's scared of me too, Niko thought. *No. Scared is probably pushing it too far. But he's wary. I'm still a threat.*

He felt a little ornery, stepping forward to close that space, pushing up into Kestrel's territory of nervousness. The other man went slightly more rigid, eyes on Niko warily. It pleased him. He wanted to control the situation, to remind Kestrel of the threat he very much still was, here in this place. The suit gave him a few inches on the other man, something he wanted to use to his advantage. He looked down at him.

"Why are we here, Elliott?"

"I wanted to talk," Kestrel responded. It was impossible to get a straightforward answer from him, and it chipped away at Niko's patience—which he had precious little of, due to lack of sleep.

"We were doing that on the phone already."

"No," Kestrel said loftily. "I wanted it to be in person. Unless you're going to fumble around and try to arrest me again."

Niko bit down on a slithering anger, a smirk rising unbidden to his lips. "No, this time, I won't fuck around."

"Come inside," Kestrel said. Niko's pulse beat along his skin. If this was indeed a trap, this was the moment he'd be walking into it. Kestrel turned and wandered inside the nearest door, leaving it open behind him. Niko hesitated a moment before following, every nerve burning with anticipation, ready to fight for survival.

Instead, he walked into a furnished apartment that was surprisingly well preserved and clean, with simple black furniture and framed abstract art on its white walls. It seemed to have been spared so far from the inevitably encroaching overgrowth and seismic destruction. From the lack of anything out of place, Niko knew this wasn't where Kestrel had been staying. In fact, it probably wasn't even on this planet at all, with its unstable tectonic activity.

Of course he's playing it safe, meeting somewhere else, Niko chided himself. *What did you expect? For him to pull something stupid like you would?*

"Have a seat," Kestrel said. "Make yourself at home. I don't think the owners will mind." He sank into a minimalistic wingback chair, crossing one leg over the other. There was something absurd about it all.

Niko glanced warily around the living room, half expecting to find someone else there, or something hidden behind a chair or couch. There was nothing, only the quiet stillness of an abandoned dwelling. Even the usual sniper rifle Kestrel carried was nowhere in sight.

Niko knew this was a man who relied on illusion and stealth regularly, though. Not seeing anything hardly was reason to let his guard down.

"Please tell me you're not going to hover there awkwardly," Kestrel said. Niko's irritation flared again, but he understood it now—this was another game, a way for Kestrel to subtly regain his own control over the situation. A way to rearrange them so they were sitting, Niko no longer bearing down on him, and kept several feet apart.

Clever.

But he would still play this game. He had no reason not to, yet.

Niko sank slowly onto an equally minimalistic couch, the aged thing only emitting, to its credit, a quiet groan under the weight of the suit. He realized he must look awkward and out of place sitting in such a domestic environment—covered in armor, loaded with guns—and briefly wondered if being pushed into a sense of displacement and incongruity was just another angle of Kestrel's game.

"Why are you killing people, Elliott? Why go through all this effort? And what the hell is Honeybliss?"

Kestrel's gaze drew inward, becoming cold. The odd loftiness to him, as though he'd somehow caught some of the unburdened winds of Sunorrna within himself, vanished immediately. He frowned, but stayed quiet.

"You brought me all the way out here to talk. So, let's talk."

"I wonder," said Kestrel, his voice detached, his eyes not focused on Niko, "if you would believe me if I told you."

Niko willed himself to be patient. Kestrel had wondered the same thing multiple times aloud to him already. This wasn't part of a game. He really was struggling with something, retreating deep inside himself. Prying it out of him wasn't going to get the answers Niko sought.

He softened his voice instead. "I'm here, aren't I? I want to understand, Elliott. Why do something like this? This—this is extreme. You mentioned them not being innocent. You accused them of trafficking people. How is that possible?"

Kestrel hesitated, worrying his bottom lip with his teeth. Niko could see it, the way he held onto something and rolled it through his mind, as though testing whether to tell—and what to tell.

"They are trafficking people," he said finally. "Honeybliss is a network and a club for the galaxy's elite. The wealthiest and most influential. People who have no conscience but have enough money and power to inflict their cruelty and bored sadism on others. Everyone in it protects everyone else. And they have the money to make anyone who opposes them disappear.

"They're all beyond the law. They practice trafficking of every sentient species. They take slaves. They rape and break and kill people, because it entertains them and because no one stops them. Every year, thousands go missing because of them. They're never found again. They've done it for decades. Possibly longer."

It was quite the accusation.

"That sounds," Niko began slowly, "like a conspiracy theory."

"It's not a conspiracy," Kestrel spat, his sharp gaze snapping up to meet Niko's.

"Do you have any kind of proof to back up these claims?"

"I do," Kestrel said. "I started researching them three years back. Security camera feeds, personal phone footage. Recorded conversations. Sightings of missing people. I have it all."

That stunned Niko into silence. He was prepared for a deluge of empty conspiracy talk. After all, Kestrel's files held ample history of his obsession with different groups. But if he had actual proof, somehow, that would change everything. "How the hell do you even know about any of this?"

"I—" Kestrel hesitated. "Let's just say it's a little bit personal."

Again, dancing around the answers.

"What about the EverView Files?" Niko asked, bringing up one of the other conspiracies from his case file history.

Kestrel blinked at him.

"Uh, Nine Hatch? The Ascendance of Norovi? Secret Xaarthan Empire?"

Kestrel was scowling now. "I don't know what you're saying."

It was Niko's turn to stare, dumbfounded. "You don't... know what any of those are?"

"No. I don't. I think I've heard of the Norovi thing? Some kind of ancient alien conspiracy that predates the modern species?"

Niko was speechless.

"If you think this is anything like that, you're unfortunately very mistaken," Kestrel said. "Here." He began typing at a small hologram, then sorted through countless files with deft fingers. A moment later, Niko's phone chimed. "Go home. And look at it there, if you want. It's all on there—the evidence that they deserve everything I've done to them."

Niko frowned. He wanted to open the compressed files here, to explore whatever it was Kestrel claimed to be hard evidence that leaders around the galaxy were engaging in the worst sort of crimes known to sentient species. He wanted to press the other man on it, to pick apart anything flimsy. To ask him how it was personal, how he knew any of this. Why it drove him to assassinate.

But Kestrel had told him to go away and look at it in private.

"Why not here?"

"Because if I have to see any of it one more time, I'm going to lose my shit."

"Haven't you already?" Niko asked, leaning back on the couch and draping his arm across the back of it. He eyed Kestrel. "Lost your shit."

"Oh, no," Kestrel said. "You misunderstand me. What I'm doing is to keep myself sane."

What the hell is on these files? Niko almost dreaded to know. The room felt airless. Whatever this data contained was enough to make Elliott Kestrel call systematically killing the galaxy's luminaries keeping himself sane.

"Why do you do what you do, Niko?" It took a moment for Niko to register that Kestrel had spoken. He blinked at the other man.

"Hunt bounties, you mean?"

"Yes. It's not for the money." It wasn't a question, but rather a statement. Kestrel propped his chin in his hand, leaning against the arm of the chair as he regarded Niko. "If it were only that, we wouldn't be having this conversation."

"No, you're right. It's never been. I—" Niko hesitated, painful memories surfacing from the placid dark deep inside of him. He was about to lay himself bare before Elliott Kestrel of all people, to tell him what he'd shared with almost no one else. "Someone close to me was... was killed."

"Lover?"

"No. My mom and brother."

"So, you want to protect people now."

"Yeah, I do. I want to stop it from ever happening to anyone else. I know that's not realistic. But if I can spare even one family from losing their mom, or son, or sister, I know I've done my job."

"And that's why you've been fighting so hard to stop me," Kestrel said. He eyed Niko, chin in hand still, expression as impassive and unreadable as a cat.

Niko shifted uncomfortably. "It is. You're—"

"Killing innocent people? Ruining lives? Harming families? Look at the files and tell me if that's what you still think."

Niko looked at him. Sitting in the chair across from him, one long, slender leg draped over the other, he looked hollow. Inwardly drawn, pulling in all the light and sound in the room, holding some sort of maelstrom inside himself that he wasn't yet willing to let out to Niko.

"You could have given me these files over the phone," Niko said slowly. He wanted to know why. Why bring him here just to deliver a file? Why sit in sullen silence and refuse to answer almost any question straightforwardly? Why question Niko on the motivation behind his work? The fact that this *wasn't* a trap was almost more concerning to Niko than if it had been.

"I wanted to see if you'd come," Kestrel said simply.

So, this had been a test. To see how willing Niko was to listen. How sincere he was when he'd said he wanted to understand.

"Go on, then. That should answer all of your questions. Or most of them." He paused, before adding, "You'll see what happened to my sister, too. Since you were so curious."

Niko sat a moment before rising. He felt awkward and strange. He'd been fearing, dreading this moment. Anticipating it, not having any idea where it would lead. Kestrel was predictable in ways—Niko was learning him as rapidly as he could. But in other ways, he remained confounding, drawn inward, a mystery. In his myriad imaginings the night and morning before he arrived, Niko had envisioned their meeting to be anything but a simple talk. Yet that's—mostly—how it had gone.

It was all oddly amicable. Especially given how their exchanges tended to go.

It took several minutes to unpack all the compressed files. Niko gestured away the case documents he'd left hanging open above his desk, making room for what Kestrel had sent. He watched as the progress bar crept along, disturbingly slow. He hadn't had to wait so long to process data since Zann had sent him Galapol's original bulk of research on the Kestrel case.

A case that was disturbingly full of lesions in the truth its data claimed to bear. Kestrel hadn't even heard of the conspiracies Niko listed off to him. His surprise and irritation were sincere. Yet—those same fictional cabals and Kestrel's supposed historic insistence on them were the central key to a mental unraveling that Niko found didn't synchronize with the man much at all. It was like the person Niko had had so many exchanges with and the man described in medical histories and interrogations were completely separate people.

It would be easy to paint a person as incoherent and unbalanced if someone had access to rewriting their history.

Especially if that person were a legitimate threat.

That hardly explained Kestrel's parents, though. His ex-boyfriend, his former boss, even old friends. His Graceleaf University professors.

That was a whole other enigma to unpack. One person lying under testimony was believable, but everyone Kestrel had once held social ties to? Even his own family. The idea sent a chill rippling across Niko's skin. There had to be an easier, simpler explanation. The assassin was, after all, more than capable of taking lives without hesitation. It may just be that the collected, sharp, and cautiously trusting man Niko had begun—*somehow*—consorting with was merely one facet of a greater, more unstable whole.

If whatever was on these files was valid, however, it would prove the man wasn't at all deranged.

When the data was ready, it revealed a holographic list of hundreds upon hundreds of folders, all named after various people. He recognized many of the names—renowned politicians, celebrities, leaders, and others of influence among them. Most were still alive. Some had already fallen to Kestrel's bullet. Even countless more names, Niko had never heard of. Each folder contained copious amounts of images, documents, sound recordings, and videos. He was intimidated by the sheer number of folders, but started with the first in the long, long alphabetical list: Giannis Alexopoulos.

Niko recognized the man's name. He was a human vlogger who had rocketed to galactic fame through his supposedly hilarious film, game, and art reviews. Niko himself had never watched his material but thanks to the internet, could recognize the guy's face from a crowd.

The folder revealed dozens more files.

Niko opened the first video. It appeared to be taken on someone's personal phone camera, the shot shaky and amateur, often out of focus. Giannis's face was painfully familiar, just as he was in all the videos and internet memes Niko had come across in the wild. But unlike the lighthearted jokes and art videos, nothing else about the man was familiar here. He had a wholly different look to him—eyes cold, expression displeased. He wore only a pair of pants with the button and fly lazily left undone.

A pair of people—a Heenva man and woman—were tied up on their knees, pleading and crying. They had no clothing on. It was clear from the setup of the room itself what was going on. Both were covered in dark bruises, their hair matted from what looked like days or more of suffering with no access to proper hygiene. They both begged him to stop. To spare them. To please just let them go.

Giannis took a swig of bourbon straight from the bottle, then violently smashed it across the woman's face as though she were nothing but an annoying object.

Then he grabbed the man's face and freed himself from his pants.

He...

Niko looked away. It was horrifying. It was sickening. He wanted to vomit, his entire body gone cold as ice at everything that was searing itself into his mind now.

He forced himself to watch. It was awful.

The cruelties and violations enacted on that pair were horrific. And the man—the same man who frequently went on camera and made lighthearted, sarcastic jokes about movie premiers or paintings—was an animal. He was a monster. He had no empathy, no consideration. He took what he wanted from them and they had no way to fight back, no way to stop it.

And when he was done, he killed them. Whoever held the camera handed him a pistol and Giannis simply shot them both, the woman screaming and the man not even uttering a sound, too broken by what had happened to him.

Niko wanted to wreck him. He wanted to take Giannis by his throat and wring the life out of him. He made himself look through the other files, through anything on the two Heenva—they had been a married couple, with three children back at home. Children who would never see their parents again.

It wasn't just Giannis.

The entire long, long collection of folders was a compendium of nightmares. Again and again, Niko struggled to even watch it in glimpses, but made himself, regardless. For the victims. For the people who had once been living, breathing, real. Who had just been minding their own lives. Who had never done anything to hurt anyone. He made himself watch and see what had been so seamlessly hidden behind a well-paid hush campaign wide as a galaxy. Artists, actors, politicians, kings. There were so many. So many faces that Niko had been familiar with through the media, had even grown up seeing on TV in some cases. People who smiled and charmed and donated to charities and when the cameras weren't on them, they inflicted the cruelest acts imaginable on what seemed to be an endless supply of lives, likely floated straight to them on vast sums of credits. Credits they had in such abundance that they could waste and not even miss.

Horu Duu'mari. The Gheroun Imperator Khaathra, the very one Niko had fought so hard to save. Even Princess Vhee-vaala. They were all here, and they all inflicted suffering in their own way. Some chose violence. Others chose a sexual sort of violence. In the end, they all had one thing in common: they had reached a status so lofty, so high, so untouchable, that they had turned to rending, ripping, and tearing their power from others, simply because they could. Because they were bored, maybe. Because they were randy and didn't want to try for a real connection with another being or go through the effort of paying a sex worker. Niko didn't know. It didn't even matter. What mattered was that they did it. And they did it again, and again, and again, all bare and before him in file after file after file.

It was misery, spelled out in videos, pictures, and sounds.

Honeybliss had always been real.

Several hours passed and Niko sat in his chair, still forcing himself to watch as much as he could. He felt he owed it to the victims, to Kestrel. To the truth. Honeybliss had worked hard to wipe all the blood away, but here it still was, a little stain, caught in digital form. Niko wanted to see what they had tried to hide away forever.

His body alternated between ice and burning, his forehead pricked with cold sweat. He didn't eat, didn't give himself a break. He just kept watching.

At the end of the long, long list was a single folder different from the others. It had a single, short name on it:

CLEO.

Niko paused, hand hovering over the folder before he finally opened it.

His heart began hammering in his chest, hard enough to hurt. He felt it in his throat, in his wrists, in his hands—the beginning of a deep panic attack that lurked beneath the surface, like a whale swimming through dark waters, waiting to crest.

This was different. This was—

You'll see what happened to my sister, too. Since you were so curious, Kestrel had said.

Let's just say it's a little bit personal.

Niko felt sick. To think he'd ever accused and had even tried to wound Kestrel with Cleo's death filled him with a shame he couldn't crawl out from under.

With a trembling hand, he reluctantly opened the first of her videos. Like many of the others, it was taken with someone's phone, as though they'd wanted to record it and found it amusing. Or titillating.

Cleo was in a warehouse of some kind, her hands and feet bound. Like the Heenva couple with Giannis Alexopoulos, and many of Honeybliss's other victims, she pleaded. She screamed. She tried to reason and ask why. Tried to even make deals, exchanges.

Uru Taal stood before her, the hideous, gargantuan Toliai crown prince. He gave her a sickening grin, one that held no warmth nor empathy whatsoever.

Niko closed the video.

He couldn't bear to watch Cleo Kestrel's harrowing final moments of life. The humiliation, the pain. The indignity. He looked down at his hands, realizing they were grasping the edge of his desk tightly, and that they were trembling.

Elliott Kestrel had lived with this knowledge for years. He had probably watched this footage of his sister's torture. He'd compiled all the data. Had suffered through watching every video, saw every photograph that linked world leaders to trafficking of innocent people for their own pleasure. Niko had only been exposed to that deep dark for hours, and it already ate away at him.

Kestrel had never been deranged. He'd been *noticed*. They had seen that he'd seen. And they'd painted him as broken, unstable, unreliable for having used his voice.

Niko had gone to a speech of Uru Taal's, early in his hunting of Kestrel. But Kestrel hadn't shown up. Taal had even been present at the Deura-11 parade Niko had argued with Zann about, but Kestrel had gone to the concert instead.

If there was anyone in this galaxy the man must want to eat a bullet most, Niko couldn't imagine it being anyone else. So why hadn't he killed him when he'd had the chance? Why, in fact, hadn't he made it a priority to go for Taal above anyone else in this devouring mission of revenge?

Niko pulled up their text window and wrote to him. *Uru Taal is still alive. Why didn't you go for him first?*

Because I want him to know I'm saving the best for last, Kestrel replied.

CHAPTER NINE

THE OLD-FASHIONED WAY

NIKO LAY IN BED, the sounds of late-night traffic humming outside his window. It had been three days since he'd first seen the files Kestrel had sent him. He hadn't slept more than four consecutive hours before waking again. Every time he closed his eyes, the videos replayed themselves through his mind, unbidden. He couldn't push them away, couldn't erase what had been seen.

On the second night, he had gotten so ill he'd grabbed the nearest trash can and thrown up bile; his appetite had vanished and his empty stomach twisted into a tight knot. When he was able to sleep, he dreamed about what he'd seen. Sometimes the images mixed themselves with memories of his own mother and Ryen. When he'd woken up from that, he stayed awake, too sick and shaken to attempt going back to sleep.

On the third day, he'd watched some of them again. They were already a part of him, ingrained despairingly into his mind. What Kestrel had sent him truly was the worst of the galaxy's bottom feeders, acts so heinous and disgusting he didn't have words for them. Adults, children. Male, female, nonbinary. Honeybliss didn't discriminate in their filth and cruelty. They, in fact, reveled in it.

Whoever the Honeybliss network hired to clean up their records and sweep their sickening truth under the rug was immaculate at their job. Not a trace of these acts existed online, in the media, nor even in discussion forums anymore. How Kestrel had managed to get it at all was a feat of rare skill. And it was clearly a labor of... *love* was hardly the right word. Dedication, maybe. Determination. The files were thorough, they were damning. They were well organized and documented.

How had Kestrel lived for years with this knowledge? These images?

If I have to see it one more time, I'll lose my shit, he'd said.

And Cleo—

His own sister was in those files. Kestrel had never killed her. He had never been violent towards her. Uru Taal had, by some unfortunate chance of fate, chosen her for his sadistic desires, and she never came home.

And now her brother—abandoned in her absence and helpless to stop what had happened—was killing her killers.

Niko couldn't blame him anymore.

In some ways, it felt familiar to his own story. He had been there before. But the abyss that Niko had traversed once, Kestrel was making a home in. Settling in for the long haul.

Kestrel was headed down a path that he could never return from. Even in his incredible skill, it was unlikely he would ever make it so far as Uru Taal. Galapol, hunters or mercenaries would get him long before that. Multiple civilizations wanted a piece of him now, because he'd taken from them the people they truly believed were good. And where the anger and outrage stopped, the unfathomable bounty began. Niko wouldn't be surprised if Honeybliss itself contributed a sizable chunk of that money.

It was all wrong. There had to be a better way than this. Niko knew Kestrel just needed to be heard. It wouldn't forgive him to the public—nor from the law—for having taken lives into his own hands. But it would at least shine light on Honeybliss and open an investigation that he knew would shake the galaxy to its core. And maybe he could help Kestrel slip away somehow, disappear from the public entirely, somewhere he would never be found.

Niko had made a promise to his brother that he would put an end to this. Maybe it would just be in a way neither of them had expected.

He had to talk to Kestrel.

Niko opened the phone hologram. The time read 4:41 in the morning. He swiped through his contacts until he landed on Kestrel's, then hesitated. He wanted to reach out, to ask if the other man was alright.

Of course he's not, Niko thought. What would even be the answer to a question like that?

He swallowed, then opened their text history.

Elliott? Niko sent. His gaze raked across the long shadows of his bedroom.

The notification chimed at him. *I'm here.*

We need to talk, Niko typed. *Please. Can you meet me again today?*

There was a long pause, Niko left only in the quiet of background traffic and the dark of his bedroom. He was aware of its walls suddenly, how they boxed him in, pressed down against him.

I'm preoccupied today, Kestrel finally sent. Niko had a feeling he wasn't referring to attending a party. Or maybe that's exactly how Kestrel thought of this whole thing.

Niko knew today, Jande Seiiren was on the list, the next name and event to come up in chronology. He had seen the sickening things the Heenva painter had done, using his victims to sate his lust. His appearance at the Duskdream Art Festival had been canceled, the man cowardly—though smartly—hiding away. More and more on the list were catching on, beginning to cancel their appearances and events.

Seiiren won't be there today, Niko sent.

Another long pause lingered before the phone chimed again. Niko tried to imagine what the other man was doing—preparing for his next kill, maybe. Checking that his weapons were loaded, that his cloaking device still functioned. Checking and double checking, probably. Maybe the hologram of their conversation was in the air beside him as he worked, and he absentmindedly looked at it every time a ping came through from Niko's end. Or maybe he was sleepless too, lying in bed somewhere, mind turning over again and again with the same dark images that afflicted Niko now.

He wondered if Kestrel was quietly waiting for every response the way he himself was.

I know that. It doesn't matter. I'm tired of waiting, if they're going to be cowards.

Niko's heart sank. This time he hesitated, staring at the bleary transparent blue of Kestrel's words as they hovered in the air, a menagerie of ghosts.

Elliott, can we talk about this? I saw the videos too. Everything these people did is despicable. It's given me nightmares since I— He deleted the last line. *I don't blame you for what you're doing. I see you and I hear you. But there has to be a better way than this. What you're doing has only one way to end. These people need to be brought to justice. The public needs to know what they've done. I can help you get these files out.*

He thought about Zann. His brother was a single file transfer away. Niko could have all of the damning evidence of Honeybliss in his hands in moments. Galapol needed to know. It certainly wouldn't absolve Kestrel in the eyes of the law, but it would open the doors to a deep, sordid web of secrets and crimes masterfully kept under wraps for decades.

But something made him hesitate. Sending this would show Zann he'd been talking regularly with Kestrel. His heart leapt at the thought. Would Zann see it as a betrayal? He probably would.

Would it be something they could recover from? Niko wasn't so sure.

I am bringing them to justice, Kestrel sent.

Niko sighed. He ran a hand over his face; stubble was already covering it. He was losing track of time again. *Maybe I should just let it grow,* he thought.

Right now nobody knows why you're doing this. It all just makes you look unhinged and cruel. People need to know about Honeybliss. They need to know that the leaders and celebrities they believe in and love aren't who they think they are.

You think I haven't tried? Kestrel shot back. His replies were getting quicker. Niko imagined his eyes narrowing, sharp and angry and intelligent. The same look Niko often found himself on the receiving end of. *Every time I tried to get this out, I was silenced. They've bought their own hackers who built online AI to scan for and delete references or files. They pay off people in the media to stop the truth from getting anywhere. I have tried. And tried. And tried. That route isn't possible. So I'm making my own.*

We can work together on this. I know somebody at Galapol who's trustworthy and who will listen. Whatever you're about to do today, please just rethink it. Talk to me instead. Niko rubbed at his chest. He hadn't realized how hard his heart had started hammering.

He waited. And waited. Thin lines of gold stretched and shrunk across the wall as a passing car's light trickled through his blinds.

Elliott?

Kestrel wasn't responding anymore. Niko held his thumb over the phone icon and after a small delay, his call patched through. He waited, frozen, as each soft ring narrated the passing of slow seconds. Eventually, an automated voicemail prompt took over and he hung up.

Answer the phone. Or respond to me.

Nothing. Niko sank back against his pillows, staring up at the murky ceiling. He closed his eyes, heart galloping still, breath flowing in and out as he waited for a reply.

"Hnh?" Niko grunted out as he woke, eyes blinking open to see his room dimly illuminated with sunlight that stubbornly permeated the blinds. He hadn't remembered falling asleep. He couldn't remember what he'd been doing, disoriented as consciousness flirted with him, but he knew it was somehow important.

Then it came back to him. Sober clarity flooded in quickly, as though he'd been plunged into ice water. He craned his neck to look at the hologram which still hung in the air, ephemeral, from hours before.

10:18 in the morning. There was a single reply from Kestrel, delivered hours after Niko's last message.

I will never stop. So stop wasting your time trying.

Unfortunately, Niko had never been very good at giving up either.

He called again, clearing the hoarseness of sleep from his throat. Just as before, the call rang through unanswered. He tried again, then a third time, with no response.

Okay, he thought. *The old-fashioned way it is.*

He opened a new web search to try and locate Jande's residence. As expected, the painter kept his address out of the public eye. It would be easy to ask Zann or anyone at Galapol, and in the past he would have done just that. Jande's address would be over to him in minutes. But that would start to raise questions, and those were something Niko still wasn't ready to face yet. So he would have to work for it.

He switched over to the dark web, a process that took time and care, but was one he'd grown familiar with over his years as a hunter. After half an hour, trawling it yielded up what seemed to be coordinates—rather than an address—for something that was half home, half compound on Valaevanas, the oceanic home-world of Loolae and the Xermotl people. He tested it against several other sources and maps, and it appeared to be reliable information. He had a location now. If Kestrel was going for Jande Seiiren today, this is where he'd be.

The idea of going to Valaevanas made Niko's stomach ache. It was an oceanic world in the truest sense, with only two percent of its surface comprised of land—jagged, tiny islands which were rocky, barren, and frequently eaten away by salt.

To add to the pleasant nature of the planet, due to the lack of shore to break up the constant, churning ocean, frequent rainstorms and swelling, monstrous tidal waves made the surface of Valaevanas a particular horror for anyone who didn't possess a set of gills.

Niko had poured obscene amounts of money over the years into modding the *Soñadora* though, something he was silently thankful for now. Its feet were equipped with heavy anchor weights and solid clamps for inclement weather and uneven land. Even the wild, endless ocean of Valaevanas wouldn't make it budge once he'd grounded it.

Niko himself on the other hand might be a different story.

This is going to be fun, he thought. Kestrel really was out of his mind—just in a completely different way than his files had suggested.

He dragged himself out of bed, every movement making his abused body ache in protest. The paltry few hours of sleep he'd snagged barely made a difference, his thoughts cloudy and sluggish. Niko couldn't afford to be anything but at his sharpest and best when he made it to Valaevanas—Kestrel would undoubtedly be. And if Niko had any chance of convincing him to reconsider things, he had to match the other man.

A cold shower, omelet, and two energy drinks later, and Niko felt as ready as he was ever going to be for whatever lay ahead on Valaevanas.

Niko landed the *Soñadora* on the flattest patch of rock he could find, trying to keep a good distance from the compound. The last thing he wanted to do was immediately announce his presence and create hysteria. He wanted to reach Kestrel before he embarked on his kill, and reason with him. Maybe they could avoid the entire thing together—it never hurt to be optimistic.

He'd seen countless photos, videos, and films of Valaevanas as it was miles below its churning surface. It held an exotic, incredible beauty, its animals and citizens existing in the weightless, gliding splendor that only water could bring. Their cities were built of great, bulbous glass structures, with many city sections kept sealed and supplied with oxygen for tourists and visitors who only breathed air.

The surface of Valaevanas was something entirely different. Waves thrashed and assaulted him as he climbed down out of the ship, a heavy lavender cloud cover pelting him relentlessly with horizontal rains and strong winds. The rocks on which he stepped were jagged, slippery, and porous. Why the hell Jande Seiiren thought this was the special place for his forever home was an enigma to Niko. The man was a Heenva and would drown just as easily as Niko could.

His compound-slash-home was deeply *isolated* though, and if he'd wanted to embark on less than legal deeds that involved trafficking or slavery, this would probably be the place to do it. The whole thing made Niko sick to think about.

He made his way along the rocks, careful not to slip. His suit was heavy and he would sink instantly in it—and had no illusions he could swim the intense, churning tide without it. Especially when he could only rely on his arms.

He spotted Kestrel in the distance, his heart leaping in a strange fusion of relief and anxiety. Kestrel wasn't using his stealth tech yet; Niko had likely arrived at the same time he had. He was standing at the edge of an observation deck, eyeing the compound's door. The rain pelted him as well, his usually wild hair hanging in limp waves around his face.

Niko made his way over.

Kestrel turned to look at him. There was something new to the other man's gaze Niko had never seen before—a deep seated fear. He looked rattled, eyes a little too wide, corners of his mouth drawn taut, his features awash in the lavender light of the ocean planet, sea and salt and rain soaking him. He looked, for the first time, afraid of Niko. "We have to stop meeting this way," Niko said, aiming for a bit of levity.

"Shut up," Kestrel said tightly.

"Elliott," Niko began, taking a small step towards him. "Listen. I need you to listen right now. You can't do this anymore. I can't let you hurt or kill anybody else. I have close connections in Galapol. If I tell them to look into this, they will.

"This isn't the right way. And it's a path to self-destruction. Eventually, it's going to all catch up to you. Galapol or another hunter will get you. It's a matter of when, not if. Your bounty skyrockets with every kill. They won't be kind to you."

"And your 'connections in Galapol' will? You think I should surrender? Turn myself in?"

"No. I can help with that. I can find a way to get you a new ID and—"

"I don't care about what happens to me. I accepted that outcome the day I started. I don't have anything else left to live for except this. Nothing else matters. And I won't stop until every fucking animal in Honeybliss is gone. They won't take anyone else's family away."

The last line made Niko's head swim. He could have said it himself, a handful of years ago. Maybe at some point he had.

We're more alike than you think, Kestrel had said.

"It doesn't have to be like this." Niko was pleading now. "We can find another way. This is just... unchecked vigilantism."

"I've already tried everything you've suggested, Niko. I told you. It's all a dead end. I won't let anyone stand in my way now. Not even you," Kestrel said, the words coming sharper. More bitter. Niko's heart ached in his chest. Despite everything. Despite *everything*. He took another cautious, slow step closer.

"Elliott, I can't let you."

Kestrel looked at him coldly, gaze closed off and hard, intense and intelligent and focused all on Niko. A dangerous wall was rising, not unlike the tidal waves building around them. "Are you saying you're going to try to stop me? After everything I showed you?"

"I have to."

Kestrel sprung on him. It wasn't the stratagem of a sharp tactician. This was sloppy and emotional. It was personal. Niko had betrayed him.

Kestrel shoved into him hard, aiming punch after punch towards Niko's exposed face, his neck, the vulnerable joints between his armor plates. Sometimes he even struck the plates anyway, his hands coming back bloodied. The wounds he was inflicting onto himself didn't even slow the onslaught he gave. This was genuine rage. And hurt, unlike Niko had seen from him so far.

"Please, just fucking listen to me!" Niko struggled to get him under control, to overpower him. He struggled against the other man's lithe strength, even in his armor. He didn't want to hurt Kestrel any more than he needed to, trying to simply overpower him, let him wear himself out. Kestrel kneed him hard in the crotch, something that Niko felt an echo of, even clad in the suit. He grunted and shook Kestrel roughly by the shoulders. It was hard to keep a grip on him in the unforgiving, horizontal rain. Kestrel slipped free and elbowed Niko in the face, sending him staggering back.

"*No*," Kestrel snarled, the vitriol in his voice thick and caustic. "*You listen to me*. You saw *everything* and you're still trying to stop me. You think I didn't want you to watch it there because I couldn't handle seeing it? Please. I've seen it all so many fucking times I have it memorized. I could recite you every plea, word for word. I just didn't want to watch yet another asshole figure it all out and then just turn away. I can't handle it anymore."

Niko held his face where he'd been struck. It was going to leave a bruise. "I'm not turning away from this, Elliott." *I'm not turning away from you*, he'd wanted to say. "I'm trying to help you."

"Help me? You're not even listening to me. All you're doing is getting in my way. It's all you've ever done."

Those last words grated under his skin like gravel. Irritation flared up through Niko, white-hot. "I'm getting in your way? I could have brought you down ten times over. That's my fucking job. But instead, I've stopped to actually listen to you. Don't give me that condescending prick bullshit. It's getting old."

It wasn't what he'd wanted to say. Niko was losing his grip on the situation quickly, slipping to exhaustion and emotion. He wished he could take it back, that he hadn't turned this into a petty insult match. It wasn't why he'd come all the way out here. "Elliott, I—"

"I should have killed you back on Vhesa," the other man seethed.

"That isn't you and you know it, Elliott. Don't do this." Niko said it without thinking. He paused, wondering when he'd come to apparently know and understand Kestrel so intimately.

Kestrel seemed to have the same thought, also pausing before his expression twisted into an even deeper rage. Niko had definitely fucked up. Again.

"You don't know anything about me."

"I know that you're not actually a bad person. I know that, outside of Honeybliss, you're not a killer. You spared civilians, officers. Other hunters, even. I saw how repulsed you were when Bubblegum caused civilian casualties."

"Bubblegum?"

"The, uh, the pink haired—"

"Ah." Kestrel's tone grew flat at the memory. "Right."

"My point is—" A bullet ricocheted sharply off the chestplate of Niko's suit, just below his neck. Mere inches higher and it would have taken off half of his face. For a brief second, he and Kestrel stood, stunned, staring wide-eyed in the direction of its source.

Then hunters' instinct kicked in and Niko pulled Kestrel to the ground with him, trying to shield the other man with his own armored body. He unlatched his rifle. Jande Seiiren stood in the entrance of his compound, pistol in hand and something that glinted silver clutched in the other. He wore nothing but a loosely tied silk robe and swayed slightly on his feet, branching antennae glowing a dull blue, expression sour and determined as rain pelted him.

"You hit the wrong person, you stupid bastard," Kestrel shouted. Niko heard the telltale sound of his stealth tech switching on.

"I'm ready for you," Jande slurred. He sounded drunk. If a masterful assassin were out specifically for Niko's head, he might help himself to a few drinks too. "I'll be damned if I let you take me too."

"You should have thought of that before you started keeping sex slaves," Kestrel retorted. Jande fired twice more on them, sloppy shots that both missed.

A sharp, blaring siren cut through the air, the entire observation deck flooded now in red light. Niko glanced up to see a bright crimson hologram hovering above the western railing.

WARNING: TIDAL WAVE IMMINENT
RETREAT TO SAFETY

"Oh shit," he muttered.

"I got a special present for you," Jande drawled as he slipped around the doorframe and out of sight.

"And it's not even my birthday," Kestrel said. "I hope it's not one of those drunken paintbrush convulsions you call art."

"Nope. Something even better."

Kestrel's tone darkened to a low purr. "Or maybe it's your head on a platter? Because I would find that gift very, very touching. You're going to die today, Jande."

Jande fell back on his native Sala Heenvan dialect. *"Piece of shit dick-fisting fuck-sandwich."*

Kestrel seemed to always bring out the best in people.

"I'm impressed," he said. Niko was surprised he apparently knew Sala Heenvan too. "That was creative. But you're still going to die. Are you afraid?"

"Fuck off, murder-cunt. I'm gonna make you regret ever coming here," Jande slurred, still hiding around the doorframe. Niko knew he was trying to work up courage of some kind.

"Elliott..." he started warily.

"Why don't you come out here and give me my present, then? I don't think I can handle the anticipation much longer," Kestrel said.

A second later, a small silver grenade clinked against the floor beside them.

"Oh *shit!*" Niko said, more enthusiastically this time. He scrambled to get away but the thing went off beside him. There was no violent explosion—rather, a controlled electromagnetic pulse erupted outward from it in a shockwave, knocking Kestrel right back out of stealth. Niko wasn't the only one catching on, it seemed, to his tricks.

He was crouched beside Niko, sniper rifle trained on the door. Niko saw his banter with Jande for what it was now—buying himself time to line up the perfect, single shot.

The sudden exposure forced Kestrel's hand. He fired quickly and missed, the bullet ricocheting off the doorframe, not even leaving a mark. Whatever material the compound walls were made of, they definitely weren't concrete.

Jande disappeared inside, and Kestrel sprang up after him, sprinting hard across the deck as the thick doors slid closed.

"No, Elliott—" Niko tried to stand and follow, but his blood turned to ice as a deadly realization occurred to him.

He couldn't move his legs.

The EMP had knocked his suit's neurotech out.

"Elliott—? Elliott, I can't—"

Kestrel was already gone, pressing into the compound after Jande. Niko's throat squeezed shut in fear as he frantically willed his legs in vain to carry him to safety. Kestrel had no way of knowing he couldn't follow. He couldn't help Niko now—if he would even want to.

The alarm sounded again and the hologram changed.

WARNING: TIDAL WAVE ARRIVAL
RETREAT TO SAFETY

He focused his gaze beyond the hologram, out into the western ocean. He could see it now on the horizon: a gargantuan, unfathomable wall of sea.

He needed to move. Now.

Niko glanced at the compound door. It wasn't a viable option; the thing was thick and solid, meant to protect from the relentlessly battering waves. And Jande had probably sealed it shut behind them.

The only option was his ship. He looked towards it now. It was far. Too far. But if he started now, he could possibly make it.

Knew this was going to be fun. He swallowed, trying to steady himself, and reached out with trembling hands to pull his weight across the observation deck. He would have to crawl the distance—he had no other choice now. If he stopped for even a second, he'd be swept into the depths of an endless sea he had no hopes of swimming in.

Niko dragged himself along, an arm's reach at a time. He forced any other thoughts from his mind. There was only the next pull of his bodyweight ahead of him. And then the next. His ship grew slowly larger in view. Too slowly. He needed to pick up the pace if he had any hopes of making it. His lungs burned as he drank in ragged breaths. His arms screamed out a plea of exhaustion, every muscle aching. The wind and rain battered him; from the ground, constant splashes of sea nearly choked him.

He made it off the deck and onto the jagged, natural stone ground. It was a new challenge, one that made his life harder and easier all at once. He was grateful for the protection of the suit. Without it, he would undoubtedly have torn himself to shreds on the unforgiving rocks. But their tiny holes and spires made for spots to grip, and he found himself making quicker progress than he had on the flat, slick surface of the deck.

Niko told himself not to. But he looked anyway. His heart leapt at the sight of the great wave, half the distance already closed. It bared down on him now. Even the first sight of it from the horizon hadn't been able to suggest the sheer size of the thing. He had to go faster.

Niko pulled himself along the rocks, ignoring the constant spray and splash of saltwater in his face, ignoring the pain and the way the jagged stone drove between the plates of his suit. His chest ached—he wasn't getting enough air to keep up with the exertion. But he pushed himself anyway, pulling, then pulling again, long past the point of exhaustion.

The ship got closer with each drag of his body, until he finally reached the front anchored leg. He used it to haul himself towards the door, sitting up and tearing off his glove to activate the biometric lock. It took several tries, each one grinding a searing, wild anxiety deeper into him. He finally reached high enough to satisfy the scanner, and the door opened, extending its ramp down to him.

"*Thank fuck*," he panted, lungs too deprived to push out more than a whisper. He pulled himself up the ramp and reached back to slam his palm against the door panel. It quietly slid closed and sealed behind him. Niko slumped against the wall, resting the back of his head against it. He closed his eyes as he struggled to catch his breath.

When he opened them again, he realized he could see the wave through the ship's tiny windshield. There was no sky, there was no horizon. All he could see now was a wall of blue. It was humbling.

Something knocked against the door. He froze. *Kestrel?*

It knocked again, this time the obvious pattern of a hand pounding frantically against the metal.

"Ell—"

His external camera activated, a live holofeed of someone standing outside the ship, anxiously glancing around and rocking from one foot to the other.

Giannis Alexopoulos.

Niko was speechless. He hadn't expected him here, but it made sense now. Giannis had been publicly open about his close friendship with Seiiren, both men influential in the art community.

Giannis pounded on the door again, desperate.

"Hey!" he called. "Please let me in. I need out of this place. You—you're a bounty hunter, right? He's here. The—the Kestrel. He's killing people. I need to get away from here. And the wave is coming. Please."

Niko froze, staring at the hologram. Images flashed through his mind of Giannis. He had a particular sadism, and the depraved pleasures he'd enacted on his weeping, devastated victims would be seared into Niko forever.

Every one of those people would never go home. Every one of their families were broken forever after. Niko couldn't unsee it.

Maybe.

Maybe Kestrel was right.

"Hello? Please? I saw your door closing earlier. I know someone's in there. You're a hunter, right? I'm just a civilian. I don't want to die here. The—the wave is really close." Giannis pounded against the door again.

Niko swallowed. Every muscle of his body was frozen. He could save this man's life—with a simple press of the door panel, he could let him in and close it again before the wave crashed down. He could even bring him to Zann, bring him in as a criminal to be processed. After all, he had the hard data proving Giannis's guilt.

But he didn't want to. He didn't want the man on his ship. He didn't want to open the door for him. Maybe it would be easier to let the wave wipe him from the galaxy, just as he'd erased the remains of the poor souls he'd ruined.

"H-hello? I have money. Lots. I can pay you. I'll pay you all of it," Giannis pleaded. His voice was escalating, his tone growing shriller with panic. He started to cry. "I'm—I don't want to die."

Funny, Niko thought. *That's the same thing somebody once said to you.*

Niko said nothing.

Seconds later, the wave arrived, the water slamming into the ship like a wall, shaking and jostling it hard. The lights flickered and for a moment, all Niko could see through the thick windshield was a torrent of raging water, but the anchors and clamps held true. Giannis was gone in an instant. He watched it all on the holofeed as it flickered and glitched too. One minute the man was huddling into himself, wild with despair, and the next, he was simply gone, nothing but churning tide in his place.

I killed him, Niko thought. *By not helping him, I killed him.*

He expected guilt. He expected shame. But instead, all he felt was a mild disdain, buried under layers of numb exhaustion.

He sat in silence as the water slowly receded in the windshield and holofeed views until the ship was no longer submerged. Then he pulled himself to the wheelchair at the back of the ship and sat in it, still in the dead suit. He wheeled his way to the flight console, switching the engines on. There was nothing more to do here. If

Giannis's fearful depiction of Kestrel's murderous exploits was to be believed, the assassin was doing just fine for himself.

If Kestrel's ship had been washed away in the wave, Niko knew there were undoubtedly plenty of other options to choose from, probably sealed away in a parking garage. He withdrew the anchors, released the clamps, and navigated the ship into the air. There was nothing more he could do to help Kestrel here now.

And there was nothing more Niko could do to get in his way.

He wasn't sure he wanted to anymore.

CHAPTER TEN
SWEET DREAMS

"Tina, check for new messages," he mumbled at T1-N4. It was probably the sixth or seventh time he'd asked that day, but he didn't want to count. Counting made it more embarrassing.

"You have no new text messages, Niko."

Of course not. Why would Kestrel reach out to him?

And why had Niko spent the morning hoping he would?

He leaned forward, smearing a hand over his face. T1-N4 floated around him, ambivalent.

"You seem under the weather lately, Niko! Here is a suggestion. In the last two months, you've spent ninety-one hours and four minutes online searching for Elliott James Kestrel. You exhibit the highest signs of engagement and wakefulness when researching this person. It's good to engage in what makes you happy. Would you like me to read you the latest news or facts about Elliott James Kestrel?"

"No. *No.*"

"I can also tell you an internet joke about Elliott James Kestrel: how do you know if the infamous sniper likes you?"

Niko's lip curled.

"He misses you!" T1-N4 exclaimed.

Niko desperately felt around the desk for a projectile. Anything would work at this point. His hand landed on an old beer can and he hurled it towards T1-N4, striking true. With a sharp *clang*, the little bot was knocked out of the air, bouncing off the floor before righting herself with her extendable arms. It all brought Niko much more joy than hearing T1-N4 recite Kestrel facts would.

"That wasn't very nice, Niko," she said, rising back into the air, engines whirring on overdrive. "As an Autonomous Assistance Bot, I am programmed to see to your physical and emotional needs. Using aggression is never okay!"

Niko grunted.

T1-N4 resumed her ambivalent floating, this time making her way out into the kitchen to discard the beer-can-turned-projectile. Niko switched his phone back to private mode, opening the text interface. His heart leapt into his throat as a new text came through.

It just as quickly sank when he saw it was from Zann instead.

So get this. Niko stared at the onslaught of text. *Fucker got two more yesterday. He's changing up tactics. Went right to Jande Seiiren's residence this time, no fanfare. Painted the wall with Seiiren and we have intel that Giannis Alexopoulos was present too but is missing. They think he tried to flee and was lost at sea. I'd say we might have a real fucking problem on our hands now but we've already had one for a long time. Anyway, you'll see it in the news soon enough. I've updated your files.*

Niko didn't know what to say. *Getting real tired of this asshole,* he replied. He was grateful for the exchange being through text, afraid that any stiltedness in his voice would give him away.

You're telling me. Come on, Niko. Work me some miracles here. Use your magic bounty hunting powers and make this guy fuck off.

You have no idea, he wanted to tell his brother.

He wondered what Zann would say if he told him he was the one to let Giannis Alexopoulos die. That the man had been begging for help, sobbing in fear, and Niko let him drown.

He wondered what Zann would think if he told him he couldn't have cared less about it, either. Or that he actually saw what Kestrel was getting at with this whole thing.

I'm trying, he sent instead, then closed their exchange, swiping over to the contact of a black market armor technician named Noori, the other correspondence he'd been anxiously awaiting all morning. She'd promised to text him as soon as his suit was ready for pickup.

Niko had gone straight to her shop after departing Valae-vanas—the armor was integral and he needed its neurotech functioning again. Noori charged an excruciating premium—as most black market denizens did—which Niko paid out of pocket instead of Galapol's funding, but she worked fast, and she worked quietly, and he was promised the suit back next day. Zann would never need to know where or when or how it was damaged.

Niko had been avoiding his brother a lot lately.

There were no updates from Noori, either, so he swiped over to Kestrel's contact now and stared at the black hole image. Then he did what he knew he shouldn't.

He called Kestrel.

Soft, impersonal ringing filled the quiet of his living room until it terminated unsurprisingly with the automated voice prompt. He hung up quickly. Of course Kestrel wasn't going to answer—the man had been livid. He had been more than that. Niko had betrayed him.

He exhaled sharply, stewing in the miasmic silence. Then he called again.

And didn't get an answer again. This time, though, he left a message, brief but to the point.

"Elliott. Call me. Please call me."

Niko leaned forward in his chair, resting his forehead against the simple foldout desk. He'd fucked up on Valaevanas. He'd only succeeded in angering Kestrel and driving a wedge between the delicate truce that was building between them. He knew that much. And if Kestrel didn't hate him already, he definitely did now.

His phone rang, the sound of it cutting straight through the light haze of sleep that had already begun to seep in. Niko sat up immediately, reaching forward to answer, heart hammering.

"*Elliott—*"

"What?" Zann's voice cut through the silence, pulling all the air out of the room.

Niko froze, his arms and chest going numb. Silence stretched between them, cold and strange as Niko searched frantically for an explanation and came up short again and again.

"I—I don't know. I think I nodded off. I'm so tired lately."

It was paper thin, and Niko knew it. But it wasn't entirely a lie—since he'd started hunting again, Niko felt tired in a way that went somewhere deeper than just the physical.

"You're overdoing it again," Zann said.

"Only way to keep up with this bastard," Niko said. His voice sounded watery. Zann had to see right through it.

"Listen, Niko, I— Shit. What?" Zann's voice grew muffled as he spoke to someone in the background. Niko could just make out Fourier's voice and tensed immediately.

"Can you give me a damn minute?" Zann asked Fourier. "Right now? Fine. Okay." His voice grew clearer, directed back at the phone now. "So, I need to address something right now but I've got some new case info for you that just came in. Stuff I don't want to summarize through texts. Will you be around later?"

"Yeah," Niko said.

"I'll talk to you," Zann said, and hung up.

Niko sighed, staring at the phone hologram when a notification caught his eye. He'd had a missed call when talking to Zann. He opened the notification; it was Kestrel.

Fuck.

He called him back, full of nervous energy now, tight as a wound spring. Kestrel answered on the third ring.

"Yes?" he asked, tone icy.

"Elliott, I—I'm sorry. For what it's worth."

Silence hung between them again before Kestrel replied. "Are you?"

"I just— I see why you're doing it now. But I thought— I just wanted to—"

He was losing himself, the words becoming jumbled, a tangle of rapidly swelling fear.

"You wanted to what?" Kestrel said, each word precisely delivered.

Niko shook his head.

I wanted to protect you. The thought was so ludicrous, so *outrageous*. He was supposed to be hunting Kestrel. Now all he wanted to do was keep him safe, protect him from a galaxy righteously enraged. Regardless of how frustrating and stubborn the other man was. Niko felt he was back on Valaevanas, no ground below him, only the churning sea.

"I just thought there had to be a better way than this. I— Meet me again. On Sunorrna. Tonight. Will you?"

The only reply he got was silence.

But Niko wasn't going to give up. "Elliott. Meet me. I'll be there tonight. I'll be waiting for you."

The line went dead, leaving Niko alone again.

Niko stepped off the *Soñadora*, back in his suit again. Noori had finished her work late into the afternoon and he'd swung by her shop to collect it on his way out to Sunorrna.

He had no weapons on him this time. Whatever state Kestrel was going to be in—if the man even deigned to show—Niko wasn't here to fight. Though he knew Kestrel might be.

But he couldn't bring himself to take the guns, nor any other weapon. They sent a message, one he didn't want to carry tonight.

This time, it was night on Sunorrna—a rare occurrence with its double suns. Night lasted three hours, and only came every four days. Or so he had read in his hours of sleepless research. A brilliant tapestry of stars filled the sky. Miles of empty skyscrapers stood, dark and silent silhouettes like gravestones of the world's former potential.

The wind was stronger now than it had been in the day, tossing Niko's hair around, into his eyes. All around him, the city streets stood silent, occasional rare lights on in windows, giving a bizarre impression that someone still lived there. He had learned the power grid still functioned in many intact areas.

As he approached Tulnath Boulevard, Niko could see the open door to the third-floor apartment cracked open. The light was on inside, spilling warm and golden onto the balcony railing. His heart skipped a beat at the sight as he tried to remember. Were the lights on the last time he'd been here? Did Kestrel turn them on after he'd left?

He climbed the stairs, his arrival announced with each heavy step, and paused before the cracked door, pushing it open.

Kestrel sat in the same chair he'd been in last time, hands draped over its arms. They still bore faded cuts and bruises from when he'd punched Niko's armor. He looked expectantly—blandly—towards Niko.

That he'd gotten here first—Niko didn't know what to make of it.

"You came," Niko said quietly. Something panged in his chest, something warm and liquid.

"You wore the suit," Kestrel replied. "Even though you asked *me* here."

"I..." Niko glanced awkwardly down at himself. He would take it off. He would pry it off piece by piece, a show of cautious trust, if he could. But it wasn't possible.

Niko moved to sit on the couch again, glancing around the room. It was as pristine and preserved as before, gentle lighting emanating from a crisscrossing, artsy chandelier. He half expected its owners to come walking out, demanding to know what they were doing here in their home. But they never would—Sunorrna and everything that remained on it of evanescent civilization was liminal now, slowly sinking out of galactic memory.

"Niko," Kestrel said, his jaw set. Niko could see him fighting against his own frustration as he spoke. "I know you're trying to help me. I know you're doing what you think is best. I can't express how grateful I am. I'm sorry for lashing out at you on Valaevanas."

"It's alright," Niko said. "You were right. I wasn't listening to you. I want to know why you won't even consider what I'm saying either, though."

"I'd like to explain something to you. Though I don't know if you'll listen."

"I'll listen. I'm listening."

"No one is coming to help. No one ever will."

Niko wanted to argue, but held his tongue.

"Distributing these files won't do anything. Going to Galapol won't do anything. Appealing to the press won't do anything."

Niko couldn't help himself, leaning forward. "Why do you think that? People are going to care about something like this. This is terrible. These people should be tried for their crimes. They should be investigated. This— What you're doing. It just makes you look like a nutjob. It paints them as the victims."

"Their reach extends to the media and the internet. Even the dark web. Besides, they've already made me look like a nutjob. I've seen the news. It's hardly anything new. I've dealt with it before that, as my life rapidly imploded. They took everything. Every ally, every friend. Every single connection I ever had. They isolated me from society. No one believed me. Or if they did, they were threatened by entire governments. Or paid well off to help ostracize me further."

Niko hesitated. "Your parents—"

"My parents are probably doing this for a payoff. I doubt they even needed to be threatened, but if they were, they'd cave easily. Frankly, I think they'd do this just for fun, though. Getting paid would just add incentive to what was already there."

"Why would they do that to you?"

"Because my parents are cruel, stupid people, who have always hated and abused their children. Cleo—" He struggled to even say her name. "Cleo used to get the worst of it, because she was older. She'd stop them from coming after me."

Niko ached for them both. "Elliott, um," he started. "Have you seen the Galapol files on you?" He knew Kestrel was more than capable of getting information when he wanted it—he had, after all, thrown Niko's own license number back at him.

Kestrel tensed. "I haven't."

"I can show you. I have a copy directly from someone in Galapol. Everything in these files—it's the only information they have to work off of right now."

Kestrel went quiet. He picked up a bottle of water from the floor beside the chair and uncapped it, taking a few swallows. Niko recognized it as the same tactic he'd been using on Jande Seiiren. The same one that had been used on Niko himself on Uula. Kestrel was buying himself time to think. He set the bottle on the coffee table between them.

"Show me. I want to see it."

Niko hesitated. Showing him this was a shattering breach of trust between Zann and himself. *But so is even being here at all*, he thought. *Why draw the line there?*

He sighed, knowing he was beyond the point of turning back now, and thumbed through his own files. A moment later, Kestrel's phone chimed as he received what Niko had sent.

Like the Honeybliss files Kestrel had sent him, it took a moment to load, both men sitting in silence as it did. Once it was ready, Kestrel opened it slowly, methodically, his gaze dull, apathetic even. He began making his way through each file, gesturing quickly through holographic images of himself. He paused briefly only on pictures that contained Cleo as well. Then he began scrolling through a medical and professional history that Niko was beginning to understand was somehow full of fabrications.

Niko watched him in silence. It was a rare moment to see the other man at rest, not staring back at him warily, but rather engaged in something else. He forced himself to look away, wondering with a chill if anything in the files had ever been real at all. Job histories, master's degrees. Even the interrogations with supposed former colleagues, employers, and his ex-boyfriend. Were any of those people even someone Kestrel actually knew, or were they hired actors from Honeybliss?

A soft snort escaped Kestrel, drawing Niko's gaze back to him. Niko realized he had made it to some of the particularly egregious parts—specific mentions of a history of violence against his sister, and that she'd disappeared from the public eye in fear of him. Theories that he'd buried her somewhere on their shared property.

Niko noticed he never once looked surprised, though.

When Kestrel reached Liam's interview, his mouth turned downward in quiet, subtle displeasure, as though he'd tasted something particularly sour. It was the most he'd given away during his entire search through Zann's files, the carefully bland expression cracking in a hairline fracture to reveal something that lurked deeper. Niko weighed whether to ask him or not about it, before opening his mouth to speak.

Ringing tore through the still and silent room, making both men startle. Kestrel eyed him sharply, warily, like a cornered animal. Niko glanced at his interface, the blood draining from him at the sight of Zann's contact number.

"I—I'm sorry. I need to take this."

"Of course," Kestrel said, looking back at the files and resuming his scrolling.

Niko stood awkwardly and wandered out onto the balcony. He closed the door behind him, but knew the city was silent enough that his voice would carry anyway. He could probably get pretty far before Kestrel would be unable to hear him.

He answered.

"Niko? Sorry about earlier today."

"It's no problem."

"Where are you?"

"Um..." It wasn't a question he was expecting to be asked.

"I dropped by your apartment. I was in the area for Ch'ua's Chicken and figured it would be best to just stop by instead of call. Are you nearby?"

"I, uh, needed some fresh air," Niko said awkwardly, wincing at himself. His heart leapt into a sprint, hammering in his chest. "So I took the ship out to Saanas Park."

Zann paused. "Hey, you doing okay, Niko?"

"Yeah. I'm alright, Zann."

"Well, it's too bad you're out there. I got you some nachos but they're all mine now." He laughed. "Nah. I can drop them off in your fridge if you want."

"No, it's okay. You can have them. Thanks, though." The idea of Zann looking through his apartment while he wasn't there made Niko's skin crawl, the realization sending a jolt through him. He and Zann had keycards to each other's homes. He'd never had a problem with Zann dropping things off, being there alone before. Seeing anything Niko might have on file.

He'd also never lied to Zann about a bounty. Especially one as pivotal and elusive as this.

Everything was different now, and Niko was the only one who had changed. Zann was only doing what the two of them had done together for years.

"You sure you're okay? Never saw you pass up free nachos."

"Yeah. I'm just not hungry."

"This shit isn't real chicken anyway," Zann continued. "You're probably better off not eating it. Anyhow, we got some good intel on where this fucker's going to be next. I think it's pretty solid. My team has been piecing patterns together and they've got a ninety-three percent certainty that he's going for Iincha'cul next." He abbreviated the Dvaab leader's name, knowing Niko wouldn't remember the whole thing anyway. Iincha'cul had such renown among his people that there weren't enough letters in the alphabet twice over to spell the whole thing out.

"The, uh, chancellor of Neema?" Niko tried to sound surprised. He knew Iincha'cul was next. He was among the Honeybliss files and had a speech coming up that had made Niko's original list. His files had been particularly distressing to Niko, and had involved legitimate cannibalism.

"Yeah. So, we're planning to go all in on this. We're using all our resources. We've even made the chancellor aware. He was freaked out and wanted to cancel, so we discussed an idea to trap Galactic King Fuckface when he inevitably shows. We gave Iincha'cul the okay but we're going to be there en masse, undercover. I think this is it. We can trap him here. We're making a plan that I can show you. We're going to cage this bastard and finally take him the fuck down."

Niko glanced back towards the apartment, his throat tightening. "Okay." He was unsure whether it was best to lean into the enthusiasm more or push it away. He had no doubt Kestrel could hear him. But Zann could too, and Niko had already fucked up enough times with him that day.

"Hell yeah," Niko added, pushing more color into his tone this time. "Let's end this. I'm ready."

"Yeah. I want to see this guy get fucking canceled. I need you there, Niko. I know you're tired, but this is going to be the last time. Let's give him a real bad day."

"Yeah," Niko said.

"You'll be there, right?" Zann asked.

"You know I will."

"Good man," Zann said. "Anyway, I've got some 'chicken' to eat and we're making prep. Tomorrow at the station?"

"Let's make it happen," Niko said.

He hung up, and stayed out on the balcony a few moments, closing his eyes and letting the wind caress his face, his hair. He felt stifled in the suit. His whole body was on fire. The entire vast, silent planet suddenly felt too small, too oppressive. Too crowded.

Niko finally went back inside, eyeing Kestrel warily. The other man glanced at him. He had already made his way through most of the files, his face as dispassionate again as ever. Niko's insides tied themselves into knots. He wanted to do anything but sit, but everything else felt awkward. Reluctantly, he sank back onto the couch.

"My sponsor. The one who, uh, ironically gathered those files," he offered.

"Your 'Galapol connection,'" Kestrel said.

"Yeah."

Niko was bursting, the energy and urgency inside him too big to contain. "Elliott, you need to take this to Galapol. You *have* to. They need to see. You— No— No. I'll do it."

Kestrel raised his gaze from the files, meeting Niko's own blankly. "You'll do it? And let them know you've been having these little trysts with me?"

"This is bigger than me," Niko said. "It doesn't matter."

Kestrel paused, a frown rippling over his brow, breaking the curated stoicism he'd been wearing. He stared at Niko in silence, as though expecting anything but that.

And then it was gone again. The blandness that returned to Kestrel's face had a particular edge to it, like a dull razor.

"I already did, Niko."

"What?"

"Galapol already know. They know all of it. I went to them two and a half years ago. I tried again and again. I reached out to different branches. I sent them everything you've seen. They *know*. They know why I'm doing this. The moment they figured out who I am, they knew the motive. It may have taken time for the right hand to catch up with the left, but they're there by now. They don't care. They never did. They have to bow to those governments too. In fact,

I'm certain they had a hand in orchestrating my public undoing. When I made too many waves, I woke one night to assassins in my house. Maybe that was their hand too. They probably fabricated the history you see in these files."

Niko stared at him. All the air was pulled from his lungs.

"They're likely not even the full extent of their real internal research, either. It's just what you needed to be shown to do your job."

There was no way. They couldn't all know. Not everyone. Zann had given him the files—they contained more than he was legally allowed to be shown.

"Even if you brought the evidence to them," Niko said slowly, "it doesn't mean that everyone in Galapol knows. The guy I work with didn't know. He's a good man. He cares a lot about injustice. Sincerely. I've worked with him a long time. I— He's my brother."

Kestrel stared at him, something akin to pity in his eyes that drove Niko mad. He felt like he was scrambling. Every explanation Niko grasped for only brought him further from believability, it seemed.

"No. It's not like that. When our mother and brother were murdered, their killers were let off. They got a slap on the wrist and nothing more. They disappeared to some back corner of the galaxy. It wasn't even legal, but he worked with me and we tracked them down. It took years. We gave them the justice they didn't get but that they *deserved*. That's who Zann is. He understands."

"Niko," Kestrel said, his tone softening. Something panged inside Niko at hearing him say his name, at hearing it framed inside his handsome voice. "You're telling me you hunted down your family's killers, even when it wasn't legally sanctioned."

"Uh. I. Yeah," Niko said, not liking where this was going.

"If someone had asked you to stop, would you have?"

Niko felt himself flushing. "No," he admitted, uncomfortable now. He saw exactly what Kestrel was getting at. He swallowed, his dry throat clicking.

"Why did you do it? Why did you even have to?"

"I..." Niko ground his jaw. He fought tooth and nail to keep from admitting it, but the truth was the truth, ugly and hypocritical or not. "They were never given justice."

But Kestrel didn't dig in. Instead, he just looked at Niko for a long moment before glancing passively away. "You have a lot of faith in your brother. I hope that you're right."

Niko sat in his discomfort a while before speaking again, eager to switch the subject away from himself. "Is anything from those files even true?"

Kestrel shrugged, closing out the files. The room dimmed with the lack of hologram light. "My birth name. Where I worked. Where I went to school. My stay in the hospital. And such."

Niko's eyebrows shot up. Of all the things that he'd have particularly pegged as fabricated, that last one was top of the list.

Kestrel noticed his surprise. "It wasn't for the reasons it says. I was..." He paused, taking another drink to pace himself. "My grief was unbearable. After she died. When no one would listen to me. When no one stood by me. When I realized my sister was never coming home again. That she had no future anymore. That everything she had ever worked for was gone now. That I was profoundly alone. I—I couldn't function anymore."

Niko winced. He wanted to reach out, to comfort the grieving man, but didn't dare.

"Cleo was my world. She was my only family. She took on the worst from our *genetic donors* and moved out when she was sixteen. She took me with her. She raised me. She put me through school. She gave me a home.

"I've been alone since. They took my friends. My accomplishments. My dignity. My employment. Even my boyfriend. Then they tried to kill me, because what they did to me wasn't enough. I—"

Kestrel laughed breathlessly, a broken smile on his lips as he looked at Niko. When he spoke again, it was barely a whisper. "Niko, I've been so... *alone.*"

Niko swallowed again, his throat sticky and dry from the stress pressing in on him. Memories of taunting Kestrel with cruel accusations of killing his sister sat in a different way entirely now that Niko knew the truth.

"I thought," Kestrel started, "you were going to be like everyone else. That you'd learn the truth and then just... turn away. Everyone else has. Everyone. I thought that's what it was when you showed up there. When you wanted me to relent."

"No, Elliott. I'm still here."

He glanced at the bottle of water. It looked dangerously inviting.

Kestrel noticed. "Have some."

Niko hesitated before taking the bottle and chugging down most of what remained. "Sorry," he mumbled. Kestrel only shrugged.

He was burning up now, all too aware of the restriction of the suit, of how tight and encasing it was. Normally, it was a comfort—the suit gave him protection. It gave him freedom. But it felt like a furnace now, like a modular sarcophagus. He unlatched the gloves, the cool air of the room a balm on his skin, and massaged at his fingers.

Kestrel's attention fell to Niko's hands, his gaze seeming to wake up, attentive now, the moment of raw emotion gently falling away. To Niko's surprise, the other man let out a soft laugh, another faint smile—sincere and amused this time—creeping across his face.

He stood and crossed the room, closing the distance between them. Niko's heart sped up all over again. He sat, staring up at Kestrel. There was a softness to the other man's gaze now, the careful apathy and pain both tucked away. If Niko had shared rare moments with Kestrel before, this was the most exceptional of them all. He reached out and took Niko's hands in his own. The gesture was startling. He held them palm down, trailing his thumb along the backs of Niko's fingers. Kestrel's hands were warm—the only sensation in the room now. Niko hadn't been ready for this.

Kestrel tilted his head, half-smile still present. "Really?"

"Really what?"

"'*Killjoy?*'"

"Oh." Niko felt sheepish suddenly. Kestrel had noticed the old tattoos that adorned his hands—myriad symbols and markings, including a compass along the back of his left hand, and letters printed one each across his fingers, spelling out KILLJOY. He winced. "Yep. Got that one when I was a little drunk."

"Is that what you call yourself? Killjoy?" Kestrel's smile grew.

"Used to be, uh, a name I was known for around the black market."

"It's not enough letters to even cover every finger. What's this last one?" Kestrel traced his thumb along the left pinky. Niko shifted on the couch, a new kind of heat overtaking him.

It was surreal, bizarre, this sort of simple closeness. To be explored by Kestrel. To have his hands held. It was like Uula all over again, the sudden shift into something *different*. Something that Niko wouldn't let himself look at head on. He couldn't. Kestrel eyed him like he was an amusing toy, or maybe something for his engineer's heart to pry apart and study the pieces of.

"It's, um, a skull. But it's faded pretty badly over the years. I use my hands a lot, so it kind of deteriorated quickly."

Kestrel exhaled in amusement, and Niko watched as a stray blond strand took flight at the movement of air. "You... use your hands? A lot?"

He was getting stupid and flustered. "I—I—uh, my job—and—"

It was over as quickly as it began. Kestrel let go of his hands and took a step back. Niko still felt the ghostly echo of his touch as the warmth faded.

Kestrel eyed his armor up and down.

"Do you have more tattoos under there?"

Oh boy, Niko thought. *That's a hell of a loaded question.*

"Yeah," he commented neutrally. "I'm pretty inked up." He couldn't go there. He couldn't afford to. He slowly drew his hands closer to himself, then reached for his gloves and fastened them back into place.

Kestrel took another few steps back. "Cleo always said to avoid men with tattoos. She said they'll break your heart."

Niko snorted. "Sounds personal."

"It was. Are you a heartbreaker, Niko?"

He couldn't go there.

He couldn't let himself this time.

Niko stood. "Elliott. You need to listen to me. You can't go after the chancellor tomorrow. They're expecting you. They're going to throw everything they have at you. It's a dead end. This whole thing is a setup and they're aiming to finish this. It's a trap and they're going to kill you. I'm going to have to be there. And I can't let you go if they're there."

"Stop coming after me, Niko. Tell them you don't want the bounty anymore."

"Just let me talk to Zann. Please. He's different. He's like me—if people are being hurt, he'll listen. If he agrees to open a real investigation into this, will you reconsider?"

"I am never going to stop until either Uru Taal or I are dead. Walk away from this, Niko. Go home. Just go home and live your life. You're going to get hurt if you don't."

Niko went to Kestrel and took him gently by the shoulders. "Why? Why won't you let me even try? Zann isn't like the people who've let you down. You're not listening to me either."

Kestrel glanced away, his expression turning impassive. He was silent a moment before speaking. "Kaapra-19, Station Twelve. Right? That's where he works from?"

"I— Yeah."

"Niko." Elliott spoke quietly, slowly. "Station Twelve was one of the ones I sent the files to. All of them. They have everything. They have for years." Niko couldn't breathe. The ground fell out beneath him, leaving him in a vertiginous freefall. He swallowed, trying to make sense of what Kestrel said, trying to pry it apart, find the holes in it.

"He— If he knew, then he'd have known exactly where to anticipate you every time." Memories of arguing with his brother over the concert versus parade flashed through Niko's mind. He'd been frustrated at the time, had felt unheard, untrusted. Yet in the end, he'd been the one in the right. The thought was irritating at the time, but now it only left him relieved.

"I don't think even they know who all is a part of Honeybliss. Galapol is just another tool they pay off sometimes," said Kestrel.

Zann couldn't have known about any of that. Zann probably hadn't been shown those files; he was busy working on other cases then. It probably would have been around when Niko had his accident, when they'd finally caught who'd killed their family. Just because Galapol had that information didn't mean every individual who worked there did. He wouldn't have had high enough clearance then, hadn't been promoted yet—

Zann couldn't have known. Not with what they'd gone through with their own family.

"No." Niko shook his head. "He couldn't have seen it. I know." He wasn't arguing any further. Zann was his best friend, his last remaining brother. They had been through the dark together, left to pick up the pieces of senseless violence. They had chosen to make a difference, side by side, to make sure it never happened to anyone else. As a team.

As brothers.

Zann wasn't like that. He wouldn't turn a blind eye to all of that.

Zann wouldn't *help* Honeybliss.

"I want to try. Just let me try. Someone there must have seen them, but he didn't. I'm going to show him these files."

"Okay," Kestrel said simply.

Niko didn't know what was right anymore. It didn't feel good to fight Kestrel on this. Not when he had been there himself. To continue on his path would only end in death, though. And Niko, despite everything he knew he had been hired under contract for, didn't want Elliott Kestrel to die.

He couldn't think anymore, his thoughts a jumbled tangle of intentions, feelings, needs and fears all roiling together. Niko moved towards the door.

Kestrel was there before him, blocking the way out. There was something a little wild to him now that he'd realized Niko was going. Something desperate.

"Leaving already?"

"We're done talking." Niko didn't want to talk, didn't want to think about the implications talking led to.

"We don't have to talk."

Niko's breath caught in his throat. He couldn't go there.

Kestrel bored his gaze into Niko's, alive and searching. Bright, feverish.

"We can fuck each other," he said, voice low and liquid. "Isn't that what you want?"

"Elliott."

He reached up and caressed Niko's cheek. His touch was warm and electric, even more than when he'd held his hands. "Tell me how you like it. I'll make it good for you."

Niko took Kestrel's wrist in a tight grip and pushed the other man back against the doorframe. Kestrel's breath hitched.

Stop. The word was on his lips, on his tongue. He knew that he should say it, should put an end to this now. But Kestrel wasn't the only one lost and alone.

"On Uula," Niko said instead, "what was that?"

Kestrel was silent.

Niko tightened his grip. He was tired of games, of secrets. "Tell me what it was."

"A diversion," Kestrel said quietly.

Niko tilted his head forward until he was inches from Kestrel, sharing the other man's air. Breathing his breath.

"Was that all it was? If it was, tell me. Say it."

Kestrel hesitated.

"Say it, Elliott. If that's all it ever was."

"When I wrote 'you can't stop thinking about it,'" Kestrel said haltingly, "I think I was just talking to myself."

"You couldn't stop thinking about it?" Niko let his thumb wander along Kestrel's wrist now, tracing the tendon there, the dusky veins.

"I couldn't stop thinking about it," Kestrel said. "I can't stop thinking about it."

"And that *picture?*" Niko breathed, the memory of it burning through his mind. He wanted it again, wanted it even now: Kestrel bare and ready and perfect before him. He could do it so easily, could pull off the thin layer of clothing that was the only barrier between the conservatively dressed man before him and every memorized contour of that illicit photo.

"I wanted you to think of me too."

Niko's entire body was alight in agonizing fire, a desperate need and hunger clawing up out of the long drowsy depths. He wanted to fight it, but it was winning. And for the first time, Niko found himself tired of fighting. He leaned down to meet Kestrel, pressing his lips to the other man's, sliding his tongue along his bottom lip. Kestrel was just as ravenous, pushing back into Niko, kissing him again and again, relentlessly.

Niko fumbled with unlatching his glove and reached out to touch him—anywhere, everywhere. At the ridiculous untamed cowlicks, at his regal cheekbone, his neck. His shoulder. He pushed the collar of Kestrel's sweater down and stroked the lovely exposure of pale skin with his thumb. The fluttering pulse of Kestrel's heart met his touch.

"I thought of you. I thought of you all the time," Niko murmured into Kestrel's ear. The scent of the other man's hair made him high. "I can't stop thinking about you, Elliott."

Niko couldn't handle it. He couldn't handle the burning that flared through him now. It woke him up and brought his body to life with a terrible vibrancy he needed to answer.

There was nothing in the entire galaxy he wanted more than this.

Niko brushed his lips against Kestrel's neck. He begged kisses along his throat until they turned into greedy licking and sucking at the delicate skin. Niko wanted to mark him, and the honey-dark thought of Kestrel wearing proof that Niko's mouth had been on him beneath those black turtlenecks he wore seared hot through his mind. Kestrel moaned in response and tipped his head back, enthusiastically letting Niko help himself to it all. The vibration of his voice rippled against Niko's mouth in a way that drove him nearly hysterical. He was beyond losing himself now. He was already lost.

A heavy and metallic snap rang out between them, loud against the quiet of the room. Niko froze in place, cool air flooding in now through the front of his suit. Kestrel's hands had been just as greedy and wandering over his body too, and he hadn't even noticed, hadn't felt it through the thick armor plating at all. His clever engineer's fingers had managed to seek out the latch to unfasten the chest-piece.

If he pried it any further from the rest of his suit, the neurotech that allowed Niko to walk would disable.

A chill settled over Niko as alarm and unease crept in. He felt, suddenly, vulnerable. Exposed in a way he wasn't used to. He reached up instinctively and grabbed Kestrel's hand to keep him from going further.

He couldn't go there. This had been a mistake. It was worse than the alleys of Uula.

Niko thought about what this would lead to if he let it continue: being left without a way to walk, stranded on empty Sunorrna, a mile out from his ship. No chair, no suit if Kestrel so saw to take it from him. Letting himself be at his most vulnerable before someone who had used him before, had worked his deepest desires against him.

This wasn't what he needed to be doing. If he let himself fall into Kestrel now, he could never go back. Zann would be waiting tomorrow at the station, to talk about how to kill or capture the man. In the end, this might just be another diversion after all. Kestrel's last-ditch effort to buy time, keep Niko from being swept up in whatever was about to go down tomorrow.

Niko pulled away from him, quickly refastening the loosened chestpiece. It reconnected with another solid snap. He took a few uneasy steps back, still dazed and drunk but sobering.

"Why?" Kestrel said, slumping back against the doorframe. He reached up and touched absently at the blushing mark Niko had left on his neck before tugging the collar of his turtleneck up to cover it.

"I—I can't, Elliott. We can't."

"Why not?"

"I have to talk to Zann. We only have a day before they lay this trap, if you won't reconsider. I have to get these files to him, talk to him. Let me help you, Elliott."

"You *were* helping me," he said flatly.

Niko flushed. "No. Not like that. Trust me. Please. Let me help you bring them to justice. He'll listen. The others might not have, but he will."

"Niko. I don't want to stop killing them. *I like it.* Every creature in Honeybliss is already getting exactly the justice they deserve."

Niko closed his eyes, not wanting to get caught in this fight again, this cyclical impasse. "I'm going to try anyway, Elliott. I have to."

"Just go, then."

"Elliott..." Niko tried to reach out for him. It was stupid, but he couldn't help himself. It had become instinct to want to reach for Kestrel. The other man shrugged away from him, retreating further into the empty and silent apartment.

"Don't." Kestrel's tone was descending from flat to outright vicious now, rough at its edges with disdain. Niko's chest tightened at hearing it. It was Valaevanas all over again.

"Give me some time. I trust Zann. We can bring Honeybliss to light."

"Then go do it," Kestrel said. "See where it gets you. I hope your brother is everything you've built him up to be."

The moment Niko was back in the *Soñadora*, the door closed tight behind him, he patched a call through to Zann. He waited, desperate, as the ringing seemed to stretch on forever. Finally, Zann answered.

"Niko. What's up?"

"Zann. I've been doing research and there's more to this case than we thought."

"What do you mean?"

"Honeybliss. It's real. It's a real thing. And the people who've become victims—"

"Niko. I told you. I don't give a flying Toliai's lumpy ass about that right now. I don't give a shit about motives right now. I'm just ready to end this. We can interrogate him about motives later on, if he doesn't eat a bullet tomorrow."

Niko hissed in frustration. "You're not listening to me, Zann. There's a whole other dimension to this we aren't seeing. Cleo Kestrel is dead, but Uru Taal killed her. There's video evidence. All the targets so far have been trafficking thousands of people every year. They're enslaving people. They're—they're raping them, and killing them to hide the evidence. They're torturing people. The fucking chancellor of Neema is eating people—"

"How the fuck did you even find any of this out? Are you still at Saanas Park?"

"I— We'll talk about that later. But this shit is legitimate. I have proof of every single one. Even Princess Vhee-vaala—"

"Niko, let's talk about this after tomorrow. Right now, I have so much on my fucking plate. I need to focus on bringing down this asshole and then we'll talk about whatever footage you have. Deal?"

"Zann. This is important—"

"We'll talk about it. Okay? I promise you we will. Right now, I need your head in the game. We cannot afford to fuck this one up. He can't get away again or I'm going to space myself. I am ready to be done."

Niko wanted to throttle him through the phone. He paced back and forth, still in his armor. The ship felt too small. "Zann. I'm going to send you these files. Please take a look at them."

"Fine."

"These people— I— They *deserve to die.*"

Zann was silent.

"When I said it's like Mom and Ryen all over again, I meant that in every way imaginable. I can't even blame Kestrel for what he's doing, now that I know this. Every part of this is some sick miscarriage of justice. And no one cares. It's like what we did. This is just like what we did."

"You shouldn't say that over the phone," Zann said slowly. "Electronic records, and all."

"Fuck. I know. I just—"

"Niko. What do you want me to do about it?"

"We can launch an investigation—"

"That's not what I'm asking here."

Both men fell silent, only the soft background static of their call filling the void between them.

"What do you want me to do about it?" Zann asked again. "Should I tell my guys to back off? File a formal appeal? Should I tell them it's okay, and that he's cool because the renowned politicians and celebrities he's knocking off are *bad people?*"

Niko was stunned. "I— What if we could work with him, somehow?"

"Do you think that's even close to realistic, Niko? This is far beyond that. Whatever his motives, he's gone too far. This isn't like Mom and Ryen and what we did. We were careful. We covered our asses. He, instead, has just shit the galactic bed. I have one job—and that is to bring Elliott James Kestrel to justice. Whatever form that takes. Are you with me?"

Niko didn't have words.

"Are you *with* me? If you're not, you need to step down from this. I will pull you off the case."

"I'm with you, Zann," Niko said. He paused before asking what lay heavy and dark on his mind. "Did you know about this?"

"About what? That he's out blowing the brains out of planetary leaders with complicated, ugly histories?"

"About Honeybliss."

"I've heard a few rumors."

"Rumors?"

"Yeah. That it's some 'big elite group' conspiracy that might have a miniscule fraction of a chance of being real."

"How much did you know?"

"I don't know— Niko— I—I have so much on my plate right now—"

"Zann. *Zann*. Answer the question."

"—but we'll talk about it, okay? When this is finally over. We can launch an investigation—"

"You knew they existed. And what they did."

"Yeah." Zann's voice was clipped. "Yeah, Niko. I did. Okay? I know they did some fucked up shit and I promise you we will look into that. After tomorrow."

Niko sat down in stunned silence, his heart ripped out of him.

"We went into this to help people," he murmured.

"Don't do that to me, Niko. We did go into this to help people. We're still helping people."

"Did you know who's in it? Did you know he's been targeting only them?"

"No. No, Niko. I didn't. I don't know who the fuck is in it. How do you know any of this?"

"Black market exchange. Their terms were anonymity. I'm sorry." He wondered if Zann even considered the flimsy lie a possibility.

"Fuck. Of course. Yeah."

Niko fell quiet.

"Niko. We'll talk about it. All of it. I promise you. Right now, we need to stop this first. Kestrel is not helping people. Regardless of his reasons, he cannot do this. He is breaking entire governments. Entire fucking planets, in some cases. He only ever dug his own grave and he dug it deep."

Niko was at a loss for words. Zann was just as set on his path as Kestrel was.

He wasn't going to listen. And even if he did, what could he do about it? In the end, Zann's hands were tied. He'd been right when he said he couldn't ask them to stop.

"Yeah. You're right. It's not the same, is it?" There was nothing else to say.

"No, Niko. It's really not. Get some rest, okay? Focus on tomorrow. Then we'll talk."

He sent the files anyway.

He sent them just before going to bed once he'd gotten home. Zann would have all night and tomorrow morning to read and watch them—if it made any difference. Niko didn't even know what he was asking of his brother anymore. Of course Galapol wouldn't pardon Kestrel. Of course Zann had no power to even try asking that, even if he'd wanted to. Niko had told himself getting these files to Zann would be the first step towards bringing Honeybliss to justice, but what had he even tried arguing with his brother? It felt more like he'd been begging him to spare Kestrel himself.

That was what Niko wanted.

Icy unease crept through him when he thought about what lay ahead tomorrow.

He texted Zann. *I hope when you see these, you're reminded of the real people they've been hurting. It's not just a rumor.*

Once the files were sent, he found himself swiping again to the contact that had become so familiar. He wanted to text him, to call him. What would he even say at this point if he did?

I miss you. I want to talk to you. I hope you're okay.

Or, *Please don't go. Reconsider this.*

Or maybe, *I'm sorry I left you alone on Sunorrna. I'm sorry we didn't finish what we started.* Was he still there? Or had he packed up his scant belongings and left on his own ship to prepare? What was Kestrel thinking? What was he doing? Niko hated how much he wanted to know.

Thinking of you, he found himself typing. He hesitated, then deleted it. After leaving him like he had, it was too impertinent. Too unkind. Even if it carried the weight of what sat heavy in his chest.

Instead he wrote, *Goodnight, Elliott,* and closed his eyes, not expecting a response.

He was startled from the edge of sleep by a ping.

Goodnight, Niko. Sweet dreams.

CHAPTER ELEVEN
NO WAY OUT

DESPITE ALL HIS APPREHENSION, it was the first full night of sleep Niko had gotten in a long time. He'd had feverish dreams of Kestrel, ones that constantly shifted, intangible, ephemeral. He spoke with Kestrel, again and again. He dreamed he spoke to him in the indigo-tinted fields of Kaalan-10, sitting together under an old tree. He dreamed he talked with him aboard the *Soñadora Despierta*, the two of them sitting in the pilot's and co-pilot's seats. Kestrel was in his apartment, perched on the edge of Niko's bed. He was on the warm beaches of Eanan, the ocean matching his eyes.

In every dream, Niko begged him not to go, tried to explain why it would only lead to his death. Kestrel was quietly adamant. Every time Niko finally came close to convincing him, the dream shifted once more to someplace else, and he had to start all over again.

He went through the motions that morning, before suiting up and meeting Zann and the other agents and investigators at the station. Fourier gave him a *'Good morning, sunshine,'* that Niko didn't bother responding to.

They spent two hours discussing the plan of action and strategy, with even the chief, Kamira Salas, who'd agreed to fund Niko's work joining in. They stood leaning against the big oak table, blonde hair slicked back, hands in their slacks pockets. They nodded once to Niko and he returned the gesture. There had always been respect between them, since Niko had first begun hunting. Kamira knew Zann and Niko's story, and had helped train Zann up to be the investigator he was to this day.

Blueprints and maps covered the conference room walls, and coffee was ordered and passed around in generous quantities. Zann looked again like he hadn't slept all night. Niko watched him quietly as tactical placement of agents was discussed. If Zann had seen the files, he made no mention, and with the station in such an anxious frenzy in anticipation of finally trapping Kestrel, Niko was given no chance to speak with him alone.

Niko, for his part, was expected to play the role he always had: he would enter separately, and be left to his devices. He'd gained a reputation for being able to sniff out the elusive assassin with uncanny instinct alone, so he'd been given the task to locate him for Galapol.

He glanced around at the officers and agents gathered, at the old faces who he'd become so warmly familiar with over his years working to bring bounties in. How many knew about Kestrel's files? How many in this room knew exactly what he was fighting for—and why? How many knew the grotesqueries the chancellor had committed, and were choosing to let him walk free—defend him from Kestrel, even?

Niko's thoughts drifted to Kestrel and got lost there. He wondered what the other man was doing right now. Probably preparing for the speech, just as Galapol was. Was he nervous? Was he lonely? Did he even care at all?

This wouldn't be like his other assassinations. He wasn't going to make it back from this one. He didn't stand a chance. Galapol was pooling everything they had into this effort, to try and end his deadly endeavor swiftly and for good.

Niko was going to have to see him be brought in—or killed. It didn't matter which way it went down, in the end. Apprehending Kestrel led to the same grim fate, just drawn out with courts, fanfare, and his inevitable execution before the eyes of billions.

And Niko was going to have to help them do it. He might even have to be the one to do it himself.

The meeting concluded, the crowd in the room dispersing to their various roles and preparations. Niko had mere seconds with Zann before the other man had to leave as well.

Zann looked at him, his gaze flickering briefly to lock on Niko's own. He reached out and grasped Niko's shoulder, giving it a shake.

"We'll talk."

And then he was gone.

The speech was being held on the small, deep azure moon of Neema, a colony-world of the Dvaab. Its conference center lay beneath the thick, sweltering atmosphere of dense blue cloud cover. Its architecture was traditional Dvaab design—sleek and full of spirals and swirls, which the Dvaab greatly favored and considered holy, as they formed the very pattern of the lifegiving galaxy itself. Like the Quwa-quay, the Dvaab culture was steeped in religion. Whereas the Quwa-quay worshiped their Grand Sovereign as an incarnate of their god, the Dvaab found holiness in the universe itself, shunning the idea of mortal gods entirely. They considered all things sacred.

All things, Niko figured, except probably Elliott Kestrel.

Especially if the presence of a phenomenal amount of Dvaab authorities wandering the grounds of the conference center was any indication.

He knew Kestrel was here, waiting somewhere, alone and silent in the rafters, perched like some patient and predatory bird watching mice scurry below. Niko needed to see him. He just didn't yet know what to do when he finally did. It was, after all, why he was here, and what Galapol was counting on him to do.

Niko glanced up at layers of spiraling walkways and stairs that gracefully orbited one another in a double helix, wondering if somewhere above, Kestrel was watching him now. Something in him ached at the thought.

He made his way up along the nearest winding staircase, climbing the great spiral from which warmly glowing ornate lamps hung low, and glanced back down at the people below. Niko had never seen so many Galapol agents at any event before. Between the agents,

Dvaab security, and perpetual swarm of scattered bounty hunters, the place was a festering sharks' den. All of it made Niko nauseous. He'd barely touched his breakfast that morning, too sick to eat.

This definitely wasn't how he'd imagined things going when Zann had asked him to take up hunting again.

Niko reached the top of the curving stairs; they gave way to a walkway that circled the entirety of the grand room. All along its walls, beautiful lanterns hung, with ornate spiral patterns carved into their crystal. Security drones floated to and fro around the vicinity, but he knew they were as good as useless. They had been, on Uula. Niko glanced around quietly, looking for Kestrel. He hoped he didn't see him. He hoped he hadn't shown.

His life would be so much easier if he hadn't.

"It's a nice view, isn't it? The Dvaab always have beautiful architecture."

The voice came from just beside him, familiar and handsome. Niko closed his eyes for a moment as his heart sank. He forced himself not to turn a reactionary glance towards the stealthed man. It would only bring attention. Instead, he cast his gaze slowly around, appearing to still be looking.

When he replied, it was in a murmur. "I was hoping you wouldn't show."

"I was hoping the same of you."

"Seems we're at an impasse, Elliott."

"Why did you come, Niko?"

A million answers pushed for dominance in his mind.

I had no choice. That wasn't true, though, was it? Zann might have been disappointed, but Niko could have recused himself, backed out of the hunt. It was no secret that he'd not been doing great since he'd begun pursuing Kestrel, too many old memories unearthed, too many old ghosts. And now, new ones to add to the haunted collection.

Maybe, instead, *I wanted to see you one last time.* It hurt too much for Niko to even get the words out, his chest constricting tightly, breathlessly, at the thought.

He settled on a frustrated, biting, "Why did *you?*"

"You know why," Kestrel said.

He did know why. Because no one else would. Because no one had listened to Kestrel. Because he had committed to this stubborn plan and one way path, and was taking on a galaxy alone.

Niko glanced away, out at the walkway around him.

"Just... walk with me for a moment. We've got a while before this starts."

He continued along the circling path, moving slowly, pretending to gaze around for the assassin who kept beside him. He could hear the quiet footfall of Kestrel, the only sign the other man hadn't abandoned him completely. He wondered what was going through that beautiful, brilliant, headstrong mind right now.

Niko passed another hunter, an obnoxious young Xermotl who lit up her patterns in rippling, flashing rainbows—the uniquely Xermotl version of the middle finger. "That bounty is mine," she said.

"Good luck with that," Niko murmured. He kept walking.

Another drone floated by, pausing to scan Niko before continuing on. They had so little time. Niko had so many things he wanted to say, memories of his feverish dreams and their repeated arguments running through his mind. He had mere moments before Galapol would start wondering. Moments before the event would be getting underway and Iincha'cul would make his appearance.

"There's no way out of this, Elliott," Niko murmured. "Not this time."

"Don't give up on me so easily."

Niko ached. Frustration swelled rapidly in him. He found himself instinctively turning towards Kestrel, then glanced around in paranoia to see if anyone was watching. "You might be able to leave now. If you do it before killing the chancellor, they'll never know you were here. You can come back for him later, go to his home like you did with Jande Seiiren. You can survive this. We could—"

Something silver flashed past Niko and landed on the floor with a clink. He recognized it immediately: an EMP grenade. It was pure instinct to get away from it as quickly as possible; Niko didn't want a repeat of Valaevanas, didn't want to be left stranded, unable to walk.

It detonated, frying Kestrel's shields and knocking him out of stealth. Niko pulled his gun without thinking, training it in the direction the grenade had come from, adrenaline pumping through his veins now as he readied instinctively for a fight.

No one was there.

A shot rang out from seemingly nowhere. Niko saw the bullet tear through Kestrel's shoulder, a stream of blood flying through the air as it struck. Some of it spattered him. A second bullet lanced through his side, more dark blood spraying Niko. Kestrel jerked back from each impact. He dropped his sniper rifle; it clattered to the floor beneath him. He staggered, then collapsed, the ground sticky with pooling blood.

No. NO NO NO!

Niko's pulse pounded in his ears, his entire body going numb as fear constricted him rapidly. He trained his gun quickly to the east, the source of the shots, ready to fuck up who-ever had dared. He didn't care at this point. Hunter, Galapol agent—Niko wanted to break them. It wasn't another hunter at the business end of his barrel, though.

It was Zann.

Niko partially lowered his gun, confused and conflicted.

He'd appeared seemingly out of thin air, pistol aimed at the fallen Kestrel. Clipped to his belt was the same cloaking device Niko had often seen worn by Kestrel.

The Galapol agent. The one Kestrel had left cloaked and unconscious on Uula, when Niko had given him no choice. They'd retrieved it.

How long had Zann been listening? How much did he know?

Zann's eyes bore a cold, obsidian glint. He approached Kestrel, his pistol aimed straight at the fallen man's head, seeking to finish the job. Niko acted before he could think, all wild fury, passion, and instinct. He was running. He slammed into Zann with all his weight, hard as he could.

Zann's pistol was knocked from his hand, where it fell off the edge of the walkway, down into the crowd far below. He held his own, to his credit, and staggered but remained standing.

"Wait!" Niko backed away from him. Zann backed warily away from Niko too, cool and untrusting eyes fixated on him now. Niko hated seeing that look aimed towards himself. "Don't kill him," he pleaded, his voice thick with fear as he fought to control the rapidly unraveling situation. "We can work with him on this, Zann. It doesn't have to be like this."

"That's bullshit, Niko. There's no future for this guy and it's time you come to accept that. He did this to himself."

Zann reached into his coat and pulled a second pistol out, aiming it down at Kestrel. Instinctively, Niko's own gun was up in an instant, trained on Zann. Zann quickly turned his pistol on Niko instead. Niko's heart leapt into his throat, his blood turning to ice as he stared at his brother. Both men found themselves at a standstill.

"Don't you fucking do this to me, Niko," Zann said, voice a low warning, laced with pain. "Are you going to pull that trigger? You're going to shoot me over this piece of shit?"

Niko's pulse beat wildly in his ears. Sweat trickled down his neck. He hesitated, slowly lowering the rifle again. "I— No— No, just— Please. Please, don't do this. Zann. The people he's killing are *monsters*. It doesn't get any worse than what they've done. I know you know that."

"It doesn't change what he's done to galactic civilization as a whole. He's taken justice for this into his own hands. He's kept everyone fucking terrified. Nobody feels safe anymore. He's ruined entire worlds, Niko. You're defending a murderer! You *know* this, Niko!"

"How is that any different from you and me and what we did to Mom's killers—"

Zann cut him off. "You told me to trust you. That you'd make this right."

"I'm *trying!*" Niko pleaded.

"I trusted you, Niko! I waited for you to fucking do something about him. I watched you. You've had a clear shot of him this whole time and you didn't take it. Instead, you've been chatting it up with him like you're best friends now. Giving him advice on how to kill."

"I—"

"Black market anonymity, my ass. I knew something was up with you. You were always better than this. I couldn't figure out why you kept coming so close and letting him get away. Again and again and again. The Niko I know would have had Kestrel or any other murderer six feet under long ago." Zann murmured into his earpiece. "I need backup. Upstairs. Top level."

Fuck.

"This isn't right, Niko. And it's not good enough. You fucked up bad. If they find out you've been chumming it up with Kestrel, you're fucked beyond belief. So just step away from him and keep your shit to yourself when the backup arrives." He paused, then said, "I want this son of a bitch dead so he doesn't tattle on you."

Zann turned his gun towards Kestrel again, and Niko acted once more without thinking. He threw his weight into Zann again hard, all frenzy and movement. Zann's shot missed, ricocheting off the floor.

"I'm sorry, Zann." Niko punched him hard enough to knock him unconscious. Zann's legs gave out from under him and Niko caught him mid-fall, gently lowering him to the ground. Niko pulled the cloaking device from him with trembling hands, but it had been damaged in his assault. Up close, the thing looked surprisingly fragile.

Damn it. It would have been useful. He tossed it over the edge of the walkway; it would break into pieces from the long, long fall. It was all he could do to keep anyone else from repairing and using it against them again.

He heard voices from below, dangerously close now.

"There!"

"He's up there!" He was out of time.

Niko sprang up, running towards Kestrel now, and lifted the fallen man off the floor and into his arms. Kestrel was both somehow lighter and heavier than he'd expected. His head lulled back, face pale, eyelids fluttering but ultimately remaining closed.

Niko was beyond rational thought at this point, driven by mere reactions mixed in a slurry of adrenaline. He took off running across the high walkway, as hard as he could. It was a dead end—the only way to go was down. He hugged Kestrel tighter against himself.

Damn, this is going to suck.

Niko pushed the thought from his mind. It was better to just not think about any of it—the steep drop that lay below, and the now hostile crowds that mingled down there.

He leapt from the walkway, hugging Kestrel tightly to his chest, the dizzying rush of weightlessness gripping him as spiraling ramps and one story after another rushed by them in a blur. He struggled to switch Kestrel's weight to his left arm, grabbing him tightly against himself, and fumbled for the compact grappling hook at his waist with his free hand.

Niko didn't let himself think about how much this was going to hurt. He focused only on the task in front of him, on Kestrel heavy in his arm, on aiming the grapple at the lowest balcony.

He aimed, fired, and struck true, the thing clamping on tightly. The rope went taunt as they swung, Niko's arm erupting in pain, muscles pulling from the sudden strain of bearing his own weight and Kestrel's too. Kestrel was jerked around like a ragdoll in his arm. Niko almost lost him—his grip was beginning to slip against the other man's blood.

I've got you, Niko promised him silently.

He released the grapple and landed among a gathering of wealthy Dvaab with a heavy thud. They froze, staring at him with shocked, green and leathery faces as their brains struggled to process what exactly they were seeing.

He was fortunate that understanding of what had transpired above hadn't reached the civilians just yet.

Seeing an armored bounty hunter was hardly unusual at big events these days. But Niko was holding Kestrel against himself, and Kestrel was bleeding out, dark crimson smearing across Niko's chestplate and gloves, dripping from him to the ground below.

Confusion spread to Galapol themselves, too—Zann had called for backup, had indicated the assassin was here. But he'd never said a word about Niko being involved, nor that Kestrel had been taken down. Niko found himself in a surreal moment as ground agents spotted him and began to make their way over—not as hostiles, but to try and aid him.

He had no interest in their help.

Niko inhaled, readying himself, and burst into a full run now, woe be to anyone in his path. He knocked people out of his way by brute force, other attendees ahead catching on and quickly getting out of his way. He drove straight through the crowd, only further sowing confusion and alarm. People were catching on that *something* wasn't right, now. They just weren't sure what. Murmurs surrounded him as he ran.

"Look, he's got him."

"Someone finally caught him."

"What's going on?"

Other voices came too, louder, more commanding than the guests'.

Galapol.

"Hunter, stop. We're going to commence arrest now."

"Niko!"

Niko ran, ignoring them all. He was close to the exit doors, close to getting outside. If he could make it to the *Soñadora*, he'd be golden.

It was, of course, easier said than done. Niko felt the transition, the slow change in mood as all around him agents caught on that he wasn't helping, but rather defying. Aiding the very one he'd been sent to bring in.

Their voices turned to shouts, warning him to stop, warning him that if he kept going, he'd be considered uncooperative with the law. Warning him they would open fire.

He kept going anyway, hugging Kestrel close to himself. He was too far gone to stop now. He'd made his choice. Niko burst through the front doors and sprinted through the ship parking deck, Galapol hot on his heels now. The warnings ceased as they made true on their promise—bullets pinged off the back of Niko's armor, some so uncomfortably close to his head that they grazed his hair. An explosive round detonated against the back of him and he stumbled but managed to right himself.

Niko kept running.

Nothing would ever be the same again.

He could never return from this.

Niko could see the ship in the distance, pushing himself with all that he had to cross the final distance. He made it, climbing inside and locking the door behind him. Bullets and explosive rounds pinged and crashed against the windshield and the sides, but the *Soñadora Despierta* was the best out there for a bounty hunter. It deflected them all, taking the onslaught like a trooper.

Niko quickly sat Kestrel in the co-pilot's seat, where the man slumped into himself. He didn't look good, his skin outright ashen now. Niko would have to apply what bandages and pressure he could from the ship's quaint med kit when they were clear of this place, but right now, he couldn't afford the time.

He seized the flight controls and within seconds was airborne, the ship wobbling unsteadily under the rapid handling and sloppy, adrenaline-guided driving.

Niko took off at a reckless speed. The gates to the parking deck began drawing closed, likely at Galapol's command.

He'd have mere seconds to make it out.

He pushed the ship even faster, their surroundings hurtling past them in the windshield, grateful for the credits he'd poured into speed modifications in years past. He was flying only on instinct now, twisting the ship and dodging other lazily floating vessels that were coming in to park.

Security bots, Galapol ships, and quick-responding hunters who'd made it to their own crafts were fast on his tail now. The huge metal gates of the deck drew further and further closed with each beat of Niko's pulse, until only a small sliver of blue cloud beyond peeked through.

He floored it.

The *Soñadora* hurtled through the last remaining sliver between the gates, just in time. In the rear cameras, he watched them slam closed, effectively trapping anyone who was still inside. That would buy him some time.

He had to think quickly. Kaapra-19 would be anything but safe now. Within hours, his apartment would probably be searched inside out, turned upside down. Galapol worked quickly.

He could never go home again.

Niko was only just now beginning to grasp the level of truly *fucked* he'd made himself today. He'd made an enemy of his only living brother, had allied himself with public enemy number one. But he couldn't bear to have stood by while Zann killed Kestrel. Stopping that had been worth every consequence.

I'm sorry, Zann.

Niko knew where to go. There was a place from his old days hunting, a safehouse for people like him who needed to lay low with no questions asked.

He scrolled through his list of old, old contacts from another lifetime, one spent in and out of black markets and strange places, with even stranger allies.

He opened the man's contact when he found it, the Gheroun's name floating in bright holographic blue before him.

Niko put a call through to Baouban.

After a few rings, Baouban answered, his voice breathless and awed.

"Holy shit. Niko? Is that you?"

"Yeah. It's me. Listen, Baou, I'm going to need your help with something."

It had been over three years since Niko last saw Baouban. The man looked a little older, his posture more slouched, the folds around his three eyes deeper than Niko remembered. He still favored patterned button-up, human-styled shirts, though, wearing a blue one now with a scattering of little orange cats on it. He maneuvered up the ramp into Niko's ship once it landed, already at the old safehouse and waiting, tentacles grasping his way up into the *Soñadora*.

Baouban and Niko looked at each other. "Wow, it's been a while. I really did think you might be dead."

"Felt like it, sometimes," Niko said. He didn't have time for old introductions, though. "Did you bring the RapiGel?"

"Yeah. And a lot more." Baouban held up a small briefcase. "Where's he at?"

"On the bed in the back." Niko was already moving. "I patched him up, put pressure on the entry and exit wounds. I think he has a bullet in him though. And he's still bleeding out a lot."

"We'll get it taken care of," Baouban said, moving after Niko. His bulk and dozen tentacles filled up most of the free space of the ship. They approached the bunk, which was built into a small nook in the wall, and Baouban sighed. "Look, I hate to say this, but this might work better if he's on the floor. Do you have a towel or blanket?"

"Yeah, I'll use the ones from the bunk," Niko said. His chest ached. He moved towards Kestrel, lifting him with gloveless hands enough to pull the sheets and blankets out from under him. They were already soaked dark with blood, the scent of copper thin on the air.

Niko spread them out on the floor, then moved to take Kestrel. Baouban crowded in beside him, snaking out four tentacles to wrap around Kestrel's legs. "I got it, let's move him."

Together, both men carried him to the center of the cabin, then laid him gently on the floor, face up. Niko tried not to think about how pale Kestrel had turned.

"Alright," Baouban said, awkwardly moving into a crouch. "Where are we gonna..."

Silence hung thick in the small ship, every one of Baouban's eyes going wide, each one focused on Kestrel's face now. Niko thought he saw him turn a paler shade of green.

He *may* have neglected to mention on the call exactly who he'd needed emergency treatment for.

"No shit," Baouban murmured. Niko swallowed back a lump in his throat.

"Yeah. It's him."

"No shit," Baouban said again. He looked nervous, drawing back from the unconscious man lying on the floor as though Kestrel might injure him just by existing.

Niko shifted his weight. "We're still good, right?"

"This is nuts. You're damn lucky I always liked you, kid. We're alright," the Gheroun said. "Hey, good for you, though. I'm not surprised that if anyone could get him, it was you."

Baouban unlatched the briefcase and began digging through it.

"Let's start with this one," Baouban said. He unscrewed the vial of RapiGel and, after slipping on a sterile tentacle cover, pulled away the blood-soaked bandage Niko had tied on and began carefully administering globs of the translucent green gel down into the entry wound in Kestrel's shoulder. Niko winced, trying not to think of how painful and invasive having someone's tentacle jammed in a raw wound had to be, and was glad Kestrel wasn't conscious for it.

He watched as the gel quickly hardened, forming into a thick and rubbery bond inside, stopping more blood from coming out. RapiGel was the colloquial name for the sticky secretions of a specialized gland found only in an endangered creature called the Kanau-vaanat. Its magic lay in an enzyme which naturally stimulated the healing of soft tissues. The fact that it also quickly plugged open wounds and stopped continuous bleeding was only a bonus.

RapiGel was nothing short of a miracle, and every black market peddler knew it. Each drop of this was about to drain whatever Niko had left in his account. A *premium* service from Baouban. He figured it didn't matter anymore—Galapol would have a freeze on all his accounts and assets by the end of the day anyway. May as well put it to a good use.

"Turn him over and hold him there," Baouban instructed. Niko did, gingerly lifting Kestrel and turning him over onto his side, where Baouban applied RapiGel deep into the exit wound. A single hook-shaped, old scar ran up Kestrel's right shoulder blade. Niko had noticed it when applying his own sloppy bandages on him and had had no choice but to cut off Kestrel's shirt. He'd tried his best to clean the blood off him.

"We'll hit the next one first, then finish these up with gel and stitches. The gel's good, but stitches give it extra hold."

Niko nodded. Baouban fished through his briefcase before extracting a long pair of bizarre-looking forceps designed for use with tentacles.

"You jacked him up pretty good," Baouban said. "Guy kinda deserves it, though."

The white lights of the ship were too harsh, the walls too cramped. Niko wished he could be anywhere else.

Baouban repositioned himself—a notable feat, given the Gheroun's size and what little space there was for him in the ship's cabin—and unceremoniously plunged the forceps into the bullet wound at Kestrel's ribs. Niko tensed. "Get ready with some of those sheets."

He dug around with the forceps and Niko could hear metal on metal. Baouban started talking, his tone buoyant, like this was an everyday occurrence. For all Niko knew, it probably was.

"So, you back to working with Galapol now?"

"Yeah, something like that."

"It's good to see you back, kid. You used to be the talk of the town once. Everybody was confused when you up and vanished. What happened?"

"I, uh," Niko hesitated. "I finally caught the guy I wanted to catch. The one who got me into hunting in the first place."

"Right, I remember you telling me about that guy. Well, what brought you back? It's been years."

"Galapol is desperate. They called me in, asking if I could take Kestrel down. They're throwing everything they can to see what works."

"Yep. Well, they found something. You. Everybody wanted their chance at him. I heard even the Legend is back from retirement trying to take this guy down," Baouban said. He huffed in frustration.

"Bullet's being stubborn. I've almost got it, but it keeps worming deeper. Gotta be careful not to tear anything."

Niko swallowed back a swell of rising bile at the thought.

He made himself ask it. "Do you think he's going to make it?"

"Oh, sure," Baouban said. "Didn't hit anything vital, it looks like. Lucky for you. Bounty's higher when you bring 'em in alive. I've patched up dozens of guys worse off than this in my years. He lost some blood but he'll be fine."

"Good."

"So, you back in the game now? People are gonna be real happy to hear about you."

"I don't know. This was kind of a special case."

"Well, at least go let Lady D know you're still kicking. She was especially vexed when you disappeared."

Niko forced a wan smile. The former hunter everyone called Lady Death was someone he owed favors to and never had the chance to let her collect on. Of course she wasn't going to be thrilled he had left that world behind—whether through retirement or the permanency of death. Letting her know he was back wasn't Niko's particularly favorite idea.

People tended not to like when their debts weren't paid up.

"Got you, you son of a Toliai," Baouban grunted, prying the bloodied bullet out of Kestrel. "Sheets."

Niko didn't have to be told twice. He rushed to press a fistful of sheets over the wound, fresh blood welling up from it now that the bullet had been freed. The whole ship smelled like copper now; it permeated everything. Niko's hands were slick with blood.

"Alright, when I say ready, let him go," Baouban said. A moment later, he hovered in again with the vial of RapiGel. "Ready."

Niko let go and the Gheroun closed the gap, administering a dab of antiseptic before stuffing globs of the gel compound straight down into the wound. Several seconds later and the flow of blood stopped as the gel solidified within Kestrel.

"Stitches time."

"I miss it," Niko admitted as he watched Baouban start threading a suture now. How he managed to do such careful work without fingers always perplexed Niko. He realized he was sweating and wiped his forehead. "I've been missing it the whole time. Life isn't really the same without hunting. It's like I've just been sleepwalking."

"You're not the first guy I've heard say something like that," Baouban said. "They try to leave the life behind, thinking peace and stability will be waiting for them on the other side. But all they get is emptiness. Most of 'em go back. In the end, the dark market is always waiting."

Niko didn't comment, and Baouban spoke again. "You'll always have a place here, Niko." Once stitches were finished, Baouban slathered on another coating of RapiGel. He wrapped a fresh layer of clean bandages around Kestrel's shoulder and ribs. And then he was done, sitting back on his tentacles.

"Thanks, Baou," Niko said, relief washing over him. Kestrel wasn't going to die. "Bill me whatever you need."

"Just don't forget me when you cash in that big bounty," Baouban joked—or maybe he didn't. The man was loyal until the end, but he still, as any denizen of the black market, had a special love for money. "Turn him over again."

Niko gently turned Kestrel onto his side again so that Baouban had access to the fresh bandages over the exit wounds, but the other man ignored them entirely. Instead, the Gheroun seized Kestrel's arms and bent them behind him, then produced a cable tie from his briefcase and pulled it tight around his wrists, binding them. It dug into his skin.

Niko froze.

Baouban scooted himself towards Kestrel's legs now, gripping another cable tie.

"What are you doing?" Niko blurted out before he could think better of it.

Baouban paused, turning to eye Niko oddly. "You don't want him running off on you or trying anything when he wakes up. Don't give him that chance."

The idea of Kestrel waking up somewhere unknown to him, bound and unable to move, sinking rapidly into panic and despair made Niko's chest ache. He couldn't help himself. It was probably smarter to let Baouban keep his assumptions, but the truth would be all over the news within hours anyway, if it wasn't already.

"Baou," Niko said. "No. Not like that." He pulled a jackknife from his utility belt and sawed the tight binding from Kestrel's wrists. It had already left a faint, red indent on the delicate veined skin.

Baouban stared at him, unmoving, heavy silence filling the small ship. Niko felt the other man's gaze on him as he was looked up and down. Then Baouban merely shrugged, tucking the extra cable tie away back into his briefcase.

"Okay, sure. Whatever floats your spaceship. I won't ask questions."

They cleaned up together in silence, and Niko paid the bill. As he expected, it drained most of what he'd had left from years' worth of savings, for the combination of a week at the safehouse and Baouban's *premium* services. Niko saw his rates had increased significantly since he'd last worked with the Gheroun—or maybe Baouban was just double-charging him for giving the galaxy's most wanted secret safe harbor. In the end, Niko didn't care. He got what he needed, and no one would keep a secret like Baouban would. The man charged a hefty price and always had, but the cost earned an unbreakable trust. And a relief that Niko needed right now.

"Pleasure doing business with you again, Niko," Baouban said once he'd packed up his briefcase again and moved to the door of the ship. He extended a tentacle, which Niko shook. "Welcome back."

"Thanks again, Baou. I'll take care of the place."

"You were always good for that," Baouban said. "You get a week. I can't guarantee protection for you after that."

"Got it."

The other man left, his ship ascending—with a small and friendly wave—past the view from Niko's windshield, and Niko was left with a silence he hadn't realized he'd needed. He exhaled slowly, looking down at his bare hands. They were covered in dried blood.

He moved to the back compartment of the ship where Kestrel still lay, towards the tiny corner bathroom to wash them, catching his reflection in the mirror as he did. His forehead was smeared with blood, too, where he'd wiped at it. The man who stared back at him looked tired and a little lost: dark shadows under his eyes, a scattering of bruises, dark bronze skin turned paler now.

Hands clean, Niko moved back to where Kestrel lay, looking down at him. He was quiet and still, the subtle rise and fall of his breathing the only movement to him. He didn't look peaceful. He looked worn down—far worse than Niko, even—with dark circles under his blond lashes, and skin an ashen white with loss of blood. Unruly strands of gold hung limp in his face.

Niko knelt and picked him up, gently as he could to not aggravate the wounds, and carried him down the ramp and outside of the ship. He was tired, but the weight felt good in his arms. The scents of petrichor and wood filled the air, towering blue-leafed trees half as thick as houses swallowing up the back of the small, simple cabin that stood before them. It was a rule to park around back—it kept the ship hidden from sight in the unlikely case anyone happened by.

Niko carried Kestrel around to the front, struggling to reach for the doorknob. The old, wooden sign still hung on the front door, same as it always had, though faded now from the elements.

WELCOME HOME, it said.

Chapter Twelve

IT ALL TASTES THE SAME

Kestrel stirred and let out a grunt of pain as he woke. Niko had laid him on the bed, an old and creaky but marginally comfortable thing that he knew had to be the same bed since the last time he'd stayed in the cabin. Kestrel's shifting made the springs groan beneath him. Sunlight spilled over his face in slats from between drawn blinds; his hair fanned around him on the pillow like a wild halo. The faintest wisp of blond stubble graced his cheeks.

Niko shook his head, pulled from half-sleep himself. He sat forward in the makeshift bedside chair he'd stolen from the small dining table setup. The cabin offered a far more comfortable couch, but he wanted to be near when the other man woke. Even so, he felt a rush of unbidden nerves as Kestrel opened his eyes. He looked tired—no, exhausted—though some of the color had already returned to him. Baouban's emergency patching had done the job. He'd been unconscious for two days.

Niko's suit beeped in warning. He was running low on battery charge.

Kestrel twitched at the sound, turning his head sharply towards Niko and moving to sit up. Pain seemed to stop him in mid-movement, and he reached up reflexively to touch the bandaging across his shoulder and ribs, his breath hissing out through his teeth.

"Hey," Niko said, slowly rising from his seat. The movement coaxed another warning beep from the suit. "It's just me." He briefly wondered if that was as reassuring as he'd meant it to be.

"Where—?" Kestrel asked. His voice was thin, hoarse.

"We're at a safehouse. Nobody else knows where this place is."

Kestrel lay still a moment on the bed, his tired, half-lidded look turning more vibrant, sharper, more acutely aware. He blinked rapidly, then pushed himself, though slowly this time, to sit up.

"Hey, take it easy," Niko said. "You were shot."

"So, this is what it feels like," Kestrel said quietly, as though the irony of the idea amused him.

"Yeah, it's not one of my favorite experiences, personally," Niko said.

Kestrel glanced at him. "Someone managed to shoot you in that thing? I want to know their secret."

Niko grunted. "Believe it or not, the suit's a new addition. Most of the hunting I've done was without it."

"RapiGel," Kestrel observed, his attention back on his wounds. He peeled the bandaging back over his shoulder and prodded at the rubbery glaze over darkly bruised and sutured skin. Niko winced at knowing how much the gesture had to hurt, but the wound looked clean and was already closing.

"Yeah, the guy who owns this place helped you."

Niko could see the muscles in his bare back tense sharply. The old and faded scar peeked out from beneath his bandages. Kestrel turned to look at him, eyes cold and sharp. It was the same distrust Niko was used to seeing pointed at him. "You said no one knew about this place."

Niko glanced around at the cabin. It was small and plain, with a scattering of aged, dinged-up furniture and wooden walls. He'd drawn all the window blinds closed, though late afternoon light still slipped through in stubborn patches. "Baouban won't sell us out. He charges premium but never gives away the secrets trusted with him. I've stayed here before a few times. This is a house for people who don't have anywhere to go. No questions asked."

Kestrel didn't look convinced. He glanced away, his gaze trailing over the trappings of the cabin. Niko wondered what he thought of it all. He wondered what Kestrel thought of a lot of things.

A heavy silence fell between them that lingered.

Then Kestrel tensed again, turning a sharp and urgent gaze towards Niko suddenly. "Your phone."

"What about it?"

"Give it to me."

Niko hesitated before popping the slender, transparent glass chip free from his suit's arm compartment. He held it out to Kestrel, who took it quickly.

"I have it shut off, so you'll need to turn it back on first—"

"Good," Kestrel murmured. Niko heard him release a quiet sigh that he could only think of as relief. Kestrel hunched forward into himself, fingernails digging and prying at the tiny and delicate wiring laced throughout the glass phone. Niko wanted to ask but didn't dare speak, merely observing him in the silence of the cabin. Finally, Kestrel pulled a single, silvery-blue thread of wire free, thin as a human hair, then crushed the fragile thing between his fingers. He held the chip back out towards Niko, glancing up at him again.

Niko took the phone and turned it over in his hand before slotting it back into the arm compartment of his suit. The suit beeped in warning again at all the movement. "So, what was that about?"

"Tracking wire. It's a good thing you didn't have that on, or you'd be sending out a beacon to anyone who can access your service provider. You won't have to worry about it anymore."

"Right. Thanks." Niko wasn't used to being on the run.

He bent down to dig through a duffel bag he'd thrown together—various supplies he carried with him on jobs that might be useful—and pulled out a small bottle of painkillers and a folded, spare gray t-shirt. He opened the bottle and handed two pills to Kestrel.

"Here, take these. It'll help."

Kestrel did, swallowing them with a glass of water Niko had already put at the bedside table in anticipation of his waking. He rolled and shifted his shoulder, his expression turning tired and thin again. He looked at Niko, and Niko caught a light sheen of sweat on his face in the striped light of the bedside window. He held the shirt out to Kestrel, who took it and pulled it on. It was at least one size—maybe two—too big for him, hanging off his narrower frame.

He still bore the mark Niko had left on his neck, though significantly faded. Niko had to look away, or it would kill him.

"You helped me," Kestrel said after a long silence.

"Yeah, I did."

"Why?"

"It was the right thing to do," said Niko.

"Was it?"

Niko stared at him. "It's what I wanted to do."

Kestrel drew quiet for a moment. "That was your brother."

The air left the room, leaving nothing to breathe. The cabin felt suddenly like it was suspended in space, rather than drenched in sunlight. Niko didn't have anything to say.

Kestrel had been conscious during their argument, after all.

He looked up at Niko, unexpected sorrow slanting his brow. "You're close to him."

I was, thought Niko. He cleared his throat and sank slowly back into the bedside chair, his suit issuing another warning beep. "Yeah, I am."

"Will you tell me about him?"

It wasn't what Niko expected, but Kestrel never was. He was always shifting, slipping through Niko's grasp every time he thought he had a hold.

Where to start?

"So. There's a lot here. I hope you don't have anywhere to go." He offered a wan smile.

"I don't think that will be a problem."

"Zann's actually my half-brother. We weren't really that close as kids, or anything. I loved him, of course, but we were just very different people. He was quiet and broody and didn't have a lot of friends. He buried himself in school and got top grades in his class. Meanwhile, I just wanted to play football and occasionally beat people up."

"Oh," Kestrel remarked. "That's not surprising. So, you were the school bully?"

"Eh. Not really. I just liked looking for reasons to fight. I actually knocked some of the real bullies around and kept an eye out on the kids they targeted. I looked out for Zann and my baby brother, Ryen, too. Zann got it bad sometimes. He was a smart little dweeb and a magnet for assholes. Even though we weren't close, I still made sure that somebody always had his back. Though I think he mostly just found me annoying.

"It wasn't until, uh, until Ryen and our mom got killed that Zann and I started to really bond. Ironically, he's my best friend now."

Or was. Niko had no way of knowing how things stood with Zann and thinking about it made him feel ill.

"You mentioned that about your mother and brother," Kestrel said softly. "Back on Sunorrna."

"Yeah, uh. It's actually why I got into bounty hunting."

"What happened?" Kestrel asked. Niko sighed, slumping into himself heavily. The deaths of his loved ones were precisely the *last* things he wanted to talk about right now. But wasn't it grief and loss that had set them both on this very path that led to being here now? Their losses were the gravitational pull that had drawn them into orbit around one another. Niko felt he had to honor that.

"My mother, Yesenia, and brother, Ryen, were out running errands together when two guys accosted them. They wanted money. My mom just tried to give it but my brother—he was only thirteen at the time—put up a fight. Tried to protect her, I think. He gave them some trouble. The whole thing escalated and they both got hurt. But in the end, the guys got the money anyway. And could have left. They could have just *left*.

"But they didn't. As they were leaving, one stopped and… and seemed to reconsider. He turned around. Ryen had given him a bloody nose. I guess he just didn't like that. There was no reason, though. No reason to take their lives. But he did. He shot them both, right on the street. And then they fled."

"Niko, I'm so sorry," Kestrel said quietly, his eyes full of grief and sympathy. Niko figured if anyone could understand losing their world to senseless violence, it was him.

He shook his head and continued. "We had footage of it and everything, but they were never actually judged guilty. They caught a loophole in the system, some plea deal where in the end they only got convicted of theft and assault. And due to their cooperation, they served a whole *two fucking weeks* in jail with a month of community service. They skipped town after that. Ended up on the other end of the galaxy… counting their lucky stars. I guess."

Kestrel said nothing. Niko could only imagine him being hardly surprised at hearing justice often failed those who needed it most.

His insides twisted in shame as he thought of how he'd kept trying to use that very reliance on upheld justice to convince Kestrel to stop.

He'd just wanted there to be a better way than the dark and deeply isolated path Kestrel was on.

"Zann and I were livid. We didn't want to just sit around and do nothing. We couldn't. He ended up in the force and I became a hunter. He's always had an investigative mind. When— After they died, even though Zann was just a teenager still in high school, he demanded the footage. We both watched it." Like the Honeybliss recordings, that footage was something that had burned itself into Niko's brain for the rest of his life. He still had nightmares about it sometimes. "But he watched it over and over, trying to dissect it. Trying to see if there was something we'd missed.

"Anyway— We worked together like that for years and it was great. He sent me after guys like them, trash who needed to be brought down. I never took small jobs on petty shit like theft. I only went after the absolute worst. The people who were truly a stain on society. It became my niche. I was known for it over time. I took jobs other hunters didn't even want to touch. I honestly loved it. It was the first time I felt alive since what had happened.

"All the while, we worked together in private to find where our family's killers ended up. It took a few years but eventually we did. Had to pull some strings in the black market, even. It wasn't... it wasn't entirely *legal,* but I hunted them down. I found them and I killed them. It wasn't for Galapol that time. It was for Zann, and for me. It was for Ryen, who never got to grow up.

"I got the first one, but the other guy—the one who'd actually shot them—he was a real son of a bitch to get to. Quick and tough and just wouldn't die. I kept after him. I was unstoppable. I was a monster. I didn't sleep, I hardly ate. I'd been shot and just kept going. Nothing else mattered but getting to him.

"I finally did. I had him cornered in a skyscraper he was squatting in on Celelast. He'd gotten me disarmed so I was on him and I—I saw my chance. I slammed him right through the window. We both fell. It was nineteen stories."

Niko laughed out his exasperation. "He broke my fucking fall. I don't know how, but I survived. I shouldn't have. People don't survive falls like that. He ended up a stain but all I got was a shattered spine. I was lucky."

Kestrel watched him quietly. "You were prepared to die for it," he said.

"Yeah. Yeah, I was. I did things like that a lot." *Still do,* Niko thought sardonically, and continued. "Stupid shit to make sure I got my mark. But this was different. Everything about this was different. All that mattered was that I saw it through to the end, at any cost. Even myself."

"I understand," Kestrel said. "I knew I probably wouldn't survive this the moment I decided I was going to do it. It's the other reason I'm saving Uru Taal for last. Other than hoping he hasn't slept a night since I started. I thought it would be good motivation to not let myself give up early. To keep going and living no matter what."

"Seems it's worked out well so far," Niko said.

The small, sly smile that graced Kestrel's lips flooded Niko with utterly disproportionate warmth at the sight. He found that he liked making Kestrel smile. The man looked far better wearing a smile than the cold, bitter expression he usually carried when Niko crossed paths with him.

His smile faded and he eyed Niko. "Can I ask you something?"

Niko swallowed. "Yeah. Of course, sure."

"I understand why you did everything you did regarding your family's killers. Even to the point of going out that window. I'd probably have done the same. But I— You're someone who understands what it's like when your family is taken away by people who couldn't give two fucks less."

Niko glanced away. He knew where this was going.

"In your own experience, you had to take it into your own hands. Because no one else would."

"Mmh," Niko acknowledged.

"Then why? Why all the insistence on going to Galapol for justice?"

Niko cleared his throat. *Because I thought if Zann knew, he would make a difference. Because I wanted to keep you safe—from yourself. From everything that wants you dead now. Because I'm selfish. Because I've been there before, and in the end, it only left me broken.*

In so many ways.

"I guess I just wasn't ready to let go of the hope that there could still be good out there. I'm sorry, Elliott. For being a hypocrite. For trying to stop you from doing what I would have never even let anyone else stop me from."

"It's alright, Niko. You did what you felt was right. I can't fault anyone for that."

"No, it's not just that." The words launched themselves from Niko, frustrated and sharp before he could take them back. "I *have* been there before. I know what it's like. You can't look away. It's all you want to do. You live for it. The revenge becomes you. But then, one day, it's over. And either you end up dead, like I almost did, or you end up having to live with the fucking void that comes after."

Kestrel fell quiet.

Niko ran his hand over his face and the suit beeped again.

"What *is* that?"

"It's my suit. It's about out of battery and every time I move it uses a little bit more."

Kestrel looked at him oddly. "Why don't you ever take it off? You never do." A thin smile crept across his lips again. "Am I really that scary? I guess I should be flattered."

"No, it's..." Actually, he wasn't entirely inaccurate. The idea of Kestrel seeing him without his armor *did* terrify Niko. But not for any of the reasons the other man could probably have guessed. Niko felt a swell of anxiety, monstrous and consuming as the waves of Valaevanas, rise up whenever he thought of Kestrel seeing him in the chair for the first time, unable to do the feats he regularly pulled in their skirmishes.

There was also still the non-zero chance that Kestrel might weaponize his condition and leave him stranded when Niko couldn't stop him.

But in the end, what scared him most was the idea of Kestrel seeing him as somehow... less. The very thought stole his breath away. It hurt.

But he had no choice now.

"I—" He swallowed. "I can't walk without the suit. You know how I said I fell? Broke my spine? I didn't really recover from that. I have paraplegia. The suit's a custom commission my brother bought me that has neurotech. It lets me walk, but I can't feel my legs when I do, so it's tricky."

Niko forced himself to look at Kestrel. He had to know. Kestrel looked shocked at the revelation, but his gaze quickly shifted to fascinated—even outright impressed. "So, you're telling me that every time you ran after me, jumped, fought, you couldn't feel what you were doing?"

"Uh. Not really, no."

"That's impressive, Niko. You're quite audacious."

Stupid, more like it, he thought. *And stubborn.*

"I'm going to go charge it. There's a port in the ship I hook it up to. I have a chair there."

"Do you need any help?"

"No." Niko stood and walked out of the cabin and into the clear, late afternoon air of Vorna-12. Great trees towered all around him, their trunks rivaling the cabin in width. Their lofty canopy served to keep the safehouse obscured. The suit beeped at him again and he glanced at the indicator on his arm. It read six percent.

"Shit," he mumbled. *Closer than I thought.*

Niko entered the *Soñadora* and unlatched the suit, piece by piece. He hooked it up to its charger and transferred to the wheelchair he'd kept folded beside the charging port. Then he simply sat for a few moments, trying to clear his head. Kestrel knew now. He hadn't taken the opportunity to dig into him. Niko hated how much he cared about that. It was like he was ten again, afraid his mother wouldn't accept him for who he really was.

Zann, Loolae, and anyone else he'd actually kept communication with over the years since he fell had given nothing but encouragement and reassurance. But Niko still couldn't grant that grace to himself. Even when he'd needed it most.

He made his way back down out of the ship, trying to steel himself, when he nearly startled at the sight of Kestrel outside. The other man stood against the doorframe of the cabin, his wounded shoulder slumped against it for support as he peered up into the trees. He was lithe and beautiful and perfect there in the sun. His wild hair shone in the dappled light as it poured in ribbons through the canopy.

Niko froze for a moment, his fear asserting control of every muscle. He looked at Kestrel and waited.

"Vorna-12?" Kestrel said, his gaze still cast upward.

"Yeah. How'd you know?"

"I took a biology course that focused on the flora of alien worlds. I recognize these trees."

Niko was more of an 'in one ear and out the other' kind of guy when it came to school. He hadn't been able to graduate high school fast enough and had zero inclination to ever go further with it. "Sounds riveting."

Kestrel turned his green eyes on Niko finally. A pleased smile spread across his lips. "It's good to see you without the suit. You're not just an abstract heap of armor. There's a man underneath there after all."

Niko felt himself flushing. The way Kestrel referred to him as a *man* was oddly thrilling. The fear that had wound itself tightly through him finally began to relent.

He tried for a gentle jab back at Kestrel. "Yeah, and you look better without that stupid assed bird mask. What was that, anyway? Cosplaying your own name?"

The clever clapback he'd anticipated never came. Instead, something dark shifted in Kestrel, the other man drawing into himself and looking away. His face drew into a startlingly bitter scowl.

"E-Elliott? I didn't mean—"

"It was actually a present from my sister."

Niko winced. *Oops.*

"It was the last thing she ever gave me. We were supposed to be going to a costume party together and she bought it for me. She thought it was funny, because of our last name and everything. We never got to go, though. She died the night before." He hesitated before continuing. "I—I thought if I wore it, I'd feel closer to her somehow. Like she was with me through this. It's stupid."

"It's not stupid," Niko said. A sullen and uneasy quiet fell between them, until he spoke again. "Are you hungry? It's been days since you last ate anything. I'll make us some food."

"I'd like to help," Kestrel said.

Niko made his way into the kitchen—a small corner of the cabin with dilapidated cabinets. One didn't hang right any longer, settling at an angle. The place had certainly seen wear and tear since he'd last been here four years ago. It had never been any semblance of luxury, nor had Baouban advertised it that way. But it did what it needed to do, and when you needed quick and reliable shelter, this was it.

He'd once heard a mercenary call Baouban's safehouses 'the most premium hovels in the galaxy.' She hadn't been wrong.

Kestrel followed shortly after, closing the door quietly behind him. Niko sifted through the cabinets, having to fight the crooked one. It was never much, but Baouban kept the place stocked with food and supplies, and from what Niko could see from his chair, the cabinets looked to have a decent selection of dried goods. A particular bag caught his eye and Niko couldn't help the wide grin that spread across his face.

"Baouban, I could kiss you."

Tortilla chips.

"Hey, Elliott. Do you like nachos?"

"Sure. That doesn't sound like much of a meal though, if I'm being honest."

"You haven't tried them how I make them. Hey, could you, uh..." He pointed to the bag of chips which peeked out from a higher shelf. Kestrel reached up and handed it to him. Niko felt a blossom of warmth as he did—Kestrel was decidedly a much better assistant in the kitchen than T1-N4.

Niko froze.

Tina. Galapol had undoubtedly combed every inch of his apartment long since by now. Including the little assistant bot—and all of the deeply incriminating texts synced to her. And call records.

And a certain picture.

If there had ever been a chance of turning back before, it was gone now.

"What is it?" Kestrel was staring at him. He looked nervous and Niko realized it was likely a mirror of his own expression. He forced himself to appear neutral and shook his head.

"It's nothing." Niko maneuvered to the refrigerator and opened the freezer, praying for any sort of frozen meat. He didn't want to go there, didn't want to talk about everything that now lay exposed to Galapol. It would only bring the mood back down, and at this point, there was nothing either of them could do about it.

"Bingo," he said, reaching into the back of the freezer and procuring a pack of gray, frozen meat encrusted with freezer burn. A single sticker on the front read: CHICKEN THIGH, with something else in Dvaab printed beneath it. Niko examined the meat closely; given that Baouban probably restocked the place through black market vendors, it was likely this was one of the myriad counterfeit 'chicken' meats that actually came from weird little alien fauna.

In the end, it all tasted the same. If you didn't think too much about it.

They scraped together a scattering of ingredients. Niko would have loved to have had fresh vegetables and aromatic herbs, the way his mother had used when cooking. But he had to make do with a jar of dried cilantro flakes, shredded cheese, two old onions, broth, cumin, salt, and canned tomatoes.

They cooked together, Kestrel processing the vegetables as Niko cut the meat. Niko boiled the shredded meat and onions in broth until they were tender, then mixed it all together over a generous bed of tortilla chips and topped it with heaps of melting cheese. It didn't escape him that the more the cabin filled with the scent of cooking food, the more Kestrel stared at the pot, pupils blown. He was definitely hungry.

It was surreal to be immersed in such a simple—*domestic*—task with the galaxy's number one most wanted. Surreal, but not unwelcome.

This was something Niko could get used to.

When they sat down to eat, Kestrel was ravenous, digging into the food the moment his plate touched the table. He didn't stop until every last scrap was gone, working out a *'Diff if rully good'* through a mouthful of chicken. Niko swelled a little with pride, trying to ignore the fact that Kestrel technically hadn't eaten in days, was probably famished, and would likely have given the same response if Niko had plated a raw potato for him instead.

After they were finished, they sat together at the little dining table, where Kestrel picked curiously at a vulgar engraving so ancient it predated Niko's first stay here. He was already looking better, the color returning to his complexion.

"Elliott," Niko said. "I told you about Zann. Will you tell me about Cleo?"

The light left Kestrel's gaze and he stayed silent a while. Niko thought he had stumbled yet again and loaded up an apology, when the other man began speaking.

"Our parents really were awful. Our childhood home was dysfunctional and chaotic at best. Terrifying to be in on occasion. I don't know why. They've always been that way. They would fight and scream and hit each other, and when it got particularly bad, it would spill over onto us. That started happening more and more the older we got.

"Anything could set them off. My mother was a ticking time bomb of anxiety and rage and any little perceived slight sent my father into violence. It's probably good I got out when I did, because if I'd been there as a teenager, I think I would have started goading him on purpose. I'm like that. I can't help but push back when people are awful. I don't take it lying down. Neither did Cleo. She never antagonized them, though. But the moment either of them—especially our father—turned their rage on me, she was there, stepping in between us. She knew how to manipulate the situation, knew how to draw their attention and anger to her instead.

"I fought for her too, but she always hated it. I remember the first time I did. He was... he was choking her. She'd tried to keep me back but I was on him, punching and hitting him in the leg until he had no choice but to stop. I'd gotten his wrath too for it, of course. Later, Cleo was so upset at me for doing that. She always admonished me if I tried to pull their anger back away from her. She wanted to keep me innocent, I think. As innocent as growing up in that fucking household could ever be."

Niko winced, nausea threatening to give him an unwanted encore of his cooking at the memory of Mary Kestrel telling the interrogator that Elliott had done that same violent act instead. Everything they'd used to paint their son as a monster was projection. They were the only ones who had ever harmed their children. There was never confusion nor derangement, only parents who didn't deserve the family they'd been gifted. No wonder Elliott had changed his shared middle name the moment it was legal.

"She would send me away when it got really bad," Elliott continued. "She had a method. I had terrible anxiety when I'd hear them start fighting. We knew all the tells. We knew when it would spill over onto us. So, Cleo would take me by the hand and lead me into her closet and put her favorite headphones on me. They were her birthday present. They were pink and had incredible bass. She really loved music. She'd turn on her favorites—pop songs from girl groups and idols and boy bands—and calm me down with it. It blocked out the shouting. The other sounds too.

"I still turn to music to this day when the anxiety gets to be too much. I put on her old songs and shuffle them with new ones. I've been fond of Hayura and Kuliedi Taan lately. It really helps me calm down and reminds me of her. She would have gone nuts seeing them collaborate."

"So," Niko interrupted, "do you always listen to music during your assassinations?"

Kestrel eyed him oddly. "I do."

"Picked up your music frequency on Yhanwe-ha," he explained. "It's how I knew you were nearby."

"Oh. That makes sense."

"Does it give you anxiety? Going out there and doing, uh, what you do." Niko had imagined Kestrel cool and detached as he picked out his vantage point. As he lined up that pivotal shot.

"Of course it does," Kestrel said. "Sometimes I can hardly stand it. I get panic attacks over it. I'm scared I'll fuck up. It's so much pressure. And once I'm actually there and not just planning it out anymore, it hits me every single time that this is all happening right now. And that it's all very real."

Niko blinked.

"What? Not what you expected?"

"I guess I imagined something far more aloof. You talk like you relish the work, even."

"Oh, don't get me wrong. I do. Every time I spray one of those bastards' gray matter, I celebrate. But it doesn't mean I'm not scared, too."

Niko thought about that for a moment, then tried to bring their thread of conversation back to Cleo. "You said when Cleo was sixteen, she finally got out of there?"

"Oh. Yes. She'd been auditioning with talent agencies in secret and wanted to represent herself. I'm not sure what strings she pulled but I think her agent realized she was in a pretty bad place and made some things happen for her in the background. In the end, Cleo was allowed to represent herself instead of as a minor with parental permission. The moment she got her first big check, she got an apartment. There are hardship laws on Delevia, where we lived, for people fifteen and up who are in a legitimately dangerous situation, so she got it for a discounted rate. After that, she was free. And she took me with her. I think in the end, our parents were relieved to not have to attempt taking marginal care of us anymore. We shared a cramped little studio for a while as she saved up. She was on me like a hawk. Made sure I stayed in school, that I kept my grades up, that I didn't end up in some unsafe situations when I hit puberty and discovered other boys. She kept an eye on me. She was more of a mother to me than my own had ever been."

"You mentioned she put you through college."

"Yes. I wanted to get a job to help pay for it, but she fought me and said she wanted me to focus on doing the best I could at my studies. She was always telling me how smart I was, how capable, how far I'd go. How proud she was of me. But I wanted to do more. I wanted to return the favor and help her too. My dream was to one day be able to pay her back for everything she'd ever done for me.

"But I—" His voice grew quiet. "I never got to. Instead, I— I—"

Niko ached. "Elliott. She wouldn't have wanted you to." It was quite a presumptuous claim about someone he'd never get to meet, but Niko knew. "Your sister just loved you that much."

A tremor of grief crossed Kestrel's face, and if Niko didn't know any better, he would have thought Kestrel just took a third gunshot wound. Then it was just as quickly gone, suppressed again somewhere deep inside.

Silence fell over the cabin now, the air dour and oppressive. Even the light had at some point faded, giving way now to the early evening symphony of nocturnal insects and little creatures outside the cabin walls. To Niko's surprise, Kestrel spoke, though. "Thank you. For letting me talk about her. I never get to."

Niko swallowed back a lump of emotion. He got it. How long had it been since he got to talk about his mother? About the kindness of her smile, or the way she'd struggled to get up and going any time before ten in the afternoon. How she'd loved to cook for others. How she had once brought the law down on a young and spindly Zann after he'd mocked Niko for a rejected and broken heart in his sophomore year. In that moment, she'd made Niko feel seen and heard in a way he hadn't been cognizant of before.

People often didn't know how to treat others who were grieving. He knew that intimately now. They skirted infinite circles around the subject, never wanting to offend, to stir up sorrow.

No one talked about the lives of the departed. No one asked about Niko's favorite memories of them. They just stopped talking about it at all. Even Zann had, too.

"Sure, Elliott. I'm glad I asked. She sounds like a phenomenal person."

"So, what happens now, Niko?"

Niko felt the room spin. He hadn't been prepared for such a hard-hitting question. He had no plan and no direction. Once his time at the safehouse was up, he officially had nowhere to go. "Well, for right now, we should probably both clean up. I don't think either of us has showered in two days."

"I mean after that," Kestrel said. "You don't get to stay in this safehouse forever, do you?"

"No. I don't." Niko fell quiet.

"We'll think of something," Kestrel said, rising from the table.

We. The word burned bright as a star. He'd said *we* instead of *I.*

Chapter Thirteen
GRAVITY

Night was settling in now, and Niko was wide awake. But Kestrel had been injured, and though RapiGel allowed a body to heal itself faster, it came at the cost of demanding more energy, too. He'd heard the other man yawn a few times already.

"There's, um," Niko started awkwardly, a flutter of nerves rising in him all over again. Anxiety wasn't finished with him yet today, it seemed. "There's only the one bed here, so you should take it. I'll stay on the couch."

"You should have the bed," Kestrel commented.

"Don't be ridiculous, Elliott. You're injured."

"It's honestly not that bad," Kestrel countered, his expression bland. Niko knew he was lying, though. He wore it in subtle ways through his body language. The way he'd leaned against his chair as they'd talked. How he favored one arm.

"El—"

"Or," Kestrel said, cutting him off. "We could stop this posturing and share it. Unless that would be a problem?" He looked Niko right in the eyes as he said it in a way that Niko absolutely couldn't bear, his soul about to astral project straight into space.

Niko forgot how to speak. He nodded, then realized that nodding might be interpreted as him having a problem. "Uh, I—I mean, that's okay. To do that. Not, you know, that it would be a problem, or anything."

Nice one, dumbass. He wanted to sink into the ground.

Kestrel made him feel sometimes like he'd never been around another person, had never once engaged in conversation before. Like he was scrambling to speak in a language he'd just only barely learned on the fly.

Niko had never been like this around anyone before.

They showered, Kestrel first and then Niko. Niko was despaired to see that the other man was still awake—face cleanly shaved and damp hair hanging as he boredly gazed around the cabin, sitting on the bed—when he'd emerged from his intentionally very, *very* long shower. Kestrel had helped himself to another round of pain pills, the bottle moved over to the other bedside table now. He apparently hadn't been so tired as Niko had assumed.

Niko pulled himself out of his chair and onto his designated side of the bed, grateful that it at least was sufficiently wide. He arranged himself until he was comfortable—acutely aware of how awkward he undoubtedly appeared with having to shift himself around—and lay on his back, staring up at the ceiling.

He reached over and switched off the bedside lamp, painting the cabin in darkness that his eyes slowly grew accustomed to.

"Niko?" Kestrel's voice came softly from his right. Niko glanced over at him. His features were lost in the long shadows of the night. "Thank you. For helping me. For..." He hesitated. "Everything."

There was so much Niko wanted to say.

"I've got you, Elliott." It was probably too much. "I'll watch your back. We're kind of in this together now."

"Are we?" Kestrel asked.

"I mean, I guess I could walk back into Station Twelve and ask Galapol if my contract's still good."

"I would honestly appreciate the audacity, if nothing else." After a moment, he added, "Niko. I'm sorry you've lost your standing with Galapol because of me. I'm sorry you had to turn against your brother."

"It's okay, Elliott. You didn't force me to do anything. I made my choices."

A lull fell between them. Niko still wasn't tired.

"Hey," he said. "Do you remember Giannis Alexopoulos?"

"Are you being serious right now?"

"Okay. Fair. But— Did you know that I killed him?"

He felt Kestrel's gaze drill into him, even in the dark. "What? Really?"

Niko didn't miss the subtle jubilation in the other man's tone.

"Did you really?" Kestrel asked again.

"Yeah." Niko sighed. "I mean. I didn't shoot him or anything. But he'd been there that day. And when I'd gotten back to my ship, he started pounding on the door, trying to get in. Pleading with me.

Talking about paying me 'lots of money.' In the end, I just kept the door closed. And I waited. The wave came and it washed him away."

"Exquisite," Kestrel purred. Despite himself, Niko huffed out a sudden laugh. It was so absurd—all of it.

Niko didn't tell him about the near fatal struggle he'd had himself while trying to outpace the wave. It would only drive guilt into the other man, and it wasn't what he wanted. Kestrel hadn't known then what it had meant for him to be caught in the EMP and left behind, and to Niko's relief, he hadn't appeared to put the pieces together. He'd be just fine if Kestrel never did.

"I still have it recorded on my ship. I'll show you sometime."

"*Ooh*, security footage and chill."

Niko laughed again and shook his head. It was just the amount of absurdity he needed to let him finally relax against the background horror of freefalling with nowhere to go home to anymore. In spite of it all, he felt comfortable in that moment, there on the bed with Elliott Kestrel in Baouban's safehouse cabin, in a way he hadn't in a very long time.

He gazed at Kestrel in the dark, faint features shrouded from view, but clear in memory. He could see every little feature in his mind's eye now. A strange courage came over him and he spoke before he could censor himself.

"I can't stop thinking about you wearing me on your neck. Every time I see it, I remember how it was. How you tasted."

Even speaking of it was an evocation, and Niko felt a white-hot hunger start to rouse low in his belly, in his groin. Here, without the armor restraining him, he was getting hard. He heard Kestrel's breath hitch, then quicken in its carriage.

"I really want to fuck you," Niko said.

Kestrel swallowed, a sound so subtle, Niko almost missed it. Then he said, "I want you to fuck me, Niko. I've been practically begging you to."

He pulled himself over towards Niko, closing the distance between them. Niko craved him. His hands found him quickly, touching at his chest and stomach, reaching up under the shirt to do it. He was careful, gentle, paying mind to avoid the other man's injuries.

Kestrel propped himself up with his good arm and hovered inches above Niko. Then he leaned down and met him in a kiss, warm and liquid and scintillating in the dark.

Niko let out a low hum of appreciation, trailing voracious kisses along Kestrel's jaw now. He moved to sit up, unable to get enough of the man before him, desperate to press his body against his. Kestrel's fingertips trailed along Niko's hands, down his arm. Over his chest and stomach. It was too much. Niko could almost lose himself right then, just from the idea of it all.

Kestrel unfastened Niko's pants with quick and masterful fingers, sliding his hand eagerly under the hem of his boxers. Niko felt him take hold, the hot touch of his hand divine as Kestrel pulled him gently free, stroking. He groaned as Kestrel worked him and greedily let his own hand wander into Kestrel's pants to return the favor. He found him there, just as fervent as Niko was. Kestrel felt so fucking good just to grasp, to touch. Niko could feel his hot pulse in his hand and he loved it.

Kestrel pulled away though, and reached over to switch the bedside lamp back on. Niko squinted in the light as his eyes adjusted, and Kestrel bent to kiss him again, murmuring.

"I want to see you."

He scooted back until his lips were agonizingly close to Niko's cock. Then he leaned down and licked its length slowly. Niko gave a strangled grunt as Kestrel parted his lips and took him into his mouth—hot, slick, and perfect. He started sucking him off.

It was excruciating for Niko; he wanted nothing more than to reciprocate, to get down on his own knees and swallow up Kestrel's hard length. The very thought, feverish in his mind, nearly drove him to the edge and he gripped Kestrel's wrist tightly. Kestrel pulled away again, sensing how close he was. Everything he did was maddening to Niko. It was too much.

"No. Not yet," Kestrel murmured, wiping his mouth with the back of his hand. Everything about him was heady—was *thrilling*—and Niko felt alive at his touch. Just thinking about Kestrel was enough to bring a soft groan to his lips.

Niko had wanted him for a very long time.

Kestrel tugged Niko's pants and boxers off and tossed them aside, careful while moving and lifting his legs as he did. He paused to look at and trace his fingertips along the myriad tattoos adorning Niko's legs, which made Niko's chest blossom with warmth. He loved that Kestrel liked his ink, liked how he looked.

Then Kestrel hastily removed his own clothes, leaving himself beautifully, beautifully bare. Niko was blessed with a full view of the lithely sculpted body in its whole, Kestrel's rigid hunger blatantly on display. It wasn't like the photograph. It was so much more.

His white bandages cut jagged across his otherwise flawless body. Niko couldn't keep his hands off him, running his own calloused fingers along Kestrel's side, over his hip, playing along the slit of his ready cock, which dripped with pre-come.

Everything about him was beautiful. He was breath and body, air and life.

Niko had never needed anything more.

Kestrel moved again, this time closer to Niko. He swung his leg over him and straddled his lap. Niko leaned forward to meet him again, lips messily claiming every inch of collarbone, neck, and his good shoulder. He buried his lips against Kestrel's throat and started sucking another welt onto his skin. Niko wanted to devour him.

Kestrel was careful with him, though—delicate, even. He seemed afraid to put his full weight on Niko's hips, instead hovering gently above him and hesitating like he wasn't sure what he could and couldn't safely do. Niko took him by the hips and pulled him down hard onto himself, then growled, voice gravelly, "Don't. Don't treat me like glass. Don't hold back with me. I want everything you can give."

Something in Kestrel's eyes changed, a bright, vivid hunger alighting in them. "You like it rough," he murmured.

"Yeah."

Kestrel moved his hips, rubbing himself along Niko's cock. It felt so good. So fucking *good*.

None of his lovers had felt this way before. None of them had been somehow inseparable from hunger. Not like this.

But then Kestrel paused, the building momentum between them stilling. "I don't have any lube," he said plainly. "I never expected to have sex again."

The words shook Niko to his core and he froze, heart in his throat. It was such a simple, almost innocuous statement. But the weight and the depth of it struck hard.

Kestrel had been truly prepared to die. The simplicity, the gravity of it wounded Niko in a profound way. Kestrel had told him he knew he probably wouldn't survive it all. But this simple, startling detail made it so much more real somehow. Niko pulled him into an embrace, heartbeat to heartbeat, simply holding him for a moment as he stroked the other man's back. Kestrel wove his arms around Niko in response, his long fingers trailing gently along the nape of his neck in a way that left Niko lightheaded.

For a moment, they just held each other.

Niko wanted to make love to Elliott Kestrel. He wanted to fuck him, to give him pleasure like he deserved. To make him feel good, to make him feel wanted. Like Kestrel deserved.

No.

Like *Elliott* deserved.

Niko couldn't think of the man in his arms as Kestrel anymore. That was a surname, something from detached case files and news reports. Impersonal.

Niko wanted to be the one to give him what he'd been prepared to never experience again. To make it all mean something to him. He kissed his neck and moaned his name into it, reaching up to pet the man's soft, golden hair.

"Elliott."

Niko had what Elliott didn't. He reached over, still planting kisses on and stroking his hand along Elliott as he fumbled desperately through the duffel bag he'd left sitting by the bed. His hand eventually closed around the small bottle he'd been seeking and he poured warm lubricant generously into his palm. Niko stroked himself with it, then Elliott. He reached behind and spread it along Elliott's opening, slipping a finger inside. The other man moaned, arching his neck back at the touch.

"Is this how you want it?" Niko murmured.

"Please. I just want *you.*"

Niko slid one more finger in, then another, loosening him up slowly, fucking him gently with his hand, getting Elliott used to him. Elliott let out a sharp breath and stifled moan, hungrily nipping at Niko's lip. His reactions alone were enough to almost send Niko again.

Elliott was ready. He took over, positioning and lowering himself slowly onto Niko with a soft sigh. They paused, adjusting to one another. It was too much, too much to be inside him. Niko gripped Elliott's hair tightly, gripped his arm. He reached down and stroked him as Elliott began moving, pushing Niko deeper inside and pulling out again, creating a darkly delicious rhythm and friction between them. Niko wished he could take control, could thrust into Elliott again and again, hard, until the other man fell to pieces. But Elliott didn't seem to mind, ardent in his quickening movements as he rode him. Niko gripped his hips and ass, helping to lift and lower him.

The shitty old bed groaned beneath them with Elliott's movements. It was all Niko could do to hold on, to pace himself, to keep from spilling inside him at the warm touch, at the connection to this beautiful man. He wanted it to last.

He couldn't last.

"I—I'm going to—"

He felt it coming, the hot spill, too early, but too far gone to stop it now. He dug his fingers into Elliott's thigh, gripping him as he came inside. Then Niko sank back down onto the bed, his cheeks flushed dark, burning hot in shame. He'd meant to hold back longer, meant to make it last for Elliott. He couldn't even give him that. He felt like a teenager again, awkward, fumbling, unable to pace himself or make it good. It had been too long; he had gone too long without a lover. Or maybe Elliott just did that to him.

"I— Elliott, I'm sorry, I—"

A crescent smile snaked across Elliott's face. He bent down, still sitting on Niko, and kissed him again, slowly, tongue against tongue. "You liked it that much, did you?"

"I'm sorry."

He touched at Niko's chin. "Don't be. I like knowing you couldn't last with me."

"Let me make it up to you," Niko said, taking Elliott in hand again and stroking him.

"I won't say no."

Niko pulled him forward until Elliott straddled his chest. He leaned forward, hands roaming the small of his back, his hips, his thighs now, and took him in his mouth.

It was delightful.

Niko had always liked giving more than receiving. He loved the taste of cock, loved the sensation of it filling his mouth. He especially loved watching his lovers come undone piece by piece. He wanted to see Elliott, wanted to know if his agonized expressions and sounds would stay subtle or give way to something more passionate when he'd reached his climax.

No. This wasn't enough. Niko wanted it to be more.

He pulled back, looking up at Elliott. "Fuck me," he murmured, his own voice emerging rough and low, "in the mouth."

Elliott peered down at him wordlessly and trailed his thumb along Niko's bottom lip, then smeared it sloppily across his cheek. "You're sure?"

"I can take it."

Elliott's gaze grew dark and hungry at that.

He leaned forward, grabbing a fistful of Niko's hair in one hand and balancing himself against the wall with the other. He pushed himself slowly into Niko's mouth, drew back out, then slid even deeper along Niko's tongue.

Niko loved every second of it. He loved Elliott taking his pleasure from him, setting the pace, controlling the situation.

Surrendering to him felt thrilling in a way Niko was afraid to think too much about. With each thrust, Elliott went a little deeper, until the next time, he was down Niko's throat, buried to the hilt.

Niko watched as Elliott's more reserved expression quickly crumbled, giving way to a half-lidded pleasure. His breath escaped him in soft pants through barely parted lips, each gasp escalating until it became a quiet moan. He lost himself briefly, thrusting into Niko hard and fast, gripping his hair.

"Oh—*fuck*—Niko—"

The sensation of his come sliding hot and salty down the back of Niko's throat—delivered with a strangled gasp—was enough to make Niko rouse again. But when he looked at Elliott, he could see the man was nearly translucent and exhausted now, collapsing into himself and panting harder than he should have been. Elliott reached up, gingerly touching at his bandaged shoulder.

"Was it too much?" Niko asked, caressing him.

"No," Elliott murmured breathlessly. "No."

"Here. Just let me—" Niko started, beginning the awkward rearranging necessary to get himself turned over.

"Right, sorry." Elliott climbed off him and took the opportunity to clean himself up. He switched the bedside lamp back off and darkness settled over the room again.

"Come here," Niko said once he'd settled onto his side. Elliott sat beside him but didn't lay down yet, reaching out to stroke Niko's hair as he gazed down at him. It was bliss.

"Turn over," he said softly. "The other way." Niko hesitated but did, turning over to face away from Elliott. The other man finally lay down and wrapped around him, burying his face in the back of Niko's neck and planting a light kiss there. His body was still warm and vibrant against Niko's. It broke Niko's heart to be held like this. He had been so lonely.

"Are you okay?" he asked.

"Yes. Are you?" Elliott murmured.

"I'm—I'm great, actually."

"So am I."

"I should have been more careful with how we did this," Niko said. "You're injured."

"It's not that bad."

Niko knew he was lying. He took Elliott's hand in his own and kissed the back of it, letting his lips linger, exhaustion already creeping in. He inhaled Elliott's scent, unique and intoxicating, mixed with Baouban's cheap body wash. Despite everything, Niko felt a peace he didn't know he could experience. His eyes grew heavy then, sleep finally calling him with its siren song.

Half in a dream, Niko remembered a documentary he had seen once. Two galaxies were colliding—vast and ancient, older than anyone. They cast and entangled their stars in the violent gravitational tides of their collision, each twisting around the other again and again as their new orbits tightened. They fell into each other's gravity until the stars of one galaxy were no longer separate from the other, spiraling evermore into a single, unified point.

It was inescapable now.

CHAPTER FOURTEEN

THREE POINT FOUR BILLION CREDITS

"Niko," Elliott whispered.

Niko shifted to bury himself deeper into Elliott. He couldn't remember ever being so comfortable. Nothing hurt when he was in Elliott's arms.

"Yeah, babe," he murmured. The word had come out in the thoughtless way half-conscious language did, and only a moment later did he realize he'd even said it.

"Niko?"

Elliott's body was stiff around him, each muscle taut with a quiet, tightly strung tension. He gave Niko a small shake. Niko opened his eyes, met by the darkness of night filling the cabin.

"What's wrong?" Niko murmured, wakefulness quickly returning to him as his skin prickled with unease.

"There's someone outside. I heard something."

Niko was wide awake now, adrenaline flooding his body. He swallowed. This shouldn't be possible. This safehouse was one of the most secure locations anywhere in the galaxy. No one was supposed to know about it. And it was miles upon miles from the closest settlement. There was no reason for someone to come across it by mistake. Any foot traffic would have to be intentional.

Maliciously so.

He hoped it was an animal. That Elliott was just paranoid due to how he'd probably had to live for the past several months. That the sound of something rustling around in the forestial dark was enough to make him wake Niko.

All the same, they couldn't risk ignoring it. And Niko didn't want to discredit Elliott, to doubt his judgment.

"Okay," he murmured slowly, craning his neck upward to look for any movement in the cracks of the old blinds. There was nothing. Only the sounds of insect song filled the silent seconds as he waited.

"I can get to your ship. Your weapons are there, right? Do you have a code to get to them?" Elliott asked.

"It's a biometric scanner. I'll have to be there. And I'd feel better with my suit if this is going to be a fight."

"Let's go," Elliott said, sitting up. The distinct loss of his warmth made Niko ache, but he knew this wasn't the time to dwell on it. Elliott was quick, already up and throwing on clothes, silent as a ghost. He tossed Niko his own, which Niko tried to pull on quickly, though it was always a little awkward for him. Niko looked over at his chair, steeped in heavy shadow, and fought back a groan. The thing was not exactly the epitome of stealthy movement.

Elliott glanced around the room, straining to see in the dark as well. "I had knives—"

"Kitchen counter. Drawer under the coffee machine," Niko mumbled. The number of hidden weapons and tools he'd found on Elliott when removing his shirt and initially bandaging his wounds was both impressive and not surprising. In the least. Niko had shoved them in the kitchen drawer for the time being. It hadn't been the most creative spot, but mostly he'd wanted to ensure they weren't within Elliott's grasp when he woke. Niko had no idea then how the man would react, waking in a new place, confused.

Elliott slipped off quickly. Niko didn't even hear the drawer open and close before he came padding back, the pale glint of a silver blade clutched in his hand. Niko unfortunately hadn't been able to save the sniper rifle; it had been a casualty left back on Neema, dropped by Elliott when he'd collapsed. Niko had only been able to carry so much then, and Elliott had been his priority. By far.

Even so, tactical knives weren't going to cut it, either. Not if this was going to be a real battle. Niko had seen firsthand what Elliott was capable of carrying out with a knife alone, but that had been under the benefit of stealth and surprise. And Niko was at a distinct disadvantage—no weapon at all, his armor locked away, charging aboard the ship. They needed to get to the *Soñadora*.

Elliott crouched and moved to the window by the bed, slowly parting the blinds to peek through before shrinking away again. He glanced at Niko, holding up four fingers. Niko winced. Any hope he'd had that this was just the clumsy approach of an animal vanished.

How? He couldn't stop wondering. This safehouse was the best you could find. This shouldn't be happening. Baouban protected his people. He had old world honor that was rare these days. Increasingly so.

This shouldn't be happening.

Even Zann didn't know about this place. Was he being tracked, somehow? Had Zann suspected him enough to—?

"There's a hidden door in the back of the closet for emergencies. It should lead straight to where the ship's parked," Niko said.

They made their way to the small closet and out through an even narrower external door, Niko's heart rate briefly spiking as his chair was barely too big to fit through. Elliott paused and turned to help him, though, quietly maneuvering it back and forth until it cleared the door frame. Once outside in the night air, Elliott slipped ahead again. Niko's nerves burned with panic as he tried to follow, both swiftly, but quietly. They reached the ship and Niko was grateful the chair hadn't been as loud as he'd worried it would be. This was the first time he'd ever had to navigate an active situation in it, rather than his suit. He hoped it would be the last.

As the door to the ship slid open, the leaves of several trees to the front side of the cabin shook as something gargantuan thudded on the ground.

"*Idiot!*" a feminine voice hissed. "*You'll wake them!*"

Niko and Elliott exchanged glances.

Toliai, Elliott mouthed.

Oh fuck, Niko thought. Toliai were by far the largest and hardiest of all known sentient alien species. They stood almost a story high and had a scaled hide that was close enough to bulletproof.

The *Soñadora* lowered its ramp and they both quickly ascended it, Elliott stubbornly waiting for Niko to get in safely first. The door closed behind them. Niko glanced towards the ship's console, with all its screens and holograms shut off, still and silent. They could try and take the ship, leave now. But he needed to *know*. He needed to know who'd managed to follow him here. And he needed to check, first, if the *Soñadora Despierta* had a tracker. If he couldn't take care of that first, it didn't matter where they went. They would always be followed.

It was going to have to be a fight.

He moved to the back of the ship, where Elliott was already waiting, antsy, and let the locker scan the pads of his fingers. The door yielded to them and Elliott helped himself to a secondary rifle Niko didn't often favor, inspecting it and checking if it was loaded. It wasn't.

"Ammunition's to the right, on the bottom," Niko said, and wasted no time getting back into the suit. It still wasn't fully charged, but it would do. It wouldn't die on him any time soon.

He felt a rush of relief as the sensation of protective armor fastened tightly around his limbs. A moment later and he knew the neural implants had locked in and around the skin of his legs, tiny, sensitive needles sliding unfelt under his skin, all announced with a pale hologram activating at the wrist of his suit that read *CONNECTED*.

Nothing *felt* different when he was connected to the suit. He would never be able to fully feel his legs again, but he had a palpable relief at knowing he could stand now for as long as its battery allowed. He did, pulling on the gloves last and locking them into place.

All that was missing was the helmet, still. But he'd never get that back unless he had a new one made, the original crushed somewhere in the great core of Uula.

He walked over to Elliott, who reached in and handed him his usual rifle.

He pays attention, Niko thought. Then again, Elliott had been the very target at the other end of that same rifle many times, Niko realized. He probably had it memorized well.

"Are you ready?" Niko asked, loading the rifle and switching off the safety. "It's no sniper rifle. Do you know how to use it?"

"I know how to use it," Elliott said dryly. Niko thought he detected a hint of irritation in the other man's voice.

"Sure you're going to be good with your shoulder?"

"*Niko.*"

"Okay, okay. But I want you to stay behind me," Niko said.

"I'm not—"

"You don't have any armor and I do," Niko cut him off, moving to the exit.

"I was going to say I'm not an *idiot.*"

Niko couldn't help but smile. No. No, he wasn't an idiot. He was *the Kestrel,* probably the more tactically minded and clever out of either of them. Niko just tended to react in the spur of the moment when it came to combat, all intuition. That instinct had kept him alive so far, for the most part. Maybe not whole, maybe not unscathed. But it had kept him alive, and that was good enough.

As they reached the door, a series of rapid-fire gunshots rang through the air outside of the ship, clearly aimed at the cabin. The sound of wood splintering and glass shattering joined in, filling the air with a cacophony of noise. After a moment, it fell quiet. Even the insects had stopped singing.

"Well, we're awake now," Elliott quipped. Niko snorted. He glanced over and realized he'd instinctively put a hand on the other man's chest the moment the gunfire had started. He retracted it.

They exited the ship, both men readying their guns, Elliott dutifully keeping a few steps behind Niko.

Niko saw the Xermotl first, a lavender colored man with blue patterns, wielding an automatic rifle. He was creeping around the back of the cabin—which was now standing in disarray, windows shattered, blinds hanging askew, entire chunks of wood missing. The whole thing was peppered with holes. His four legs crunched quietly over broken glass shards. Niko got a surprise headshot on him, just as the man looked up in startlement. Niko grimaced, sending a silent apology to the Xermotl as he folded into himself and crumpled to the ground. He didn't prefer killing, but he would if he had to, and their lives were in real danger.

And they hadn't been left with much choice. He recognized these guys as other bounty hunters, maybe mercenaries. They had no uniforms, and Galapol wasn't likely to send a hulking, ground-shaking Toliai in the middle of the night for an orchestrated surprise attack.

The first had been easy to take down, but the other three heard Niko's shot and responded expertly. He heard their voices, the quiet: "*Oh shit. Behind the house.*" And: "*They're here.*"

Elliott tapped Niko on the shoulder and gestured into the forest, left of the cabin. Niko swept his gun in that direction, but was met with only the still of night. Gunfire erupted from the trees, the bright starburst of someone's firearm going off, a single shot followed by another. Niko shot back, both hunters missing their marks in the moonlight. The other shooter had likely ducked behind one of the hardy trunks, so Niko took the opportunity to book it for the cabin, crouching down at the corner, just out of sight of whoever was shooting from the trees. Elliott swiftly followed, keeping close.

"I've got your back," Elliott murmured. Niko kept his gaze trained on the forest before him, trees extending back until he lost visual, their silhouettes melting into the dark. He heard something behind them, turning just in time to see the long, pale gold arm of a Quwa-quay tossing a grenade towards them.

Fuck. Oh fuck—

Elliott was there, suddenly. Eyes on it, he caught the thing in mid-air and whipped it back. It detonated near its source, eliciting a shriek from around the cabin's corner. Niko gaped at him in disbelief, his brain struggling to process what had just happened. He had seen guys try to pick up and throw back grenades that had landed by them before in his line of work. It never ended well—there just wasn't enough *time* to complete the action.

But this was the first time he'd seen someone outright deftly intercept it mid-throw and hurl it back in time to avoid certain destruction. Elliott wasted no time getting on with the battle though, raising his rifle and disappearing briefly around the corner, a single gunshot cracking through the air as he finished off the Quwa-quay who'd thrown it.

Another gunshot grazing Niko's hair reminded him of what he'd actually been doing before getting baffled by Elliott's insanity—and skill. He pressed against the back of the cabin, making a mental note of where the shot and telltale starburst flash of light that accompanied it had come from, and shot once, twice, three times into the dark of the forest. The third shot hit, a high pitched, feminine cry of pain echoing from the trees. But his assailant wasn't dead yet. She returned another two more shots, both dangerously close and pinging hard off Niko's chest armor.

He wished he had his helmet. Niko would feel a lot more confident if he did.

He waited again, one breath, then two. Elliott scurried back beside him, sinking down into a crouch. Niko knew this game of hiding, shooting once, then hiding again. It could go on for hours. He'd wounded his opponent, but didn't know where. She could have RapiGel. She could keep at this, stalling him for as long as she needed. The trees shook with another few lumbering steps from the Toliai. Niko didn't have time to wait.

"Stay here," he mumbled. Before Elliott could respond, Niko leapt up, running as hard as he could straight into the forest, zigzagging as he went to make aiming on him harder. Bullets zinged past him, the bright flash of each shot telling him exactly where to go.

They never expected to get rushed. It was one of the reasons Niko relied on it so much. Nobody expected their opponent to throw sanity to the wind and go charging head first into active ranged combat.

He slammed into the woman—tall and gangly, a Heenva—and knocked her to the ground. Her branch-like antennae glowed and pulsed with her distress. He wrestled her gun out of her hands.

"Fuck you!" she yelled in Sala Heenvan, scrambling to pull a secondary pistol on him. Niko wrenched it from her hand and hit her upside the head with it. She fell unconscious beneath him, her struggle over. A quick glance showed him he'd only gotten her in the arm with his shot. If she treated it when she came to, she'd live. He got off her, confiscating her guns for himself, then moved back quickly to join Elliott. They still had the Toliai to deal with.

They exchanged glances, Niko murmuring for the other man to keep behind him now. Toliai were nothing to fuck with. He'd always dreaded jobs where they were his mark. Guns did little to them. Explosive rounds *might* start making wounds. He struggled to think of his options, when Elliott held something up, clutched tightly in his hand: another grenade. He must have taken it from the Quwa-quay's remains.

Of course he did.

Niko couldn't help but grin. This might just give them a fighting chance after all.

"Hope you have good aim," he teased.

"Are you kidding me?" Elliott said. Niko peeked around to the front of the cabin, where the lumbering creature was glancing around, clutching an oversized, heavy-looking gatling gun. He'd clearly been the one to go all out on the cabin.

"I'll distract him," Niko whispered. "I'll go around the left and you take the right."

"That gun is going to do some damage if you're not careful," Elliott commented, but slipped off around the back and towards the other side. Niko inhaled, nerves rising. He peeked around the cabin's side again and started shooting at the Toliai, aiming for his face. The gargantuan alien snarled in rage and opened fire. Niko barely had half a second to duck behind the cabin before it erupted into splinters of wood again, bullets zinging straight through the structure and past him. He felt a few ricochet off his back, and kept his head ducked down.

It was enough time for Elliott to act. Niko heard the explosion as bullets rained down on him—and then stopped. He moved around the corner again, rifle trained on the Toliai, just in time to see the gunner clutching desperately at his smoldering face. He stumbled back into the trees, letting out a deep roar. The tree he fell against cracked under his weight, but ultimately stood.

The Toliai gunner slumped against the tree, unmoving. Where his face had once been was a ghastly sight now—even more ghastly, Niko thought, than what the typical Toliai face looked like.

The elation of victory rushed through Niko's veins as the forest fell quiet again. He felt triumphant, as he always did when being the last one standing in battle. Working with Elliott was... it was *fun*. He was used to this kind of high-adrenaline skirmish in his work, but he'd never gotten to work with a partner before. Especially not one as masterful as Elliott. This was something Niko could find himself getting used to.

But Elliott came up behind him again, gluing himself to Niko's back, gun sweeping the dark trees.

"Don't get too excited yet," Elliott murmured. "There's still one out there."

Niko froze. "You said there were four."

"I hadn't accounted for the Toliai."

Shit.

Niko raised his gun again, short-lived triumph giving way to tension. The night was quiet, nothing around them but heavy, heavy silence that the insect symphony was still wary to fill.

Where are you?

Niko stepped forward and heard leaves crunching ahead of them in the dark. He and Elliott both trained their guns in the direction of the sound.

"Hey, uh," a familiar voice called out, nervous and shaky. "So, listen, I'm sorry about all that."

"Baouban?" Niko gaped.

The hefty, sage-colored Gheroun slithered his way out of the dark before them, from behind the dead Toliai, all his tentacles not currently used for walking held up in surrender. He wore a button-up shirt with strawberries on it. "Please don't shoot."

"This was *you?*" Niko said, incredulous. He was outraged.

"What are you waiting for?" Elliott murmured under his breath.

"Whatever happened to honor?" Niko asked, ignoring Elliott.

"I'm sorry, Niko. I am," Baouban said, keeping a good distance from them, tentacles still held aloft. They jiggled in fear. Niko could see miserable regret in his three eyes. "But there's *never* been a payout this good. Nobody's ever seen anything like it. This bounty is something generations of your family could thrive off of. A number like that changes everything, Niko. That kind of money is a wild card now."

"You sold us out for his bounty," Niko spat, disgusted.

"N-no," Baouban said nervously. "Not just. Yours, as well."

"What?" Niko paused. That meant—

He had a bounty now too. Posted by Galapol.

"Since a few days back, there's been a hefty bounty on your head too. The two of you are now the highest paying job the galaxy has ever seen, by far."

Niko couldn't help but ask. Morbid curiosity rubbed through him like sandpaper, grating. "How much?"

"Three point four billion credits."

Holy shit.

Niko was both aghast and—well, honestly, he was impressed. Was he really worth that much? "For me?"

"Ah, ha ha, no," Baouban laughed awkwardly. "Most of that's for him." He gestured a tentacle towards Elliott before quickly raising it towards the sky again, where it quivered. "One hundred twenty million is you."

Niko scoffed. He was worth far more than that. He was easily on par with Elliott. He was skilled, and dangerous, and—Niko shook his head. None of this mattered. He didn't even *want* a bounty on his head. The implications it carried were horrifying.

"Are you going to shoot him now?" Elliott asked, loud enough for Baouban to hear. "Or should I?"

"Whoa! Wait wait wait wait!" Baouban pleaded. "I have fourteen spawnlings!"

"And you have a fatal case of backstabbing," Elliott said, taking aim.

"Elliott," Niko said, sighing, and Elliott reluctantly lowered his gun. He stared out at the quivering mass of tentacles with disdain. "I trusted you, Baouban. People came here knowing they were taken care of. You'll never get that back."

"I know," Baouban said quietly, glancing towards the ground.

"I would have had your back through anything. We took care of each other, in another lifetime."

Baouban nodded. "I suppose 'sorry' doesn't really cut it."

"Not this time," Niko said. He lowered his gun too, and Baouban visibly sagged in relief. Niko stared him down, unimpressed at the miserable alien before him who had once been a champion of those in need. "I thought you were one of the real ones, Baouban."

Niko turned away, stepping into the splintered remains of the cabin. The place was destroyed. Cabinet doors barely hung on to their hinges, shattered shards of glass darkly glittering all along the floors, the tables, the bed. Stuffing leaked from the mattress, some of it still floating through the air. Niko went over to his bedside bag of supplies and picked it up, giving it a quick look over. It had a few holes but had managed to survive the worst of the damage. He zipped it closed and slung it over his shoulder, heading back out to where Elliott still eyed the Gheroun warily.

"Come on," Niko said.

"You're going to let him go?" Elliott asked.

Niko started towards the ship, but paused to cast one last glance back at Baouban, a man he'd once respected, even thought of as a good friend. "Everything he had rested on his reputation. In the end, he made a gamble and lost. Let's just go."

He called out, a little louder, "Baouban. There's a hunter out about ten yards east of the cabin." Niko pointed. "She's wounded but alive. Get her some RapiGel. Or make her buy it, if money is all that matters now."

Once they had the ship cleared of Vorna-12's atmosphere, the infinite, perfect black of space before them, Niko sank back into the pilot's seat of the *Soñadora*. He wanted to banter and laugh with Elliott about how the fight had gone down, how he'd taken on a live grenade and lived. How they'd worked together to take down an armed Toliai. But laughter wasn't something Niko felt capable of right then, and despite the man sitting in his co-pilot's seat, Niko found he only wanted to retreat inside himself, nothing to say.

Baouban had dealt him a low blow, but he'd also given him an invaluable lesson. If even someone like him were willing to turn on Niko for this bounty, there was *nowhere* safe for them now. Three point four billion credits was a lot to turn down—maybe even an impossible amount.

Everything was about to change. Or maybe it already had, and Niko was just struggling to admit it.

They'd given a quick look over inside and out of the *Soñadora* before taking off. There were no tracking devices and the ship was clean.

Elliott looked over at him. Despite everything, he wore a faint smile, eyes squinting. "I was right," he said.

"Yeah?" Niko asked, wanting to humor him despite his own mood.

"We work well together."

Niko snorted. He couldn't help the smile he felt taking possession of his lips. They'd endured so much, and had no stable ground beneath them to stand on, flung adrift to the stars. But Elliott Kestrel was *here* with him, smiling at him. Had watched his back. Had kept Niko alive.

They'd worked as a team and it had been… amazing. Fulfilling.

Before he could reconsider, Niko found himself pulling his glove off and reaching towards Elliott, taking his hand in his own. He ran his thumb along the back of it.

"I like your hands," he admitted.

"Do you?"

"Yeah, they're, uh, handsome."

"*Hand*some hands? Really?" Elliott was smiling again, though. "I like yours too. I like the tattoos on them. I like the ones everywhere else, too."

It was nice. Niko hadn't been complimented on his looks in so long. And it meant especially much coming from Elliott.

They settled into silence for a while before Elliott spoke again. "Are you alright, Niko?"

"I don't know how to answer that," Niko admitted. "I'm trying to think of where we could go. I thought I knew a few places, but this is making me question all of them." He stared out the windshield at the infinite obsidian that lay before them, bejeweled with stars.

"Money makes the galaxy turn," Elliott mumbled. He hesitated before finally speaking again. "I know a place."

Niko looked up at him. He was so beautiful, sitting there in Niko's oversized t-shirt, hair all but a disaster from the combination of fucking, sleeping, and getting caught in an unexpected shootout. On his long neck was a constellation of blushing bruises that Niko had left him mere hours before. He looked tired but relaxed, and it was nice to see him like this instead of wearing the usual cool scowl Niko met him with when he'd been hunting him.

The sight of him like this made Niko ache. He was the one point of gravity Niko could hold steady to when everything else was rapidly falling apart.

"It's where I've been staying," Elliott said.

Niko couldn't help but smile again at that. All the countless, tireless efforts Galapol had made trying to track down Elliott, trying to find his nefarious base of operations and coming up empty-handed again and again. It had driven Zann nuts. There was an illicit thrill at being able to see its secret unveiled.

"All this time?" Niko asked.

Elliott smiled wanly. "All this time."

CHAPTER FIFTEEN

WHERE THE MAGIC HAPPENS

NIKO WATCHED IN SILENCE as the icy moon before them grew in the ship's windshield view. It was a small, barren thing that didn't even have a formal name, so far from its star that it remained in perpetual night, despite its rotation. The ship's coordinates listed it as simply RM-9832642G. The solar system it resided in was similarly named, simply a string of numbers and letters to classify its location. No one lived in this system. There were no settlements, no cities, no ports. The entire system Elliott had come to reside in was silent and still, each planet and moon constituting billions of miles of emptiness.

It definitely made for a good hiding spot, at least.

Niko guided the *Soñadora Despierta* down to hover above the surface of the moon; it didn't possess an atmosphere, nor breathable air of any kind. Below him as the ship flew were towering loops, spires, and jagged cliffs of rock frozen in eternal ice which stood dark under the dim light of its distant star. A large crescent filled the western half of starry sky, a quiet, rocky planet that was a deep red and bore a similarly dispassionate string of numbers to identify it among the vast sea of celestial objects.

"It should be just past this outcropping," Elliott murmured. Niko glanced at him. The man's voice came dull and quiet, his eyes matching his tone. Since they'd entered the solar system, everything about Elliott had turned inward and bland.

"You doing alright?" Niko ventured.

"Yes. Why?"

He hesitated, not wanting to press it. If Elliott didn't want to talk, that was fine. Instead, Niko glanced out at the silvery structure on the horizon, exactly where Elliott had said it would be. It looked to be an abandoned research facility of sorts, with signs and logos printed in heavy, blocky Quwa-quay along with an industrial sort of hangar entrance. The entire thing was built for function over form, dim lights lining the outside and flooding the icy ground below in a wash of ghostly white. It stood like a silent eidolon among miles of emptiness.

"So, how'd you find this place, anyway?" Niko asked, maneuvering the ship down and slowing it as he approached the hangar doors. They opened on their own, some sort of automatic sensor, likely. Niko couldn't imagine anyone else living here to consciously open and close the gates.

"It was an old Yhanwe-han mining facility. Apparently, this moon has ample deposits of rare elements. It was abandoned decades ago along with dozens of other classified mining operations the Quwa-quay lost funding for. It had all been initially for experimental weapons crafting. I found out about this when I was research-ing Honeybliss. I found out a lot of interesting tidbits of dark government projects along the way. Every planet and nation has their fingers dipped in something."

Interesting, Niko thought. *But not surprising, either.*

He guided the ship into the hangar, setting it down gently into a space that was far too large and far too empty. He was used to crowded hangars full of ships, with people wandering to and fro. The bright and flashing lights of neon advertisements, the little pop-up shops of convenient toiletries and supplies for weary interstellar travelers. Food stalls that smelled of fried and crispy treats. None of that was here now. The only contents of the hangar besides the *Soñadora* were two small utility ships with Quwa-quay printed along the side, parked near the back of the hangar. They looked like they'd been there a while.

Elliott must have been using one of the mining ships to get to and from his marks.

Niko heard a soft sigh beside him, a quiet exhalation of held breath. Elliott gazed out blankly at the vast, silent hangar ahead of them as the gates slid closed and oxygen cycled through again. His gaze was unreadable, everything about him turned sharply inward.

"Home, sweet home," he murmured. "Is it what you imag-ined?"

"I—" Niko started. Thinking about it, he realized he had no idea what to expect of where Elliott had been working from. Imagining it had simply drawn a blank. "I don't know, actually."

Once the chime and announcement in Quwa-quay sounded, clearing them to safely exit the ship, Niko moved to the back of the cabin and hooked his suit back in its charging station, then switched over to his chair. "This place is Quwa-quay made. So I assume stairs aren't a problem?"

"There aren't any," Elliott confirmed.

He helped Niko haul up his supplies. Then they exited in silence. Outside of the ship, the heavy stifle of the place pressed down on Niko even more. He was dwarfed by the size of the empty hangar, with its five-story-high ceilings and expansive space. Each movement echoed in the vast chamber. There were no announcements over comms, no purring of ship engines, no looping advertisement tracks or jingles or catchy music. The entire experience was bizarrely inviting of agoraphobia. Everything felt erroneously too big, like it had been designed wrong. Niko briefly missed the small, familiar walls of his cramped apartment on Kaapra-19. The earthy, sage green of them. The decades-old holiday cactus he'd kept in the kitchen that had once been his mother's.

He wondered if Zann had managed to get a hold of it. Probably not.

They made their way through the hangar and up a metal ramp towards a set of double doors that Elliott unlocked with deft fingers over a number pad hologram.

The doors slid open and they entered the facility proper, another huge control room that was equally too big and too quiet, the overhead lights blinking on one by one as sensors caught their movement. Niko could hear their soft, electric hum. Along the far end of the room were metal benches, chairs and consoles, and a single small window with half-a-foot-thick glass revealing the frigid, dark landscape beyond. Every wall was bare, except for old instructional and cautionary signs posted in Quwa-quay.

Niko thought it would be more exciting to see the infamous Kestrel's secret lair. He hadn't been sure what to expect—something matching the wit and cleverness of Elliott, something that had more quirkiness. Spite, even. *Anything.* But all he was met with here was a disarming silence and emptiness, devoid of any traces of personalization. How long had Elliott spent in this place, countless miles from the nearest person, plotting to avenge the death of his sister? Months at the least. But likely even years. The isolation must have been agonizing.

Nothing about RM-9832642G's research facility was stimulating. It was, instead, horrific.

"It's, um. It's *quiet* in here," Niko commented. He swallowed and heard the click of his throat. He could hear his breathing and became painfully conscious of it.

Elliott moved to one of the consoles, punching in a few commands and waking the screen up. A moment later and the heavy silence was banished, a wash of sparkling pop music and rhythm flooding the room from overhead speakers that were once likely used for internal communications.

"It can't keep me down, can't hold me,
Gravity can't touch me when I'm with you.
Free me, love me, take me, remake me."

The music was familiar and Niko couldn't help but laugh. The conjoined voices of Hayura and Kuliedi Taan sang to them in harmony. It was the new music they'd made together, the very same song the starlets had debuted when Elliott had gone for the CEO of StarSeam on Vhesa Station.

"Really?" Niko asked, incredulous.

Elliott smiled wanly—though sincerely. "I mentioned I'm a fan. I love their stuff."

"Not what I expected, honestly."

"No? What, then?"

"I don't know. Metal? Something angrier."

Elliott made a face. "Oh, god, no."

Niko laughed again at the bizarre irony of it all, at the idea of Elliott Kestrel, decked head to toe in weapons and gadgets aplenty, waiting in the private balcony to fuck up Matteo Ricci's day while tapping his foot in time to the sparkly music that flowed below. Enjoying it. Stealing a little moment of private delight before his work began.

"What about you? What do you like?" Elliott asked.

"No, I want you to guess," Niko said, feeling a little ornery now.

Elliott pressed his lips together in thought, staring hard at Niko. He clearly took the question seriously. After a moment, he said, "I don't know. Rock? Blues? Classic rock."

Niko laughed. "Nope. Rap."

"And?"

"No, that's it. Just rap. I like the harder stuff. Royce RG and Lord Fukkaho are what I had on repeat lately."

"Lord... Fukkaho."

Niko grinned.

"I wish I'd thought to make an alias for all of this, after all. I could have gotten so creative," Elliott lamented.

"What was it Jande Seiiren called you?"

"'Dick-fisting fuck-sandwich,'" Elliott said, reveling in it. They both laughed, despite the lightless mood Elliott had seemed to fall into since they'd arrived.

"You could call yourself the Dickfister. 'Oh, did you hear? The Dickfister came for him last night. He didn't make it.'"

Elliott burst out a peal of laughter, tilting his head back. It was beautiful to Niko to see and hear it. He could drink up that sound. It left him relieved to see a stubborn joy breaking through Elliott's quietude. It pushed back against the walls of the empty, huge room and transformed the place.

"He really was an artist," Niko said.

"Too bad it never translated to his 'paintings.'" Elliott was still smiling, eyes squinted.

The song switched to another familiar track, pulsing through the speakers, filling the still and empty room around them. It was going to get stuck in Niko's head and he knew it. It did every time he heard it.

"*When you're lost, my love will guide you home. I've got you, baby.*"

"You know, it's kind of funny," he said. "I was so convinced you were there for the singers that night. My brother and I had this big argument over it, over whether you'd show up at the concert or this

Toliai political parade that was happening at the same time. But I'd picked up your music on Yhanwe-ha and was convinced they were next. It was this same song."

"No. I just knew Ricci would be there. But I won't lie and say I wasn't excited to go, too."

"I wish I could take you to a concert," he said.

Elliott smiled, but it was thin and languid again. "That would be nice."

Niko knew he'd fumbled, that it had only served as a reminder of what Elliott could probably never do again. The emptiness of the facility had returned, cold, vast, and utilitarian.

He wanted to take Elliott's hand. He longed, oddly, to dance with him—a strangely spontaneous impulse. He wanted to sweep Elliott up and move to the music with abandon, just the two of them here alone, the only two beating hearts and conscious minds in trillions of miles. If they couldn't go to concerts, they could make their own enjoyment together. He wheeled the chair closer, but Elliott turned and walked across the room.

"I'll show you around," he said flatly.

Elliott led him up another ramp and to various hallways lined with empty rooms. He passed quickly over most of the rooms, showing him only the first, then explaining they were abandoned labs, recreational lounges, and storage areas. Some hallways had internal windows leading to the labs. Niko could see a glimpse into one of the common areas, where several shriveled, dead alien plants sat under a wash of white, fluorescent lighting.

"Kind of bright in here for a Quwa-quay setup," he said. He'd expected something artificially crepuscular, for every corner to be steeped in heavy shadow to accommodate the former workers' light-sensitive eyes.

"I replaced many of the lights myself, early on. It was hard to see what I was doing without it."

Music still played over various speakers throughout the facility, though when they entered the cafeteria, which sported huge windows fully displaying the frigid and fatal landscape of black rock and jagged ice that surrounded them just beyond these plain walls, Niko felt the music for what it was—a flimsy bandage taped over a gaping, raw wound. It covered and obscured, but didn't change what really lay underneath.

The cafeteria was equally huge and equally empty, save for a vast stack of crates and bags along the far corner near the kitchen.

"I stocked up before I began," Elliott said, apparently predicting the question on Niko's tongue. "I ran calculations on how long something like this would take at maximum and gave myself an extra two months just in case. I have just enough to see this through. The same goes for weapons and other parts. I have extra ammunition for practice."

Niko ached. The music no longer served its purpose at all anymore, was no longer acting as even a flimsy balm. A new song started, peppy and layered and *fun,* but none of it reached him. It all felt wrong in this empty place. The signs were everywhere: in Elliott's speech, in his mannerisms. In how he'd calculated and prepared. He saw his life as reaching its coda soon. There was an end date in sight, a finality. Elliott had orchestrated everything, his death the final preparation.

He wanted to speak, but didn't know what to say.

Elliott briskly continued on their depressing tour, leading him next to another—to Niko's great and total lack of surprise—huge and mostly empty room, the longest one so far. Niko guessed it must have once been the main equipment and supplies warehouse. The uncanny size of this one had been put to good use, however: target posters and dummies stood lined at the furthest end of the room, bullet holes peppering them.

"Shooting range," Elliott said.

Next were the residential quarters. He opened one door to a tiny room that had a small pile of dirty clothes cast on the floor and two half-emptied water bottles on the plain nightstand. The blankets were pulled back, clearly previously used, the only sign of recent life Niko had seen so far in the entire place. Niko recognized the gray sheets as the same from the photograph Elliott had sent.

"I've been sleeping in this one. Do you want to stay in here?" His question came quiet, stilted, and with maybe a hint of self-consciousness.

"Yeah," Niko said, watching him. "I do."

Elliott looked relieved, something in his gaze turning a little less withdrawn. He took Niko's bag from him and set it on the bed.

He led him down the hallway to a simple bathroom with a walk-in shower that had a built-in bench.

"Towels are in there," Elliott said, gesturing to a plain, gray locker. "I stocked up on hygiene supplies too. There should be extra toothbrushes."

Niko reached up and pried open the medicine cabinet above the sink, the plain mirror swinging open with a groan. It was impulse and curiosity, but he felt Elliott stiffen beside him and wondered if he'd made a mistake to help himself to exploring, instead of waiting to be shown.

Inside the cabinet were several bottles of sleeping pills. Niko winced as he thought about Elliott needing them—the man clearly had trouble sleeping often. He'd mentioned anxiety before.

Maybe Niko could help him with that. He wondered if Elliott would find it easier to sleep wrapped in his arms, body pressed against him, no longer despairingly isolated anymore. He felt his cheeks grow warm at the presumptuous thought, and closed the medicine cabinet again.

Elliott stared dully at Niko, gaze hollow, somehow even more devoid of life than before. It was like talking to a shell now, the person inside somewhere else. Elliott had become a chameleon in this place, just as empty as his surroundings.

Niko decided he wasn't a fan of RM-9832642G nor its facility. He especially wasn't a fan of what being here clearly did to Elliott.

"Laundry is down the hall." Niko nodded. "The last place is my workshop."

Elliott led him to what must have once been a laboratory of sorts, full of island counters, tables, shelves and consoles. He had since taken over and converted it to a multifunctional workshop, with weapons and tech parts scattered in a chaotic mess on the counters and stacked upon the shelves, replacing whatever had once been there. In the back of the room, lining an entire wall, was a mixture of holographic diagrams and information—schedules, maps, and architectural blueprints. Niko recognized the layout of Vhesa Station on one of them. Elliott must have hacked and collected maps, plans and diagrams months ahead of time in conjunction with a curated schedule of public events. The preparation behind it all was, to say the least, impressive to Niko.

Some of the blueprints had handwritten notes, all in the same despairingly awful, illegible handwriting Niko recognized from the original photograph everyone had mistaken as mentioning 'the Kestrel.'

So, he really did write that piss-poorly. Niko shook his head.

To the right of the maps and information was a grid consisting of dozens of photographs, each a portrait of the Honeybliss members from Elliott's files. The first ten portraits had a thick, messy red X scratched across them. Niko recognized them as the figures Elliott had successfully eliminated. A tactical knife was driven into Imperator Khaathra's portrait, straight in the middle of her three eyes.

Niko grimaced and Elliott noticed. "I may have imagined your face instead of hers at the time," he commented airily.

"Remind me not to piss you off," Niko mumbled.

"A plan of this complexity and scale is always going to have a high chance of unforeseen obstacles along the way." The memory of their first encounter came to Niko's mind. The irritation, the easy, strategic pivot. *Not again*. Niko had just been one obstacle of many, then. He wondered how many times he'd forced Elliott to have to readjust on the fly since.

"I'll go back and take care of her later," Elliott added, his voice clipped. It was back once more: the sharp turn inward, the dulled expression. "Chancellor Iincha'cul too."

Niko's eyes wandered further along the room, his gaze falling on a single sign that hung on the wall opposite of the maps and portraits—the first true evidence of Elliott in this place. It was purple, covered in cheap glitter, and looked like the kind of tacky thing you could find at any five-credit store. It read:

This is Where the Magic Happens

Niko barked out a laugh. *This* was what he'd expected, anticipated. Elliott glanced at him, a sly—pleased, even—smile touching his lips, a ghost of tension slipping away.

"Nice."

"Thank you. It felt fitting in my Murder Room."

Niko shook his head. Here was one, tiny glimpse of Elliott: dry and witty, even a little petty. Here was the man behind the mission, the human being underneath the anger, resentment, and isolation. The life that preceded its meticulously-arranged expiration.

He swept his gaze around again. On one of the consoles hung a printed photograph of Elliott and Cleo. It carried the same spirit as the graduation photo, though in this case, it appeared to be Cleo they were celebrating instead of the other way around. Cleo wore a slick, asymmetric designer dress, silver earrings dangling, glinting like tiny stars. She clutched a bouquet of pink roses to her chest with one arm, grinning triumphantly. Elliott was beside her, clad in upscale clothing as well—a nice, soft gray turtleneck, vest, and slacks. He stood beside his sister, both siblings with one arm around the other. Elliott smiled alongside her. He looked proud.

Elliott was younger there—maybe eighteen, or twenty, his hair trimmed shorter, the cowlicks not yet so aggressively taking over like golden weeds. Behind them was a crowd of models, judging by their clothing and makeup.

This had been from one of Cleo's fashion shows. Her brother had gone to support her.

"Did you buy her the roses?" Niko blurted before he could think on it. Elliott went stiff, the color draining from his face as he looked over at the photograph.

"I did," he said after a long silence. His voice was so quiet, Niko could barely hear it over the music. "I wanted to show her how proud I was of her."

Niko ached.

"We always supported each other," Elliott continued. "I came to every show. That's the last picture I ever got of her."

It was a far throw from the abused and terrified sister Elliott's doctored files had painted. The cruelty of it all made Niko sick. It wasn't enough that Honeybliss had taken Elliott's world from him. They'd had to rub his nose in it and humiliate him like a dog.

They stayed silent for a long while, Niko looking back towards the wall of data, the grid of targets. All of this—the galaxy as a whole forever changed—had been driven by a single woman's death.

Niko had first learned Elliott through assumptions and cold facts—mostly incorrect, even outright fictional. Through detached police files and a corrupt, invented history that had cast him as unstable. He held, still, base facts about Elliott. Niko had learned he was an engineer, the top graduate of his class. He learned where he'd worked and who his professional associations had been.

Then Niko learned him in a new way, a deeper way: slowly, instinctively through their orbit as hunter and hunted—the methods he favored, the brilliance of his tactics. How he sometimes did crazy things like Niko did, thinking on his feet. The way he, also like Niko, tried to avoid unnecessary deaths.

Now Niko was being let into a deeply intimate space, and learning Elliott Kestrel as a person. As a man. He was a patient but passionate lover, enthusiastic and responsive. He liked Niko's cooking, and his tattoos. He liked pop music. He was funny.

He was surprisingly empathetic; his entire assassination plot had been orchestrated all along in the name of putting a stop to what no one else would. He wanted to protect other families from the type of pain both of them had had to endure.

He was shockingly, painfully isolated from everyone and everything.

Niko had it bad for him.

And that terrified him. Being at Elliott's side came at a steep price. He'd traded a galaxy to be near him. He'd traded Zann. He'd traded stability and safety. Society. Normalcy. And Elliott still spoke in circles around one, terrible deadline: the end of his mission. For him, there wasn't a *what comes after*.

"Come here," Niko murmured. He held out a hand to Elliott and the other man hesitated a moment before crossing over to him. He took Niko's hand and Niko tugged him over, right into his lap.

He wrapped his arms around Elliott, pulling the other man against him. Elliott obliged, leaning into the embrace, seeming to sag against him as though he were letting all the horrible weight he carried settle onto Niko instead. Niko was glad to bear it. He stroked Elliott's hair in silence.

Niko wondered how long it had been since anyone had held Elliott. This facility had already begun to crawl under Niko's skin and get inside of him. This was a liminal space—like Sunorrna, it was abandoned and lonely, the kind of place Elliott haunted. The only kind of place he was allowed to haunt now.

"Can I just hold you a while?" Niko murmured in his ear.

Elliott snaked his arms around Niko until he was tightly embracing him too. "Only if I get to hold you, too," he whispered.

Niko stayed like that a while, simply holding Elliott, pleased he could be a bulwark against this maddeningly empty, isolated place. He could feel Elliott's heartbeat against his own chest, steady and slow and dutifully marching on, writing his life's story one beat at a time.

Niko had worried how things would be after they'd slept together. He'd expected awkwardness, perhaps distance. Maybe uncertainty. But Elliott gave his affection freely, easily even; he didn't keep away from Niko, didn't do the dance of discomfiture. It surprised him.

It hurt, too. Niko knew that whatever happened now, whatever his future might bring, he wanted to protect Elliott. He wanted to be there for him. They were in this together now, two fugitives from a law as wide as a galaxy. His gaze trailed to the photo of Elliott and Cleo, looking again at the woman so full of jubilation as she held a bouquet of roses gifted by the brother she'd protected. She'd carved out a home for Elliott when neither sibling had had anyone else to rely on.

Niko wanted to take up her mantle, her fight. He wanted to protect her brother, to put her ghost to rest. To carry on what Cleo Kestrel had fought hard to do in her tragically short life. He met her eyes in a silent exchange. They were confident, smiling, forever caught in an eternal moment of joy. It felt like she saw him now, as though she were smiling only at him as he held Elliott in that moment, locking gazes through time.

Knowing.

I promise I'll take care of your brother, he thought. *He's not alone anymore. I've got this. You can rest now, Cleo.*

He wanted to give Elliott Kestrel something to keep living for.

Niko woke disoriented, not remembering where he was. He opened his eyes, his whole body stiff and heavy, his right arm asleep.

Memory returned to him slowly—they had fallen asleep, embracing, Elliott sitting in his lap. Elliott was gone.

Niko cleared his throat and glanced around before seeing the other man in the far corner, quietly adding some sort of modification to a rifle scope.

Elliott glanced up at him. "I didn't want to wake you," he said softly.

"I don't even know what time it is," Niko said hoarsely, the haze and blur of sleep still in his eyes. "I don't know that it even matters at this point."

"It's four thirty in the morning," Elliott said. "We slept for about four hours."

"More than we got the night before."

Elliott leaned forward, examining the scope. "It's a shame we had to leave the other rifle behind. It was my best one. I had a lot of experimental mods on it. But I had spares, just in case."

Niko wheeled over to get a closer look. Elliott held it out to him and Niko turned it over in his hands. He wasn't a sniping kind of guy himself, but could still appreciate the beauty of a well-made, well-modified weapon. And this rifle was a thing of beauty. He whistled, handing it back.

"My old one was named *Parley*," Elliott said. "This one is *Repartee*."

Niko smirked. "Hey. Come get something to eat with me. I don't know about you, but I'm starving."

Elliott hesitated, looking like he wanted to argue, his gaze falling back on the gun he'd laid on the table. After a moment, he relented, nodding.

Niko went to the kitchen with him, another oversized room made for several cooks working together to serve an entire staff of researchers, miners, and scientists. Elliott moved to the walk-in freezer at the back.

"Don't get too excited. I only have the nutritional basics. Canned legumes and tuna, frozen lean meat. Oats, rice. Frozen vegetables," said Elliott.

"No sauces?"

"No."

"Herbs?"

"No."

"Salt?"

"I do have that."

"What about drinks?" Niko tried not to hold his breath over the hopes of a cold beer.

"Electrolyte water and caffeine tablets."

Right.

Niko worked with him to cook up a meal of chickpeas and onions and tomatoes with—real, actual—chicken breast. It was plain, and in the end, overly salted due to Niko being desperate for any semblance of flavor. But it was a meal, and it was edible.

They sat together in the inappropriately vast cafeteria, in front of the thick windows overlooking the most harrowing vista Niko had seen in quite some time: dark ice and rock with occasional jagged spires, under an airless vacuum of black sky.

There was an odd silence between them, heavy and full. It carried a certain edge, a shift in mood that had been slowly and subtly building since they'd arrived at the facility. The inward turning vacuousness that had begun creeping over Elliott had dug in, settled deeply. When Elliott was down to nothing but scraps of sodium-drowned chicken left on his plate, he spoke, the same hard edge to his voice as the silence that swam through the cafeteria.

"I'm going out again in a day. It's Yuuorta's turn."

Niko was startled. Some part of him had almost forgotten, as though together they could just hide away here from everything. His being here now didn't change any of that. Elliott was still determined to finish his mission, to make his statement, to keep anyone else's family from going through what he'd had to.

He leaned back in his chair, his heart doing a flip in his chest. Elliott was quiet and still, a tangible tension there inside him. Niko felt the unspoken questions; they didn't need to be spoken.

Are you going to try and stop me?

Are you going to help me?

He thought about how crazy, disruptive, and frankly suicidal Elliott's path of vengeance was. The public executions, always evading Galapol and every hungry bounty hunter ambitious enough to turn their sights his way. The idea of going with him, of *helping* him was madness.

They were at an impasse of wills. It was becoming familiar now. But...

Everything Elliott was doing was exactly what Niko had been craving, had been missing for three years. He had been sleepwalking through life without the hunt, without the adrenaline. Without knowing he was out there doing something to leave the galaxy a little bit better off than it had been. Niko didn't know how to stop, and frankly, he didn't want to.

Though completely controversial at the least, Elliott's work was something Niko couldn't bring himself to disagree with. He had seen the videos, and still had nightmares about them. They still regularly crept into his thoughts, unwelcome memories of little cruel details he didn't want to think about.

Above everything else, Elliott was clearly unwilling to capitulate. He was determined on a set course, and that course was the punishment and execution of every last living member of Honeybliss. Elliott wanted to put an end to a behemoth that was ruining lives and reveling in it, with no one lifting a finger to stop them.

All he'd wanted was to be heard when no one else would listen and his life was quietly erased, rewritten, destroyed from the ground up. In the end, the real enemy all along had been Honeybliss and every degenerate trash pile that bought its way into their elite club. *They* had been the arrogant ones. *They* had been the ones taking lives carelessly into their hands. Elliott was only doing what no one else would.

Niko couldn't argue with it.

And he couldn't bear to leave Elliott to take them all on, on his own. The idea of standing by while Elliott put his life stubbornly in danger again and again made him feel ill. Niko was more than capable. He had been one of the best hunters in the galaxy, before his hiatus. He was strong, intuitive, and experienced. He could help Elliott survive this. He had once been excited to go toe to toe with Elliott and match their skills. But now he wanted to see what they could do working together instead.

It was crazy to even entertain. But he had already come this far—had already chosen to throw the life he'd known away to be at Elliott's side. To save his life and give him a tomorrow.

Niko had promised Cleo Kestrel he would take care of her brother, an unspoken vow.

He was already headed down a path he could never return from, but this was launching himself straight into freefall. How far down the ground was couldn't be seen.

But wasn't that what he'd always done?

"Elliott," Niko said slowly, looking over at the other man. Elliott still sat tensely, his hands on the table as he stared down at his plate, not looking at Niko. "Let's *do this*. I'm with you."

He had Elliott's attention now.

The other man stared at him, eyes wide and intense, the overhead lights of the cafeteria catching in them. He searched Niko's face, profound shock written in his own expression. He clearly hadn't expected to hear those words. And Niko couldn't blame him—for someone as carefully, deliberately ostracized as Elliott had been, how many years must it have been since someone had told him they were on his side?

Niko reached over, resting his hand atop the other man's. Elliott's hand—tight and rigid with tension—relaxed. He turned it over, grasping Niko's in his own now.

"Elliott, let's set the galaxy on fire."

He had committed himself. There was no going back now—Niko's life was now on a singular trajectory. He was no longer fighting to stop Elliott from killing yet another renowned figure.

He was, instead, going to help him keep doing it.

If Zann didn't hate him before for clocking him out and running away with Elliott Kestrel, he would now. The thought of Zann made Niko's heart tremble, the truths Elliott had reluctantly dragged into the light haunting him. Elliott had gone to Galapol years ago. Galapol knew. Galapol had always known. Zann had admitted he'd known, too.

But how much did he actually know?

Elliott and Niko had showered, changed, and gone back to the so-called Murder Room, where Niko had a suspicion Elliott spent most of his time when he wasn't sleeping, eating, or training. Out of anywhere else in the vast, quiet facility, this room actually felt lived in. Niko envisioned him there alone, working away on a new strategy after yet another wrench had been thrown in his plan, under a sea of sparkling, upbeat love songs delivered over comm speakers, pushing himself until exhaustion and falling asleep there at the table.

"Yuuorta's going to be... Let me remember," Niko said, looking at the grid of portraits. He had gone over his own list enough times to have the next few events and dates memorized by now. "At the Civic Community Center of Egleesa. The, uh, panel on establishing interplanetary relations between new colonies."

"Right," Elliott said, casting him an impressed look that Niko tried not to feel too pleased by.

"I did my homework," Niko said.

"You wouldn't have been able to keep up if you hadn't."

The irony of someone like Yuuorta—a controversial and hideous little Gheroun who had inherited his nepotistic position through his aunt's influence rather than qualifications—playing ambassador between alien nations and worlds while being one of the most grievous offenders in Elliott's collection of videos appalled Niko. There'd been multiple videos of Yuuorta's exploits around the galaxy—the man was so sloppy, he barely even tried to cover up his revolting behavior. It was often swept under the rug or, as Honeybliss had done to Elliott, his victims and their families were discredited, blamed and sullied in the public eye by lawyers and goons of his wealthy aunt—who had died the previous year from issues with her second and third hearts.

Niko felt no qualms sending Yuuorta to a family reunion. Not after the years of worthless destruction the man had wrought. Not after what he'd watched unfold over several clearly captured videos and a dozen more images. Removing Yuuorta permanently from society was doing the galaxy a kindness no one else was making happen.

They discussed the community center building, the schedule of speakers. When Yuuorta was expected to speak. Elliott had all the architectural blueprints. He brought them up on display between the two of them, where they hovered luminous and complex. It was fascinating to Niko to be on the other side, to hear and witness and watch how Elliott worked. He'd had to try to learn Elliott on his own, to guess his next move, his angle and approach. It was fascinating to go over the plans with him as they were made, and together, they came up with a combined approach to get the job done.

Niko suggested using the ventilation shafts to get to a small decorative interior balcony; Elliott agreed. Elliott's stealth tech would handle any drones, and in the case that stealth failed, he had a backup scrambling device that worked on their frequency.

Niko suggested using the few EMP explosives he still had to create a diversion, knock out the lights, and secure them an easy exit.

They both agreed it was vital to utilize earbuds with a private frequency for communicating with each other.

The research and preparation that went into this mark alone was astounding to Niko. Not only had Elliott had to compile a list of events each Honeybliss member would be at, he would have had to research each location, get the blueprints, research the types of security and authorities that would be present. He had to account for changes on his feet as he went, too—the introduction of drones and the ever-increasing swarm of bounty hunters. The diligent presence of Galapol.

"How long have you been planning all of this out?" Niko asked.

Elliott fell quiet, lost in thought before answering. "I first had the idea two and a half years ago after trying to get the files out went nowhere. I committed over a year back."

Before Niko could ask any further, Elliott said, "Let me show you this." He went to another small table that was scattered with various electrical and machine parts and picked up a small device. When he returned, he held it out to Niko.

"So," said Elliott. Niko took the device, turning it over in his hands. It had all the telltale signs of being crafted by hand, wires and scrapped parts visible that were far more function than form. He recognized it as the same thing Zann had worn on Neema. "This is my Ophthalmic Refraction Apparatus."

The words may as well have been Dvaab to Niko, but he could hazard a guess. "So, this is how you go invisible?"

"Yes. I've made a few, because they keep getting fried."

"How does it work? Show me."

"There's a switch here— Yes," Elliott said as Niko fumbled around with the device, trying to learn it on his own. The moment his thumb hit the small switch, an odd sensation vibrated through the air and Niko watched as his own hands and body disappeared before him, leaving only a bent visual distortion to silhouette him. He waved his arms, gazing right through his own hand at the wall beyond in fascination. He was marginally easier to see in movement, and all but disappeared when he was still.

Niko was *delighted*.

"This. This is great. I could get into so much trouble with this thing."

He glanced up, watching Elliott attempt to fight off a stubbornly persistent twitch of the lips. His eyes smiled, though. He looked pleased with himself and Niko loved it.

"You'll get plenty of chances for that."

"Wait, I get to *use* this too? Out in the field?" Niko heard his voice pitch higher in excitement. He felt like a child again, giddy with a new toy he was about to inevitably go on a rampage with.

"Do you like it? I designed it myself. The shield generator too."

"Of course you did," Niko said. "Yeah, Elliott. I like it a lot. That's an understatement. Though it made you a real pain in the ass."

"Good. Then it's doing its job."

Niko flipped the switch on and off, again and again, blinking in and out of existence like a human strobe light. Elliott emitted an offended hiss.

"You're going to break it. Stop."

Niko grinned, but relented, setting the ORA on the counter.

Elliott let him test out the shield next, which Niko *really* got excited for, giving a boisterous whoop when it activated. "God, if I'd had this back when I was hunting regularly—"

"You don't need it now," Elliott said. "You have the suit. It's bulletproof."

Niko looked up at him. "I'll be your personal bodyguard. Your shield. Nobody will get through to you anymore."

Elliott swallowed, eyeing him up and down. "That's hot, Niko. My own bodyguard."

"I aim to please." Niko grinned, though it faded as he thought of the severity of the real danger that lurked ahead of them. "You're going to need the protection now. Every kill you make drives the bounty higher, brings out more ruthless hunters and mercs, sets governments' and Galapol's gazes on your every move."

Elliott glanced around in thought. "I'm surprised they haven't canceled it, actually. The panel."

Niko thought about that. It would have been the easiest course of action—to cancel events for every Honeybliss member in Elliott's data.

Can't cancel events forever, Niko, Zann had told him at the beginning of all this.

"I think," Niko said, "they're pushing the offensive instead. Building a trap. They can cancel every event on here but they know you'll still come for everyone who remains on the list. Like Jande Seiiren. Best to get it over with quick than draw it out and try to constantly anticipate when and where you'll show up."

"Niko," Elliott said, "no matter what happens from here on out, I'm grateful to you."

"I wish I'd listened sooner," Niko said. "Instead of making it harder for you."

Elliott shrugged. "I'm just glad that you're here."

CHAPTER SIXTEEN
LEGEND

"So, the only problem," Niko said, "is that this suit is loud as hell." He looked with trepidation at the external ventilation entrance. Elliott—like Niko—was safely hidden away by their ORA stealth cloak, but Niko could feel the other man's stare boring through him.

Niko shrugged. "Hey, sneaking around isn't usually my style."

"I know," Elliott said. "You're very loud. And *present*."

"It's never been a problem until now."

"Well, we'll just have to be careful. Move slowly through here and try not to knock against the sides."

Easier said than done.

Elliott had cut a hole big enough for them to slip through its grate with what looked like a small, ultra-heated laser of some kind. It was another of his many homemade inventions that Niko found grudgingly convenient.

Once they were inside, Niko did his best to maneuver through the vast, corrugated metal pipe that formed the ventilation shaft into the back of Egleesa's Civic Community Center. His metal boots knocked hard against the floor beneath him with each careful step though, the *clank, clank* echoing around the tunnel like a hammer on steroids. Elliott stopped walking, a fact Niko only discovered when he slammed straight into the back of him and nearly knocked them both on their asses.

"*Niko,*" Elliott hissed. "Are you even trying?"

"You try walking in this fucking thing. And tell me when you're going to just *stop* like that, because I can't see you."

"You should have worn slippers instead of those boots."

"The neurotech doesn't work without the boots attached."

"Then we should have taped cloth to your boots before we did this."

"It's not that loud," Niko insisted.

"It's that loud."

They made it—somehow—to the great fan at the center of the tunnel. It was huge, so large it rotated slowly enough to leave brief second-long gaps between the sweep of each blade.

Niko would have preferred a much more direct approach—blocking the fan, disabling it with an EMP. But Elliott insisted even a brief interruption of it would trigger a notification to whomever was tasked with manning the quiet background systems of the building—a risk they couldn't afford.

So they, instead, would have to rely on timing and swiftness.

Niko groaned.

Elliott went first, helping himself. Niko saw his outline pause before the gargantuan metal blades, then slip through the brief gap with ease. He released the breath he hadn't realized he was holding, his shoulders sagging in relief that he wasn't about to witness Elliott end up as long division.

Then they tensed all over again when he realized it was his turn.

"Niko. Come on," Elliott whispered.

Niko hesitated. The suit *might* save him from the massive pressure of what must be at least a ton of sharp-edged metal. But it wouldn't be pretty.

The more he thought about it, the worse it was. So, he did what he did best, and stopped thinking. Niko watched the fan blades and the moment the next gap came around, he swiftly leapt through.

And lived.

When they reached the decorative interior balcony that circled above the event stages, Niko's heart sank. This was time for the part of the plan he liked least of all. It had been one thing to discuss it in theory; it was a whole other experience to be about to follow it through in-person.

"I'm going to make my way down and start planting the EMPs," Elliott murmured. Niko's heart panged at the idea. He found he very much disliked letting Elliott go off on his own now, where Niko couldn't help him if anything went south.

He swallowed the stubborn displeasure and unease that were tying a knot inside him. "Where's your hand?"

"Right here."

"Where's 'right here?'"

A moment later, he felt Elliott's hand gracelessly knock against his armor as he grasped through the air for Niko.

We might need to work out the kinks in this stealth thing.

"Here," Niko said, and handed over the EMP grenades. "Elliott—"

"Yes, Niko?"

"I know Galapol, and I know they're going to go all out on this. So just... be careful. Don't take any risks you don't need to, and get back here quickly. I can't help you when we're that far apart."

Niko almost didn't feel it beneath the armor, but a hand grasped around at his waist, awkward and searching, before landing home. Elliott's arm snaked around him.

"I'll be back in no time," he said.

And then he was gone. It was almost difficult to tell, since Niko couldn't see him. But he *felt* Elliott's absence, like a dull ache. He felt the loss of his arm around him, even if it had only come as a vague sensation of pressure through the suit.

Niko waited, casting his gaze at the sea of people below. Security drones hovered around the vicinity, one sweeping so close to Niko that he had to lean back to avoid it grazing his face. The thing paid him no mind, though, continuing to hover on to somewhere else. Niko briefly missed T1-N4 and the way she'd perpetually floated through his apartment, not so differently from these drones.

"Place is crawling with Galapol," Elliott whispered through Niko's earpiece. *"You called it."*

"Be careful," Niko murmured. Unease wormed through his body as he looked down at the mingling, watchful crowd below. It was swarmed with Galapol agents. Niko imagined Zann out there somewhere, bitter and betrayed, looking for Niko the way Niko had spent the last months looking for Elliott. It made his throat tighten.

"Moving to east wing to plant the EMP," Elliott said over their frequency.

"Just— Be careful, Elliott," Niko said. He was repeating himself now, going in circles from anxiety. His chest and limbs were tight. The idea of Elliott being discovered was unbearable to him. Niko had to restrain himself from breaking from their plan and making his way to the other man. He wanted to shield him from any harm that might come his way. Instead, he was useless, stuck here. Niko exhaled slowly, trying to settle the electric sea of roiling nerves within him.

Elliott was an expert in subterfuge and stealth. How many times had he outwitted Galapol—and Niko—at these events before? Yet Niko was antsy, ridiculous. Wanting to hide him away, protect him.

He couldn't help it. Elliott was profoundly capable, but if Niko had his way, he'd take over and do the rest of the missions himself while Elliott stayed back at the facility, if it meant knowing the other man was out of harm's way.

He figured admitting that out loud wouldn't earn him Elliott's high opinion, though.

He had to trust in Elliott's capability. Niko was used to doing things himself, taking on the danger, the pain. It was agony to stand back and let Elliott work solo, out there slipping in and out between the crevices among a sea of hypervigilant Galapol and undoubtedly twice as many bounty hunters.

Niko looked out at the panels going on, among the center of swirling activity. Yuuorta was due to speak soon. Politicians, ambassadors, and activists mingled together on stage to discuss policy.

He had become all too used to these sorts of big events lately. But this was the first time he was here *with* Elliott, on the other side of things. This time, he was working with the very man that he'd been hunting. And the man—Ambassador Yuuorta—who he would typically protect was now the hunted.

Context made a hell of a difference, it seemed.

Now, if they could just get everyone else to see the same context Niko had been given.

"Elliott?" Niko murmured. Another drone floated right past him and he found himself going stiff, holding his breath, but just like the first, it paid him no attention. Neither did the crowds below, nor the scattering of Galapol agents whose wary gazes swept the very balcony on which he stood. He was, truly, invisible before a crowd of thousands. This wasn't how he normally worked, but Niko would make the best of it.

"Here. Moving to the north wing for the second plant."

Another two agonizing moments of silence passed before Elliott's voice filled his ears again. *"Moving back to you now. ETA five minutes, if nothing comes up."*

If nothing comes up. The words were so innocuous, but they made Niko's skin crawl at the implications. Anything could happen now. He wondered if Elliott was feeling the same nervousness, the same adrenaline-driven tension he felt. If the other man was, he did a phenomenal job of not showing it. His calm demeanor was somehow both reassuring and infuriating.

Niko checked the time, squinting hard as he held his wrist display almost up against his eyeballs. Pale numbers barely showed through his stealth, indicating three minutes had passed.

Then four.

Five.

Six.

"Elliott?"

Seven minutes.

Niko had never been great at waiting around, at simply anticipating results. Patience wasn't his personal virtue. He debated again trying to intercept Elliott. Below, Yuuorta was already maneuvering onto the stage to wide applause. Elliott was nowhere in sight, his end of the line dead. Niko's pulse began hammering.

"Ell—"

"Behind you."

Niko spun, gun raised reflexively. The slender outline of Elliott stood behind him, subtly distorting the scenery. Niko hadn't even heard him approach. He let out a long breath as he lowered the rifle again.

"Do not fucking do that again unless you really want to be shot."

He heard the smile in Elliott's voice. "You haven't managed to do it yet. Even when it was intentional."

"Yeah, well, let's keep it that way. What took you? It's been almost eight minutes."

"It's hot right now. I had to take the long way around. And I couldn't respond because I had to keep quiet."

"Had me worried," Niko murmured.

Elliott was quiet for a moment before speaking. His tone was lighter, a tinge warmer. Fond, even. "I know what I'm doing, Niko. This isn't my first time."

It *was* Niko's, though. He knew he should relinquish his possessive, protective anxieties. He knew that Elliott had done this countless times now. Niko had been his biggest challenge before. But he couldn't help it—the idea of Elliott being hurt drove him senseless.

"He's on stage now," Niko said, craning his neck to look down at Yuuorta. The man was so pompous and arrogant, with what were clearly tentacle implants and filler. He had a particularly slimy smile that Niko hated. Image after image of Yuuorta's violations and hedonistic escapades at the cost of others filled his mind as he stared at that smile. He wanted to wipe it off the ambassador's face.

Elliott moved to Niko's side, peering down at Yuuorta in quiet contemplation. "Disgusting creature, isn't he? You watched the videos, didn't you?"

Niko wished he hadn't. The things he saw there stuck with him in the quiet moments between distractions. He figured they probably always would, to some extent. Everything in Elliott's files was darkly and maliciously haunted. "Yeah, I saw them all."

"Well, let's not keep him waiting," Elliott said after a moment. He picked up the sniper rifle and switched off the safety, which Niko caught in glimpses of distorted surroundings and through sounds.

"Hey," Niko said. "No matter what happens from here on out, I have your back now."

"Niko." It was there again, that wash of warmth in his voice. "Did you ever stop to think I have yours too?"

"I know, babe."

Below, another round of applause erupted as Yuuorta began talking, tentacles wrapped partially around the podium. He cracked an icebreaker joke that made Niko want to punch him in those over-plumped tentacles.

Niko thought all of it would feel different. It was strange, of course, to be on the other side of things now, with Galapol as his enemy. But in many ways, he was only doing exactly what he'd always done. Yuuorta was a monster and, together with Elliott, Niko was cleaning the galaxy of him. They were stopping him from being able to hurt and torment and kill behind closed doors ever again. They were protecting the vulnerable, taking up the mantle that Galapol had let slip. He thought he would feel more guilt, more uncertainty.

But he didn't. Just like with Giannis Alexopoulos.

And it felt, in many ways, great to be here, at Elliott's side. It was an honor to be so trusted by him, and let into his world. The man so many—including himself, once—perceived as coldly evil was giving all that he had to bring a desperate justice and end to what the proper channels and authorities had failed to. Niko couldn't fault him for it. Even Galapol, the galaxy's established protectors, created by a banding together of every known sentient species working for a better society for all, had chosen to turn away from this.

So, Elliott and Niko were taking it into their own hands.

"Will you do the honors, lover?" Elliott asked. It took a moment for Niko to realize he was holding out the small kill switch that would activate all his painstakingly placed EMPs. Niko had watched him work on the device, carefully threading a wire through the pins on each grenade that would be triggered to pull them free at the flip of a switch. It was like dark magic woven in an esoteric language of machine parts, wires, and delicate computer chips—fascinating to Niko, but ultimately confounding.

He took it carefully.

"Gladly."

Niko could see his shape move into a crouch as he cradled the sniper rifle against his shoulder and lined up his shot. It was fascinating to be here, to see him work his art. His form went so still that Niko couldn't see him at all anymore; he heard a slow, calm, exhalation of breath. He found himself holding his breath along with Elliott.

A single shot fired. It was quick, the sound thundering through the building. Yuuorta stood for a moment at the podium, clinging to it with his plump tentacles. Then he simply slid down it, knocking it clear over as he fell against it. He lay there on the floor, dead, teal blood pooling beneath him. It was beautifully, perfectly done. The shot was so clean that it was merciful in comparison to the sorts of violence Yuuorta had enacted on his victims before they succumbed.

He would never hurt anyone again.

The crowd below began to freeze, then frenzy in panic as Niko had become used to seeing. He flipped the switch and the planted EMPs erupted at once, their shockwaves knocking the power out as the building sank into only the dim emergency light of backup generators. None had been close enough to affect his suit, thankfully. He could hear the confusion and fear from the audience below, his only regret in this. Niko wished he could show them why they were doing this, why they had resorted to these measures. He wished he could explain that civilians were in no danger from himself nor Elliott.

Elliott was already up. "Let's go."

Niko wasted no time. They grabbed their things and left. Niko kept close to him, trying not to accidentally step on the backs of the other man's feet. It was hard to tell exactly where Elliott was, given the cloaking.

They swiftly made their way back through the ventilation tunnel, their route quick and easy now that the fans had been shut down in the loss of power. Thirty more yards and they would be out.

The tunnel shook around them, rocked by an explosion that burst bright and loud right up against Elliott's energy shield. Niko grabbed for him instinctively and held him tight to himself. The impact was enough to knock them out of stealth though, and he could see the shield glitching as it faltered.

"Fuck," Elliott hissed. He looked nervous and annoyed, scowling down the tunnel at four silhouetted figures who now stood blocking the exit. "Not again."

Those words made Niko do a double take, but he didn't have the time to pause. He trained his gun on them.

"Get behind me," he commanded, pulling Elliott back before the man had a chance to protest. Only a second later, bullets ricocheted down the tunnel their way, pinging and scattering in every direction. Niko crouched and held his arm over his face to shield it.

He could feel the bullets as they hit his wrist, chest, and legs. He could feel Elliott behind him, making himself compact as he pressed up tight against Niko's back. Another explosion rocked the tunnel, falling just short of them this time.

He had a feeling this wasn't Galapol, nor security. The sloppy nature, combined with the careless use of explosives suggested other hunters. But Galapol would be there soon enough—the explosions were sure to draw attention.

Niko hated doing it, but they had no choice. He had to get Elliott out of there or they would be swarmed. They'd bought themselves precious minutes with the EMPs and confusion they sowed, but the hunters were going to stall them.

The second their bullets stopped and they were forced to reload, Niko seized the moment and opened fire. Elliott lined up a shot over Niko's shoulder, and he saw one of their silhouettes fall.

Another explosion made the tunnel shudder, this time too close. Niko could feel the scorching heat against his skin, the roaring sound of it leaving an intense, whining ring in his ears. He had to close the distance or the next was going to hit.

"We're going to do something a little crazy, Elliott," he said. "On the count of three, we're going to rush them."

"Wait— I'm sorry, rush? As in, *towards* them?"

"You got it."

"Niko, I don't think—"

"Three. Two. One. *Go!*"

Niko sprang up and burst into a run, hard and fast as he could. It was exhilarating, despite the insanity of it. For a moment he felt weightless, boundless, like he was a high school boy playing football again. He could hear Elliott's footfalls behind him as the man kept close. At least he hadn't abandoned Niko to his crazy act alone. Elliott was, it seemed, truly ride or die.

Niko appreciated that.

They never expected it when he charged. Almost every time. He could see the shock on the man's face—a particularly short and haggard Dvaab, covered in faded tattoos—as Niko came barreling down the tunnel towards him, and he scrambled to shoot Niko. The bullets pinged off his armor uselessly.

"Oh sh—"

Niko body-slammed him to the ground, then knocked the guy clean out as he grabbed him by the neck and gave him a good secondary knock against the floor.

"Beastly," he heard Elliott marvel. "But effective."

Niko was up again instantly, crashing into the other nearest hunter as he threw his armored weight fully into her. The human woman pulled a knife which she tried to drive desperately towards his face. He overpowered her instantly, wrenching her arm back and knocking her out too with a solid *thunk* against the curved tunnel wall.

Elliott took aim for the remaining hunter, his bullet ricocheting uselessly off the man's armor. Niko looked towards the hunter, ready to destroy him, and paused, blinking.

"Wh— Legend? *The Legend?*"

"What?" Elliott said.

The old man—human, in an armored suit of his own, his front teeth missing and with tattoos all along the right side of his olive-toned face—wheezed a laugh. "The very one and only. Now, if it ain't Killjoy. Been a while, kiddo."

"You know this man?" Elliott mumbled.

"I—" Niko paused, a temporary truce between them. "You retired. You've been retired for years."

The Legend chuckled. "I heard you was retired too. A special somebody brought me back." He gestured towards Elliott with the barrel of his gun.

Niko frowned. "Uh, yeah, me too."

"His bounty was worth dippin' my toes back in for. 'Sides, I missed it. No good sittin' around, just twiddlin' my thumbs."

Niko winced. The Legend was, well, a legendary hunter who'd brought in more bounties than any other in recorded history. Niko had met him several times before, had even shared drinks with him in an old and shady black market bar as the man traded stories until they were both too drunk to stand. He'd even gotten some pointers from him, when he was green and new to hunting.

He didn't have the heart to hurt—or kill—the guy. "I don't want to do this," Niko said slowly.

"I do," said Elliott. "We need to go."

"You know how this goes. Business is business, kid. Ain't nothin' personal," the Legend said.

Niko knew that. But he hated it. There was no way around it—old bounty hunters like the Legend were full of pride and honor.

He couldn't be talked down, and offering an alternative or consolation prize to that glorious bounty would only bring insult.

The alternative meant having to kick an old man's ass.

Elliott was clearly growing exasperated. "Can you just... run at him? Do your thing?"

Niko suppressed a groan. The Legend was ancient by now. This would be like giving someone's great-grandpa a full-on linebacker tackle. But Elliott was right. They were running out of time, and needed to move.

Their brief truce was over, the Legend opening fire on Elliott. Niko was in his way instantly, soaking up the hits with his armor. If Zann didn't hate his miserable guts until the heat death of the universe now, Niko would have to thank him for the suit.

He surged forward, straight into the Legend's gunfire.

"Hey, I taught you that move—"

Niko body-slammed the old man with a silent apology. The Legend went down with a wheeze as all the air was knocked out of his lungs. "Holy shit, kid, you're heavy," he choked out.

"It's over. We're going now," Niko said, pulling his weight off the senior citizen he'd just undoubtedly sent to chiropractic hell.

"You can't just leave. At least kill me first," the Legend said.

"Wh-what? No. Nobody's killing anybody here."

"You bested me. I ain't what I used to be. I wanted so badly to be. Thought I could do it, still. So just do me the honor and put me out of my shame."

"No," Niko said. He seized the Legend's gun and tossed it out of reach. The Legend had truly been an unrivaled hunter once, before

Niko had come into his prime, but time had clearly won the long battle against him. Niko almost wished they could have a fairer fight, but now wasn't the time. "I'm not going to kill you. Just— Come back later and we can do it again."

"You're serious," Elliott marveled.

Niko stood and held a hand down to the old man, but he refused it, slapping his hand away. "You may as well have killed me. Never lost a bounty before. I ain't worth shit now."

"Just—" Niko hesitated. "Just be careful. Go see a doctor. That can't have been good for you."

"Piss off," the Legend said.

Niko glanced back at Elliott and they continued towards the exit, hurriedly stepping over the unconscious bodies of the other hunters they'd downed. Niko could hear voices in the background, likely Galapol catching up.

Elliott gave an awkward glance towards the Legend before stepping over him too. "I'd say it's a pleasure to meet you, but it's not."

"You can especially piss off, asshole," the Legend said.

They slipped out the grate and back to the *Soñadora*, no other obstacles in their way.

CHAPTER SEVENTEEN
GOOD FOR YOU

Once they'd cleared Egleesa's atmosphere and were safely on their way back to the ice moon, Niko winced, holding his gloved hand over his face. "I seriously just annihilated somebody's granddad. That was the guy who *taught* me to rush people."

Elliott laughed. His smile was reminiscent of the old photographs Niko loved from his case files—briefly unburdened by gravity, luminous as the stars—taken before Elliott's life had ever fallen apart. He had a way of tilting his head back and closing his eyes when something really amused him.

Niko felt himself grinning too. It felt good—no, *fucking great*—to have gone into the fray alongside Elliott Kestrel, against all of Galapol and the galaxy's best hunters and win the day. They got a clean shot on Yuuorta, and the sadist would never hurt another person again.

And Elliott—

Elliott was *radiant*. Handsome and untethered. His movements were loose and easy, his face carrying a sly little pleased smile.

He seemed genuinely happy. Niko wanted to kiss that smile up, to taste the lips that framed it.

"We did it," Elliott said.

Niko held his hand up. "High five."

Elliott leaned languorously against the wall, peering over at him, his eyebrows rising. "Are you serious?"

"Do it. Come on."

"You're a dork." Elliott relented, though, slapping his hand hard into Niko's, the gesture making his smile widen, despite his teasing. "I see there's a certain type drawn to bounty hunting. Maybe when the Legend dies, you can rename yourself that."

"You're the real legend here. I'm just a converted fanboy."

"You're my fanboy?"

"Hey. We're a team now. So, we should have a cool name too, to reflect that."

"Like what?"

"How about Starhawk?" Niko asked.

Elliott frowned. "Why Starhawk?"

"Well, Estrella means 'star' in Galactic Standard. And Kestrel—"

"Is a falcon, not a hawk."

Niko grinned. "It's close enough. Predatory bird."

"It's not the same thing."

"Come on, Elliott. It sounds so cool."

Elliott shook his head and laughed again. Niko could lap up his laughter. He could live off the sound alone.

He stepped closer, looming down now over Elliott as he slumped back against the wall. It felt good to look down at him instead of up for once. "Come on, Elliott."

Elliott peered up at him, eyes searching. "I'll consider it. You're still a dork, though."

"And you're hot as fuck," Niko said. "You want to know something stupid? The first time I saw your face on Vhesa, I forgot what I was even supposed to be doing. You were that offensively gorgeous."

"You want to know what else is stupid? I felt the same way when I finally saw yours on Uula."

"Mmh, I remember that going a little differently. I remember you throat-punching me and running away. Wasn't great for my self-esteem."

Elliott grinned. "Well, I didn't want to die either. So there was that."

"You were so fucking phenomenal tonight, Elliott. You always are. It was thrilling getting to see you work," Niko murmured. His voice turned low, wilderness clawing at the edges of his words. "It made me really want you." He had Elliott's full attention now, the other man's smile gone, something else there now, darkly watchful and hungry.

"It was *thrilling,*" said Elliott, throwing the word back at him, "getting to see you toss everyone around like they weighed nothing. You went a little feral."

"I can't help it," Niko said. "When you're threatened, I go a little feral."

He backed Elliott against the wall, pinning him there under his own weight. Elliott gave a small gasp. Niko closed the narrow gap between them, his lips meeting the heat of Elliott's as they parted, permitting, inviting.

Niko wanted it bad, wanted to take him, to turn him over and pump him full right there against the wall, standing. The idea made him feverish, made him hot. He couldn't keep himself off Elliott, and his desire was fully reciprocated at every step, Elliott kissing him, reaching up to grasp a tight fistful of hair.

It didn't go as Niko usually tended to do things.

This time, Elliott pushed back against him, planting his own hungry, dominating kisses on Niko's mouth. Before Niko realized it, Elliott had driven him back against the bunk bed compartment, the mattress hitting the backs of his legs. He fell back onto it, looking up at the other man.

Elliott loomed over him before crawling forward onto the bed, one knee beside Niko. He continued his insatiable kisses, hands moving exactly where they needed to be, unfastening the pieces of Niko's suit snap by snap. He stripped them off Niko and set them aside, never once letting up on trying to devour him.

It left Niko lightheaded. He loved being so wanted, so desired. He ran his hands over Elliott, sliding them up under his shirt, along the bare skin there.

He saw the straining, voracious bulge in Elliott's tight pants, felt it push against his stomach as the other man leaned against him. It was delicious. Niko wanted him, wholly, vivid memories of their last time together resurfacing. He wanted it again, wanted to make it last longer for him this time. He—

"I want to be inside you," Elliott purred in his ear. "I bet you feel so fucking good, Niko."

Niko's breath caught in his chest, his body seizing up as a wave of trepidation spread through him.

Elliott sensed it and paused. He leaned back, giving Niko a few inches of space, and reached up to cup his face in his hands. He looked at Niko searchingly, breathtaking eyes of dusty green full of concern.

"Is that alright? Do you like that?"

"I—" Niko hesitated.

It was always that way. He'd let himself bottom before, a few times in his early twenties, but had never been able to enjoy it. Not nearly so much as he'd enjoyed topping. Niko liked to control the situation, to be the one to fuck into his lovers, to pleasure them. Any other way made him feel inexplicably insecure and nervous. He wasn't used to giving others that sort of power over him.

Normally his answer would be easy. But—

Something about Elliott was different. Niko's face flushed, his heart racing at the memory of what he'd requested Elliott do to finish himself off during their previous lovemaking. He was shocked at himself that he'd even asked. The memory of it left him achingly hard now; he could feel himself dripping.

He remembered the shifting fantasy he'd had of Elliott after the picture had gotten under his skin. The way Elliott had felt in his mind. It was where his thoughts had all driven towards, in a single direction. It had been the destination. The very thought of it made him feel faint, made it hard to swallow. It was that good.

And it was hard to refuse Elliott when he'd... well, worded it like that.

Fast rising hunger warred with nebulous anxiety inside him, until finally Niko nodded his consent. "Yeah. I—I want you to."

Elliott stroked his cheek. The tenderness and warmth of it made Niko want to melt into him. Some of his strange anxiety quieted.

"You're sure?"

"Yeah. I'm sure."

Elliott leaned in and kissed him again, slowly this time, passionate. Niko felt some of the tension relinquish its tight hold on his shoulders as he leaned into Elliott, returning his kisses.

"I'll make it good for you," Elliott whispered. Goosebumps prickled along Niko's skin in thrilling anticipation, which was now beginning to win out over his nerves.

He wanted this. Maybe he had all along.

Elliott pulled Niko's shirt off, then his own. His gunshot wounds were looking much better now, thanks to the expedited healing of the RapiGel, ruddy and scarred patches of skin all that signaled where deep injuries had once been. "Lay down, lover," he said.

Niko obliged, lying on his back with an anxious swallow. Elliott reached up and unfastened Niko's pants, then carefully removed them.

He took his time. He helped himself to a handful of Niko's own bulge beneath his boxers, giving a gentle squeeze that made Niko's breath catch in his throat. Then he pulled the boxers off, Niko's length springing free. Elliott didn't touch him there again though yet, instead trailing his fingertips down Niko's sides, his hips, his legs. The touch transitioned from fully felt to mere faint electric pinpricks as his fingers traveled.

Elliott tilted his head, eyes roaming the length of Niko's body. He studied him like he was a fascinating gallery piece on display. Like he was something beautiful. Niko felt his cheeks and chest flush with heat at being looked at like this. Then Elliott took hold of Niko's leg and lifted it. He merely held it, exploring with his hands, the touches gentle, worshipful even. He looked at Niko with a mixture of affection and awe, then bent his head forward to kiss his scarred and tattooed knee with such tenderness that Niko's throat nearly closed up with a pang of emotion.

Niko couldn't feel any of it. But the sight of Elliott as he held his cheek against Niko's leg, eyes closed, before trailing more long, sensual kisses along it made him hurt in a profound way.

He'd spent so long stuck in a complex shame about himself and the image of his body. Particularly his legs. To see Elliott giving such attention—such *love*—to the part of Niko he'd wanted to ignore or throw away made it hard to breathe.

If Niko had felt deeply for him before, it crossed into something wild and fierce now. Something with wings that beat in time to his human heart.

"I—"

"Are you alright, Niko? Do you want me to stop?"

"No. No. I— Just." It was hard to speak. "Thank you."

"For what?"

"I don't know."

"You're so beautiful, Niko. I've never seen someone so beautiful as you."

Niko had to look away. He had always worn his emotions on his sleeve, and they were threatening to surface now when he didn't want them to. He wanted to enjoy this moment, here with Elliott, about to get fucked by him. About to be made love to by him. He didn't want to let himself fall apart.

He wanted to hold onto Elliott and never let go.

Elliott set his leg back down, then briefly stepped off to rifle through Niko's duffel bag which sat on the counter. Once he found the small bottle of lubrication, he returned, quickly undoing and shaking off his own pants, then underwear. He stood handsome and bare now. Niko would never tire of seeing it. He loved every part of Elliott.

Elliott rubbed himself with lube, then moved between Niko's legs. He lifted one again, bending it at the knee, getting access to all of Niko now. Niko swallowed again in anticipation of the touch he was about to administer. Elliott planted another slow, soft kiss against his knee before taking his hand and rubbing lube onto Niko's entrance.

It felt good—and strange, and alarming—to be touched there like that. Elliott rubbed him, then pushed a finger in.

Or tried.

"Niko, I'm going to need more than that. You need to relax."

It was easier said than done. Niko inhaled slowly, then let out a long breath, willing himself to relax, to yield to the other man's touch which he wanted so badly. Elliott gently let go of the leg he was holding and brushed his hand against Niko's erection, then took hold of him and began to stroke him. His touch drew a small sound from Niko's throat, and he relented a little until Elliott loosened him up. He did that for a few moments, until he apparently felt Niko was ready, pulling his hand away.

Niko's pulse hammered in his throat as Elliott climbed onto the bed and positioned himself between his legs. The other man took himself in hand and pushed against Niko.

And went nowhere—again.

"Niko," Elliott murmured, pausing again to run his hand along Niko's chest. He took his hand and held it. "Relax. Let me in."

Niko mumbled an apology, letting out another exhale, then tried to force himself to calm back down.

They waited a moment, then Elliott tried again. Little by little he entered Niko, slowly, pausing frequently to allow him to get used to it. It felt—

It hurt. But it felt fucking phenomenal, too.

Elliott gave him a moment once he was fully in. Niko could feel him, feel every inch, feel the heat and the hardness of him. He loved it in a way he didn't think he ever could. He liked it even more than their first time.

Elliott bent forward to kiss him, long and slow, passionate, but Niko was having none of that now—he pleaded wordlessly to Elliott with his own starving kisses, his hands roaming the other man's body, running through his hair, touching him everywhere.

Elliott smiled against him, then took Niko's legs gently in hand, holding them to give himself access. He started moving, slowly, pulling out, then pushing deeply into him again. Niko felt full with him, like a part of himself had been missing all along and only now was whole again.

Elliott moved in him, slowly, a delicious rhythm, gentle and considerate.

"Elliott," Niko said, his voice emerging drunk sounding with desire. "I want—"

"What do you want, Niko?" Elliott murmured.

Niko wasn't used to begging. "I want more. Give it to me. Please. Just— Fuck me hard."

"If that's how you like it," Elliott said, his own voice lush and dark in a way that told Niko he liked it that way too. He obliged, his thrusts becoming harder, faster, until he was railing Niko relentlessly, his whole body rocking as Elliott met him again and again. Niko wrapped his arms around him and held him, his hands on Elliott's back, feeling every muscle as they worked and strained. His fingertips trailed the old hook-shaped scar there. Niko met him tongue against tongue, the secondary penetration into the other man's mouth making him dizzy.

Niko made himself endure it all, this time. He *forced* himself not to give in too early to the pleasure that ravaged him like a sultry fire, though Elliott made every cell in him feel aflame. It was everything he could do to barely keep himself together.

"Harder, Elliott," Niko begged. "I want to feel you days from now."

Soft sounds escaped Elliott, betraying his own heady indulgence of Niko and what they were sharing. Knowing his lover was so enjoying himself in him sent a rippling chill of pleasure through Niko. It was almost enough to send him over the edge, but he fought it.

Elliott came first, giving Niko a brief thrill of triumph. He felt the other man spill hot into him with an agonized moan. Elliott dug his fingertips in him, clinging hard but unfelt to Niko's legs as he lost himself. Then he slid out, not missing a beat, moving to take Niko in his mouth.

"Mmm," he hummed as he licked Niko's cock. "Niko, I don't know what you do to me."

The feeling was mutual.

Niko came shortly after, finally letting himself succumb to Elliott's warm, wet mouth. The other man swallowed, his Adam's apple shifting as he did. He wiped at his lips, then cleaned them both up before crawling across the bunk and collapsing beside Niko.

Niko pulled him into a tight hug, burying his face in Elliott's hair.

He felt warm. He felt alive. He felt resplendent in a way he couldn't remember.

His emotions sat tangled and heavy and burning bright in his chest: appreciation, affection, need. Companionship, belonging—

"Niko. I really, really like you," Elliott said. "I don't know how I got so lucky."

An even deeper warmth, all golden honey, spread thick through Niko's chest. "Combination of shield generator and me being a piss-poor shot," he joked. "At some point I had no choice but to give up shooting and just listen instead."

Elliott smiled. It was wide, sincere, unburdened, his eyes squinting in a way that Niko knew would leave crinkles at the corners one day, when he was an older man. The thought made him smile too.

"Thank you for being here," Elliott said. "This— It feels different now."

"We're a team now," Niko said. "You're not alone anymore. I'll be here."

Elliott's smile grew. "Niko. Was it... alright?"

"Yeah, babe. It was great."

"You're sure?"

"I'm pretty fucking sure, Elliott. I can't fake things like that." Nor did he want to. Niko couldn't bear to live inauthentically—for all his flaws, he knew he could rest easy one day, knowing he had never pretended to be anything but himself.

Elliott planted another lingering, wet kiss on his collarbone. "You were incredible. You felt so good. I loved fucking you. I love— I love being with you."

"It's mutual, Elliott."

The light of what they shared permeated even the ice moon facility, where even the plain gray walls and too-empty corridors couldn't stifle it. Niko was happy. Elliott seemed relieved. He joked and smiled.

The days passed by, luminous, even in the moon's eternal dark.

Elliott showed him how to use the sniper rifle at the makeshift shooting range, putting Niko to shame when it became competitive. Niko distracted him with hungry kisses and seeking hands.

Niko invented new meals from the meager range of foods Elliott had, some being a little more disastrous than others. But Elliott was a good sport—or didn't want to waste the limited resources available to them—and ate it all anyway.

He introduced Elliott to the fine artistry of Royce RG, which he blared loudly over the facility's speakers and out into the desolate icy night of RM-9832642G. It made Elliott groan, but Niko caught him mumbling some of the lyrics to himself in the kitchen—and Niko found himself doing the same with the annoyingly saccharine songs of Hayura and Kuliedi Taan. They were growing on him now, and almost gave him a strange nostalgia. He couldn't hear their music without thinking about Elliott now.

They made bets on what their collective bounties must have reached by now and discussed what they would spend the money on if they turned each other in—Niko's idea being to use the money to bail Elliott out again, and Elliott saying he'd take a vacation to the beaches of Eanan.

Niko's birthday came and passed; he would have forgotten it completely, but Elliott surprised him with a sweetly-made but hor-rific-tasting cake he'd engineered from the scarce food supplies they possessed.

Their work continued on for two more successful kills: Jori Tauldaath and Kunathad, absolutely nothing of value lost in the galaxy with either of their deaths. Niko made it a habit to witness their files before embarking on each kill. He wanted the reminder of what these people did, wanted to see again for himself the horrific reality they hid behind prestige and shining public image. Together with Elliott, they were cleaning up the galaxy and giving it a better future, cutting a tumor free.

He and Elliott worked well side by side—more efficiently, even, than when Elliott had worked alone. Niko acted as his bodyguard and bulwark, ready to defend him at a moment's notice. They got out quickly and quietly, not needing to fight either time.

Niko found working with him thrilling.

As the morning of the next event came up, however, Elliott had begun to retreat back into quietude again, some of that luminous high dissipating from him. Niko found him looking out the thick windows of a quiet, empty lounge. He stared out into the unchanging, empty night, his pale reflection peering back at him, earbuds in his ears. Niko could hear the soft music even from feet away.

Elliott startled when he realized Niko was there, pulling the earbuds out. He turned the music off, the room filling with silence. Niko wrapped his arm around Elliott's waist and Elliott leaned into the touch.

"Hey, babe. Something on your mind?"

"Mmh," Elliott acknowledged. Niko thought that was the only answer he was going to get, until Elliott finally spoke again. "Duuru Orkan."

"Yeah?" Niko looked up at him. "He's next."

"He is." Elliott looked unwell.

Something clicked in Niko's memory. "Wait— Isn't he—?"

"Uru Taal's son." Elliott craned his neck to look down at him.

Niko blinked. He'd completely forgotten the two massive Toliai were related, both in succession to the throne of Thoro.

"He grew up to be just as much a disgusting worm as his father. Clearly." Elliott gripped the window ledge so tightly his knuckles turned white. His voice held a faint tremor. "I can't wait to hurt him."

Niko didn't know if he was referring to father or son.

"Hey. Come here," he said, gently tugging Elliott over into his lap. He half expected the man to shove away from him, his whole body tense with anger, but instead he relented, sinking into Niko's lap and resting his head against his shoulder. Niko stroked his hair.

"They—they were both there when—"

Niko made a soft sound. "It's alright, Elliott. We're going to make sure Duuru doesn't hurt anyone ever again. Maybe now we'll have his old man's attention, too."

"I hope so," Elliott seethed. "I hope he feels what I had to feel when my family never came home again."

It worried Niko. He would be a liar to deny that it did. And he understood. He very intimately understood that all-consuming drive for revenge. But he also knew how poisonous it was, too. If Elliott disdained Honeybliss, the sheer contempt and vitriol he possessed for Uru Taal and his son were on another level entirely. Niko just hoped it wouldn't burn through him like a star on the edge of its supernova, all fire and energy and rage and nothing left enduring once it was over.

There was a special kind of emptiness that came after. One that Niko had only barely survived.

"I'll be there with you," Niko said. "I'll be there when you do it. It's okay, Elliott. We'll take him down together. We'll keep him from hurting anyone ever again."

Elliott relented finally, his body relaxing into Niko.

"Niko... I—" he said slowly, quietly. "I l—"

He hesitated a moment, seeming to reconsider his words. "I'm glad you're here."

"There's nowhere else I'd rather be," Niko said, and meant it.

Chapter Eighteen
What You Wanted

The 114th Starlight Awards were held on Haneen, the rocky, mountainous moon that the Gheroun hailed from. Haneen was a landscape of peaks and valleys as far as the eye could see, the conical architecture favored by the Gheroun fitting in much better here than it did on Uula. Here, it blended seamlessly with the mountains, part of the landscape itself. The same hardy, curled trees from Uula's decorative floating platforms—which had, to Niko's fascination and horror, withstood explosive rounds—dotted the grounds outside the Greela Indoor Botanical Gardens where the awards ceremony was being held.

Above it all, in the deep green sky, Uula hung half visible, bands of pink and lavender along its vast surface.

Duuru Orkan was being awarded today, for being the Galactic People's Choice for Favorite Toliai. It made Niko sick to think about. More than that, it made him angry, the sort of deep, acidic rage that had worked its way under his skin and wouldn't mollify.

Duuru was more an animal than a man—but that was unfair to innocent animals who didn't deserve that kind of comparison.

Once Niko had remembered who Duuru Orkan even was, he hadn't been able to stop thinking about it, nor about what today meant to Elliott. He had a tradition of watching the victim videos, but couldn't bring himself to, this time. Niko still couldn't bear to see it happen to Cleo. It was agonizing enough seeing it all happen to strangers, but Elliott's sister had been his world—the only person who, before Niko, ever gave a damn about him, it seemed.

Just knowing Duuru had been there for her end was enough.

Today would be the last day of Duuru Orkan's life. He may have unfortunately wormed his way into getting a people's choice award, but he also had earned Niko's personal choice award to die.

The awards ceremony was a little more unpredictable than previous hits had been—unlike the political speeches and discussion panels, this one drew a particularly large amount of public interest and eyes. Niko was almost glad for it. No one knew—to his regret—why they did what they did. But Niko particularly disdained this creature and wanted his death to be seen by millions.

Elliott, it seemed, was rubbing off on him. Or maybe he just refused to tolerate that Duuru himself had personally helped ruin Elliott's life.

The Greela Gardens interior was a beautifully curated fanfare of colorful alien flora, which often hung from little decorative balconies and tiny floating platforms, similar to the ones Niko had found himself leaping from on Uula. Crowds gathered and mingled, all in their most stunning attire for the awards show. He recognized several big celebrities among them. It was one strange aspect of hunting Elliott—and now working alongside him—that Niko hadn't prepared for. He was used to seeing actors, singers, directors, politicians, and artists on the regular now. That was just the nature of Elliott's kills being carried out primarily at impactful public events.

They filled the curving hallways of the Gardens, rows of chairs and a stage ornately set up and flanked by flowering plants that glowed in place for the award winners and hosts.

Niko knew there would be an even higher presence than usual of Galapol, bounty hunters, and security, so they'd made sure to prepare by bringing every tool and toy Elliott had at his disposal. Niko even got his own shield generator this time, just in case. They were likely going to have to think on their feet with this one, which was more Niko's style anyway.

They decided to keep to a thin, decorative balcony, from which sprays of plants and waterfalls trickled down. It circled the central awards chamber, though there wasn't much room present to work with. They'd have to make do. It was high enough that even if they hadn't had stealth, it would be difficult to see them up there from below if they crouched low. A review of their blueprints revealed a small maintenance shaft inside the walls that led up to the balcony, likely for plant curators to tend to the foliage there.

Galapol had an agent stationed at the balcony though, just past the hidden maintenance door.

Niko and Elliott crept through, then paused.

"We need to get rid of him," Niko murmured.

"I have an idea," Elliott whispered. "See his radio? I can use that. Like I did on Uula. We can make a diversion and report sighting us somewhere else."

Niko saw what he was getting at. "We make a false alarm, send people that way, then take the shot in the clear."

"Precisely."

He pressed his back against the wall, letting Elliott slip past to do his thing.

Niko froze as he looked over at the Galapol agent blocking their way. His back was turned to them as he scanned the mingling crowds below, muttering into his radio. From this angle, he could have been Zann—tall and thin, with a narrow frame. Dark skin and tight coils of black hair. Niko briefly wondered if it was, his heart aching. His brother's name died in his throat, desperate to come out and call to him, to get him to turn and talk to him. But it wasn't Zann, and Niko couldn't afford such a blatant mistake.

He watched as the air seemed to distort before him. A moment later and Elliott had the agent grabbed tightly from behind, chloroform-soaked cloth pressed over his mouth and nose. The man went limp in his arms and Elliott carefully laid him down, taking his two-way radio. It disappeared into nothingness as he pulled it behind his own cloaking radius.

It wasn't Zann. Niko could see the man's face now—thick eyebrows and a goatee.

The radio sounded from *somewhere*, making Niko jump. "Agent Adebisi, report for routine check in. Over."

He heard the eerie sound of two voices talking in unison—Elliott's, and the altered version that came out across the radio, matching the murmurs of the agent from only a moment before. It was something Niko didn't know if he would ever get used to.

"This is Agent Adebisi reporting in. West balcony is all clear, over."

"Excellent. Please give the new passcode cycle, Agent. Over."

Niko could feel Elliott's pause without seeing him, he had grown so attuned to the other man. He froze as well, heart skipping a beat.

Passcode cycle?

Elliott crouched and began desperately patting the agent down—Niko could see the man's vest and clothing as they moved, the distortion of light as Elliott pawed through his effects in search of whatever might generate a passcode. They were catching on. They'd learned from Uula that Elliott had this sort of technology and could mimic agent voices.

Galapol had caught up to his tricks. They'd come prepared.

"Agent? The passcode. Over."

"One second. I'm trying to get— I think I dropped the damned thing."

Niko winced. It was a flimsy excuse, an attempt to buy Elliott time. He saw him pat at the man's ears for any sort of earbuds.

Below them, a hearty roar of applause started as Duuru Orkan was announced by the host. If they could just get a clear shot of him—

But the Toliai still wasn't anywhere to be seen.

"Try, um," Niko murmured. "One of the other frequencies."

Elliott did, switching between stations until he reached one where a feminine voice prompted him.

"Five-minute check in code. Please provide your password and agent ID to retrieve."

Elliott was silent. Niko could only imagine what was going through his mind right then: fear, panic. Trying to outsmart the problem rapidly strangling him. But they'd been too prepared, setting up their agents with regular check-in intervals and unique passcodes. Ones that required another set of credentials to even retrieve.

Galapol had finally learned to outmaneuver them.

There was a long silence that fell between them, both men at a loss. Niko felt ill, goosebumps prickling along his skin.

"They're coming," Elliott said. His voice was tight and laced with fear. "We need to go. Now. We can't do this tonight. It's too hot now."

"Wait. Hold on." Niko was thinking.

This was their chance. This was *Elliott's* chance. Uru Taal and his son Duuru had been a pestilence on Elliott's life, the very stains responsible for setting every event since into motion. Being here had meant the most to him of any of his cumulative work so far. And Duuru was about to come on stage. They just needed a clear shot and could be gone. They just needed time for Elliott to set it up.

"Niko, we don't have time!"

"I have an idea. We can still finish this."

"What?" Elliott sounded breathless. Niko hated hearing the horror in his voice.

"They know we know they're coming. It's logical for us to retreat. If we split up, I can make some distractions. Loud ones. They won't know where to look, and you can set up in a new spot and tag him."

Below, Niko could already see movement as several armored Galapol agents came their way.

"I don't— I don't like this, Niko. We can just come back for him later."

Elliott's grand plan was falling apart, one aborted kill at a time. Imperator Khaathra, Chancellor Iincha'cul, and now Prince Duuru Orkan. Niko wasn't going to let it all start unraveling now.

"Trust me, okay? We don't have time to argue. They're almost here. I'm going to draw them away and you work your magic." Niko slipped off before Elliott could say more, back down the maintenance shaft and into the central auditorium. Sure enough, there were a dozen Galapol agents making a beeline in his direction now. They didn't see him yet, but they'd find Elliott if they made it up the maintenance shaft. If not there, then wherever he was currently heading.

Niko was going to have to get messy.

With a silent apology to the civilians he was about to frighten and for the damage he was about to cause, he pulled a grenade from his utility belt, then glanced around. There was a verdant courtyard to the east, walled-in by glass, which was currently closed to public mingling. No one would be in there to get hurt. Niko tried the double glass doors, but they were locked tight.

He didn't have time for this.

He smashed the lock with a single, hard punch, the delicate glass shattering around him. Several quizzical, alarmed looks drew his way but he ignored them, shoving the doors open and lobbing the grenade inside. Seconds later, it exploded in a flash of fire that rocked the courtyard and corridors around it, sending splinters of hearty plant debris pelting into the glass that encased the courtyard.

He definitely had Galapol's attention now. And everyone else's, too. Already, people were beginning to make for the exits.

"What are you doing?" Elliott asked, incredulous, over their frequency.

"Drawing them away from you. Can you get the shot in?"

Niko was already running, trying to keep to the outer fringes of the crowd, still cloaked by Elliott's ORA. He would have to kiss him later in thanks for it, the kind of kiss that would sweep him off his feet. Niko pulled another grenade from his belt and held it ready.

It was working. The agents changed their route, heading straight to the damaged courtyard now.

"I can try. I— No. Shit. There's Galapol getting on stage. They're surrounding him."

"Can you try to get a clear shot? I can pull them away from him." Niko had to get closer. He slipped straight past horrified crowds of glamorous celebrities and towards a fountain which aquatic plants grew in. Like the courtyard, it was generally off limits, roped-off from the main crowds. Whoever had set up the event clearly didn't trust celebrities and influencers not to start touching everything.

Niko threw the second grenade; seconds later, it exploded too, the entire room rumbling. The fountain crumbled apart as water flooded out now, soaking the grounds. He gave another silent apology to whoever had diligently curated and cared for the display.

He was definitely getting more attention now, as Galapol and hunters alike ran his way. Niko was already on the move again. Since they'd started working together, this was the most reckless he'd been. It reminded him of the days before, when he'd hunted regularly. When he threw himself into the fray and got his jobs done no matter what. This had always been his style: wild, careless. Intense.

"Elliott? Did it work?"

Elliott made a soft, frustrated sound over their frequency. *"No, I still can't. They're fucking escorting him away, Niko. They're escorting all the nominees away. We need to get out of here. This is bad. They're everywhere now."*

"No," Niko growled, rage and determination grinding and cracking against each other like hard teeth. He didn't like to back down. "We're not done here yet."

Elliott had come here for Duuru Orkan. The same man who had been present for the cruel and pointless end of Cleo's life. The one who had shattered Elliott's world.

Niko wanted to deliver him up to Elliott for sacrifice—a courting gift.

A flash of scaly brown caught his attention at the far end of the stage, before disappearing quickly around a corner, flanked by several armored agents. Niko swiftly followed, murmuring to Elliott as he did.

"I think I know where they're taking him. Northeast corridor. Check your blueprints. You can catch up with him. I'll draw them away from him."

"Niko," Elliott said. *"Let's just go. It's not happening tonight. This went south too quickly."*

"It is, Elliott. It can still happen. I'll draw them away and you take that sick fucker down." It was hard to keep his voice to the murmur required for stealth. He was too angry. He was so mad at the idea of Duuru getting to worm his way out of his fate that he was shaking now. "Isn't that what you *wanted?* Isn't that what you said meant more to you than anything?"

He was met with only silence before Elliott finally spoke, voice flat.

"Fine."

He could do this. Niko had a squadron of angry Galapol and desperate hunters all honed in on him now. Elliott would be free to work unhindered.

He rounded the corner to the northeast corridor, a long hall flanked with big windows looking out into another tangle of forestial courtyard. They were there—Galapol, quickly moving Duuru Orkan along. Niko wanted to break him. The sight of the gargantuan, scaled, repulsive Toliai as he nervously shuffled along in cowardly self-preservation made him want for violence.

"Elliott? You'll have a chance. Are you ready?"

"I'm ready," he said. His voice came from beside Niko now, rather than over their frequency. He'd caught up.

The agents were flanking Duuru defensively, protecting him with their own armored bodies. It was impossible to get a shot through to him while they were there. Niko needed to get them away, to break their formation. He had one grenade left. He wouldn't use it on them—they hadn't come here to kill or hurt anyone who wasn't Duuru Orkan. So, he would have to work a little harder.

"I'm going to slip ahead of them and divert. I want you to get the shot in, then head west, back down towards the original maintenance shaft. I'll meet you there. We'll get out quick and clean."

"Understood."

"Get the shot and go."

Niko moved back down the corridor and wove his way around to cut them off, relying on attempts to memorize the blueprints he and Elliott had poured over in the afternoon. He managed to get to the cut-off point before Galapol and drew out his last grenade, throwing it into the empty hallway ahead of them where it detonated harmlessly, its only casualty the dented and scorched walls.

He turned to make his way back to the maintenance shaft now, when he was stopped short.

The group of agents he'd diverted through the grounds had caught up, cutting Niko off suddenly from the way he'd come.

Well, shit.

Before he could get out of the way, an EMP was lobbed in his direction. Niko tried to dodge but the thing went off, sending its shockwave coursing throughout the hallway. He winced, bracing for the fall of his suit and legs giving out, but it never came. The shield generator seemed to have taken the brunt of the hit, disabling along with the cloak, leaving him revealed and vulnerable now. But he could still walk.

This was bad.

He was in the plain now, visible and out of explosives. And quickly being corralled away from Elliott again. They were funneling him now, pushing him into what was likely a trap.

Niko's heart sank. This had so quickly turned south. Elliott had warned him, had seen it coming a mile away.

"Elliott," he said over their frequency, trying to keep his voice calm. "Get the shot and go. Take the *Soñadora*. I reprogrammed it to recognize you—"

"What?" Elliott breathed over their connection, barely more than a whisper. *"Niko? What are you saying?"*

"I... Elliott, I'm sorry. I think it might just have to be you who gets out of this one." He sure as hell wasn't about to let Elliott be taken down for his stupid mistakes and swollen ego. His inability to quit. He still wanted Elliott to have the victory he deserved, the revenge he craved. And to get out and live another day. It was all Niko could offer him at this point—the agents were closing in. And it was a matter of time before they used another EMP, and cut off his ability to flee at all.

"No," Elliott said. *"No, I'm not leaving you."*

"You have to, Elliott. We don't have a choice now. I can buy you the time to get out. You can use the ship for your work. It has—"

"No!"

Niko turned, but there was nowhere else to go. A line of agents filled the hallway, both behind and ahead of him. He was trapped now.

He gave a heartbroken grin, gun still up but not willing to fire on them. They weren't who they'd come for tonight. They were just people, doing their jobs, hopefully trying to make the galaxy a little bit better of a place than they'd found it. Just like Niko had. He didn't want to think about how many there tonight probably knew about Elliott's files on Honeybliss.

"Hey guys," he said, hating how nervous his voice sounded. "I don't want to hurt anybody."

"Drop the gun and get on your knees!" one of the agents yelled. Niko didn't recognize her.

Elliott hadn't gotten his shot in yet, hadn't lined it up. He could still see Duuru at the far end of the hallway. Still flanked by Galapol, still unfortunately living. But he could grant Elliott one last favor.

He still had one trick up his sleeve.

Niko turned and barreled towards the line of agents who had been behind him, arm raised to deflect bullets from hitting his face. Some small part of him wanted to scold them on their flimsy formation—he had always used brute force in his work. They should have come equipped knowing this, and not stood single file, shoulder to shoulder. Their bullets pinged off him and he slammed straight into their formation, knocking two right off their feet. He stumbled, but kept running as more bullets pinged off the back of his armor.

It was only a matter of time before they would manage to hit him with another EMP, and then this little second wind, desperate game was over. But it would buy Elliott the time he'd need.

Niko rounded a corner and saw even more agents coming his way. Every Galapol special ops officer in the vicinity had managed to figure out they'd needed to get here, it seemed. He readied himself to try and meet them head on again, unsure if he could make it through their ranks this time.

And then he saw it—a flash of silver that spelled the end of his journey. The EMP grenade sailed through the air towards him, Niko instinctively turning away and shielding his face with his arm in vain. The thing exploded, but once more, he still stood.

Niko lowered his arm, confused, when he saw what had stopped it. Elliott stood before him like a bulwark, their roles reversed. The man had caught up somehow. Whether straight around the chaotic mess of agents or through some other clever path, he was there. And had used himself to shield Niko. His own shield and cloak vanished in the hit, leaving him woefully exposed. It made Niko ill, made his heart ache.

Elliott trained his gun on the nearest agent, and Niko did too. If they could make themselves look like a threat, still, it could keep them from risking openly shooting Elliott on the spot.

"Drop your weapons!" one of the agents yelled. Elliott ignored her, so Niko did too.

"Elliott," Niko whispered. *"Why?"*

"I'm not leaving you to die."

It hurt.

"But—but the mission—"

"I don't care about that. I'm not leaving you, Niko." Niko was stunned, breathless, a dizzying pain blossoming throughout his chest that almost left him wondering if he'd already been shot and just hadn't realized it yet.

Elliott had once told him that it was all he lived for now. That it was all that mattered to him.

No. No, no...

One of the agents pushed through, wearing a full suit and helmet himself. He had a rifle drawn on Elliott as well, but reached up with one hand to pull his helmet off and toss it aside.

A familiar face and slicked back, dark hair greeted Niko. Fourier smiled widely at him.

"Niko. Long time no see, huh? The armor makes a little more thematic sense here."

Niko kept his rifle trained on Fourier. From the corner of his gaze, he could see Elliott did too. He was staring Fourier down with a cold, tense rage.

"Where's Zann?" Niko asked.

"Zann is off the case. In fact, he's out of Galapol. I got promoted to Lead Investigator. So, here I am."

"I want to talk to him."

"Not possible. But if you surrender now, you can both make it out of here today alive. No guarantees for later though."

"Why are you doing this?" Niko asked.

Fourier laughed. "Why are *we* doing this? I think the entire fucking galaxy wants to ask you two degenerates the same thing."

"You have the files. I sent them. Elliott sent them over two years ago. Galapol knows what these people have done. What Duuru Orkan has done. Why aren't you investigating this? Why aren't you arresting that man and bringing him in? Why aren't you fucking doing anything about the *thousands* who go missing every year?"

Fourier smirked. "I don't know what you're talking about, Niko. He roped you into his conspiracy shit too. That's really too bad. Your brother talked you up like you were his hero. Unsurprisingly, he turned out to be an idiot too."

"I want to talk to Zann. I'll negotiate with Zann. Over the phone."

"No. I don't think so," Fourier said. Niko's heart was in his throat, a nauseating mixture of terror and blinding rage both. He hated this man. How he was even allowed to talk the shit he was as an officer and agent of Galapol was beyond him. It was like the man only wanted to escalate and was getting off on it.

Niko had no doubt he knew all about Honeybliss. He probably had all along.

"Put your guns down and you won't get shot. You can plead your case at the station."

"I..."

There was no way out. There had been a chance, and it was gone now.

They were surrounded on all sides, and outnumbered. There was no way out of this. And it was all Niko's fault.

He had made a promise to Cleo. He had vowed to her that he'd keep her brother safe. Take care of him.

Trust me, he'd said to Elliott as the man had argued with him to flee with their lives.

And now he'd gotten him killed. Elliott had sacrificed himself to try and protect Niko from his own mistakes, his own arrogance.

Maybe—

There was still a chance. He could try to negotiate and plead. Trade his own life for Elliott's, take the blame. The galaxy wanted blood and maybe he could satisfy it with his life alone. Maybe he could even say this had been his idea all along. Niko was a terrible liar, but he could do it for him, could say they'd had connections before any of this had started, that he'd coerced Elliott—

"If you do not put your weapons down, we are going to open fire. And you're very much at a disadvantage. It's over now, Niko. Come on." Fourier said the last words like someone might talk to a dog they were trying to coax into obeying.

Niko's hands trembled. It was hard to stand, hard to breathe. The weight of everything had caught up to him, was falling down on him now. He was suffocating. He dropped the rifle on the ground in front of him.

"Now, kick it away."

Niko nudged it with his foot towards the wall of agents. One stooped and picked it up.

"And now you." Fourier looked at Elliott.

Elliott stood silent beside Niko, gun still trained on Fourier. Niko saw he was shaking too. His view of Elliott distorted as tears filled his eyes. He couldn't stand it, couldn't stand to see the fear in him. Couldn't stand to know he was the one who'd brought them to this sudden end.

It had all been so avoidable, if not for ego.

Niko swallowed back a lump in his throat. When he spoke, his voice emerged hoarse and pleading. "Elliott. Just do it. Maybe we can..." Elliott only gripped his rifle tighter, hands trembling. Niko could see it in his eyes, on his face. Written all over, in the tension of his body. He had come to read Elliott so perfectly now. He knew he was going to do it.

"Elliott, this isn't you. This isn't who you are. We're not about that. We don't kill anyone but Honeybliss."

"*You,*" Elliott whispered, his gaze burning straight into Fourier. He ignored Niko's pleas. "*You always knew. And you did nothing.* Galapol watches us call out to our loved ones as we die. You watch us suffer. You watch us disappear. You just don't care. Because the ones perpetuating it are more powerful than you. Because they have more money than you. You always knew. Every one of you. You couldn't care less. And you never will."

"And you," said Fourier, "are clearly batshit fucking crazy."

Niko saw it the second it happened: the tightening of his hand over the trigger, the movement of tendons. He threw himself on Elliott, tackling the other man to the floor beneath him. Elliott's gun went off, the bullet perforating the ceiling instead.

A cacophony of shots rang out around them as Niko buried himself in Elliott, trying to cover him entirely, his only goal to shield the other man with his own armored body. He heard and felt bullets ricochet hot off his suit.

And all at the same time, there was another sound. One he hadn't expected.

An explosion. And then another, so strong the entire room rocked, windows blowing out around them as shards of glass rained down on Niko. Then more gunshots, followed by another two explosions. The world came apart around them, and all Niko could do was hold onto Elliott and pray he himself took whatever damage came their way instead.

Then quiet descended over the corridor. For a moment, he was too terrified to move. All that existed was Elliott, his only awareness, the only solid anchor to which he clung.

"*N-Niko,*" Elliott breathed out in bewildered terror. Around them, Niko heard the sounds of bodies falling, slumping over. The last moans of the grievously wounded as they slipped away. He could smell viscera and blood, freshly spilled, a copper tang filling the air. He was afraid to look.

But he made himself do it.

Niko craned his neck and glanced over his shoulder, trembling. All around them lay dozens of dead and dying Galapol agents, peppered with gunshot wounds, blown partially into pieces by the onslaught of explosions. Niko gaped in horrified awe.

All of them. Every single one. Even Fourier.

A whole special ops squad of Galapol agents had been cut down with ease, caught off guard, their attention focused on the galaxy's now pair of most notorious assassins.

He heard footsteps—boots crunching on broken glass as each step drew closer. The creak of leather. They came into view—sky blue combat boots with ripped jeans over thin, human legs.

Niko looked up and saw a bright shock of pink hair. Machine gun clutched in her hands, Bubblegum stared down at them. She glanced around the corridor at the casualties she'd made. One agent, a Gheroun woman, was struggling to stand back up. Bubblegum casually moved towards her and shot her in the head. Niko shuddered at the sound and the merciless violence of it. The Gheroun slumped forward, falling onto her face, and didn't move anymore.

Niko pulled Elliott up to sit with him, still wrapped tightly around the other man, trying to keep himself in between Bubblegum and him. Elliott was silent and dazed, possibly in shock.

Niko swept a quick glance around—maybe if he could grab one of the fallen agents' guns... But the nearest was a good five feet away from him. Even Elliott's rifle had been knocked away when Niko seized him.

Bubblegum turned and regarded them again blandly. "Well, you better get a run on. The Galactic Police are gonna be real pissed when they find out you guys are killing cops now."

"We didn't kill them," Niko spat.

Bubblegum smirked. "Sure you did. Because that's what this is all gonna look like."

Elliott seemed to have found his voice again. "Why did you help us?"

"Because I'm not going to let Galapol waste that bounty on your pretty head. With each new death you two dipshits rack up, the higher it gets. And it's really going to skyrocket now, because Galapol *hates* a cop killer. I want it even bigger..." She walked over and kicked the gun nearest to them away for good measure, having the same idea Niko—and probably Elliott—had. "...Before I come back for you and cash in. Because I will. But for today, enjoy your good fortune."

A pitiful, rumbling groan came from the far end of the corridor, catching the attention of all three of them. Duuru Orkan was still alive. He stood fearful and shaking as he stared out at the bloody sea of carnage that had once been the only thing standing between him and death by a sniper's bullet.

"I—I'm going. I'm going to leave—"

Bubblegum sighed. "Toliai are so fucking irritating." She pulled a small, clearly homebrewed pistol from inside her bright yellow jacket, then shot Duuru in his left eye. The Toliai began screaming. He clawed at his face and thrashed, his giant scaled body shaking the floor as he collapsed in agony. Niko looked away as the familiar, acrid scent of bog-theun toxin filled the air.

Then she trained the gun on them. Niko held Elliott tighter, all instinct.

"Now get the fuck out of here, before I change my mind. Your corpses are still worth a whole lot of credits."

Niko glanced at Elliott, who mirrored the look, eyes wide still with shock and horror. They quickly stood, legs shaking and unsteady beneath them. Niko refused to let go of Elliott; he forced himself to relinquish his embrace, but held tightly to his arm.

"Hey," said Bubblegum. "And take your shit. They'll wonder why you left it behind, otherwise."

After a moment of hesitation, they retrieved their weapons from amidst the chaos and gore. It made Niko ill to look at. He tried not to think about the faces there he recognized.

Another gunshot rang out as Bubblegum dropped a wounded agent who had started to subtly reach for her own gun.

It was long past time to go.

The horror of their situation kept them both silent on the ride back to RM-9832642G's facility. Once Niko got the *Soñadora* docked, Elliott quickly stood, grabbed his things and made his way briskly down the ramp. Niko paused, still in his suit, and watched him go from the ship's doorframe. Elliott disappeared into the facility, the door to the hangar sliding shut behind him.

Niko felt ill.

He took his time removing and charging the suit, took his time locking all his weapons away. The suit was coated with the blood of the fallen agents still, little shards of shimmering glass embedded between the protective plates. He would have to clean it later, when he could stomach the task. Then he simply sat in the ship, the silence of the eerie, empty hangar almost tangible.

He sat for an hour, maybe longer, not wanting to go inside yet, not wanting to be anywhere or do anything. He wanted to talk to Elliott and beg forgiveness, wanted to hide from the other man and pass out in one of the spare, unused beds and sleep until the days melted into oblivion.

He'd almost gotten Elliott killed. He'd almost gotten them *both* killed. They were alive purely by bizarre chance. If he'd only listened to Elliott, who had done this time and time again, expertly, rather than his own ego and inability to yield, none of it would have happened. They'd be discussing a new strategy. Instead, Niko was left in cold silence and Elliott couldn't bear to be near him. And now, to the galaxy, they were cop killers, on top of everything else. He swallowed back the sensation of rising bile.

Hiding wouldn't change anything. Sleeping wouldn't save him. He had to talk to Elliott, had to see if, at this point, there was anything he could still salvage.

It was the last thing he wanted to do, but Niko took hold of the wheels and slowly eased himself out and down the ramp, then into the quiet facility. Like the hangar, the control room was silent and still. Niko had stayed on the *Soñadora* so long that the lights had shut themselves off to conserve power, flickering back on as he moved into the room.

He made his way to Elliott's bedroom—it didn't feel entirely like his own right then—and knocked.

There was no answer.

Niko cleared his throat. "Elliott? Can we talk, please?"

He was, again, met with only silence. Niko reluctantly opened the door, but before him lay only an empty room, just as they'd left it that morning: messy sheets, Elliott's half-emptied bottles of water with one uncapped, and a pile of dark clothes lying in the corner.

Niko backed out and moved down the hallway to the cafeteria. Its lights almost seemed to struggle to kick on, sluggish in their activation. Elliott had insisted the generators were set to power this place for years to come, but Niko wondered.

He wasn't here either.

His last option before searching the halls aimlessly was the research-lab-turned-murder-room. When its door opened, Niko's stomach twisted in a slurry of relief and anxiety at the sight of him, diligently at work at the central island, cleaning the disassembled *Repartee.* Elliott tensed up instantly upon seeing him, his gaze harrowingly cold. Unwelcoming. He set the gun parts down and stared.

Niko's heart sank.

"Elliott, listen, we need to t—"

"You need to go."

Niko blinked. The hurt was so deep it spread through his body like a shock of ice water. "I... What?"

"I want you to *leave*, Niko. We're not working together anymore. It's over."

CHAPTER NINETEEN
FREEFALL

NIKO WAS STUNNED. WORDS left him as he gaped, wounded, at the other man. There was no warmth in his eyes. Elliott only stared at him now with cold contempt.

So, he truly hated Niko now.

"Elliott, wait—" He had to get it out, at the very least. Had to apologize. But Elliott was in a frigid fury and wouldn't let him get a word in.

"No. This is over. I don't want you here. We're not partners, we're not friends. We're not anything. You need to get out of this facility and never fucking come back. You're not a part of this anymore. Do you *understand?*" His voice grew louder with every word until he practically spat them at Niko. His hands trembled as they gripped the edge of the island.

Niko flinched. The contempt Elliott obviously had for him right then wounded him in a way he couldn't define. It was everywhere, inside him. He felt lost. But most of all, he felt he couldn't even blame Elliott for his disdain—Niko had fucked up. Badly. And it very nearly cost them everything. He'd made stupid, sloppy, arrogant mistakes that on his own, Elliott never would have. All because he wouldn't—couldn't—turn back when he should have. He wasn't helping Elliott clean up Honeybliss. He was only hindering.

He had ruined everything.

Elliott's words on Valaevanas haunted him. *All you're doing is getting in my way. It's all you've ever done.*

Shame and agony burned a scorching fire through him. If Niko was going to go, he had to at least apologize. If he left without ever being able to do that, he would never be able to sleep again. "Elliott, I just want to talk about this. If—if you want me to go, I'll go. But I wanted to say I'm—"

"Don't you see, Niko?" Elliott said. He sounded a little wild, voice tense and hoarse. "I always fucking ruin everything. And if you try to stay and help me with this, I'm only going to ruin you too. I already have, by making you lose your brother and father and colleagues. And now you almost died, too. You said yourself that this only ends one way. You never should have saved me from your brother. You never should have helped me. You should have left me to fucking die like I deserve."

Wait. What?

Niko stared at him, a new kind of horror webbing throughout his body. "Elliott? What are you talking about?"

"I almost got you killed. And it's a matter of *when* now, not *if*. Anything else is wishful thinking. You need to leave. Now. Go find a safehouse that won't fuck you over. Get a new ID like you mentioned. Anything. But I don't *want you here anymore*."

Oh.

Somehow—*somehow*—Elliott blamed himself for it all. How he'd ever managed to come to that conclusion, Niko couldn't understand. Everything that had gone wrong had been due to his own mistakes, Elliott forced to keep up and pivot to match Niko's stubborn advance.

Elliott's whole body had given to trembling now; the man almost looked like he was suffering from hypothermia.

"Elliott, no. That's not what—"

"I'm not good for you. I'm not good for anyone." Niko was growing exasperated at being cut off. "You should get away from me. Everyone else did. Maybe you can tell Galapol—"

"*LISTEN* to me for one fucking second, Elliott!" Niko hated having to shout, but he'd had no choice. The other man wasn't giving him an inch, rapidly descending into hysteria.

Elliott flinched, but fell quiet.

Niko softened his voice. "Please just let me speak. I actually came here to apologize to you. Everything that happened tonight was on me. It was my fault—"

"No—"

"Let. Me. Talk." He waited a second, but Elliott acquiesced. "It was. It was my fault. I should have listened to you. If we'd done things your way, we would have retreated like any other operation when things get dicey. You're a survivor, Elliott. You're so smart. And I'm just a fucking idiot. I—I've always had trouble knowing when to stop. I don't know how to back down. I've gotten myself hurt, and broken, and beaten again and again and again because of it. But until now, it's only ever just been me at the mercy of that carelessness.

"I'm not used to working with a partner. Neither of us are. But now, when I do something reckless, it's not just me who gets hurt. It's you, too. And I caused that today. I was too proud and too confident to back down when it was time to, and you would be dead now because of me if not for... whatever the fuck that was."

The cold rage slowly dissipated from Elliott. It was like watching a blizzard give way to clear air. He looked exhausted and hurt now, staring down at the gun pieces instead of looking at Niko.

"*I* am so sorry, Elliott. I'm sorry any of this happened. I thought you were pissed at me for it. You would have had every right to be. I thought you were telling me to leave because of the pain I'd caused you and the risk I'd put you through. Not the other way around. There is no other way around."

Elliott swallowed, his Adam's apple bobbing. After a moment, he reached up and covered his face with his hand.

When he spoke, it wasn't the mounting panic and anger from before. His voice came quietly now. "I tried to kill him. The officer."

Fourier. Niko blinked. "I wasn't going to let that happen, Elliott."

Elliott lowered his hand back to the counter. He looked ill. "But I would have done it. If you hadn't. I would have killed him. I'd chosen to. I crossed that line. And now he's dead and everyone thinks I did it anyway. It's going to be all over the news that I'm killing police officers."

"Why does that bother you so much?" Niko asked, keeping his voice gentle. Kestrel had been so apathetic towards his mangled history from Zann's files. He'd been aware that Galapol and the public alike saw him as an unhinged monster that he never was. What was one more lie tossed into it all?

"Because I've tried so hard," Elliott said, "to do this without anyone getting killed who isn't Honeybliss. It was the only dignity I had left. They took everything from me. Even myself. But when I died at the end of it all, they would never be able to say I killed anyone except exactly the ones I'd meant to. They could *never* take that from me. Even if no one ever understands why I'm doing this, I would rest easy knowing, except when we'd had no choice, that I never took a life that wasn't someone who abused and ruined others. I don't even know what I am now."

Niko ached. "You were scared. You were angry. You were in a terrifying, awful situation. And Fo— The cop escalated." Niko refused to say his name. The last thing he wanted was to compound Elliott's guilt. "He shouldn't have done that. Galapol officers receive training to keep everyone calm during tense situations."

Elliott said nothing. Niko made his way around the island to be by his side. "Hey. Come here."

Elliott went to him. Niko expected him to sit in his lap, anticipated wrapping him in his arms. But instead, Elliott quietly sank to his knees. He rested his head on Niko's thighs, eyes closed. He held onto Niko's legs. It was shockingly tender, almost reverent.

Niko stroked his wild, golden hair slowly in silence, then spoke. "Do you want to know what you're *not*, Elliott?"

"Please tell me." His voice was quiet, muffled against the fabric of Niko's pants.

"You're not the one who killed that Galapol officer. Or any of them. Since you started, you still haven't killed anyone who isn't Honeybliss or who hasn't given you a choice, like the safehouse ambush. That hasn't changed. You may have thought about it. You might have wanted to. You might have even tried. But in the end, you didn't kill him. It wasn't you. That's not who you are. That's not meant for you."

"I feel like I'm losing my mind. What if it happens again?"

"Then I'll be there to stop you then, too. I've got you, Elliott, if you still want me here."

Elliott finally raised his head to look at Niko. "I don't want you to leave. But you're such a good person. I would hate myself if you lost your life because of me. Because of this. I don't know what I would do. You're one of the most beautiful and incredible people I've ever met, Niko. I'm in awe of you."

The words shook Niko to his core. He swallowed back a lump of emotion, his eyes stinging. No one had ever said anything like that to him. *About* him. And to hear it from Elliott of all people made its impact take deep root in Niko's soul.

"You're lovely, Niko."

Those words were going to stay with him for the rest of his life.

"Let's…" It was hard to speak. His throat felt raw. "Let's take care of each other instead of turning on one another when things get bad, alright?"

"You're right."

"This is new territory for both of us, I think. You've worked alone this whole time and so have I, ever since I had my bearings as a hunter. I'll look out for you, Elliott. When it gets bad and you want to turn your gun on somebody who isn't one of them, I'll be there to remind you who you are. And when I don't know when to take a step back, I need you there to remind me so I don't get us both hurt. Can you do that with me?"

"I can do that. I want to."

"We're both fucking incredible at what we do. We should be using that. Playing off each other's strengths and taking this whole galaxy on, side by side. But we need to make up for each other's weaknesses too. It won't work out, otherwise."

The encouragement seemed to ground Elliott. He nodded and stood, then slipped into Niko's lap. Niko was finally able to give him the hug he'd longed to.

"I'll try, Niko."

"Are you sure you still want to do any of this? We could always just go to Eanan instead. Hang out on the beach and get drunk off rum and tequila. Blast some Kuliedi Taan while we watch the sunset. Tell the galaxy to go fuck itself."

That earned a small, but sad little smile from Elliott. "I'd like that. I want to build stupid sandcastles with you."

"Why do I have a feeling you'd come stomp all over mine and start a war?"

Elliott's smile grew, some of the sorrow exorcised from it. "Only because mine would be better. You have to establish dominance by being the first one to strike. That's basic sand kingdom superiority."

There you are.

Niko kissed him on the temple. They sat in silence for a while as Niko held him.

"Today took a lot out of me," Elliott admitted finally. "I think I'm going to make some dinner."

"Okay," said Niko. "I'll be right behind you."

"I'll cook," Elliott said. "You can get cleaned up or just rest." He stood and turned to face Niko, hesitating for a moment before reaching out to cup his cheek with his warm hand.

Niko couldn't help but tilt his head, leaning into the touch.

"It's been a long time, Niko, since I've had anyone on my side. I think I'm still remembering what it is to have someone near who cares."

"It's alright, Elliott. I just want us to be okay."

"We're okay, lover."

Left on his own now, Niko glanced around the room. This wasn't where he'd wanted to be—surrounded by the reminders of the day's events through weaponry, blueprints, and Honeybliss portraiture. Duuru Orkan stared at him from his photograph. Niko wheeled back out of the room and turned down a different hallway than usual, continuing until he found a small lounge area, with a

U-shape of cushy benches and big windows that looked out into the perpetual night.

Maybe someone, somewhere, had once thought adding big windows here would be soothing or picturesque when they'd designed and constructed the facility. But it only served as a reminder to Niko that he was mere feet away from an empty solar system of vast, cold nothingness.

Wonder if the workers here threw a party when they were told to pack up.

He felt all out of sorts. Greela Gardens of Haneen, and his subsequent altercation with Elliott. Duuru Orkan. Bubblegum, Fourier, Zann. It had all left Niko drained to the marrow. And now, he had learned that Zann was punished for Niko's own actions. Discomfort and trepidation seized him as he thought to confront what he'd put off since leaving Zann behind on Neema.

Niko opened his phone hologram, fingers trembling. Initially, it had been too much to bear. By the time he'd finished his call with Baouban, fleeing with an unconscious Elliott by his side, his phone had started ringing nonstop. When it wasn't ringing, texts so numerous he couldn't keep track of their number anymore relentlessly pinged at him. The galaxy had quickly found out that he'd flipped sides to save the life of the man who had murdered their leaders.

This time, there was no Zann to intercept the onslaught of calls. He'd switched it to Do Not Disturb mode, shut it off, and hadn't been willing to look at it since.

The hologram hovered before him now, casting the already weird lounge in uncanny artificial blue. Niko's incoming calls notification was capped out at 999+, his texts the same. He swallowed back a growing lump of anxiety and opened the text interface, then scrolled through thousands of messages from unknown numbers, refusing to open any.

He tried to avoid giving them much thought or attention, but occasionally the compressed preview of some caught his eye. The messages were endless.

You're a piece of shit.
You are a fucking murderer and I hope that y
WHY??? I HOPE SOMEONE ASSASSINATES YOU TOO
I represent VYYW News and would like to talk
Heard your mom got unalived. GOOD. YOU DESER
i hope u die u sick fuck
Kaana Nunnde from TWJ Media here. Can I ask
Niko, my name is Hala Vani with GNN. Are you
you assholes deserve each other
Your disgusting why would you help someone l
Hi Niko, I'm a representative of StarSeam an
you had a chance to help people but instead
I hope your family dies I hope they all get
Cerulean News would like to talk with you r
ur a fucking monster.
I'm glad your family died. You deserve it.

He didn't know how so many people had gotten his number. A leak, maybe. It didn't matter. The messages about his family made him sick, white-hot rage building like a heavy stone. He forced himself to keep scrolling through the endless onslaught, until, finally, a familiar name appeared.

Loolae. He hesitated, then opened her messages.

Niko. I heard about what happened. I don't know why you've done this. And it's probably unwise to even write to you. But I've known you for a long time as a genuinely good person and a friend, and will maintain the hope that I am ignorant to something more in your situation that led you to where you are now.

Whatever is really going on, be safe.

After Loolae, he eventually found his father. It was almost too much to open his messages; several times, Niko contemplated leaving them unread.

Niko??

Please Niko, tell me this is a joke.

Please tell me they've gotten something wrong and it's not really you.

Why would you do something like this?

Niko, why are you hurting people? What's going on?

Why are you doing this?

Please answer your phone.

If we just talk I can help you. Maybe we can speak about it all. I think you need help, Niko. Maybe there's something I didn't see before and you've been unwell. Something I missed and I'm sorry if so. Please just talk to me.

Niko, why are you doing this?

Happy birthday, Niko, wherever you are.

Oliver's texts stopped there, the last dated weeks ago on the birthday Niko had all but forgotten about. He closed his eyes, the hurt of his father's pleading messages seeping in beneath his skin. He wanted to respond, to apologize, to explain it wasn't what any of it seemed. As he reached up to type, his hands froze. What if he somehow made things worse for Oliver by reaching out to him? Got him in some sort of trouble with the law or roped him in? After all, Zann had already suffered the consequences of Niko's choices. He couldn't bear to let something similar happen to his father too.

Niko closed his text interface.

Finally, he found Zann. His messages weren't from his usual contact—rather, they appeared to come from a burner phone. *Smart.*

this is zann

fuck you niko

He'd been drinking when he wrote that one. Niko knew his tells—the man had a disdain for poor grammar, but his own seemed to slip when he got drunk regardless.

we both know i shouldnt be contacting you but just want to let you know your little neema stunt got me put on indefinite hiatus so thanks for that

asshole

now they have me under investigation because of the shit i sent you

i hope the dick was worth it. that better have been the best lay of your entire fucking life

well when youre ready to stop hiding away like a little bitch lets talk. ps dads getting death threats now but im taking care of it

Niko winced. Death threats. Everyone close to him was getting trampled by his actions. Elliott, Zann, their father.

In joining with Elliott, he had a chance to give countless forgotten victims justice. And he could prevent anyone else from ever falling prey to bored and sick elites with too much power and too little conscience.

But at what cost?

He sent a message to Zann's burner phone. *Let's talk.*

Almost instantly, a reply pinged through.

NIKO.

Niko's fingertips hovered over the keyboard interface. He was suddenly at a loss. There was so much to say and he didn't know where to start. Zann beat him to the punch though, seeming eager not to lose the rare contact Niko had reestablished.

You have pulled some utterly batfuck crazy shit lately, Niko. But I know you and I'm going to give you the benefit of the doubt that you are not a cop killer.

I'm not, Niko typed back quickly. *We didn't do that. He doesn't kill anyone who isn't Honeybliss. It was another hunter who wanted to spike the bounty. She killed Duuru Orkan too. This is turning into a big clusterfuck.*

It's been a big clusterfuck from the start, Zann sent. *What's her name?*

I don't know. She never said. She was on Vhesa Station too and made civilian casualties. She can't possibly be registered.

Description, then?

Human. Short, skinny. Dark eyes, pale skin, and bright pink hair.

I'll look into it, Zann wrote.

Thanks. Niko paused, heart seizing, before he made himself write it. *How's Dad?*

Not great. I've been staying with him though so he's not alone. Galapol might hate me right now but I got them to post guards and snipers around the place in case anybody tries something cute. I haven't told him any names or details but I mentioned there's more to the situation going on than I can legally talk about and that you aren't out just senselessly killing random politicians. That seemed to help. A little.

Niko sighed. *Thanks for looking out for him.*

Sure. You keeping tabs on the news lately?

Unease crawled through his gut. *Not really, honestly. Why?*

Check it out. You're suddenly everywhere at once. Shit's getting weirder by the day.

The unease turned to oily nausea. Niko glanced up and out of the thick window; the empty, frozen night stared back at him, unchanging. He opened the newsfeed on his phone and moved its hologram next to Zann's messages. Story after story filled his view. There had been new kills attributed to Elliott today and the day before: a Gheroun senator on the verge of retirement, an up-and-coming young Xermotl actress who was in critical condition and not looking great, and a Dvaab assistant film director, Nualan'ttee'for'nana'selvannt—the only one on the list to actually fall among Honeybliss's roster. Niko recognized his ugly, green little face immediately.

He was shocked. He scrolled down to a video of what bizarrely looked like Elliott—a man who could be his twin, with blond hair that hung around his face, lithe figure, and black tactical clothes. His visage was obscured from view by a pair of dark goggles and bandanna. He aimed a sniper rifle at someone out of view. It was footage, apparently, from the senator's murder.

This wasn't just a copycat. People were intentionally passing as him now, the goal to sow confusion. They had gotten the same idea Bubblegum had: driving the bounty higher. And whoever this man was, he likely wasn't the only one. Two of the murders had happened around the same time in vastly different parts of the galaxy. It was possible they were working in tandem—or maybe they'd just had the same idea.

Innocent people were dying now, caught up in this ever-evolving game.

Elliott was going to lose his shit. Niko had no doubt. If Galapol agents losing their lives in the chaos had been enough to stir up his self-hatred, learning that civilians were now being targeted and killed just to manipulate the price on his head was going to send him into a meltdown. Especially when, for all the public knew, he was the one killing them.

Zann, you have to convince them to cancel the bounty, he sent.

The reply came back almost instantly. Zann had always been a formidably fast typer to keep up with. *The bounty is out of their jurisdiction by this point. It's a big interstellar contribution between all the corporations, foundations, and worlds your boyfriend pissed off. And frankly, it's not clear which ones are you guys and which are copycats. Whoever's doing it is doing a good fucking job. Even got the look down. I know you can clarify it for me, but what the fuck am I going to tell Galapol when they start asking how I know any of this?*

Niko rubbed his face. They had to do something. Letting innocent people get killed due to his and Elliott's work wasn't acceptable. And Elliott's dignity was corroded every time someone dressed up as him and made that inexorable kill.

They needed people to know.

To know what Honeybliss was, and why Elliott—and himself, now—were targeting them. To know that the justice they carried out on their own was intentional, focused, protecting the galaxy from it ever happening again. And that these other kills weren't a part of their mission. They had to work in honesty and stand true.

There was someone who might just be capable of getting their message out from one end of the galaxy to the other. Someone he'd been running from for too long.

He—

The lounge door slid open behind him and Elliott stepped in.

"There you are. Dinner's..." He paused and stared at the holograms in front of Niko. At the news and texts beside them. At Zann's name above them all.

Niko flushed with horror. Instinct urged him to quickly close it all out, to try and make it vanish before he could get a proper look. But doing so would only serve to make him look suspicious, like he had something to hide from Elliott. Instead, he turned the chair around to face him.

"You're talking to Zann." It was half statement, half question. "Why?"

"Elliott, hey," Niko began, working his voice as soft and gentle as possible. "Can you sit down with me for a second?"

Elliott hesitated.

"Please?"

The other man finally relented, walking over and lowering himself onto one of the padded benches. He sat straight-backed and elegant, hands folded neatly in his lap as he stared at Niko.

Niko struggled to find how to tell him. "I messaged him, yeah. I needed to know what was going on and speak to him. The last time we spoke was before— Well—"

"Right."

"He's not with Galapol anymore. Once they learned he'd sent me all the internal research on your case under the table, he got put under investigation and let go. He led me to some updates on what's going on right now, though. And you're not going to like this, but hear the whole thing out, because I have an idea on how to fix it."

Elliott looked exhausted. To his credit, he merely nodded. Niko imagined him bracing himself as he sat there. He wanted to hold him, to pick him up and carry him off to their bed and envelop him for this conversation. But this was going to have to do instead.

"Other people are getting the same idea out there as Bubblegum. They want to drive up the bounty in any way they can." He could already see Elliott's eyes dimming with pain as the other man drew inward.

"They've gotten pretty smart about it too, unfortunately," Niko continued. "So they're making new kills, pretending to be you. Most of their victims are just innocent people. But they got Nual—uh, Nualan—the Dvaab director too."

"Well. At least they're making our job on that front easier," Elliott forced out, his tone lifeless. He looked ill.

"We can stop this, Elliott. We just need people to know what we're doing and why. We need them to know about Honeybliss. It's time they had their shit brought into the light anyway. We need people to know that we're not linked to the imitation killings and that we don't condone them. And we need to do it in a way that neither Galapol nor Honeybliss can intercept and silence."

"Oh, if I'd known it was that simple all along…" Elliott said flatly.

"I know someone capable of doing it."

"Oh?" His tone remained lifeless, clipped. Niko could tell he wasn't letting himself get his hopes up. He was almost afraid of getting his own hopes up, too. There had been a reason he hadn't tried this route before. It was a dangerous path, one full of confronting and navigating old connections he wasn't so sure were friends any longer.

Even disregarding the bounty that was on his head now.

"Yeah. There's a woman I used to know that people call Lady Death. She was a revolutionary of the Sala nation on Soorulan, back in their civil war."

"I read about that," Elliott said. "The war." He lit up suddenly, eyes going wide. "The revolution won because they were able to hack transmission towers their government had locked down and sent a plea for aid across the galaxy. I actually wrote about it a little in my thesis."

"Yep," Niko said, his chest warm with blossoming pride, despite any unresolved business that still lay unaddressed between himself and Death. "That was her."

Elliott blinked at him. "Do you think—"

"That this might actually work? Yeah. I do."

"But how? I told you, I've already tried to get this out to networks. I even tried to hack—"

"Listen," Niko said firmly, eyes focused on the other man's. "You know what she did before. And she has connections no one else in this galaxy does. She's incredibly influential and people respect her. She has a lot of friends in high places. I think she could pull strings and actually get past Honeybliss's connections in the media. It's a matter of both what she can do, and who she knows. We can't get that anywhere else."

"And you think she won't end up like another Baouban?"

The truth was, Niko couldn't say. But he opted for hope. "I've never known anyone as honorable as her. Money never mattered to her in the way it did most people in the black market. If there's anyone who would still be willing to overlook our bounties, it's her."

"That's—that's *great*, Niko."

Elliott was like a different person now, full of light and enthusiasm, eyes bright. In his excitement, he seemed younger. Knowing he was the one to bring that change out after such an excruciating day brought a contagious smile to Niko as well. They had a chance.

They had a real chance to combat this from spiraling out of control and taking more innocent lives.

And they had a chance to show everyone just who Honeybliss really was—and why Elliott Kestrel was so driven to change the galaxy forever.

Sure, Niko hadn't spoken to Lady Death in over three years. Sure, he'd ghosted her without repaying the precious favor he'd owed to her. And *sure,* there was a chance she'd turn out like Baouban. Or want his head on a decorative spike for the honorable debt he'd left unpaid. She was only one of the most formidable players in the entire galactic underworld. Niko could handle it.

Probably.

"Wait, but— How do you know the Revolutionary of Sala?"

"After the war was won, she went into bounty hunting." Niko grinned. "She taught me almost everything I know."

Elliott blinked at him, eyes full of fascination and awe. Niko found him so beautiful in all his forms, but the rare open and expressive version of him Niko liked best. It felt a little like he was being let into something deeply private, and shown the Elliott who dwelt beneath the years of pain and solitude.

"I expect this story in full," he said.

Niko smiled. "Over dinner, maybe? I just realized how hungry I am."

Niko lay in the bed they shared. Beside him, Elliott slept. He looked peaceful—beautiful—in his sleep, all the burdens and all the pain of the day lifted from him in the mercy of slumber. Niko couldn't stop looking at him. They were so fortunate to be here, to be alive. A stray golden wisp had fallen into his face and Niko gently brushed it back. When it fell again seconds later, he couldn't help but smile, a deep warmth radiating through him. He was so lucky. Despite everything. Despite the cost of it all. He was so fortunate to be sleeping beside this man.

There was nowhere else Niko would rather be.

He had never been so enraptured by another man before. Even when he'd tried to resist it, Niko had only found himself falling harder.

He lamented the pain that had led Elliott to cross paths with him. But he was grateful, too, that he'd had the chance at all. He had traded the entire galaxy for one man and found he'd make the same choice again and again and again.

Niko summoned his phone hologram, careful not to wake Elliott with its pervading light.

There were several missed texts from Zann, spread across the evening and night.

Niko? You still with me?

Did I lose you?

Thought you'd want to know in case you don't see the news—looks like the Xermotl actress is going to make it after all.

Listen. I want to talk to you. In person. There's a lot that needs to be said between us and I'm not doing that over a phone. You're my brother and my best friend. I owe you some truths, and frankly, you owe me a metric shit ton of them too.

The Duna Memorial on Celelast. Tomorrow. Just you and me.

Be there, Niko.

It could be a trap. It *could*. Niko knew it. The whole thing could be an elaborate setup orchestrated by Galapol as a way to bait Niko out.

But Niko didn't think it was. It didn't feel like it was. Since the day their family had been irreversibly shattered, Niko had had one constant in his life—a brother in blood and soul alike. Zann.

He had to believe in him. He had to know Zann was being sincere. Faith was a choice, and in a galaxy of serpents, it was often the naive one—the *wrong* one—to make. But he chose it anyway. Niko would believe in his brother, just like he'd chosen to believe in Elliott Kestrel.

I'll be there, Niko wrote. He closed the hologram and the room was drowned in shadow once more.

His eyes slowly adjusted to the dark, until Elliott's features grew clearer to him again. Niko reached out and stroked his thumb along Elliott's cheek, then brushed back the unruly strand again with tenderness. A moment later it fell back into place, stubborn and resilient as its owner.

Niko was in freefall now.

And he was falling, maybe, into something deeper.

ACKNOWLEDGEMENTS

Thank you to all of my incredible beta readers, who took time out of their lives to read this story and ensure it made sense. Thank you for helping me to grow as a writer, for encouraging me and also letting me know where I could improve. This book would not be where it is without your help, and for that, I'm eternally grateful.

I have to extend a *huge* thank you, as well, to Jon Paul and June. Your enthusiasm and ever-thoughtful critique on a regular basis helped improve my story, challenge me, and encourage me to keep going. With you guys in my corner, I feel like anything is possible. I could write a thousand novels before I would ever be able to find the words to express the depths of my gratitude to you. So, I'll settle on something simple: thank you, for your patience and your stubborn belief in me. Even when I didn't believe in myself. Thanks for being willing to be vulnerable with me in return, too, and for sharing your incredible stories with me. Please never stop writing!

I am forever in debt to Kasey, who pushed me every time I started sulking and getting lost in the tangle of my own mind. Your resilient belief in me and enduring patience as I battled unending waves of self-doubt means more than I can ever truly say.

My gratitude goes to Seaj Art for my extraordinary and beautiful cover. Getting it was a dream come true. Thank you for bringing my characters to life!

And lastly, thanks to you as well, reader, for sticking with me this long. For taking the time from your busy day to read this book. For going on this crazy adventure with Niko and Elliott. I can't wait to bring you *Killjoy*, the second installment of the *Starhawk* trilogy. It would mean a lot to me if you left an honest review on Amazon or Goodreads of this book. Reviews help boost visibility for indie authors' books, and help us continue to bring you more content in the future.

And as always, remember: *be gay, do space crime.*

Until next time.

ADRIENNE LOTHY lives in Illinois with two cats and approximately one million houseplants. When she's not writing interstellar love stories, dreaming up new plotlines, or trying to negotiate peace in the Felines vs Foliage war, she can be found journaling, photographing the sky, haunting coffeehouses, and (of course) reading.

You can read more about her, stay up to date on new content, and access exclusive free bonus stories through her newsletter. Sign up at **www.adriennelothy.com.**

She is also active on Instagram, at **@adriennelothy.**